3

Men

Alyce C. Thompson

3 Men I Chose to Love

Library of Congress Cataloging-in-Publication Data

3 Men I Chose to Love: a novel/Alyce C. Thompson- 1st edition
ISBN 0-9746411-0-3
2. A Lifetime of Pain   3. Watching Over Us 4. Through Eyes of a Black Man
5. All My Honeys'
Printed in the United States of America

emailalyce8@aol.com
www.alycethompson.com

First of all, I'd like 2 give thanks 2 my Father in heaven 4 making this possible 4 me. Without Him, it wouldn't be a me. I'd like 2 thank my mother Delores Thompson 4 choosing life 4 me. Mom u r the greatest. U made all this possible. Thanks 4 putting up with my children& me through the years. I'd like 2 give a special thanks 2 my 3 beautiful children; La'Rue Aleem Shivers, Tobias Craig Chambers and Aloni Christina Lee. U 3 have been so understanding. I can't thank u enough 4 putting up with my writing &me. It's been a long journey &u 3 endured it 2 the end. I can't express my gratitude enough. Without y'all, I don't know if I would've made it. Looking into your eyes gave me strength 2 move on when I didn't have the will 2 do so. I'd like 2 thank your fathers, La'Rue Erving Shivers, Craig Tobias Chambers & Lonnie Donnell Lee 4 giving u 3, 2 me. May their souls RIP. They were the greatest fathers 2 have. Theodore Tahai McFadden, may u RIP. I loved u like a son rather than a nephew. God has always been in control. 2 my friend Bruce Kennedy, may u continue 2 RIP. Some r gone but never 4gotten. Terrell Robinson; u will always be in our hearts. We love u 4ever. Staxxs, thank u 4 believing in my talent. U were 1 of the first 2 read my work & knew I could do it. Weldon Powell, u r the 1that pushed & helped me with my outline. I'll never 4get u calling 2 make sure I did what I was supposed 2 do. U r a friend in deed. I love u. Beetle, u read my piece & believed in me 2. We love u 4 all you've done, most important, 4 being u. U r more than a friend. Good luck with u&Connie's hard work. Jakiera&Janiesha, we got mad love 4 u 2. Eddie, may God bless u&yours. I'd like to thank Vivian Gee & her family 4 being so supportive through the years. Craig chose the right lady 2 be his son's godmother, u r the best. May God continue 2 keep u & yours safe. Grandmom Elmeretta, may God bless your soul. U were a true gem. Tobias couldn't ask 4 a better great-grandmother; u never lied. U loved him unconditionally. Christopher, may u RIP. Years may have separated us, but love didn't. U were a special uncle 2 La'Rue & he'll never stop loving u. Rodney, RIP 2. Tobias will never 4get u. U 3 live on through him. God does all things 4 a reason. He may have lost a lot, but he gained so much more. Special thanks 2 Gary, Audrey&Dana. Gary, Craig said u were a good man & although he's gone, your love didn't die with him, u kept his son close like a real man would've while others faded away but that's life 4 u; u live&learn. I'd like 2 thank Aunt Annie Dell, May, Della, Inez, uncle Danny, Kay,&Monk 4 being such a blessing in our lives. You've embraced us with the same love u embraced Boobie with. We thank u. May Fats RIP. 2 my oldest sister Corena, I love u & always will. You've endured so much through the years & God has it in control. 2 your other children, Talli, lock the writing down from inside,

3

Tedkieya, Tiana, Tyron, Taniesha, Tia & their children, Taquil, Teddy, Talli, Siani, Tallia, Rhaki, Brandon, Kayla; may God keep u in his loving care. Gina may God continue to give u all that your heart desires. Thanks 4 sharing Chantay, Tony&Aniya with us. They r a blessing. Hampton keep up the good work. U r gifted brotha&God has so much stored up 4 u. He says, "in my house are many mansions" so know that u have a place in heaven. Thank u 4 Lil Hampton, Brittiny, Daquan, De'Ja, Arman, Aliyah, big De'Ja, Tekieya&Marquice. Delia & Ebony; thanks 4 bearing my brother's seed. David, Tina & Amber, may God bless u 3 tremendously because u 3 deserve life's treasures. Never give up the faith. Delfenia I wish u the best in life. U really deserve whatever your heart desires. Never sleep on your dreams. Thanks 4 my beautiful nieces; Amiyra, Maurisa & India, I love u 3 so much. Kiesha, BJ & Kemiora Dior, may God bless u richly. Kiesha, you've been the best little sister through the years. I love u more than words can describe. Dad thanks 4 all the emails. I love u, 2. Felicia, Mel & Kim, it's been good. True sistas r hard 2 come by. Aisha & Ayinde, I love u. Aisha keep up the good work& thanks 4 all your knowledge&Ayinde do u. Symirah, I'm waiting 4 your hot seller. Natasha thanks 4 all your help&good luck with all your projects 2 come. Chris&Donna may God bless u&your fam. Mrs. Evans u r an angel, RIP. Patti&Tim RIP. I love u Ella, Felicia&Family. 2 all the people in Philly that have been in my circle at some point or another, thanks 4 being there. Only God knows the struggle&battle we fight each day. 2 my booboo Ra'Nasjah Aniyah Snell, I love u with all my heart. Thanks Rachelle 4 being a good mother 2 her. 2 the Keith family, thanks 4 putting up with the children&me. Sayeid you've been great. God knows better than anyone. NAN, RIP, we love u! Tawanda, Jawana, Tataniesha, Adrienna, Toni, Deja, Kayla & little Chris, I love u all&thanks Andrea 4 your seed. May God keep u strong. Nita, we love u 2. 2 my grandmother Alice Thompson, thanks 4 the years. It's been so good&u r stronger than what the eyes see. Thanks 4 the long life line. Grandpop Thompson RIP. May uncle Jimmie RIP 2. Aunt Jeannie, thanks 4 the years also. You've been the most pleasant aunt I've known. Danielle, Derek& the children, we love u although we don't see u all often. 2 my aunt Eva, God knows&it's all worked out. You've been a positive force in my life. Although I don't see u much, your love will never die. Be good 2 yourself. May your Ronaldo RIP. Only God knows the "time and hour." Be blessed Jonnie, Damion, Aaron, Baron & the children. Aunt Shona RIP. Thanks 4 the years of wisdom & may God bless yours; Peanut, Toni, Somari, Beene, Micah& the others I didn't name. Aunt Pinky all the way in Chicago, may God keep u safe&warm. I love u cousin David, never give up, it's written. Juanita, Delora, Paul, Dartanin, uncle Donald & the rest of the crew, we love u dearly & can't wait 2 hook up. 2 my grandmother Georga Lee Gibson, thanks 4 the long life line also. If I didn't have your feisty blood, I don't know how I would've made it sometimes. "Although small in stature, bold as a lion." Thank u&may God give u all the answers u need. May my grandfather Charles Gibson RIP. I didn't get 2 know u, but I heard so, so many good things about u & u had to be special to raise my mother&her 3 sisters alone. Some men will never know & the ones that r doing the mothers job, I salute u because it's not easy. 2 my brother Jeffrey, I love u&will never forget the time in Federal Way. It wasn't long but enough 2 carry me through the years. May God bless u&your family. 2 all my loved ones that's incarcerated, be strong&know it's bigger than us but God can do marvelous things so don't give up, keep fighting&know it's peace on the other side. Eric Allston, you've been a true friend through the years, I'll love u always. Brandon keep your head high&know that God loves u best. Bryan God is doing a new thing in u. 2 my jeweler & friend, Alex, may God bless u richly. Cousin James, I love u&may Zahir RIP. Keep the others close. I love all my little people, they r our future. 2 my new stylist Maria, thanks 4 everything, you've been the greatest. Robin&Kim thanks 4 the years of good service. Aunt Shuntaine thanks 4 the years of service, may God continue 2 bless u, Tee & the family richly. I love u all. Aunt Dawana &family, may God keep u all safe. Uncle Hamp, Uncle Bobby&Aunt Vivian, may God keep u on top. Melvin Branch & family, may God bless u. Siddiq may God bless u&yours. You've been a good friend through the years, ONE! Nephew Brandon, God loves u with an everlasting love. U can be anything u want 2 be. Korrin, Kraig, little Rodney&Ciani, may God continue 2 keep u safe. Damir, Lil Angel,&Basir, thanks 4 the years of cousinship with Aloni&Tobias. Poochie, Pop, Boochie, Pic, Maryann, Junior, YaYa,& please 4give me if I 4got u, thanks 4everything. Algie, thanks 4 the experience. Freeway, thanks 4 my first interview. Good luck with your success. Milo, thanks 4 being a true friend. Special thanks 2 my lawyer Mr. Barson. You r truly a blessing. I love u. Thanks Tariq 4 your service. U never lied 2 me. I love u 4 your honesty&hard work. It's not easy out here but the strong truly survives. Biz thanks 4 your critiques. May God continue 2 bless u&Oz with your endeavors. Farrell Anderson, I love u like a brotha. Vance, Lightfoot, Ed&the squad, God is real. Thanks2Derrick, Church, Umar, Rik&others I haven't named, I'd recommend u 2 anyone that needs work done on their homes, although they'll have 2 wait in line because u guys r so busy. Thanks Teddy 4 putting up with me. I know I can be very difficult at times. Poochie thanks 4 the paint job&I owe u 4 the old&new. Yetta, Chuck&fam. God bless u. Big I, ONE! Tanya&girls, I still love u all. Zina&Tasha, ONE! Lil Mia, I'll never stop loving u. May God give u your hearts desire, u deserve it. Stevie G, thanks 4 the years. Michelle RIP. Jamal, good luck with your talent. Ray thanks 4 being a friend . Kyle thanks 4 being a real friend. Doug, Cee, Scab&James, thanks 4 being there 4 my mom. JimJim, ur still standing strong. May God bless the Robinson fam. Ron I love u like a true brotha, bless u&yours. Joe, Jay, Reese&Marquice stay strong. Mark&Littles, thanks 4 hooking the boys up in their early years. Kahsu, Saba, Leah, Aloni's classmates&friends, Jazz, Bre,Tobias's other brothers, Tony, Mal, Brandon, Chris, Kyle, Spencel, Derrick, Man-man, Kirlem, Anwar,Yas, I love u all. La'Rue's other brothers which I've adopted as mine too; Byron, Twan, Marlon, Chink, Jim, Karon, Joe, Devon, Arnie&Henry, know that we r in trying times&we r our brother's keeper. The enemy wants 2 keep us warring against each other but we have 2 fight a good fight. It's an unfair game out here but being an achiever is the greatest reward. Dre, Keith, Kalif&Fred, I still reminisce on the old days, thanks 4the years. DeeDee, RIP. Gobe, u know I couldn't 4get u. Good luck with ur talent. TY, ONE, baby. April&my Godson Kareem, I love u. Venice, good luck with your show. El, thanks&good luck with all your endeavors. Baye, how could I 4get u this time around? ONE! Ace, it's good having u back. Noah's variety, thanks. 2 Jim's Steak staff, thanks 4 the good service through the years. Sherman, thanks&love u. Duce, I haven't 4gotten u. Rasul, thanks 4 the years of friendship, ONE! My friends around 61st&Master, Josy&children, Faye&fam, Erica&family, 72nd Street, my supporters on the lil' block. Slim-R.W, u r truly a good brotha. Hickson, much success 2 u. Rikeem, good luck. Jen, love ya. Nell thanks 4 the support from inside. To all the salons, barber shops, books stores, Liguorius, Mejah, Horizons, It's A Mystery To Me, Alkebulan, Haneef's, Empirian's, Robin's, to name a few, thanks so much. Overbrook Park Library, thanks. My sisters&brothers in Christ, please 4give me if I 4got u, I love each&every 1of u&know God is the answer. Whatever it is that u dream of doing with your life, as long as it's positive, reach 4 the stars because everyone has a talent, it's what u do with it that counts the most. I wish u all love, peace&happiness. ONE!

U can contact me by email@emailalyce8@aol.com or www.alycethompson.com. Blessed4lifeProductions.

PART I

Chapter 1
My First Love
"Cinnamon and Luke"

"Come on girl, answer the phone," cried Luke, looking at the C&L initial ring and gold rope chain that he purchased me as gifts while he worked at the school he was sent away to because of a petty crime he committed before he met me.

Luke just got busted by me, the mother of his first child, the Christian girl that went against everything her mother instilled in her. Mom raised seven children on her own once daddy rolled out. He came through town once or twice a year while on leave from the army but he wasn't holding it down like a real man. He gave mom one-hundred measly dollars a month for all of us and that wouldn't make it out the grocery store or Thrift shop for that matter.

Mom did everything in her power to make sure we were straight though. She scrambled to put hot meals in our bellies on cold winter nights and mornings when the gas was shut off. She stayed up late dreary nights sewing outfits for us to wear to school. She even made coats and hats for us in the winter.

Mom stayed on bending knees begging God to make sure we turned out like decent, healthy Christian beings. She hoped and prayed we did the right thing. She would love us with an everlasting love even when we went astray but she prayed we didn't turn out on drugs. Hopefully never molested. She didn't want to picture us stealing, killing or giving up our virginity until we were married. She wanted us to wait on Christian husbands. But most of us wouldn't make it past fifteen without getting a rock hard one.

Well, I broke the special juices for Luke at seventeen. He was the hottest commodity in the hood. Luke was tall. Something I was crazily attracted to, just like my mother because my dad was about 6'1" and she was 4'11". He was overly sexy with straight white teeth, full lips, beautiful brown eyes and bowlegged, something I died to have. Bowlegs ran in my family and I wanted them so badly but I wasn't blessed with them. Now I had a young man that had them.

Luke and I had been dating for months now. I miscarried, our first child. Now we had a beautiful son that looked just like him. Luke put in mad hours at the job my brother Malachi hooked him up with. Bringing in sufficient income for all three of us was priority but the racist boss was going to make sure Luke had it hard. She'd give everybody of her race more hours and money, leaving Luke other solutions to come up with. He had plans. He needed real paper, not funky pennies.

Luke and I were so much alike. We both loved nice things. We kept up with the latest designs. He rocked all the Kangols, Neostyle and Cazal glasses and Adidas sneaks and sweatsuits. And I rocked all the Gucci handbags, book bags, backpacks and shoulder bags. I did all the Lora Bigotti's and Emmanuel Kahn's too. The leather skirts, cashmere sweaters, you name it, I rocked it. How, my sister Shalina put me down with a lawsuit but I couldn't get, my twenty-five gees until I turned eighteen so she gave me a nice loan until then.

Competition was rough in our hood. My sisters and I had so many enemies because of our unique style and how mom raised us. We couldn't go to any of the house parties or block parties only if we snuck and when I did with my close neighbor and friend Ashley, she was shot in the back with a .45 caliber gun that was meant for one of the neighborhood rivals.

Shake Your Pants and *Glide* replayed over and over in mind. The DJ was mixing the two the night she was shot, leaving me in the street crying over her bloody body wondering where I went wrong. I would never be the same after this. I would wear her death on my shoulders thinking if only I had listened and walked the way she wanted to go, she'd never be in the street with a hole in her back the size of a golf ball with blood leaking everywhere, even down to her brand-new white Dr. Scholls that we loved wearing all the time.

My sisters and I couldn't wear pants or have boy company either. We were nice looking girls with long hair, pretty eyes, tight figures and nice complexions. I had the Cinnamon tone out of the girls. Reddish brown hair, soft light brown eyes and heart-shaped lips. My name was the perfect fit.

It was this one clique named, *Now and Later* like the candy, that despised us deeply because the same niggas that like them liked us and they couldn't begin to understand it. Their thing was, niggas had to pay now if they wanted some play or get back with them later when the money was right. We didn't have to give up the ass for a Gucci bag or two though. We shopped the stores getting all that honestly.

I would never forget the day, the leader of their squad Romaine, put her girl Meka on my sister. Although Meka was bigger than Shalina, Shalina beat that ass but that's when all hell broke lose and it was a free-for-all inside the school store. Shalina got sliced in several places and we found out who our real friends were, nobody. We didn't have any friends. We were our only friends.

After that fight, I never had a chance to fight again. Shalina beat asses left and right. And our oldest sister Ramina's man Nahum fought with us too although he beat on us when he abused Ramina. We caught hell all the way around. We fought in the house to make it, we fought in the streets to survive and we fought within ourselves to find out who we truly were.

I was confused. I had a void that needed to be filled. I needed love and thought I found it. Now I soaked the sheets because I found my first love, my confidant, my baby's daddy and friend in bed with another young woman by the name of Rose from New York City.

Rose was a bad bitch with a brother named Bud that Shalina used to kick it with. Rose had a vicious fuck game. A lot of niggas screamed her name and most women despised her because she did their men. Now she did mine but it wasn't about love. It was all about being what Luke thought, *came with the game*.

Luke started hanging tough with a young, arrogant, self-centered nigga named RJ. I wasn't feeling his style the day Luke introduced us but Luke didn't want to be chastised by me anymore. I couldn't continue to pick and choose his friends. He had to learn his way.

Week after week RJ pounded Luke about putting his hard earned money with his to buy some weed. Luke didn't want to get involved with anything illegal anymore because he had a family, something RJ could never fathom but we just purchased a brand-new 1987 Renault. We were making due with money I had from my lawsuit and my job at Clover's that I just landed to make things financially easier on Luke but being young, black and vulnerable was something Luke couldn't get around. It was a cruel, prejudice world, full of games that no one wanted to play fairly. As much as Luke wanted to remain a part of the working world, hustling could only enhance things. It could only make situations financially easier, so Luke thought in his mind.

Luke tied into the pot with RJ by putting up five hundred dollars for weed. And once he did that, the transformation began.

Luke started staying out late nights at the clubs. He hardly went to work. He began hitting me whenever he felt the need to. He wasn't my Luke anymore. He was somebody I never knew. Money and situations changed Luke. Dudes really thought it was cute to fuck the same chicks. Everybody knew Rose but again, Luke wanted to prove something to his man RJ by taking her home with him. Now he sat in his room crying and hoping I would forgive him once again, not only for the physical abuse this time, for the mental pain he caused me.

Chapter 2
THE CHANGE
"Moving Onto Something Different"

At home Luke and RJ planned to meet at the new club *5527* on Callowhill Street while I stayed in bed awaiting his return. RJ was so happy that Luke was ready to step his game up. Weed was alright but coke was the shit.

Inside the club different girls walked up to Luke and RJ giving them their numbers. They kinda looked alike since they had been hanging so tough. They both were tall and attractive but RJ weighed twenty pounds more than Luke. Luke was brown like a piece of toffee candy and RJ was light like a vanilla wafer. They both had white straight teeth but RJ had a little chip in his front tooth. And some girls liked them humble while others liked them arrogant. But as long as they got one of them, it was cool.

Carmen from north had to have Luke. She went to school with me and she despised everything about me. She watched Luke through the years and she wanted him badly. She was feeling his style.

Carmen felt Luke's dick lightly as she put her number in the pocket of his Levi jeans, then she pranced away smiling.

"What was that all about?" RJ smiled. Carmen had ass for days.

"I don't know but that bitch almost touched my wound. If she had come any closer, I would've knocked her with these crutches." They laughed at the same time then they continued to talk about their move. They needed to cop some coke.

At three a.m., Luke limped in the door.

"Where have you been?" I asked him.

"I was at 5527," he said with a slight smirk.

"Luke what's wrong with you? You're not fully healed and you went to a party. I'm so mad with you. Nothing can keep you down. I don't expect you to stay in, but I think it's too soon for you to be out. If you get hit in your wound, it'll be a total set back for you," I said.

"I'm cool. I got this," he said, throwing his crutches to the floor then I helped him to the bed. After undressing Luke, he went to sleep with a plan on his mind to get some real money. He was tired of the scrambling. He wanted to dream about billions. Like his street name and I didn't know if I was ready for that. It was too much going on in our lives already. I mean we had a second car and we were only eighteen and nineteen. I had a half carat diamond engagement ring that Luke had gotten me and planned to exchange for a bigger one, once money started flowing but things were crazy and people were simply jealous of nothing because we really didn't have much.

Luke's old girlfriend Kim was the reason why he was on crutches. Her brother shot Luke after she and her girlfriends snatched all my jewelry while I was driving with Marsha from grade school. And Luke was cheating on me constantly. I'd catch him with girls at all his little shops on Walnut Street, Chestnut Street, the one on 54th Street too. I was tired of the drug life. He wanted me bound and tucked away while he did his dirt. Nothing was the same anymore. I was more stressed than I was happy and every time I tried to go out with Sugar from the block, he'd flip out.

One month later. Luke and I were definitely moving up like George and Wezzie but RJ didn't like the fact that Luke and I were so tight again and I was expecting another child. RJ didn't have anything he could call his own so he wanted Luke to be just like him, a whore with no morals but Luke didn't get down like that. No matter what went on in the streets, he had to look out for home first.

For weeks I ran around the city with Luke dropping packs off here and there, to this person and that person and I began to bleed constantly but kept it to myself because I hated to bother Luke. He stayed in local motels with his new recruit Joe, Bee, Nas, Big Bow, Gee and KC. Big Bow and KC were cousins. Joe and Bee knew each other since grade school. And Gee and Nas were from the neighborhood and they wanted to be down so badly. I liked most of Luke's squad but some of them I simply didn't like because they were around for selfish reasons but that's the game for you. Everybody is in it for whatever it's worth to them.

I miscarried the baby and was back in church regularly because that was my refuge and strength. Although Luke accepted Christ as his savior, he was so caught up in the game. He loved the devils money and the streets calling his name was addictive. He didn't know how to break the bad spirits.

I pulled into a parking space in front of the house behind Luke's car after church. I was tired of the running with Luke. I prayed endlessly for a change. Something had to give.

Sugar pulled around the corner and parked in back of me.

"How was church girl?" Sugar asked, sarcastically.

"It was good. I paid my tithes so I feel blessed," I smiled with the glory of the Lord upon my face. Sugar and Luke looked at me at the same time like I was crazy.

"You are dumb," he said, taking the baby from me.

"Dumb! I'm far from dumb," I spat.

"Tithes. I can't believe you girl," laughed Sugar.

"I'm gonna pay my tithes no matter what y'all say. Y'all can call me foolish. I don't care," I said as I walked away. I didn't understand mom paying tithes when I was a young child and I often questioned her but she paid me no mind. She just prayed I learned as I got older and I did. "You better not take none of my money and give it to the church. I can see five or ten dollars, but not 10 percent of my earnings. Keep it up. You'll be okay," he said coldly.

"I don't care what either one of y'all say. I'm gonna continue to do what I know is right. Mom taught me well. I haven't always done the right thing, but I'm trying to do better," I said.

RJ whipped the corner in his sparkling clean black Mercedes Benz 260E like he owned the city. The coke game was doing him just fine and he was feeling himself. He parked so his five thousand dollar rims wouldn't touch the curb, then he got out and put his thousand-dollar walk on.

"I need to speak to you for a minute," he said, putting his arm around Luke's neck. He wanted to impress Sugar and me badly. In fact, he wanted to fuck both of us for real. And he hated the fact that we didn't pay him any attention. He was stepping his game up for sure, but he wasn't our type. He talked too much and he didn't know when to shut up or the right things to say. He would only learn in time. Some old head would teach him better one day. RJ and Luke walked to the corner while Sugar and I walked into the house to have girl talk.

The game started taking a toll on me and Luke's relationship. We were having problems before but the game only made things worst now. Luke started to abuse me again and I couldn't take it. I knew 5-0 was off limits but I had no other choice but to call them one day because I couldn't stand the beatings anymore and Luke eventually moved out of my mom's and in with Carmen so I started going out with Sugar regularly without Luke knowing.

Sugar came by and scooped me up to go to the ASU skating rink where all the fine brothas and hustlers were sure to be on a Saturday night. I had never been to the rink before but I knew I couldn't go wrong by going.

Sugar pulled into the lot full of Vettes', Cherokees', BMW's, Benz's, and Sevilles. My eyes lit up with excitement. I couldn't believe it. I was lost in a world of my own.

"You were right. It is packed. Everybody and their mothers are here. I have never been here before. It's alright. I have been tied up in the house too long. I almost forgot what it was like to be out," I said, checking in the mirror for any flaws. Sugar jumped out and shut her door. She was checking for a nigga. Any nigga.

"Come on girl," she said, rushing me.

"Alright, alright," I said, stepping out the car. We locked the car, and then we strutted to the door to make our entrance. We paid the fee, and then we walked in checking out the scenery.

"Can I talk to you for a minute?" asked a handsome guy rolling up showing his glimmering whites and deep dimples.

"Oh my God! That's Wayne from south. Girl talk to him. He has money," said Sugar, nudging me.

"For real. He's gorgeous, but I can't. Luke will have a fit," I said as I shied away.

"Umm, you're crazy. I would talk to him," she smirked.

"Besides, Luke is doing his thing." I turned and walked away while he watched me closely. I was something new and different. He'd never seen me out on the set before and I was hitting for something nice. Sugar followed behind me and we pranced around looking, laughing and talking about all the niggas and broads.

"Oh no! RJ and them are up here. Look at them! They are watching me," I said, pointing across the rink.

"Is Luke with them?" she asked.

"I don't know. I don't see him over there, but he might be up here. I'm ready to go," I said.

"Come on now. Lets' have some fun. We just got here and it's almost over anyway," she said as she looked around. I spotted the dude Wayne flexing his muscles on the floor. He was putting his thing down too. He looked at me with a koolaid smile and my heart skipped a beat. It was then that I realized what I had been missing in a relationship. Loneliness came over me and I wanted to be with Luke, but I knew he was staying with someone else. I smacked Sugar on the arm and said, "Dag. He can skate good girl. Look at him. Not only is he gorgeous, he can skate and he is very muscular, too. That's a plus."

She smiled, "I tell you, he's all that and some. He keeps watching you. You better get with that."

"Whatever!" I giggled. We stood around until it was almost over, then we headed toward the door to beat the crowd.

"Are you gonna wait for me?" someone asked from behind. I turned to look over my shoulder to see who was talking. *Damn, it's him.*

"I can't," I smiled.

"Why not?" He asked me.

"I just can't."

"Can I give you my number so you can call me later?" he smiled harder.

"No."

He slid a piece of paper in my pocket and said, "Here take this. Make sure you call me."

He must have had it written down already. "I will." I stepped out the door away from the crowd.

"Sugar do you think RJ and them saw me?" I asked nervously.

"I don't know. Won't you stop worrying about them?" she said, looking around trying to catch a new face or an old one, if it was worth anything.

"Right, right," I said.

We got in the car and pulled out the lot with all the other cars. Sugar raced her little Merkur hoping to catch up with all the other cars racing down the highway. The light caught us and Wayne hollered, "What's your name?" "Her name is Cinnamon, Wayne," Sugar hollered back. He smiled and nodded his head. The light turned green and he pulled off. All I could see were skid marks on the highway.

"I have been missing all the fun. I don't regret staying home with my boy; I just wish I had been getting out more often. It's so much out here to do instead of sitting around moping over spilled milk. Luke and I have had good times together, but lately he has been showing his behind. And I'm tired of the abuse," I said as I reminisced on the past.

"Don't worry. Everything will be fine," Sugar assured me as she listened to Run-DMC's, "Walk This Way."

I reclined my seat all the way back, thinking about all the times I had to put the baby in front of me as a shield so Luke wouldn't hit me. I was tired of the abuse. He was going to really lose it one day and hurt me really badly. As hard as it was to let go, now was the time.

Sugar and I walked into the house twenty minutes later and she dialed Carmen's number for me. Luke didn't know how to hide anything. He slipped up and left the number around and I never forgot it. I grabbed the phone from Sugar and said, "Let me speak to Luke."

"Who is this? The girl with the long hair and glasses," Carmen said, sarcastically.

"That's the only thing you can say about me when people mention me. I might wear glasses, but he loves me," I said.

"Well, who is he with?" she asked.

"Put my man on," I said.

"I'm gonna kick your ass when I see you four eyes," she screamed.

"Whatever you theft. That's all you do is steal," I spat.

"I sure do. And I have everything I want and your man," she spat back. I banged in her ear. The truth definitely hit me where it counted. I couldn't change who I was. Some people had it all while others got cheated.

The next day Sugar stopped by to kick it with me about a few things. She was feeling the boss from the YBM named Butch, but she didn't know how to bring it to me because he cracked on me one day while she and I were in the park. I couldn't hate on her game though because Butch had the city on lock. He was ripping it and Sugar wanted out of the ghetto. He was the big boss, not a worker or the under boss. He was the man, money, power, respect. He had it. An entourage, he had that too, old and young to build with him. They ripped the streets with no remorse. Dare to stand in their way? I don't think so. The women, they loved them. The streets feared them. The law, they were trying to break them.

15

While Luke ran around getting money, I got myself together and went downtown the next day. I felt the need to treat myself and son to something. I was worn down with Luke's bullshit and I thought this would make me feel a little better.

Inside the jewelry store one of Butch's boys walked up on me.

"What's up girl?" Ramik asked while checking out my ass in a pair of tight green Coca Cola jeans.

"Nothing," I said as I looked around.

"What you pickin' up?" he asked me.

"Nothing. I'm just looking," I said, peeping in the jewelry cases at the gold bangles.

"Did you see the bracelet that my man gave your girlfriend?"

"What bracelet and what girlfriend?"

"It's only one girl that I see you with all the time," he smiled.

"Sugar!" I said.

"Yeah," he said.

"Are you talking about that bangle bracelet that she just got?" I asked.

"Yeah."

"I saw it and I asked her where she got the new bracelet from and she said a friend, but she never said what friend," I said.

"Yeah. We was down the Row last week and we purchased a few pieces. All our main girls got big gifts and our side girls got bangles," he said, counting his stacks.

"Is that so? Y'all dudes ain't no good. Y'all have one or two main girls and then a lot of side girls. Y'all make me sick. Money really changes people and things. If you got a couple of dollars, you can get what you want, huh! That's the way it works. Some of y'all are the same dudes that girls wouldn't even talk to when y'all were walking and didn't have any money. And the girls that were with y'all when y'all didn't have anything are the ones that get the bad end of the stick most of the times. It's not right. The money isn't going to be around forever. And it's not all about the material things because when you are dead and gone. It's gonna be somebody else's. So don't cherish it. Just make the best of it," I smirked.

"Well, I'm gonna enjoy every bit of it. The hoes and the money. You only live once," he said, throwing nine stacks on the counter to the jeweler.

"Yeah. You're right, but you don't have to be a dog," I said. I stood back and wondered why my girl lied to me. Butch wasn't my man and she didn't have to spare my feelings. He was doing everybody and she wasn't the only one but she wanted to keep it tucked so I wouldn't think about fucking him because she knew she would do it to me if it was worth it. Practically all the girls we knew wanted to come up off a hustler and there was a shortage of men so we had to share most of the time.

"Give me those earrings my man," Ramik said to the jeweler.

"I'll talk to you later," I said, walking toward the door.

"Alright. Be cool girl," he smiled while checking me for the last time.

I walked in the house to a ringing phone an hour later. It was the dude Wayne. He and I kicked for an hour about everything. I told him how my son's father was stressing me and he assured me he could make me happy so I hung up with the thought of being with someone else. *Shit! Luke sleeps with Carmen every night. He can care less about me right now.* Tears fell behind my neck. *Life has to go on. He's not holding his breath waiting on me. He don't love me anymore.* I rolled over and went to sleep. I was ready to do me for a change. I loved Luke like no other but he was playing me.

1988. For weeks Wayne and I did us. Luke left the back door open for him. He got so caught up that he let a lot of time come between us. And I had to be attracted to this handsome nigga named Wayne. Luke being a part of my life for so long made me hesitant at first, but I was happy again. Wayne treated me like Luke used to treat me at the beginning of our relationship and I needed that in my life.

Once Lil Luke finished watching his favorite Sesame Street tape over and over, I got in my car and drove over to Wayne's house. I was really feeling him to be driving on black ice at two o'clock in the morning.

Inside Wayne's plush Townhouse we kicked it on his black leather sectional then he persuaded me to stay until the morning because it was too messy and dangerous outside. I never spent the night out with another man so I was uncomfortable but Wayne wasn't. He had a plan in the back of his mind. He wanted to fuck me this night.

Inside Wayne's room he lit the fireplace and turned on WDAS FM, the quiet storm reminding me so much of Luke. How could I forget the first time making love? *A Thin Line between Love and Hate* played gently in the background when Luke inserted himself inside me. That was the best feeling ever after the leaking and blood pour. I cried a river on that young boy when he hit all the right spots. *Damn! Your first love would never die. You'd take that memory to your grave and into every relationship that you ever encountered too, especially if the shot was tight.*

Wayne dropped his Guess jeans on the plush gray carpet then he walked to the bathroom. While the water ran from the shower, I lay across the bed fumbling with my fingers. I knew he was gonna pop the question or at least try to fuck me. The chemistry was there and we were feeling each other and hadn't even fucked yet. His dick wanted my sweetness.

Moments later Wayne came out with a towel wrapped around his 32-inch waist. *Damn! His body is tight*, I thought to myself. He sat next to me and passed me a tub of cream to rub on his back. I was nervous but I did it. Then he passed me bacteria ointment to rub on his blotches. The small blotches didn't take away from his smooth buttery skin. I gently rubbed and rubbed all over him even down his six pack then he dropped his towel slowly to let me see what he was working with and damn was he blessed in that department. Pussy juices immediately leaked in my panties. I hadn't felt so good in a long time and after seeing his big dick, I knew I was in for a sweet treat. It was like preparing me for my first sugar daddy taffy, difficult to eat but worth the struggle. I wanted all of his delicious caramel.

Wayne picked me up and gently kissed me all over my little body. I was stuck. I had no place to run or hide. This man was sexy, gentle and everything I longed for but I was afraid of what Luke might do if he found out. I couldn't make passionate love to Wayne. It would be violating Luke. I was "bought and paid for," so he buried in my mind.

After Wayne took my clothes off piece by piece, I could do nothing but lay back and relax. I wanted this moment to last forever. My pussy only knew Luke's dick so Wayne's wide ten inches had to gently work its way into position. He was such a prize and I wanted him badly.

After ten short pushes my pussy opened up and Wayne slid in nice and soft as I clutched his shoulders gently. I never knew another dick could feel so wonderful. Wayne's shit felt like eating cotton candy. It was fluffy and sweet. I was happy to have found a thorough nigga with it all. Wayne had the looks, money, charm and his fuck game was tight. He had it goin' on in every department and I didn't mind being his girl.

As I drove home in the morning I thought about what Luke would do if he knew I slept with someone else but I had to take my chances. It was only right that I found love again.

Wayne hooked his boy Brad up with Sugar so we did the double date thing on the regular. They were so fun to be around. I felt good again but Luke wasn't feeling too good about Carmen anymore. He took all his clothes from her room and threw them in his trunk. He was tired of her. He never stayed with a chick as long as he stayed with me. He got bored too quickly and she was fatal. She broke Luke's car windows out. She played like she was pregnant. She stalked him every time he went to the club with his boys. She fought him back then called the cops on him. She did things I never did. He had to let go. She was going to draw too much attention to him and he couldn't have that. He couldn't risk his freedom for her. She wasn't worth all that.

Sugar and I hit the skating rink in Delaware where everybody was sure to be on a Sunday night. Inside the lot I couldn't help but notice all the fancy cars and trucks. All the hustlers came out to play this night, the YBM youngins, RJ, Luke and their squad, the county niggas. Everybody that was getting money was out.

Sugar parked the car and we pranced into the doors dressed alike. We had on fine linen and leather that Sugar's tailor hooked up. We paid our five dollars at the window then we walked through another set of doors.
"There goes your girl," Sugar said, pointing in the corner.

18

"Who?" I asked, looking around me.

"Carmen and her clique," she grinned.

"That's not my girl," I said as I turned my head. Carmen had to let me know she was there. And she was mad that Luke left her alone.

"Bitch!" she said, rolling her eyes at me.

Sugar looked at me like, "check that bitch.".

"Whatever! I'm not gonna feed. How is she gonna dislike me over my baby's father? You would think I messed with her man. She acts like I violated her. She's taking him real personal and he doesn't even mess with her anymore. Please!" I said as I threw my hands up.

"She must be hurt, because she's trippin'," Sugar laughed.

"I go through too much with his little girlfriends. When he messes with them, I go through it and when he stops I still have to go through it. He needs to get himself together. If he doesn't want to settle down, then he needs to narrow it down, because somebody is going to get hurt at the rate he's going," I said.

"You're right," she said, giving me a high five.

Sugar and I got our skates, and then we hit the floor with Carmen and her clique envying us. She wanted to start some shit badly. She wanted me to make one wrong move so her clique could roll on me, but I wasn't about to embarrass myself. It was too many niggas on the scene and Wayne was on the floor doing his thing. I was not about to let him see me act ghetto after he asked me to be his. I had to represent for the few young classy chicks left on the set.

The next day Sugar called to invite Shalina and me to a party at the hotel. The big willies were doing it again. My girl Tara called out of the blue and I told her where we were going and she invited herself knowing Sugar didn't get down with her like that.

We all met at Sugar's house in our sequin, leather and furs an hour later. Then we headed down Center City and parked in the lot on 20th Street. We got out our cars and walked up in the hotel lobby. I looked around at the crowd. The money and niggas were flowing. It was definitely doing it this night.

Sugar kept her eye on Butch as soon as she spotted him in the corner with his newly purchased Mink on that cost more than some of our cars and houses. She had to have the top dawg in the city. It was a must. She wanted a way out of the ghetto.

"You were right girl," I laughed, tapping Sugar on the arm. All the wannabe's and maybes were in the place.

"I told you," Sugar said, draping her young fox over her arm. Shalina and I took our redone furs off then we walked around to kick it with the fellas. Guilt entered my mind for being out. I knew I wouldn't have been out if Luke and I were together.

When two thirty rolled around, we hit the diner for breakfast then we all separated. Sugar really wanted to go to the after party in Butch's suite but she couldn't sneak away and why was she hiding the fact that she was fucking him anyway. Nobody was dumb. I knew about the bracelet and I knew she did him too, from the streets. Nigga's couldn't hold water. It was impossible. They constantly bragged about smashin' broads.

The next day everything hit the fan. RJ caught me getting out of Wayne's McClarion after having dinner at Red Lobster's with him and after checking me like he was my man, he told Luke and Luke beat me down in mom's living room floor. I now knew what Ramina went through. It was so easy getting caught up but I refused to stay in an abusive relationship as long as she did. I couldn't let someone else control my life. Luke had to accept me moving on like I accepted all his dirt. I wanted my family but being in an unstable relationship wasn't healthy. The cycle had to change. He was destroyed by what he witnessed his father do to his mother. I was destroyed by my father leaving me. My mother was destroyed by her mother leaving her. My father was destroyed by his father abusing his mother. But as individuals, we needed to learn to do things differently. Strength, courage, wisdom, guidance and understanding could change some things.

For days I played dangerously. Luke made me stay with him most nights and I did Wayne during the day. The only difference was, I wasn't sexually involved with Luke or in love with him anymore. He was my first and he broke me down mentally. He scarred me for life.

I woke up one morning drenched in sweat. I dreamed Luke killed Wayne and I knew God was giving me a warning. The shit was about to hit the fan. I was about to get caught up in my mess.

I asked mom what to do about my prophetic dream and she warned me to tell Luke and Wayne but I didn't know how to. How could I tell Luke although he knew all about my dreams and how could I tell Wayne? He would think I was crazy so I chose to keep it to myself although I knew it was meant for me to tell.

I sat outside the next day crying again. I didn't consider myself with Luke but he claimed we were working it out and he was at his new shop on Market Street with another girl and I flipped on him and he in turn fronted on me like always. After I spit in the girl's face, he threw me in the car and left with her. He could have all the girls and I couldn't have the one man I was loving in peace.

I watched and watched, all the cars ride by the block. That's all I could do.

"Hey sexy. Come here," smiled Wayne as he pulled over with his friend in the car waking me from my thoughts. I walked to the car hoping Luke didn't pull up on the block. It was nice out and everybody was riding through in their whips. It was just a matter of time for him to make his daily round.

"Can we get together tonight?" he smiled while looking at my luscious lips. "Sure, why not," I said, happily while leaning in his window. Wayne gave me something to look forward to. Luke's car turned the corner slowly. *Damn!* "Oh, my God. Here comes my baby father," I said, nervously as I stepped back from his car. Wayne turned to look behind him. Luke parked and walked up to the car.

"Who is this?" he asked, with his eyes wide, pointing in my face. I couldn't think quickly enough. "It's my friend," I stuttered.

"Your friend?" he said, nodding his head up and down. "Umm."

"Yeah. He's just a friend," I explained quickly.

Wayne looked at me smiling like, "I'm just a friend now, huh?"

Luke looked at Wayne with a stern look and said, "This is my son's mom and I don't appreciate you comin' round here. Don't come around here no more!"

"I don't know what's going on between y'all, but I'm not a sucker. I know about you and she said that y'all ain't together no more," Wayne casually said.

"You heard what I said. Don't come around here no more!" Luke threatened him. Wayne looked at me with one hand in his lap and the other one on the steering wheel fuming.

"You ain't right," he said to me then he revved his engine and pulled off. He didn't know how I was playing. He loved me, but he was stuck because I did have a baby by this man. Luke ran to his car quickly to grab his gun. I stumped to the corner of the block with my son. I was so pissed at the fact that Luke messed up my thing with Wayne.

Wayne pulled on the corner and shook his head at me. I was a liar in his eyes. I was still fucking my baby's father for him to act this way. Luke ran by me with his gun cocked all the way back. I instantly thought about my dream and the tears started dropping. I couldn't holler, breathe or move. My circulation stopped. Luke ran on the side of Wayne's car and fired. I hit the ground while everybody on the block screamed, running in different directions. I heard Wayne's car skid away then I looked up to see where my son was.

"Your son is right here," said a neighbor while holding my baby's little nervous hand.

"Thank God!" I hollered. I didn't know what was next because Wayne was by no means a coward. It was going to be some shit. Luke didn't know whom he was fucking with but that was Luke for you. He didn't give a fuck. He'd see whomever about me and not care.

After getting Lil Luke from one of the neighbors I walked into the house to call Wayne to make sure he and Carl were all right.

Wayne and Carl were cool but he didn't want to be with me like that anymore because he couldn't trust me. I told him whom I loved and I didn't want Luke but he wasn't buying it and Luke definitely wasn't about to let me go now. As long as somebody else wanted me, he did too but when I was on the solo, he didn't pay me much attention.

Later in the evening Wayne, Brad and his boys got strapped and headed over to my house. Brad wanted to rock Luke but Wayne knew what it would do to my son and me if they killed him so he just wanted to put a little fear in Luke's heart but Luke didn't care about fear.

Luke stood at my front door with his aunt and cousins when Wayne and his boys pulled up in a gold Seville. Luke was strapped but he was out numbered. Luke's aunt jumped in front of him. She lost her brother the same way and she wasn't about to lose Luke too.

Wayne looked at me. Then he looked at Luke. He couldn't do what Brad wanted on the strength of our child so he ate his pride as a man and they walked away. I was so happy although I knew Luke was wrong. I respected his decision to spare my baby's father life. This night a new level of respect was granted. Wayne was truly a man all around the board and I wanted him even more because of the fact that he loved my son and me enough to make the choice he made regardless of what his squad felt. They killed niggas all the time and Wayne letting this one go, made them realize we had something special that no one could come between, not even pride. I loved Wayne for this.

For days I tried to forget about Wayne but it was hard. I couldn't eat, sleep or think straight. I cried until I couldn't cry anymore. I called his phone just to hear his voice and he knew it was me with all the hang ups. He was missing me too but he was going to play the game as long as he could. And Luke badgered me constantly about Wayne. Every time he pictured me giving his pussy to Wayne he flipped out and beat me unmercifully like I was somebody in the street and nobody he ever loved.

Chapter 3
WHAT'S IT ALL ABOUT
"Who's Doing What?"

Fall of 1988. I stood in the street crying my eyes out. I was so tired of Luke. He and RJ were dating girlfriends from uptown named Candis and Marcy . He really did the worst this time. He took the fifteen thousand dollars that we had in a joint account out of the bank without my knowledge. He purchased a brand-new white 780 Volvo and he put a four thousand-dollar system in it.

RJ got a new Pathfinder with a similar system in his. And they got a three-bedroom house in Cheltenham Township and he bust my car windows out because I took the beat down shit after he let his new girl drive it. Why was I going to keep letting his girl drive my car to make their runs? They had different squatters to drive so she was driving my car to spite me. She knew all about me before she started messing with Luke. All the girls did but that didn't stop them. They wanted my man.

My homie Sugar and I decided to have a big party because I was turning twenty-one and she simply loved attention. She finally hit the jackpot and was dating a nigga named John that was getting a couple dollars and she wanted everybody in the city to know it.

Sugar and I pulled up to the *Old Player's Club* on Delaware Avenue. We jumped out of her dad's black 944 Porche hyped. Her leather dress fit her petite frame perfectly and my velvet and sequin were definitely hitting for something. We would turn a few heads in the place like always. Sugar and I stayed in the hottest shit and mom hated what I became. She knew what house I was raised in but she began to wonder if I remembered because I was so caught up in fashion and she knew what she instilled in me.

Shalina and her girl Roxy jumped out of her dad's seven series cocaine white BMW. Shalina rocked a black and gold sequin dress and Roxy had that satin and lace shit on. You couldn't tell my squad nothing. We wanted a big turnout and Luke wasn't invited. We gave out 200 invitations but he didn't get one because I wanted fun for one night.

I ran my fingers through my new asymmetrical hairstyle for the fifth time. I was really nervous on the down low. The party actually made a sista sweat. The thought of not being successful at what we set out to do, killed me. I wanted everyone to show up. I wanted the party to be the talk of the town for sure.

I looked across the street only to notice a few cars.

"Nobody is here yet," I said with disappointment.

"You know nobody comes on time. Give it an hour or so," Sugar said with all the confidence in the world. She had no worries. She knew it was gonna be the shit. She knew our party had to be a bash.

"Yeah. You're right. What party do we go to that we're on time?" I said.

As soon as we walked across the street Dante's brother Damon stood in front of the club with a cake for me and fifty bottles of Dom Perion sat in his favorite cocaine white BMW with MCM interior with courtesy of Dante. I met Dante two years before while Luke and I were in Sears having family portraits taken and he was getting money, too, on the other side of town. The YBM boys wanted him to get down with them because they heard about the millions he was getting but he liked being his own man. He didn't need an entourage to feel important. He had everything they had alone, the fancy cars, the jewelry, the houses and girls but for the past year he took his hustle to another city because the Feds were on his heels and he was progressing smoothly. The girls loved him and most of the ballers respected his game despite the fact that he was stepping on their territory but they knew his name from doing business with him before. Dante was so smooth and he wanted one opportunity to show me the world but I wouldn't give him a chance because of Luke, now Luke was doing his thing.
"What's up? Have you been out here long?" I asked Damon.
"Not that long. Where should I take the cake and champagne?" he asked.
"Take it inside."
"I have to get the balloons and roses out the car," he said.
Everybody started coming through an hour later, Sugar's man and his squad, Marsha and her friends, all Shalina's old acquaintances. Roxy's squad was in the place, a couple of my friends from High School. Don was home from jail, the nigga I once had a crush on when I was sixteen but he did me dirty. He let his baby's mama steal my chain from him, then he was sentenced to five years in prison leaving me heartbroken but I got over it. I was young and learning. Now he found out about my party from a mutual friend and he wasn't about to miss seeing my pretty little face. He only wondered what I looked like now but I wasn't checking for his tired ass anymore. He played out. One of Nahum's brothers was up in the place. And Ray was an exception because he wasn't rolling with Luke these days since RJ and Luke was tight. Everybody getting money was there too, from the old ballers to the new ones. I couldn't believe the turn out. It was mad crowded and I was kinda nervous with all the people.
"RJ and them are outside. And somebody said Wayne and them were out there earlier," Sugar whispered in my ear.
"Yeah. I hope they don't start no shit," I said.
"I doubt it. They probably just wanted to see who was here. You know. Being nosey," Sugar said.
"Yeah. I just hope Luke doesn't come down here trippin."
"The photographer is gonna be snapping shots throughout the night. And if you want to take personal shots just let him know okay."

"Okay. Thanks."

The photographer went around snapping shots of everybody while Sugar and I passed out bottles of Dom that Dante sent. Everybody was getting twisted. When I reached Don, I was speechless. I didn't know what to say after so many years and he felt bad about how he left me hanging. He was young and silly but those five years in prison and studying Islam made him a better man. He was home to do right.

"Damn, you look so good," he smiled as I passed him the bottle.

"I don't drink," he smiled proudly.

"Cool," I smiled back. "So how long have you been home?"

"A minute," he said.

"Good for you."

"I know. I know. I have a lot of making up to do. Can I take you out sometimes?" he asked me.

"I'm cool," I said.

"Let me give you my number," he said as he looked around for a pen. Minutes later he got a pen from the bar and gave me his number. I put the number in my hand then I met up with Sugar on the dance floor. He would never hear from me.

Around 1:50 a.m. the lights inside the club got bright. It was time for everybody to part. While I greeted and thanked my guest for coming, RJ's cousin boyfriend Greg stepped to him outside the club about getting down with the YBM. He watched RJ come up and Butch told him to shake RJ down but Greg knew he couldn't hurt RJ because he was like family since he was going with his cousin so Greg figured RJ could get down with them instead.

I walked outside to a street full of people. The let out was just as fun. Ray stood against the wall smiling. He was so glad Luke and I was separated because he still had a thing for me.

"What's up shorty?" he said as he looked me up and down.

"Nothing. Thanks for coming," I said.

"Yeah. Who's your girlfriend?" he asked, pointing to a light-skinned girl with straight black, long hair.

"I don't know. She came with some girls from South Philly," I said.

"Tell her I want her," he said while checking out her hips.

"I don't know her," I said as I looked at her again. Her faced looked familiar but we weren't cool.

"Come on now," he begged.

"No."

He called her over and asked her name then he introduced her to me.

"Your party was nice," she smiled.

"Thanks," I said as I turned away.

"I've seen you and your girl around a lot. I mess with Des from the YBM," she said proudly as she flashed her seven carat cocktail ring that he purchased her as a baby's mama gift.

"Oh, really," I said.

"I like you and what's her name," she hesitated as she looked at Sugar.

"Sugar," I said.

"Yeah. I like y'all style. My girls don't like y'all but I always admire y'all," she said.

"For real," I said as I looked at the photographer snap more shots of Sugar and John. "Nice meeting you."

"Let me have your number so I can hook up with you and your girl sometimes. I get some nice shit and I know y'all like nice things," she said.

I gave her my number then she passed me a paper with Chocolate written on it and a number. That was the name she was given at one because she loved anything chocolate and her man Des was chocolate too.

I walked away to jump in some flicks my homie.

"Hey, hey," smiled a light-skinned brother with freckles. His Peugot was clean as the board of health and you could tell he washed it three times a day. The black showed every scratch and dent. He could stop playin'.

"Hi," I smiled as I looked across the street at the Jeeps with YBM chrome plates on the front of them.

"Come here for a minute," he said. "What's your name?"

"Cinnamon," I said, brushing him off.

"Get the fuck," he laughed.

"No kiddin'," I smirked. "And I guess your name is Mikey."

"Real cute. My name is Bill," he said.

Butch told Ramik as soon as I walked away from Bill he wanted Bill to be history. He was tired of Bill putting him off about getting down with them. Bill was down with a couple brothers from the eastside projects and they were the only ones giving Butch a hard way to go. Once he stepped to niggas and told them to get down, they did but Bill wasn't listening and Bill liked one of Butch's girls, the *Now and Later* bitch so that was even worst.

"Nice meeting you," I said as I walked away.

"Can I call you sometimes?" he seriously said.

"No. I'm cool," I said lastly then I told Sugar about Chocolate.

"Yeah, I heard about her," Sugar said.

"She gave me her number," I said.

"Give it to me. I might need her for something," Sugar said. She was about using whomever she could whereas I wasn't pressed for new friends. I didn't care about getting shit half price. I paid for what I wanted but Sugar loved a discount of any kind.

As soon Bill pulled from the curb Ramik ran on the side of his car and fired. Everybody outside the club ran. The owner of the club locked his door so nobody could get back in. I looked around for my sister and homie. I just wanted to make sure they were okay.

"Cinnamon! Cinnamon!" hollered Shalina. She knew she just saw me standing by the car that was shot. She had to make sure her sister was cool.

"I'm right here!" I hollered from between the bushes. I couldn't believe the dude I just met was leaning back in his seat clinging onto life. He was shot twenty times but he would live.

The cops came but it was too late. Butch and his squad peeled off leaving nothing but skid marks in the street. RJ knew he had to get in Luke's ear about getting down with the YBM because they didn't play no games and RJ and Luke would get more respect being down with them anyway. It would give them substance beyond their imagination.

Chapter 4
THE FAST LANE
"A New Life Begins"

Summer of 1989. Luke drove up in his brand-new 635CSI blasting his 5,000 system. I knew from the car that the coke business was doing him lovely. I couldn't control his choices. I begged him not to get down with the YBM but he did what he thought was the right move at the time.

"Cinnamon I need to talk to you," Luke said as he jumped out of his car.

"What's up?" I asked him.

"I need you to start holding a lot of money for me," he said. I looked at him and shook my head. He knew mom was a Christian and if she caught drugs in her house it would be my ass. She wasn't going for that and I respected her but I was loyal to my peoples too. I thought long and hard then I said, "not for long."

"No, not for long. I just don't know who to trust right now," he said.

"What about Candis?" I asked him. Although he and I settled our differences and were cool, I wondered why she couldn't hold his money since she had a baby with him now and he was her man.

"She's cool but I can't trust her like I can trust you," he said as he thought about her controlling ways. If he told her she couldn't have something, she took it anyway. We were definitely different from each other and Luke wanted both of us but I had to be strong. Why go from number one to seconds? When I'm hooked I'm hooked, but when I cut you, I'm through and I wasn't getting down like that but Luke wanted Candis and me. Me because he knew he could trust me. We had a history together and he knew me inside out. Candis because she was like another nigga, she would make him and RJ's runs. She would bag their coke and hold their artillery for them. And take the rap if she had to, as long as they looked out and paid all the lawyers.

"Okay," I smirked. "I'll do it for you. For you only. I'm not messing with RJ like that. I'm still waiting for y'all to pay all those ticket on the Ford."

"We got you," he said.

"Luke," I hesitated.

"Yeah," he said.

"Be careful out here. You are getting too big messing with the M boys. I told you not to mess with them," I said as I reminisced back to when he started selling weed. He said he was gonna die rich and he was definitely moving up.

Later in the evening Luke brought me 75,000 dollars in a big green trash bag and three bricks to hold for him and RJ. I never imagined them to get as big as they were getting. RJ stepped his game up and traded his 260E in for a 420SEL. He got him and Luke YBM name tags totaling 4 carat diamonds each. They funked their house out with screen tv's in the basement and living room. They got a deck built on the back of the house. They were moving up in the world and as fast as they moved their weight, Butch gave them more. He loved the young boys because they didn't play no games. They were about getting theirs.

After five weeks I couldn't take anymore. Luke and RJ came by mom's too much and it was only a matter of time that she would figure it all out. She stayed on my heels constantly about the traffic. She knew I had a baby by Luke but RJ was coming by frequently and mom didn't like his attitude so she began questioning me about their visits and I wasn't getting kicked out for them because RJ thought it was a joke.

I jumped from my favorite spot to call Luke. They had to get their stuff out of mom's house.

"What's up?" Luke laughed on the other end of the phone.

"I can't be holding your stuff because I'm not going to jail for you and RJ. And if my mom finds out, she is gonna kick me out," I seriously said.

"Just for a little while longer. I promise. It won't be long."

"I'm not playing," I said. He said that one too many times and he was bringing more and more. I had 150,000 dollars now. The bricks came and went but the money was accumulating. I hung up in the same predicament. It wasn't about me benefitting, because I wasn't getting anything and it wasn't like I couldn't, I just didn't want anything from RJ. I was being a loyal baby's mama and friend to Luke because RJ and I didn't have any ties together. In fact, there was no love between us.

Three more weeks passed by and I was sweet as cotton candy. Luke and RJ ignored my words. They kept running the money in like water. It went from 150,000 dollars to 300,000 dollars. RJ called and asked if he could come get 100,000 dollars and I told him he could get it all. I was fed up.

Twenty minutes after our conversation RJ pulled his Benz up slowly and parked.

"Can you get that for me?" he asked. I looked at him and rolled my eyes. He laughed and I got madder.

"If you need anything just let me know," he smiled while grasping his gat that he had tucked in his waist. I just remembered the days when that young nigga was scrambling, riding trick bikes, now he was smelling himself hard.

"You know I got you."

"I don't want your money and I'm not holding it for you. I'm only doing it because of Luke okay. Don't get it twisted," I spat.

"Girl, you are still crazy. When are you gonna stop trippin'?" he smirked.

"When are you gonna get some respect? You do have a sister, aunts and a grandmother and I'm sure you don't want anyone disrespecting them. You need to learn how to respect women and stop calling them hoes and bitches, as if they are trash to you. You are not God's gift to women. And one day you are gonna regret the things you say."

"Whatever! I'm the man. I'm runnin' things. These hoes respect me. They love me. I'm out," he said as he turned his back to me. I wanted to haul off and smack the taste buds out of his mouth, but it would create a bigger mess, so I withdrew. I gave him the money then I called Luke and told him he had until Friday to get his stuff.

I got up early the next morning and enrolled into The Institute for Cosmetology. I was tired of sitting around playing with my life. After going through all the necessary procedures, I knew what I needed to start, a couple hundred dollars, a transcript that I already had, a white uniform and shoes.

Back at home Luke gave me money to get the things I needed for school. I went to the uniform store first in Center City, and then I went to the bookstore to get my supplies. I now had something to look forward to. I would open up my own salon someday.

Every Friday night Sugar came by to get her nails done with Chocolate. Since our party, Sugar had been hanging with Chocolate and we became, *The Three Musketeers instead of Two's Company*. The girls in the city had more reason to hate us now because we were the shit in their eyes. We all were cute, shapely and we could dress our asses off. We kept the latest shit on. Although Chocolate had a man that hustled and gave her generously, she loved to boost. It was a habit that she just couldn't break.

Soon the silly girls figured it all out. Instead of hating on us, they gave me a play because they knew the big ballers stayed at my house getting pedicures and manicures and they figured they could come up. Every chick wanted a nigga that could take care of them instead of them struggling alone. They watched Sugar step her game up. They knew what Des was doing for Chocolate and they knew I wasn't scrambling and my baby's father was still letting me drive his cars and looking out, although he had a woman. A bond not even Candis could understand.

Chocolate pulled up smiling as I stood by the curb thinking on an early Saturday morning. I had just fucked Wayne the night before just because and I wanted my own man. I wanted what everybody else had and that was security but Wayne was playing games. He loved me but I wasn't his main girl still. Things never changed.

"Move your ass out the street!" Chocolate hollered out the window.

"Come on you crazy bitch! Park the car," I laughed, moving from the curb.

"Go with me to Wayne's to chill and watch him and his friends work out."

"Come on."

I jumped in her car, and then we pulled around to Wayne's house and jumped out.

While Wayne and two of his associates worked up a sweat, Chocolate and I sat around talking shit.

"Bitch, you better be glad I like you, cause I'd fuck Wayne. He looks good as shit," laughed Chocolate.

"If you ever try that, I will fuck you up bitch. I don't care if I'm messin' with him or not. You better not even think about it. He's off limits," I let her know. She laughed it off and I wasn't surprised. All the bitches wanted Wayne and the niggas were heated, especially Butch, because Wayne had his girl Romaine first and she was still fucking Wayne on the side. She was only with Butch because she thought he had more money than Wayne. Wayne was rippin' it, too, but he was his own army like my boy Dante. Independent he chose to be. He didn't need an entourage. And no matter how hard the YBM pressed up on him to get down with them, he had pride and he wasn't going to bow down to them. But his man Brad, on the other hand, crossed him and he was down with Butch now. Wayne was hurt. He never imagined Brad to go out like that. They went too far back and he knew the anger Wayne and Butch had between them. Nobody really had love. It was the love of money that had everybody trippin'. Everybody had a motive. Everybody dreamed of being on top. Nobody wanted to be left behind so they used whom they could to get what they wanted. It was scary and it was dangerous, but it was reality. No one played fair, the men, women or the system. It was no fair game.

Wayne came upstairs and gave me five stacks to put on a new car since RJ and Luke dogged mine and never replaced it liked they promised. Chocolate really thought about fucking him at this point. Wayne had the money, looks and I made a mistake and told her something Wayne told me not to ever do and that was, brag about his fuck game. I told her the nigga had a big dick and his fuck game was tight. And that was all that mattered to her. Wayne hit me on the ass and told us to roll. I kissed him and told he I'd see him later and then Chocolate and I went to Sugar's spot for dinner.

Early the next day Sugar convinced me to go to *Heets,* the hood's hot spot. It was a big party for one of the M boys but she claimed she just wanted a split and we could leave so I went along with her. She knew how I was about bars. I didn't smoke or drink and Luke despised me hanging in bars but that was Shalina and Sugar's twist.

Inside the neighborhood bar champagne bottles popped, chatting went on amongst everyone, cigarette smoke filled the lining of the dim room. It was fun for most but unexciting for me. I really wasn't with the set for real, for real. I wanted to leave.

"It's cool," Sugar smiled once she noticed the expression on my face.

"I'm not comfortable."

"Let me get a drink, then we can leave," she lied. She had no intentions on leaving. The night had just begun and all the ballers were out. It was her time to shine.

"All right," I said.

We sat at the bar and she ordered a split. Ten minutes later she ordered another one. I looked at her like, "come on, I'm ready bitch," then Chocolate walked in and sat down with us.

"What's up girl?" she smiled.

"Nothing. I'm ready to roll," I said.

After a couple of hours we walked outside to a wall full of niggas; some of whom I saw before and some I hadn't, picking and choosing for the night, then Sugar named all of them, one by one. Butch and a few of his boys I knew, but the others were all new faces to me.

"Hey shorty, what's up?" asked a dark-skinned guy rockin' an all white linen pants set from the finest boutique in NYC. Chocolate, Sugar and I turned around at the same time.

"Nothing," smiled Sugar.

"I'm talkin' to your friend," he smiled.

"Who me?" I pointed to myself.

"Yeah, you girl. Come here," he said, showing all his teeth.

I hesitated for a moment.

"Go head. He's cool," Sugar whispered.

"You come here," I smiled at him. He walked his sexy body across the street to me. If it wasn't for his white linen, he would've blended right in with the streets. He was the color of Hershey's Special Dark chocolate, not the milk chocolate bar.

"What's your name?" he kindly asked me.

"Cinnamon. What's yours?" I asked.

"Snoop. You sure look good," he said as he licked his full dark lips.

"Thanks," I blushed.

"Do you have a man?" He asked.

"Not really."

"Whatcha' mean not really," he said as he checked me from my head to my freshly pedicured toenails. He pictured my toes in his mouth.

"I have somebody that I kick it with, but we aren't serious anymore," I said as I looked around him.

"I don't care if you do have a man. I want you," he said with confidence as he checked out my nicely proportioned hips. He imagined me naked.

"Is that so," I said.

"I wouldn't lie. Girl you are me," he assured me.

"Oh yeah. How can you be so sure?" I seriously asked him.

"I can tell just by lookin' at you. I was watchin' you the whole night. And I like your style," he said. I was sexy, classy and cute. I would look so good on his arm.

"You like watching people," I smirked.

"No. I just like watchin' you. You got me baby. And I want you," he said with his slick ass. I was too familiar with the pimp lines.

"Well, I have to go. I'll see you later," I said as I turned to walk away.

"You sure will," he assured me.

I walked to the car and got in.

"You know who that was don't you?" Sugar asked excitedly.

"No."

"He's from Allen Woods Projects," she said.

"And," I said as I sucked my teeth. Allen Woods Projects meant nothing to me. I could care less about him and his projects.

"I'm just saying. He has things on lock down there. He's nice. I heard he's linked up with Butch now," she informed me. It was a must that we tied into their squad, us and them, dangerous. We would be the shit with them.

"What he has is his, not mine. What do I care?" I thought, staring out the window into the night. I heard her, but I didn't. Butch and Snoop linking up could only make things worst in the city. The two together only formed a stronger and bigger army. Butch needed Snoop's mentality in his circle. Snoop was a natural born killer. He had class, but he was a thug at heart with his own entourage. Snoop couldn't be moved. Butch could never order him to get down with him. If anything was to progress, it would happen with Snoop being a partner and nothing else and Butch couldn't get around that. The two had to come together. That was the only way it could be. The streets feared this black, young, confident, arrogant nigga named Snoop that wouldn't let anything or anyone stand in the way of him getting what he wanted. He wanted to take the city by storm just like Butch and he had the means to do so. And mind you, he'd kill mothers, sons, daughters, cousins and grandparents to get what he wanted. It was his world. Everybody was just *nuts'* in it.

Sugar, Chocolate and I sat around doing nothing while the city remained deserted the next day. Everybody up and left the night before to go down Virginia Beach so we decided to go too. None of us did VA before so we got lost going down but that was nothing because once we hit the strip, it was poppin' but I wasn't impressed with all the grabbing and pulling. I wanted to smack a couple niggas but I didn't want my ass on the curb so I let my lips do the talking and let it be.

"Hurry up Chocolate, make a left right there and park. They might have some rooms," I pointed to the Lodge on 27th and Atlantic Ave. She turned and parked the car fast, and then we got out and strutted into the motel.

"Do you have any rooms available?" we asked the attendant.

"No, we don't have any rooms," he answered quickly. We got back in the car and rode down the strip checking with almost every hotel and motel until we found a dump that had some rooms left on 3rd & Atlantic. We checked in, and then we went to our room to get settled in.

After settling in we walked the strip only to bump into Snoop and his gang. And Sugar loved it. Although she had John, she didn't mind having Snoop too because he had plenty of money, way more than John. Or anybody from their clique would work. What did she care about Butch? He had two girls and their squad was so deep that she could fuck more than one and who would ever notice or care for that matter.

"Where y'all stayin'?" Snoop asked, looking straight at me.

"At some dump," we all blurted at the same time like we rehearsed every line.

"We're staying at a nice hotel on the beach. Y'all wanna come stay with us?" he asked.

"We're cool," I answered quickly.

Chocolate nudged me in the side.

"Girl, say yeah. Say Yeah," she whispered all hyped.

"Y'all don't have to stay in our rooms. We have the whole floor. And they have rooms left. I'll get y'all, y'all own room," said Snoop.

"All right," said Sugar, taking control of the situation.

We went to our room and gathered our things while Snoop and his gang waited.

At the hotel twenty minutes later I slid the key in and turned the knob.

"Boy this is the best thing that could have happened to us. This hotel is top notch. I'm so glad we ran into them," I smiled, looking around the clean, comfortable room with the fragrance of citrus fruits lingering.

After we got situated, we drove the strip only to bump into Luke and Candis and RJ and their squad following ten cars deep. It hurt to see Luke showcasing Candis in VA but what could I do. It was over between us and I wasn't playing second fiddle.

My girls and I hit Venice Restaurant only to bump into Snoop and his boys once again. We simply couldn't get around them.

"Come sit with us," suggested Snoop. I looked at Sugar and Chocolate, they walked away from me and sat down with them. I hesitated for a minute, then I joined them.

Minutes later the waiter took our order and while we waited for our food we had a chitchat about different things. Sugar and Chocolate talked more than me. I did most of the listening.

"Does Des know you're down here Chocolate?" asked Snoop. He knew Des didn't like her being there but she did what she wanted to do.

"He's doing his thing, so I'm doing mine," she smirked.

"That's how it is? What about you Sugar? Does your man know you're down here?" he asked.

"Yeah," she answered, smiling from ear to ear.

He looked at me and said, "You don't have a man right?"

"I told you my situation," I said.

"Well, I wanna make you my girl. What do you think about that?" he asked.

"I'm sure you have a women," I said.

"I have friends, but no woman."

"Sure. Isn't that the famous line?" I said.

"Why don't you let me prove it to you?" he asked.

"Stop pulling my shoe. I didn't come down here to find a man."

The waiter came out and broke the conversation by putting our food in front of us. Snoop watched me closely as I ate my lobster. *Damn, I want Shorty so bad. I can eat her pussy right now. She's a bad motherfucker. I'm gonna spoil her.*

"I want you girl," he smiled. I ignored him and kept eating, then I gave Sugar and Chocolate the cue. We thanked them and left.

We walked five minutes up the strip and a white stretch limo pulled on the side of us. The dark tinted window rolled down slowly.

"Can you come to my room later?" Snoop asked me. He knew what he wanted and it was no game playin'.

"No! I most certainly cannot," I let him know.

He looked at me with a bigger grin and said, "I'm gonna have you girl before it's all over with."

His window went back up slowly, then they pulled off.

Everywhere Sugar, Chocolate and I went, we ran into Snoop and his boys. At the Pocahontas Pancakes & Waffle shop, Snoop asked me to sit under him and I was so intimidated by his presence. I didn't know if it was the age or the experience, but it was something about Snoop and I had to put my finger on it.

I ate my Belgian Waffles so fast so I could get away from Snoop. He kept assuring me that he was gonna have me and that scared me, the most. What was I gonna do with him? He was too much for little old me. He had way more under his belt than I had. I was still learning. The thought was special but I couldn't get down with him.

Snoop and I bonded the entire time in VA. I broke everything down to him about Luke and Wayne and coincidentally, he was cool with both of them but he didn't care about that. He wanted me to be his girl.

Chapter 5
Big Things
"Mafia Princess"

Fall of 1989. Snoop came back to the city and put his thing all the way down. He showered me with roses, money and pretty things. He simply wasn't letting up on little old me and I began to like the thought of what he had to offer. My homies were happy with men taking care of them. Luke and Candis were happy and he was taking care of her. Everybody I knew had somebody and I deserved the finer things too but Snoop was very dominating. Although I felt protected around him, he scared me when his mask came off. But that's the way it had to be or who would respect him in the streets, very few.

For weeks Snoop took me around and showcased me like I was his personal baby doll. He even made sure Wayne knew about us. Wayne's ego was crushed but he had his turn. I gave him more than enough time to get his shit together. He knew how crazy I was about him, but he took me for granted. Now we could only be friends. Life wasn't always fair anyway.

On my birthday Snoop surprised me with a ten-carat diamond ring and a trip to LA. Although he had business to attend to out there, it was a shopping spree awaiting me. I was so excited. I had nice things done for me before but Snoop was doing it bigger than anyone I ever had in my young life.

Before boarding USAir flight 973, Luke and I had a heart to heart conversation about everything that was going on in our lives. He was hurt about Snoop proposing to me but he had Candis and I deserved happiness too, besides, he would never try to disrespect me again ever because I was with the big boss now. I wasn't just his baby's mom anymore. I had someone that would kill for me. Snoop was my protector, my Mafia King. He and Luke were tied through the game. It was all in the family now.

As soon as Snoop and I hit LA, we went straight to Rodeo Drive to shop. I got two pairs of Gucci ostrich loafers in my favorite colors with bags and belts to match. I got a suede skirt suit from Bally's for six gees that I would wear to the Redd Foxx show later in the evening. I got a pocketbook, shoes, boots and a piece of linen from each store on the drive then I got all the new perfumes that was out.

The chauffeur dropped Snoop, RayRay and me off at the hotel. I had so many bags that bellboy didn't know how to put my things on the cart. It was too much for one trip.

Inside the suite I walked up the spiral staircase. I couldn't believe we had a house inside a hotel. We were definitely doing it big.

I walked over to the balcony to get a closer look at the scenery outside. Everything was simply gorgeous from afar and up close had to be better. The palm tree-lined street was spotless. It looked as if I was looking at a painted picture. I walked into the bathroom to jump in the Jacuzzi. My body needed to relax.

"Don't do anything," Snoop hollered into the bathroom. "A masseuse and a masseur is comin' to give us massages."

"I have never had a professional massage before. Do I have to take all my clothes off?" I asked out of ignorance.

"Yeah, but you'll have a towel over you," he said.

Within minutes Snoop and I lay butt naked staring at each other. I got kinda jealous as I watched the masseuse rub all over my man's ass and private parts. She looked to be doing extras and I knew Snoop all too well, he probably paid her extra to get extra but whatever turned him on was my pleasure. *He's daddy.*

"I have a meeting to go to and I want you to be there so get dressed when we're finished," he said.

"Okay," I said.

After my massage I got up at my man's request and slipped into a black Ellen Tracy sleeveless spandex dress then I put on a pair of black Bally's pumps. Snoop put on a black two-piece suit to compliment my dress then we jumped into the limo with RayRay and one of his associates from LA named Buggy.

The limo pulled up to dropped us off in front of *Delmonico's Lobster House*. It was his man Hasan's favorite spot.

"Come on baby," said Snoop, grabbing me by the arm. I grabbed him gently by the waist then we walked into the restaurant to be approached by an older, sharp man with plenty of class. He was sharp as a tack with his three-piece Gucci suit on. I could only imagine who he was. I stood back and watched while they all hugged each other Mafia style, then we all sat down.

"Oh Hasan. This is my wife Cinnamon," Snoop smiled, introducing us.

"You definitely have a winner. She's beautiful," he smiled as he fixed his multicolor Gucci tie.

"Thanks. I'm pleased to meet you," I stuck out my hand to shake his.

"She is a blessing Hasan," Snoop laughed. He had mad respect for Hasan. And Buggy dated is daughter so they were close for two reasons.

While we ordered lunch and waited for our food to come back, Snoop and Hasan discussed business, and big business it was, involving a lot of people. Snoop played a very important part that affected the entire city. The move he was about to make would tear the roof of the motherfucker for real. It was big, big, big business, involving millions of dollars, not one million either, 12.5 million. Snoop had to handle everything now with Butch sitting behind bars waiting for his trial to start about another drug dealer that he planned to execute because he wouldn't get down with them, but he managed to survive in a wheelchair to testify against his entire organization.

At the show we laughed and cried at Redd Foxx. I didn't know who was funnier, him or Richard Pryor. I cried so hard that I leaked in my brand-new Victoria's Secret panties that Snoop purchased me for the trip. He was hoping to make me feel sexy and freaky so he could persuade me into giving him what he was giving me but I wasn't ready for oral sex. Besides, I never asked him to eat me anyway.

After Snoop's business was complete, we boarded US AIR back home. The thought of his investment made him cockier than ever. Although tender and loving in bed, he remained hard as a rock outside. He couldn't wait to get home to give out orders. Money had to be gotten and he wasn't taking no shorts. If niggas wanted to mess up, then they had to die.

"If things go like I expect them to, we gonna be straight. Me and you girl, against the world. I'm gonna spoil you. This here ain't nothin' compared to what I want to do for you," he let me know before our flight landed. I wrapped myself in his arms and smiled. We felt like real superstars, him Romeo and me Juliet. I had a place in this world again.

Back at home Snoop gave out orders to all his soldiers. I couldn't believe the authority he possessed. He was actually their Lieutenant. He ran these dudes and they sat silently and listened. They didn't question him or give him attitude. I began to wonder what I was getting myself into. I thought I knew the nigga I was dating, but I began to realize his position for real. I was a **Young Black, Mafia Princess**. His princess but did I know the cost for real? Was I really ready for all he had to give?

After Snoop hugged his soldiers, he gave me the cue. I jumped under his armpit quickly and we left. Snoop only found peace when he was around me. Everything else in his life was too stressful. Everything he did was for others. He barely enjoyed anything. His hustle was meaningless to some.

Early the next evening Snoop and I hit the highway doing 90 miles per hour in his 300ZX Turbo, listening to Ice T's, *I'm Your Pusher*, his theme song. He had a meeting with his peoples in Inglewood and I was to accompany him. He liked the way I completed him and he felt secure with me under his wing at all times.

"Baby here comes the police. I got that gat under the seat," he said, looking in the rear view mirror.

"Okay."

We pulled over and Snoop pulled his window down for the officer.

"License, registration and insurance card," said the red neck officer hoping Snoop didn't have everything he asked for so he could fuck with him. Snoop handed the officer everything he asked for immediately. He made him look stupid.

"Stay in the car. I'll be right back," ordered the officer with his hand on his blackjack. He knew he would find something wrong once he got back to his car.

"Baby put the gat between your legs. He can't check you," said Snoop. I picked the gun up slowly and stuffed it in my pants.

"Are you cool?" I asked Snoop.

"Yeah. I'm straight. All my stuff is registered to Byran. He's cool. He don't have any bench warrants or anything."

"You're using somebody else's identity," I said.

"I have to. You know how I ride." Snoop and Byran favored, thank God. They had so many similarities and some of the same characteristics. I watched the cop as he walked back to the car. He handed Snoop tickets for speeding, then he looked closer. He had to find something.

"Step out the car for a minute," he ordered Snoop. Snoop opened the door slowly to step out. He didn't know what was going on.

"Keep your hands where I can see them," said the officer. Snoop made his hands visible and the officer called for backup. *Damn!* The officer checked under the seats to find nothing. Then he thought about the ashtrays.

"I'm going to have to take you in," said the officer.

"What!" he snapped.

"You heard me. Don't say a word," the officer informed him. He cuffed Snoop and waited patiently for backup. Snoop didn't think to hide a small bag, a five-dollar bag of weed.

At the station Snoop let me know who to contact and what to do, then I hit the highway doing 80mph listening to *Chubb Rock*. I had to get home as soon as possible to follow his orders out. He had to be out by morning.

In the morning RayRay and I went straight to the station and got Snoop out before they knew who he really was. They didn't have a clue and if they found out, he would've been fucked for a number of reasons.

The ride back to the city was serious. Snoop and I had issues to discuss. Being with Snoop meant the world to me, but we had no privacy for real. Every spot he had, at least one of his boys came through and staying at hotels were cool, but we needed a place to call home. And I was ready for big things now. Mom's wasn't where I should've been with a man getting money like Snoop was getting. And even if he wasn't getting money, it was time to step out and do things like a big girl.

As soon as we hit the spot, I sat down and waited for a solution from Snoop. He had the answers when it came to everything else so he had to come up with something for us.

"As soon as I get things straightened out, I'm gonna buy you a big house on a hill. I could get you something now, but I want you to have the best so I'm gonna wait til I make this major move," he said, laying on the buttery leather sofa, smoking laced weed, watching *Scareface* on his 60-inch screen tv.

"Whatever you do I'll be satisfied," I said and I only said it because I knew he loved me because I was understanding but it was only a matter of time for him too.

"See. That's why I love you girl. You are so understanding and you never complain about nothing I do. You're submissive just like a woman should be. I never had a women that I could take everywhere I go. They could relate to either one crowd and not the other or none of them, you though, you can relate to everybody. You know how to adjust to any situation. You have a lot of class and you also have a rough side of you. You know when and how to act without me telling you. I love that about you. We can ride out Shorty," he said, plucking the ashes into the marble ash tray. *Whatever!* I thought inwardly. I was getting tired with the lines.

In the morning I lay in bed while Snoop went to the Masjid. Snoop being raised in a Christian home like I held some values but he wasn't about to give up the Muslim religion for anything. That's all he knew. For the past ten years he practiced the religion hard. The Masjid saw him faithfully on Friday's. And although, he said he wasn't on his deen like he was supposed to be, he stood firm on what he believed. Pork I hadn't done since a young child because Grandpop's job made me hate pork, but beef I no longer knew because of Snoop. But I wasn't about to take my Shahaada for no one, not even Snoop. Now that, I couldn't do.

Before Snoop returned from the Masjid, I got up and went to Candis and Luke's place to pick my boy up. He loved chilling with his family but I missed him.

As soon as I walked through the doors, I overheard Marcy talking to Candis about still fucking Snoop on the side. I knew girls were vicious and her words may have been phoney but I couldn't let it go because I knew what kind of man I had. Women were coming at him from all angles. My homies were even jealous of my happiness when I thought they would be happy for me.

They act like I don't deserve to be happy. They want to be in my shoes. They want to wear my clothes. They wanna shop where I shop and eat where I dine. They want my man. They want to be me. I thought as I fastened Luke in the car. I couldn't wait to get home to question Snoop about Marcy. I was heated.

Before I could call Snoop to question him about Marcy, Chocolate called to deliver the news about Snoop having a girl named Nora pregnant so I had a lot to discuss with him. I was getting frustrated with all the gossip. I just wanted everybody to leave me alone whether the rumors were true or not because all things come to the light eventually. If Snoop was the lying, cheating dawg they claimed him to be, I would surely find out some day.

The niggas game wasn't that tight. His play would be up soon too. Even the best of the best get exposed.

Chapter 6
THE BETRAYAL
"Who Can You Trust?"

One month later. Nora was about to have her baby and Snoop still didn't know how to drop the bomb on me so he got me a brand-new 1990 BMW with all the luxuries and the convertible Mustang he got me with the 3,000 dollar BBS rims, would be a second car until he passed it off to his youngins'.

After I cleaned birthday cake, candy, food and ice-cream off mom's floor, Sugar, Chocolate, Spice and I jumped in Sugar's man Pathfinder to hit the skating rink where everybody was sure to be on a Sunday.

Spice was a friend of Chocolate's. They hit stores together and although I knew about her writing Luke while he was away in boarding school, I gave her the benefit of the doubt. He didn't like her anyway so I had to accept the fact that she liked my man and went for what she wanted and that was behind us now.

"Pull over y'all. Don't that look like Snoop in my car?" I shouted to my girls as we crossed 68th Street. He only looked for me to be in the Mustang. He never thought I'd be driving in a Pathfinder so he wasn't prepared for me.

"Yup. And he has a girl in there with him," said Chocolate, Sugar and Spice, at the same time.

"No, he don't. Let me out!" I hollered. I jumped in the street in front of the car. He wasn't about to run me over so he stopped and his face dropped at the sight of me. He didn't know what to say or do and the bitch knew who I was so she turned away. They were caught red handed.

"Who is your friend Snoop?" I calmly asked Snoop as he hit the button for the window to come down. I couldn't let her know what I was feeling. I had to let her think I was confident and secure with mine.

"It's not what you think. I'm just givin' her a ride," he explained.

"Well, I'm going with you," I said then I walked over to the Pathfinder to tell Sugar I was riding with Snoop while he told the girl what to say if I asked anything.

"All right. If you need us, you know where we're going," said Sugar.

"I'm cool."

I made the girl Fay get in the back of the car and I sat up front with my man. If something was going on, she felt like an idiot this night. I bust both of their grooves.

Sugar sat behind the wheel of the Pathfinder for a minute to make sure I was cool, then they sped off to do their thing for the night.

Minutes later Snoop pulled up to Island Ave and let the girl Fay out. They gave each other a fake ass good-bye greeting then she ran up her steps. I was far from stupid but what could I do. He was caught and I knew better but I wasn't going anywhere so there wasn't any use in complaining. I knew I had a fucking playa but I hated to accept it. It was just a matter of time that I got fed up with him too. All the money in the world couldn't make me stay with the lying, cheating nigga.

The very next morning Luke's aunt came and got me to go to Luke's rescue again. Ray turned on Luke to gain points from RJ. He hated their relationship and he was broke. He wanted to be down so bad so shooting Luke was the best thing for him to do to get in. If he was bold enough to try RJ's right-hand man, then he was good because he knew RJ wasn't as loyal to Luke as Luke was to him.

After seeing Luke and knowing he was cool, I went straight to his aunt's house with the rest of the family. Ray called to explain himself and beg for forgiveness moments later. He knew Luke would forgive him but he was concerned with how I felt and what the YBM was going to do next. He knew most of them had mad love for Luke and the only way they weren't going to come at his neck is if Luke told them it was cool. I kindly let Ray know that he was on my shit list because he risked my son having a father and I couldn't forgive him for that.

Before Luke left the hospital he let his squad know they didn't have to retaliate on Ray because it was merely a misunderstanding. Luke could never stay upset with anyone. He had a forgiving heart especially when it came to his friends. And snitchin' wasn't a part of the game. If you snitched, you got no respect. If you snitched, it could cost you something really nice. And Luke shot his best friend when they were thirteen and his friend never told his family. He forgave Luke because he knew it was a mistake. They were playing with the gun and Luke pointed it at him and it really went off so he had to forgive Ray like his friend forgave him.

While Luke recouped from his wounds at home, Ray ran around the city being RJ's flunky so he could earn stripes from the YBM. Being a part of them was a dream come true for him and the opportunity to show how much heart he had. RJ really thought Ray was a killer after he did what he did to Luke. He knew he wasn't a sucker and they could go on killer missions and rip the city apart.

Luke pulled his body out the bed to get a painkiller from Candis's backpack. It was hours since she'd left and the pain was kicking in again but she was at the *End of the Dove* with the bull Bones from the County and she knew he was the enemy. RJ was emulating Butch and Snoop. He wanted to be the next Kingpin in the city so he had been trying to extort Bones for months. Bones was getting money in Sussex County and he visited the city frequently and RJ didn't like it. If he wanted to come to his city and shine, he had to pay taxes but Bones kept ignoring RJ's threats. He wasn't about to a pay nigga for something he hustled hard to get. He wasn't having it.

43

Inside the front of the backpack Luke found the painkillers and a piece of paper with directions to the *End of the Dove* and Bones number on it. His heart sank into the floor. His girl was sexing the enemy while he was home hurt. How could she be so slimy? He knew she was cold but how could she cross her baby's father? He said forget the painkillers and everything else. He hopped to the bed and waited for her return. It was no explaining this one. He was gonna beat her ass with his crutches.

Candis stayed out until 12:00 a.m. Luke couldn't believe twelve hours went by and she never bothered seeing about him. She crept through the door with Gap and Strawbridges bags full of clothing. She had her story lined up.

"Where the fuck you been?" Luke asked Candis. From his tone she knew she had to put her helmet on because he was about to take it to her head. "I was out doing my thang," she smirked as she took the clothes from the bags. "I told you I was goin' to the stores."

"This long Candis. You know I told you about that boosting shit. And what the fuck are you doin' fuckin' wit' Bones!" he hollered as he grabbed his crutch.

"What are you talkin' 'bout? I don't fuck with him. Marcy does," she lied.

"Directions and his number was in your backpack," he said as he got closer.

"She had my backpack the other night," Candis said as she reached in her Guess jean shorts for her favorite pocket knife.

"I don't believe that bullshit ho! You ain't nothin' but a trick bitch! I don't know why I had a baby by you bitch," he said lastly then he swung his crutch at her head and she repeatedly stabbed him in his wounds until he fell to the floor.

"I'm gonna kill you bitch," he hollered as he reached for the phone to call his aunt. He was in severe pain and he knew he had to get to the hospital before he bled to death.

At the hospital Luke told me about Candis and Bones affair and how he made a mistake messing with her but that's the life he chose and that was that.

I left after sitting for hours. I needed some rest and I was drained with the Candis bullshit. I knew Luke did his dirt but I couldn't accept her degrading my baby's daddy. If Luke was nothing else, he was a damn good provider and she did things she didn't have to do. Luke took care of home. That was a given.

I noticed Chocolate's car in front of my mom's as soon as I turned the corner. I slid into the parking space in the back of her and jumped out with my boy.

"I saw Nora in the bar last night and she's definitely pregnant. She looks like she's due any day," she informed me.

"For real," I said in shock.

"Yup. Me and her talked for a little while. She says she knows you," she said.

"She knows me from where?" I asked her.

"From the block."

"I don't know her," I said, thinking deeper.

"She hangs with the girl that used to mess with Wayne that said something to him while y'all was at the club one night," she explained.

"Yeah, I know who you're talking about. But I still can't place Nora."

"She says she knows you and she never did like you," she let me know.

"She used to hang with Romaine and her clique too way back when."

"Is that so?" I said as I headed up the steps. Anybody that fucked with Romaine was trouble. Those *Now and Later* groupie bitches were our enemies.

"She's pregnant by Snoop, too," she said.

"I guess she told you that, too," I said and I about had it at this point. Chocolate was my girl but I began to see straight through her veil. She loved drama. And this was too much in one night for me.

"Yeah. They have been messing around for years. She says she knows about you being his girl, but she doesn't care."

"Oh, yeah," I said as I walked into the living room to call Snoop.

Snoop's phone rang and rang and rang. He was handling business so he didn't answer my call. He figured he'd pick me up later once he finished.

Snoop didn't finish his business until five in the morning so I went to sleep because I had to be to school by nine.

9:45 a.m. Snoop and Greg pulled up in my car and beeped the horn for me to come out. He knew I was pissed because he was late but he didn't know I was going to start the Nora shit so he wasn't prepared for my anger.

"Hey baby," he said happily as I got into the passenger's seat.

"Is Nora pregnant by you?" I asked him. I had to cut through the chase. I had to know. I didn't want to play no more games. He was gonna tell me something. He looked at me with sadness in his eyes but that wasn't gonna work this day.

"Is she?" I demanded an answer. "Is she pregnant with your baby? Snoop I wanna know is Nora pregnant with your child?"

"Let me explain," he said calmly. "Baby just let me explain to you."

"Explain what!" I said. "What can you explain to me?"

"I was messing with her before I got with you. And she didn't tell me that she was pregnant until a little after your birthday. I didn't get her pregnant while we were together," he explained. I added up the months for myself.

"Okay. She got pregnant before we hooked up, but I asked you if she was pregnant months ago and you lied to me."

"I was afraid I would lose you, that's why I didn't tell you. And besides, I don't want her," he said.

"You have been messing with her for years so you must like something about her," I said.

"It has been off and on for years. I would stop messing with her and she'd see me out and want to sleep with me or something. I never looked for her, in fact, that's how she got pregnant. We were at a bar one night and she saw me there and she asked me to go home with her and I did. I did it to her that one time and she got pregnant."

"Fine, but I'm still hurt. You are my man and you have somebody else pregnant. I'm humiliated."

"You have no reason to be humiliated. You're my girl. I love you," he sincerely said with tears in his strong eyes.

Snoop dropped me off at the school and I went inside frustrated. Things just weren't the same anymore. How could I function with so much going on in my life? Snoop withheld, too many things from me but I wasn't about to let Nora win just because she had a seed with him.

For two days Snoop stayed away. He didn't return my calls and he wasn't at any of the spots that I knew about. I was fed up with him. I planned to end the relationship if his excuse wasn't good enough.

Finally the phone rang at dinner time. Upset I was but I was glad to know he was breathing.

"Hello," I said.

"I was in the hospital the other day," Snoop explained before I could ask anything.

"For what?" I asked.

"I had a slight stroke on the left side of my face," he explained. I heard of that happening to someone before so I tuned in for more details.

"How did that happen?" I asked.

"I'm sorry, but when you are finished, I need to talk to you," a woman's voice said on the other end of the phone then she slammed it down.

"Who was that?" I asked.

"My son's mother," he said.

"Which one?" I wanted to know. He had seven kids and four different babies mamas. He went with maybe two of them, so he says, but the oldest three mother, was the one that he went with for years. And he claimed they weren't together when he met me.

"Emily," he said.

"Tell me something. Do y'all live together?" I asked.

"This is the big house. I bought it for her and my kids. I told you we're not like that."

46

"Okay. You tell me that, that's the big house and you bought it for her and your kids, but is that your woman and do you live there?" I demanded to know.

"I'm only here because of my kids and as soon as I buy your house, I won't be here anymore. I don't have anywhere else to stay," he said.

"That's bullshit! You have plenty of places to stay. This is another secret you withheld from me. What's next? What else am I gonna find out? What am I gonna be surprised with next? I'm tired of you and then you have the nerve to call me from there," I screamed.

"I told you it's not like that. That's why I'm calling you from here," he tried to persuade me to believe.

"Sure. She probably doesn't even know who you're talking to. You probably told her anything. I'm through. You can come get your ring. I don't want to have anything to do with you," I told him.

"I'm not lyin'. She knows about you and everything. She knows I'm in love with you. She found your letter," he said. He had to find something convincing to tell me.

"I don't know what kind of relationship y'all have, but I don't want to be bothered," I said finally then I slammed the phone in his ear.

A couple of hours passed by and Snoop came to my door begging and pleading for me to believe him and not go but I was so hurt. I wrote him a nice break up letter and gave it to him then I took my ring off and threw it in the street. He knew I wasn't playing at this point. That ring represented the bond we shared and I broke that once I threw it in the street. How could I trust a man that made me fall for him first then hit me with blow after blow? I wasn't that stupid or pressed.

Snoop picked the ring up out the street and gently placed it back on my finger then he let me know I was his **Mafia Princess**, I couldn't leave him if I wanted to and he'd kill for me.

Once he skidded off in his car I stood on the porch and cried my eyes out. I knew Snoop meant what he said. I was his and he'd kill for me. Snoop's word was his bond. He played no games and I had to find a way out. I couldn't spend the rest of my life in bondage. I couldn't stay where I wasn't happy. The excitement wore off.

For days Snoop stayed at the lick house getting high off syrup and downers. He went from gentle, patient and kind to aggressive when dealing with me now too and all the money, gifts and promises couldn't make me happy. He gave me two brand-new furs that he bought off Spice. He showed me a house of my dreams that he promised to buy me once money was right. He asked me for a chocolate girl and I wasn't about to have a baby by him now. I thought about it before when I thought I was in love but once I realized I wasn't in love with him, bearing his child would never happen. He asked me to make arrangements fast for our wedding because

Butch was home and he was marrying Megan because the FBI was on their heels but I wasn't about to go out like that. Being married to him would only cause me so much misery and grief and Megan was tripping because Butch took care of her but she shared him with Romaine for years. I was glad though because Romaine's shit hit her in her face. She didn't win in the end. That "*Now and Later*" shit played out. He definitely left her for *Later*. *Damn!*

The night before the wedding after the bachelor party, Butch and Snoop hit every bar, every after hour joint, and every chill spot in the city to get some money because a lot of their money wasn't accounted for and somebody had to pay or shit was about to get crazy. Niggas knew what it was though. Butch was home. Snoop was on his prowl like always and it was time to give that money up or *die*. *Killing your own about a dollar.*

After collecting an easy two hundred thousand dollars, Snoop and Butch both took it in for the night. They had more to talk about amongst the family. Their squad had to hit the streets early the next morning, right before the wedding.

I made sure I saw Snoop off then I went home. I really didn't want to do the wedding thing because Snoop was in it and that meant I had to sit alone and I wasn't prepared for that, besides, it was gonna be a whole lot of people there that I didn't even mess with and I wasn't good at faking the funk.

Around 2:00 a.m. Snoop called waking me from my sleep with his gangsta bullshit. He got so drunk, licked and zannied up at the reception that they took their thing to Carol's Hall for the after party but the strip was so lined up with cars and people that Snoop got into a confrontation with a man and he had his man Nice, rock the man in front of everybody outside the club. His ego would be the cause of his down fall. It was just a matter of time before somebody on the streets got tired of their shit or before the law came to indict them. They had too much going on. They were too cocky with their business and they became too lax. None of them were using their brains and I was tired of all the drama. Every time I turned around he was getting bailed out of jail for something stupid. I couldn't take it anymore.

For the next few weeks shit got mad crazy. Luke realized RJ was out for self. He never wanted Luke to outshine him so Luke broke ties with him and started his own thing. RJ was his man but it was time to move forward. They weren't kids anymore. They were men with big decisions to make and rumor had it, Candis was doing him now too so things would never be the same.

Snoops drugs didn't get into the US like they were supposed to and it was a drought so Snoop was going buck wild now. He stayed in the lick house drugged up. He smoked laced weed daily and we definitely weren't seeing eye to eye anymore. And Chocolate told me Snoop and DeRock partied Spice at the hotel and I let that *snake* drive the car he bought me.

Everybody was doing everybody. Nobody was satisfied with their significant other. Sugar was creeping with Luke's boy KC because she was tired of John's shit with his baby's mama. Chocolate was messing with my old love Wayne on the sly. *The love of money* had everybody screwed up. Nobody cared about morals or respect. It was crazy.

Although I wanted to leave Snoop, he wasn't letting it happen. He scooped me up every night to ride with him then we'd chill up in hotels until he fell asleep from his high. All that used to intrigue me didn't anymore. I was living in misery. Nora and whoever else could have Snoop's problems. I wanted out of his mess.

The hotel's phone rang at seven a.m. in the morning. Snoop talked to Butch before we went to sleep but I couldn't imagine him to call so early so I hesitated to wake Snoop but the phone kept ringing so I nudged him and he answered it.

"You're lying!" he screamed hitting the wall. The hotel manager would be charging my credit card for damages at checkout because of the hole in the wall. "I'll be right there."

Snoop hung up the phone and told me to get dressed. Des got murdered the night before. The YBM had to meet. As Snoop drove, I cried. I couldn't believe all this was happening. Although Chocolate and I weren't that close anymore, she was still my homie. My heart went out to her. I couldn't imagine life without my child's father. I didn't know what I would do if I lost Luke to the streets.

Snoop dropped me off at Luke's aunt house, then he sped off to meet Butch. Once Luke reached for me I was so grateful. I realized how lucky I was. Des's children would never feel his touch again. I had to cherish each moment while I could because what happened to Des was unexpected. We just never know.

When big Luke pulled up I was so happy to see his face. I didn't care that he was depressed. I was just so glad that he was alive and not dead like Des.

"Did you hear about Des?" he asked me.

"Yeah. Snoop just went to meet Butch."

"This shit is crazy. I don't know what to do. The game is getting shaky. Money isn't right and niggas are crossing each other," he said.

"Do you know who killed him?" I asked him.

"No. Nobody knows," he said but Des was with his boy Tyrone's girl Sheila. I told you how the game went. It was a never-ending circle. Everybody was doing everybody.

Everybody in the city prepared for Des's funeral. Snoop and his squad got black suits and Gators from Allure's and they rented ten limos for their gang.

It was mad crazy. You would've thought Des's funeral was a big party or something. All the hating chicks packed my cousin Carol's joint to get their hair done. Some of the broads weren't even cool with our clique but they had to be there. Carol's was the hottest joint for the drug dealer's girls and gossip and Des's funeral would be a come up to some.

After all the stress and tension, I decided not to go to the funeral. I knew I was wrong not supporting my man or girl but Sugar sat in for me because I couldn't do it. I couldn't stand to be around fakes and that's what most of them were.

For days Chocolate became distant. The FBI wanted to shut the YBM down so badly that they got into Chocolate's ear and told her Snoop was responsible for Des's death. She in turn told Des's people and some really believed it. To pay Snoop back, Chocolate would work for Agent Powell. Anything Snoop and I would do, Chocolate would relate back to him, if that meant hurting more innocent people then so it would be. The FBI wanted the YBM to war against each other. And all I knew is that Snoop was with me the night Des got murdered so if he sent a hit man out to do the job, I couldn't attest to that.

As the days and nights grew the gossip seemed to get twisted. All kinds of rumors were out about who killed Des and the YBM began to fall apart. Butch squad was still his squad and Snoop's squad was still down with him but a lot of people were stuck in between the two of them.

Des's boy Bear believed Butch and Snoop had something to do with Des's death so he wanted both of them behind bars. Des's death definitely shed some light on the game. I knew things were deep, but I never imagined it to be that deep.

I was so disgusted with Snoop because Nora stole the keys to my BMW while he was asleep at her house. She drove my car up and down my block to humiliate me. How was he going to fix this one? I didn't know but I knew this was the end of my patience with him. We had a big argument in front of my mom's but I let him take me to *Vinnie's* with his boys. It was Prom night and everybody was out.

After eating Snoop, his boys and I walked the lot to jump into our cars. It was a whole lot of new young boys out that didn't know who Snoop or his clique was. One of the young boys bumped into Ramik and called him a sucker and Snoop had his body laying across the black rail. I couldn't believe what transformed before me. I knew I had a gansta' but he was tripping.

Lights flashed and sirens sounded all over the place. Everybody scattered in different directions. It was time to move out.

"Baby get the car!" Snoop hollered. I ran and got the car immediately, then I pulled around to the front of the restaurant and opened the door for Snoop to get in.

"Get in!" I shouted. "Get in!"

Snoop glanced around quickly while jumping in the passenger's seat. Cops flooded the lot and entrance to find out what happened. And they were prepared. They had everything blocked off with their hands clutching their guns.

"I want you to drive out like nothing is wrong," instructed Snoop.

Troopers stood on both sides of the entrance hollering, but whatever my man said was what I wanted to hear. I had to play my part. I was stuck and I had to get us out of there. We were on the Bonnie and Clyde tip this night. "Go ahead drive through them," Snoop ordered. I looked at Snoop with his gat in his hand and I knew he was playing no games, then I looked at the Troopers waiting for me to try them. My heart pounded fast but I had to ride out with mine. He depended on me. I was his partner in crime.

"Go ahead drive through! Drive!" he shouted. "Drive through them motherfuckas."

I pressed my foot on the gas peddle and drove toward them. They drew their guns quickly. They didn't give a fuck either. It was a bunch of ignorant black people that meant nothing to them. And we kept bringing this ghetto bullshit to their territory. They weren't having it. They wanted us to stay where we belonged or act right if we came out.

"Put your head down and drive through them," he said calmly. I ducked down and proceeded through the Troopers while they let off all their rounds nonstop. Bullets flew everywhere with one hitting my left foot. Glass shattered all over the place and in my face. The tires on the car went flat immediately.

"Go! Go! Go! Don't stop!" he said, frantically while shooting back. I drove over the median and made a left turn with a burning foot. I looked over to my right to make sure Snoop was okay. Blood poured from his arm splattering everywhere.

"Oh, God!" I screamed lowly.

"I'm hit baby. Make a left and go straight down until you get to the dead end and make a right," he said.

"I think I'm hit too because my foot is burning really bad, but I don't feel any blood dripping and I can't look."

"Get us to a hospital," he begged. "Just get us to the hospital."

I drove through the park on four rims scrapping and burning the ground pass the Sergio Club where everybody stood listening to me come, even my baby's father. He couldn't believe what he saw. I was on the mission with Snoop and I had a son to live for. He just prayed for my safety. He knew I was down with mine but I was on a getaway mission with State Troopers. I was losing my young mind for this good-for-nothing nigga. What *King* would jeopardize his *Queen*?

"Hit the Avenue. I have to get to the hospital. I can't take it no more," moaned Snoop.

"Okay. Hold on. You'll be there in a minute," I promised him. I got him to the hospital on four rims quickly. He couldn't die in my presence. I wasn't going to fail him or myself.

At the hospital the doctor took care of Snoop's wounds before the cops got wind of whom he was. Pellets went throughout his arm leaving him in severe pain. I got grazed in the foot, thank God. Snoop got on the phone and ordered his my Yach to bring us another car to leave in.

As the cops pulled into the lot looking for the burgundy Probe, we pulled out in a black Cadillac, leaving them behind without a trace.

As soon as we got situated at the hotel I called home because I knew Luke told my mom what happened and I had to let her know I was safe.

Before mom hung up the phone, she let me know Snoop wasn't allowed in her house anymore because he was less than a man to have jeopardized my life like he did and she was right but I had to ride it out with mine. I was his *Princess*, his *Queen*.

For days the cops were on a serious man hunt. They knew who Snoop was and I was so miserable. I broke out in sweats at night after having horrible dreams of Snoop dying. I wanted to be down with him but all this was too stressful for me. I realized my boy needed me and Snoop would never be able to make up for the time I lost with my son.

The detectives shook Snoop's mom down and he fell for their lies and went to the station to talk to them. They never had anyone for shooting him. It was all a setup. They wanted him in for shooting one of them and I told him that but he didn't listen. He was the man and he made his own decision, besides, they weren't going to rest until they found him anyway so he did what he had to do.

For weeks things were mad crazy. The law considered Snoop ruthless and dangerous. He was a threat to society so they denied him bail. They impounded all his vehicles so I had nothing to drive. He told his man Greg to give me a car to get around in and he passed it to his peoples instead. Greg and RJ believed Snoop killed Des too so they were acting shady toward him.

Des was Butch's young boy who should've moved into Snoop's place, but it didn't happen that way. Snoop had more power and money and Butch needed that. RJ knew if Snoop was on the streets he would've never gone against him but that's how the game went. When you're behind closed doors, no one takes you seriously. People move at their pace. Your orders are just words.

After talking to Chocolate and Sugar on the three way about my business with Snoop, I got up to catch the bus to see him again. I was drained already but I made him a promise that I couldn't break.

While the train moved, Chocolate got on the phone and told Agent Powell this was the day I was transporting drugs for Snoop again. She was sure to shut us down because of her baby's father. If she was miserable, everybody had to be. Snoop wasn't going to keep getting drugs, diamond engagement rings and sunglasses from me while Des was in the dirt receiving nothing but dust. *Naw, that wasn't goin' down.*

I got off the train after a long hour. It was amazing how things went from "*Sugar to Shit*" in no time. People took things for granted and Snoop and I really had nothing. All he had was lawyer money and a few pennies when months before he had millions. Now that's crazy.

As soon as my number was called and I showed the officer my identification, she shook me down like Agent Powell told her to this time and she shook me down good but the only thing she didn't know is, I wasn't making drop offs' anymore. I told Snoop on my last visit that I couldn't risk my freedom for him because I had a son to raise so his babies' mamas or tricks could do that job and he agreed. They would be handling his business from that point while I provided the underclothes and phone tabs, the drugs I couldn't do. I was done.

After my visit I went home disgusted. I hated to be searched the way I was being searched. The long rides on the train were irritating. Something had to change or I was gonna flip. And Snoop knew it so he kept feeding me dreams of him coming home to rescue me. He cheated me and he felt bad. The cars, little money, clothes and jewels were nothing. Those things would get old. I really had nothing of any value. What he could've done, he didn't. Now it would never get done behind closed doors.

As soon as I reached the top of my steps my phone rang. It was Wayne trying to get back. He knew Snoop was never coming home but I couldn't cross him and go backwards even though Snoop wasn't shit. I just wondered if things were ever going to go back to "*Sugar from Shit.*" I just didn't know and things didn't look good either.

Chapter 7
THE SETBACK
"What a Lost"

The Penn Relay weekend. People from all over came to our city to partake in the festivities. Parties jumped all over the place. The streets were filled with all kinds of activities. It was crazy and I was chilling this year like the years before because some drama always took place at one spot or another. People simply didn't know how to act when these events came to town. They got weeded, drunk or they were on some type of high tripping so I fell back and waited to hear what went down in the city.

Bones stood in front of his full view mirror and put on his bullet proof vest then he tucked his 9mm in his holster. He was coming to town to partake in the activities regardless of RJ's threats. He was letting no one extort him for his. Luke or RJ had nothing else to say to him. But Luke's mind wasn't on Bones. He was tired of the dilemma between them. RJ and whoever else could have Bones money and Bones could have Candis, too, for that matter. Luke couldn't take anymore. He just wanted peace.

Luke drove up blasting, *Adore You* by Prince. He loved Prince and "Adore You" reminded him of me. Shalina and I watched Luke closely as he parked. He got out the car with stress written all over his face. He was simply tired of the fast life. It wasn't fun anymore. He really wanted his first family back but he didn't know how to tell me. He loved Candis for bearing their child but he knew I loved his child and I would raise both children and be a good woman to him. He made a big mistake by messing with Candis and he wasn't happy anymore. The excitement wore off and reality it was again. I was a good woman that deserved to be happy and neither of us was happy apart. We tried everything and we still couldn't find happiness or peace. If we put God first, we could learn to trust again.

"What's wrong? You look stressed out," I asked him.

"I can't wait to get my car back. RJ's aunt acts like she can't get it back or something," he said. Luke's car got impounded weeks before. Everything seemed to be falling apart for him.

"What do you mean?" I asked.

"They told her to come get the car and she didn't get it yet. Putting my car in her name was the worst thing that I did. I tell you it's nothing like having your own credit," he said.

"I feel you."

"You know I wish I never started messin' with Candis either. I'm so sorry about everything that we went through. I wish I wasn't so foolish. Leaving you was a bad move. I was so caught up in gettin' money and messin' with fast girls that I didn't realize what I had," he admitted finally. I listened

54

closely as tears formed in my eyes. I always knew he was sorry, but he never said it.

"I wish we were still together. I know you would have never crossed me. If I die today or tomorrow she wouldn't care," he said.

"Why would you say that? She loves you," I assured him.

"She might love me, but she loves the streets, too. She's caught up with messin' with too many guys. I can't trust her the way I can trust you," he said.

"Is she messing with Bones?" I asked.

"I don't know, but I'm tired of the whole thing. I don't need his money or anybody else's. And I don't want a chick that another dude has. I'm tired of the games. I just wanna be settled down with my family. I know we could've been straight together. You know how to maintain a family. She's too busy runnin' the streets and gettin' locked up all the time. I don't want my child to be raised in an unstable environment," he said, now with bigger tears.

"Well, if I can do anything for you, just let me know. If anything happens, I'll look out for your baby. Trust me. Don't be so stressed. Things will work out," I said. Tears ran down his cheeks as he stared at the sky. He wanted to grab me and hold me tight but the situation still felt awkward even though he poured his feelings out. God would make a way for us to be together so he felt in his heart.

Luke picked Shalina's daughter up and kissed her on her little chicks.

"Hey, chocolate girl," he smiled. Luke's love for children never changed. She looked at him with googly eyes and smiled. Lil Luke jumped on his back and they played until Lil Luke got tired. His daddy knew how to wear him out.

As Lil Luke lay on the recliner chair, Luke reached over and gave him a big bear hug then he kissed him on his cheek and whispered, "I love you son."

"I love you too daddy," smile Lil Luke.

"Can you get those pills?" he turned and asked me.

"What are you going to do with them?" I asked him.

"Nothing. I just need them. I have to give some to somebody. I might take one or two of them."

"Just don't over do it. You know I don't like you taking them," I said then I went in the house and got the bag.

Luke took some pills out, then he handed me the bag back.

"I'll see y'all later. I love you little man," he said to Lil Luke again as he walked away fixing his Nike head band that Lil Luke messed up while they were playing. Luke's fresh Nikes bounced quietly across the concrete then he jumped in his car and pulled off.

"He really wants you back," said Shalina.

"You think so?" I said.

"Yeah. I know so. Can't you tell?" she said.

"Sort of."

"That's why he was saying he was sorry about everything he did. He isn't happy with Candis. Would you take him back?" she asked.

"I think I would," I said. I was really missing the family thing and Luke seemed to mature a lot. Snoop sold me short and I was left hanging.

While I bathed Lil Luke, big Luke walked the strip with his friends laughing and joking. He was sluggish from the Valiums and sweating from the humidity but that didn't stop him from acting silly.

Bones noticed Luke walking toward him so he pulled his gun from his holster. Joe pointed Bones out to Luke and Luke turned his back quickly because he wasn't strapped and it was too much going on around him that he couldn't think straight. His head was spinning out of control. All he could hear were loud voices.

John pulled Bones's car a little closer to Luke and Bones fired hitting Luke in his back, thighs and legs. Luke didn't even know what hit him. He fell to the ground and Joe ran instead of shooting back.

My phone rang startling everybody.

"Hello," I said.

"Cinnamon Luke's been shot," cried his aunt. The phone dropped out of my hand immediately. A voice in my mind said, "three strikes and you're out." I couldn't believe the words that ran through my mind. I nervously picked the phone back up.

"What's wrong mommy?" Lil Luke asked as he noticed the tears in my eyes.

"Nothing baby," I lied. I couldn't tell my boy this. He was too young, sweet and innocent. He didn't deserve to be hurt this way.

"Where at?" I asked his aunt. All she could mumble is she was on her way to get me and I asked mom to watch Luke while I went to see about his father.

At the hospital all of Luke's boys crowded the entrance of the ER. I knew from the look on their faces that it was serious. They were overwhelmed with grief and they didn't know how to tell me what went down and why but they did. I had to hear the truth regardless because I would hear it from somebody on the streets that wouldn't mind hurting my feelings anyway.

While we waited for an answer, Luke was transferred to the operating room. I paced the floor crying then I walked to the phone to call the only person that I knew felt what I was feeling.

"Hello."

"Mom put Lil Luke on," I whined.

"How is Luke?" She asked me.

"I don't know yet."

"Okay. Hold on."

"Mommy my daddy is dead," said Lil Luke. He already felt his daddy's presence leave him.

"Why do you say that? He's not dead," I said.

"My daddy is dead mommy," he said, assuring me. He tried to tell me to accept it, because he already did. My little boy's mind became a man for the moment. He and his dad already said their good-byes to each other.

"Baby daddy isn't dead yet." *Why did I say yet?* "Baby pray for daddy okay. Ask God to allow daddy to live."

"Okay mommy. I'm gonna pray for daddy," he said but it was too late. The angels came down and took Luke with them. He didn't have to suffer anymore. He said his last farewell while we stood in tears. It was nothing more he could say or do. He just asked God to wipe our tears away and he begged for his children to be safe.

"Okay, I'll talk to you when I get home. I love you," I told my baby boy. My only child.

"I love you too, mommy," he said then we hung up. I didn't know how I was gonna make it if Luke died. I didn't know who would love my son the way his father did. I begged for Luke's life for the sake of his children.

The doors of the operating room opened twenty minutes later and the gray-haired doctor had Luke's blood stained on the front of his whites.

"I'm sorry. He didn't make it," he said quietly. My body dropped to the floor and I cried to the Father above. I didn't know how I was gonna tell my boy his father would never see his smiling face again.

After Luke's boys and his family talked with him in private, I did alone. I never imagined losing my child's father. I knew God brought Lazarus back from the dead so I begged him to do the same for Luke but it wasn't happening. God wanted him to part from here for good and I couldn't change that.

I checked all Luke's body parts for the last time then I walked away. I had to accept it was Luke because nobody could look just like him but his twin or possibly his children. My first love was gone forever. We would see each other again in heaven someday. He didn't have to suffer anymore.

Outside the hospital Luke's family made me get in the car. I was so torn that nobody could do anything with me. I wanted to die inside while they argued about where Candis was and whom she was fucking. I didn't care about that at the moment. Luke was dead and he wasn't coming back. Nothing else really mattered.

At home Lil Luke rested peacefully. I didn't want to wake him so I quietly moved around the room but he sensed my presence and batted his pretty eyes at me. My heart sank instantly. I saw his father in his eyes.

"Mom my daddy is dead," he stated. He already knew. He knew before I did. My heart only ached more.

"He's in heaven now."

"In heaven with Jesus?" he asked.

"Yes."

He grabbed me and we cried ourselves to sleep.

The sun rose quickly and the birds chirped outside my windowpane, asking me to wake up, but I lay numb. I didn't want to deal with reality then Snoop rang my phone and I knew I wasn't dreaming. Luke was gone and I didn't want anybody else, not even him.

For days we prepared for Luke's home going service. I didn't have much money but I had enough to make sure everything was straight. I went to Boyds and purchased Luke a two-piece cream suit for seven hundred and fifty dollars with brown crocodile shoes to match. I got Lil Luke a cream three-piece linen suit from Karls then I shopped Passyunk Avenue for shoes to match his fathers.

Sugar scooped me up and took me to our favorite mall. I got a two-piece silk skirt set with gold accessories from Cachet then I went to Bloomingdales and purchased a pair of gold Ferragomos to match. My family would be coordinated perfectly.

After Luke's aunt and I picked out his casket, Ramina came by the house to pick up Luke's clothes to take to the undertaker for me. He was her brother and she tried to remain whole and strong, but it was ripping her apart. And I definitely couldn't stand to see him again until the day of the funeral.

For days I took the Valiums Luke had given me to hold because I didn't think I could deal with reality. I lost a good friend before at fifteen, but Luke was more than a friend to me. He was my first love and I couldn't seem to accept his death although I knew God made no mistakes.

Snoop called me constantly getting on my nerves. All he cared about was his case that was coming up and Wayne supported Luke's family and me. He delivered food from his restaurant to us every day because he knew I wasn't eating and he wanted me to remain strong for my boy. He knew if my son saw me weak it would break him and he loved Luke dearly.

Bee and Joe knocked on my door to collect the goods Luke gave me, the day before the funeral. And why did they do that? Joe ran out on Luke so I wasn't giving them anything and besides, I didn't know if they were telling the truth about it being all of theirs because Luke was gone and he couldn't tell me better so I slammed the door in their faces. Snoop didn't mess with them anyway and they knew it only took a phone call for them to get seen so they walked away pissed.

I went to my room and opened the bag up that Luke had given me then I put everything on the bed.

"I don't know how much the pills go for," I thought, so I pushed them to the side. I counted out the bundles. "It's about ten thousand dollars in profit. I'll give Luke's aunt three thousand dollars of it because she sells already so she'll have no problem pushing it. And she can do what she wants with the money. I'll step to Harold and ask him to sell bundles for me and I'll give him twenty-five dollars off every hundred. I'll give my cousin Justin the rest because I know he'll look out for me."

The phone rang and it was Snoop. I told him what Bee and Joe did. He let me know he needed the pills so he would send Greg by to get them along with his jewelry. I never had to worry about Bee and Joe because he would handle them for me too.

After hanging up with Snoop I separated the pills. I kept some for myself because I became dependant on them and I separated the rest between Snoop and Luke's aunt and then I opened up my jewelry box. Snoop's YBM diamond ring and his diamond Rolex watch hit me in the face, reminding me of the words that he once spoke to me, "I might need these for a rainy day." I closed the box, then Luke and I went back to Luke's aunt house with her profit.

The morning of the funeral my family had prayer then we met the other limos around Luke's aunt house.

RJ stood outside the limo playing big time as usual with his clique. I didn't know if he was happy or sad about Luke's death because he wore a big smile that would knock a roof off a house. I saw so much guilt this day and Candis still wasn't around. She was supposed to be in one of the limos but she was absent again. Did respect and morals matter anymore?

Sugar pulled up on the limo and said, "I'll see you at the church okay."

"All right. Thanks," I smiled.

Teresa said, "Why are you still messin' with her? You know John just got her comin' round so he can see if his name come up. He thinks he's gonna be charged with conspiracy because he drove the car away after Bones shot Luke." I didn't know what to think but I knew it was just a matter of time for us to part just like Luke's clique was falling apart. I wanted to trust Sugar but I knew I couldn't because of her man and Chocolate didn't trust me because of mine so just like men handled theirs, we as women would handle ours and go our separate ways. It was just better that way. Nothing would ever be the same because too much *slime* stood in between. Everybody was caught up.

The limos pulled up to the big brick church down the eastside, twenty minutes later. My stomach got queasy and my legs began to shake rapidly. I sat still for a minute to stare at everybody in front of the church before getting out. I couldn't move. I didn't want to move. People that weren't even cool with Luke or I stood around gossiping. Like Des's funeral, it was a meeting place for some chicks to come up.

Finally I stepped out of the limo with my son. All eyes landed on my boy and me. Whispers got stronger. All people could do, was gossip about who was who and who had on what. I was so irked. I wanted to get in to see my baby's father and get out so I could be alone.

Inside the church Luke flipped out. He wanted to stay at Luke's casket and not be bothered by anyone. He kept questioning me, wanting to touch and feel his father. He knew what I said but he was puzzled. He never loved anyone that died. He really had to prepare himself mentally for this blow. "His body is here, but he is in heaven," he whispered to himself repeatedly.

Candis walked in performing and that only upset Luke more. He ran to his father's casket again and guarded it with his life. Luke's family tripped out after this. *I would never forget the cry of a mother that lost her child.*

The pastor summed up his message, and then he asked if anyone wanted to be saved. A few stood up and got saved, and then the pastor asked, "does anyone have any remarks?" I nodded my head, and then Lil Luke and I walked to the pulpit. I wrote a dedication from Lil Luke to his dad.

LIL' MAN

Daddy we shared special moments together that I'll never forget and you leaving me now isn't making things better yet. We went through good and bad times but that's what life's all about and at least I can say that I had a dad that loved me unconditionally without a doubt. No, you weren't perfect. But who is? And the most important thing is you showed me things that no one can ever replace. And hearing mommy's voice telling me you went to heaven wasn't a disgrace because I know now, that it was all done with grace. See, I know it wasn't easy for you living in this cruel world and if I had one last wish I would send you off with a kiss, having no regrets on tomorrow because it gets better than this. It's just a little hard to accept right now. Thinking back to when you were by my side when I had my surgery, promising never to let me go, feeling all my pain as if it were yours, now I'm feeling yours wanting to be a Lil Man and I'm only four. I know I'll get angry and even sad at times thinking about the person that took you from me. They'll never know how it's gonna feel for me to grow, wishing I had a dad and searching for tomorrow. I'm gonna try my best to be strong and keep all my anger inside knowing God had a better plan because it was he that created man. With all the mixed feelings that I have inside I know mom will be doing more than just praying for me because she wants me to be the best Lil Man that I can possibly be. And as for you dad, just rest in peace and know that heaven is a better place because the earth is full of grief.
Your first born and only son, Luke

I stepped away from the microphone with Lil Luke in my arms. Everything became a blur. I couldn't see the faces before me. I stumbled down the steps with Luke in my arms. My body was weak from the Valiums and from me not eating in a week. KC jumped from his seat to rescue us but I got up before he could reach me then I sat back in my seat and the Pastor closed the service after a few cards were read.

Before the funeral director closed Luke's casket, Lil Luke put a picture of him in his pocket and the dog tag we had gotten him at birth. Then Luke's squad put money, jewelry and illegal substances in his casket, like real ghetto niggas, but nobody was gonna say anything to them for doing it.

I watched as the cars stretched across the long park. And it was about forty-five deep or more. Luke was truly loved. He may have done dirt like we all have but he was a respectable young man with a heart for the elders. Some drug boys could care less about respecting others mothers or fathers. Fine, if the streets are what they chose, but have respect like you would want someone to respect you and yours.

At the cemetery I stayed around after everybody left. I needed to be alone with Luke. This would be our final good-bye and I wanted to get in all in. He had to know he was my beginning, middle and end. The love we shared would never die.

I woke up to a steaming August day. It was pass one o'clock in the afternoon. The Valiums made me sleep extra late and life waited on no one. I was living in denial, depression and I wanted my life to end but I clung onto God's word. He wouldn't let the Valiums take me over. The devil tried to take me but God stepped in because he knew my son needed me and it wasn't time for me to part yet.

Katima called waking me from my depression. Everybody around me that loved me saw the change in Lil Luke and me so they tried different things to keep us busy. They cared.

Katima begged and begged me to go to *Sesame Place* with her and her children and I kept saying no until Luke overheard me and begged too so I got up and prepared us for the day then Wayne called asking me to stop by so I did before Katima came. Besides, Luke was hungry and my family loved Wayne's cheese steaks. And I loved his turkey hoagies. He had the best hoagies around. His Amoroso rolls were always fresh and he had Black Bear gourmet turkey. Not that processed turkey.

Inside Wayne's restaurant he stood in front of the grill preparing cheeseburgers for take out. As soon as I told him what we wanted, he prepared it quickly and took us upstairs to eat.

While Nancy and Luke ate and the Rottweilers' barked, I could do nothing but reminisce about how Wayne and I used to have so much fun up in his apartment. It was nothing like old times. We had so many fond memories together and Wayne wished he never let me go because I was a good woman and Snoop never deserved me. He took me through "A Lifetime of Pain" and I needed "A Lifetime of Joy."

Before leaving Wayne grabbed me from behind with his strong arms smiling. Something about him looked better than ever but I couldn't fall with him regardless of what was going on in my life. I was weak for love but we were close friends and I wanted to keep it that way. It hurt but that was the only way it could be.

Minutes later Katima, the kids and I pulled up to Wayne's again because she wanted a water ice before hitting the expressway. He dipped the water ices and passed them to us one by one then he asked me to come back later without the kids. He wasn't about to give up on me. He really missed me and he would die trying.

While I got in the tubes with Luke, Ramik sent Des's cousins Sheldon and Blimp into Wayne's restaurant to take him out. Butch ordered the hit because of multiple reasons and it was time.

Wayne had his back turned loading sodas into the refrigerator. Sheldon came in and shot the cashier in the neck with a silencer while Blimp took cover then they both ran up on Wayne and shot him in the back four times and the head three. He never had a chance to reach for his gun that he kept so close for times like these. He hit the floor face down while they ran out with bandannas' on so nobody could identify them.

Once the sun went down Katima and I rounded up the kids and hit I95 back into the city.

"Stop by Wayne's for me," I said to Katima.

"Okay," she said then she turned on 76th Street. Yellow tape surrounded the entrance of the restaurant all the way around the corner where Wayne's cashier ran and fell.

"Oh my God! I wonder what happened," I shouted to Katima.

"I know," said Katima.

"Take me home so I can beep Wayne to find out what happened."

"Okay."

Katima dropped me off at home and I beeped Wayne's beeper back to back while I prayed. Ten minutes went by and I knew something wasn't right because Wayne always called right back when he saw my number. My stomach got queasy and tears began to form. I paced the floor nervously then Nancy called me to the television.

"Aunt Cinnamon, Wayne's store is on the news. Look! They say the owner got shot," she said. I fell to my knees and cried endlessly. I knew it was serious but I wanted to believe it was a lie and they made a mistake.

After calling around for ten minutes I finally got my answer. Wayne wasn't gonna see my face again. He wouldn't be here to walk me through this one like he did with Luke. *When is it going to stop? When are our men going to stop being targets? They fall victim to the system and the streets.*

It's a never-ending battle. And the devil plays a major roll in it all. He knows how powerful our men are so he tries to destroy them, one way or another. And it's hard out here, but the devil can be defeated with prayer and wisdom. Prayer is a powerful tool and so many fail to realize the power of prayer. I'm glad my mom laid that foundation for me. I know how to pray. Sometimes I lack prayer, but I'm here, so I pray it gets better. I hope to live to see a change. I have a son that I'm praying for every day because I refuse to see him fall victim to this madness. I pray he's not killed in vain and I pray he never kills anyone son or no one for that matter, unless he has to. I never imagined Wayne and Luke to die a month apart. How much can a heart take? I thought to myself as my heart cried sorely. I now knew what my dream meant.

PART II

Chapter 1
RIDING OUT
"Doin' Whatcha' Gotta"

One month later. Lil Luke and I sat outside enjoying the breeze. Adjusting without his father was very hard but we had to remain strong. We only had us.

Luke's 635 turned the corner slowly with someone looking just like him leaning behind the black leather wrapped, steering wheel with their cap down to their eyelids just the way Luke wore his baseball caps. My heart dropped instantly. Who in their right mind would want to upset my son and me?

"Mom here comes my dad," Lil Luke smiled. He missed taking daily rides with his partner. Big Luke chauffeured his boy around faithfully.

"Baby. That's not your dad," I informed him. I hated to shatter his dream but I had to give it to him straight. Daddy was gone and it was no coming back.

The car pulled closer and the person parked. I realized then, who it was. I pulled Lil Luke closer to me. RJ had nothing to say to my boy after all he did. RJ jumped out smiling and Lil Luke frowned. We were both disappointed.

"What's up man?" RJ said to Luke.

"Nothing. That's my dad's car," he smirked.

"Yup. That's your dad's car," said RJ, kneeling before Luke now. "Do you need anything Cinnamon?"

I looked him straight in the eyes and turned my nose up. It was nothing he could do for me.

"I don't need anything from you unless you can give me Luke back, and if not, you can't help me. I thought y'all were selling the car to give the kids the money?" I asked.

"I was, but I changed my mind," he said coldly.

"What do you mean, you changed your mind?" I asked angrily.

"I changed my mind," he said with that strong and powerful expression that he gave when he meant what he said.

"Remember. You do have a kid now. And the same way you are doing my son, somebody is gonna do yours when you leave here," I said firmly. My words smacked him in the face and cut him to his knees.

"What do you mean?" he asked me.

"You heard me. What goes around, comes back around. Luke paid for that car, not you or anyone else. But that's the way it goes. When you leave here, somebody else keeps your shit. And I understand that, but if you were a real friend, you would do what is best for his children. But it's obvious that

65

you're not his friend and you never were, as far as I'm concerned," I spat.

"Say what you want. He was my man and I loved him like a brother," he said.
"Whatever! If it was like that, why is Bones still walking around? You talk all that tough Tony shit. Now live it," I said, insulting his manhood. I was right. RJ couldn't stand the truth. In fact, the guilt was overwhelming because he let Bones pay him for Luke's death. Bones compensated everybody, except Luke's son. He thought Luke's boys were gonna do that because that's how he and his boys rolled, but Luke's camp really wasn't that cool. They were straight eaters.
"Girl, I'm not gonna keep arguing wit' you. I'm out." He pulled his cap down lower then he jumped back in Luke's car and sped off. I made him feel like the sucker he was. He let the nigga he tried to extort, kill his man and pay him off. He let Bones win. He won.
"I hate him. I hope he dies. Old son of a bitch," I spat into the air.

Days later I went to the prison to talk to Snoop because the system was trying to railroad him. They didn't want me to testify in his behalf about the shooting we were involved in with the Troopers but I had to fight for him because they were lying and I didn't like that alone.

After talking to Snoop and rationing everything out, I took the stand for my man. The DA drilled me but I didn't care. I wasn't about to break for them although they threatened to lock me up for conspiracy to shooting a State Trooper.

At the end of the week it was a hung jury. I was satisfied with that but I knew they were coming back stronger because they didn't ever want to see him on the streets again. They would do anything to see his *black ass* burn.

Months later Candis walked out of the County Penitentiary to move into one of RJ's buildings with another child. I didn't doubt the fact that she loved Luke. She was just doing what she had to, to survive. She loved herself more than anybody. And if that meant doing RJ and making his runs upstate to survive, then so it would stay and be.

I stayed at Candis's place with the kids while she made her runs for RJ. It was my duty to teach Luke's children their roots. I couldn't let them forget their father. Nothing was the same anymore. Things were crazy and Sugar and I finally broke our ties and she was hanging with Shalina. Chocolate and Candis were tight because they had the boosting, credit cards, and checks in common. Whoever imagined them two to hook up. They couldn't stand the thought of each other months before. Now they were inseparable.

RJ ran up in the apartment on me while Candis remained in the streets. It didn't surprise me that he wanted me, too. Anything Luke had, he seemed to want. But I gave it to him raw. I didn't get down like that. I wasn't Candis and I wasn't sweet. Even if things were hard, he couldn't get this. He would never be able to say he had both of Luke's baby mamas.

I walked into the kids' room early in the morning only to find Chocolate and Candis cuddled up tight. I heard some things about them and this only confirmed it. I shut the door gently and went back into the room with the kids. Nothing seemed to amaze me anymore. Anything was to be expected these days.

By two o'clock in the afternoon Candis walked into the room and asked me if I was down to go to the mall with her and Chocolate. I was hesitant at first because Chocolate and I wasn't the best of friends anymore then I said, "All right. What could it hurt?" We all liked nice things and I was tired of struggling. They could teach me a few of their tricks and I would never have to go in my pockets to pay the stores anymore. I could get what I wanted at no cost like them.

After hitting Saks, Bloomingdales, Victoria's Secret and Cachet, Candis, Chocolate and I went back to the spot to get dressed for the show. Shalina and Sugar would meet us there because Sugar still wasn't feeling Candis so she wasn't about to sit in her spot while we got dressed.

Inside the Arena everybody in the city stood around speechless as we walked through. They couldn't believe we were all together at one time. How could that happen? It was a mix and match type thing, but we all had something in common. We brushed the haters off, then we walked around like we were the shit. None of us cared about what people had to say. Our clique was tight, whether we were called *black widows, whores, or gold diggers*. We took pictures with niggas we were cool with, then we strutted to our seats to see Eric B & Rakim and KRS1.

Two weeks later Snoop was being tried again for the restaurant shooting. He needed somebody other than me to testify for him so one of Candis's old cellies volunteered because she knew who Snoop was from the streets and she needed some extra dough. Snoop was hesitant at first but he said what the hell and went along with it. What did he have to lose anyway? He had to take his chances.

For days Shayla, Candis and I sat in Candis's spot preparing for the case. We had to get him off. He depended on us.

Shayla and I did just what we rehearsed in Candis's apartment inside the courtroom. The DA drilled us hard. He came up with more witnesses too. He wasn't about to let Snoop off even if he had to lie.

Once all the testimonies were in, Candis and I went to her apartment while Shayla went home. No sooner than Shayla reached her door, the same detectives that locked Snoop up came to pick Shayla up for perjury. They found out she was locked up during the restaurant shooting and she lied about everything.

Snoop lost that case and Shayla was in again. Everything was going sour. Nothing made sense but that's how it went. You took chances and if you came up short, you had to accept it. Snoop couldn't be mad at anybody but himself. We all tried and our plan backfired.

RJ gave Candis a car and Greg finally passed me off a beat down squatter for not giving me the Cougar to get around in. I couldn't be choosey, but I was. He played me and I deserved more than a beat down piece of shit that could only get me to the supermarket and back.

Butch was still upsetting the city from behind bars. His squad had a shoot out, in front of the club *114*. Blood was everywhere. Little O and Greg got shot while Nif was put in a body bag. *Our young soldiers.*

Two weeks after the shooting Greg was up and out the hospital. He and RJ let themselves into the apartment while June and Candis sat in her bedroom kicking it. My heart dropped into the oven as I heard them run up the steps. I knew what this meant. I kept stirring the Rice a Roni in the pan. I hated to think of a shoot out with the kids around.

"What the fuck is he doin' here?" Greg angrily asked Candis.

"Yeah, bitch! You are bein' disrespectful," RJ pointed in her grill.

I ran in the bedroom to calm things down.

"Hey, look! Don't be startin' no shit in here y'all, in front of the kids," said Candis.

Greg looked at June and said, "Yoo man. You got to roll."

"Alright. I'll leave in a minute," said June. Greg reached for his gat.

"No Greg! Don't do it in front of the kids. If you wanna see him. Do it when he leaves," I begged. Greg stared at me for a moment then he paced the floor. He wanted to kill June simply for befriending Bones. He loved Luke and he wanted somebody to pay for his death. And if that meant killing June in front of the kids, then so be it because he didn't know when he would see him again. He wasn't faking like RJ. He was a killer with loyalty to his gang. He had been in the game way longer than RJ. RJ was a rookie trying to be down.

Candis whispered in June's ear, then she stood in front of him knowing Greg wouldn't shoot with her standing there.

"Ay, Jay. You better get your bitch!" he hollered. He had no problem calling Candis a bitch because she crossed all lines. She was a bitch and everybody knew it. He didn't have to respect RJ or June because Candis was out of order. She was no longer Luke's girl. Greg respected that title until she fucked his man.

"God please don't let them have a shoot out in here with the kids. Please," I prayed. RJ walked over to Candis and June.

"I want you gone when I get back," he pointed to June. June looked him in the eyes and said nothing. He couldn't, even if he wanted to or he'd die, right in front of us. RJ and Greg walked out. Fifteen minutes later June left behind them.

"Candis you are crazy. Why would you have him here knowing RJ could walk in anytime?" I asked.

"I don't care about RJ. He's gettin' on my nerves. If I didn't need him, I wouldn't be puttin' up wit' his shit," she said.

"I feel what you're saying, but you are risking your kid's lives. Say he comes in here while you're lunchin' and somebody gets hurt. You should be seeing nobody if he has keys," I said.

"Yeah, I feel you, but I'm doin' what I want. I'm not livin' for nobody, but me. I really like June. Now he's not gonna come back because he can't trust them," she said.

"What did he expect after what happened? He should know they were gonna feel some type of way about him being here. They never liked the County boys coming over here and now that one of them killed Luke, they really don't want them over here now," I said.

"I know. But I'm not gonna stop my life because of them. I have wants and needs and nobody is gonna make me happy, but me," she said and that's all she needed to say. It was her spot and I had no say so.

"I understand," I blurted aloud then I got my things together quickly. Luke and I were out for good.

Weeks later. I meant what I said. I got Candis's kids and they stayed with me. I wasn't doing her set anymore. And Snoop, he was really stressing me. I outgrew his tired ass. I was tired of faking the orgasms while he got his rocks off. I began to wonder how I got caught up with him. I guess I was intimidated by his power amongst other things. Not having my dad around made me fall for the security I thought I needed. I began to wonder if I was ever in love with Snoop's lying ass.

After thinking long and hard, I came up with a new hustle. James was into robbing jewelry stores and I met him through Candis and Chocolate so I got down with him.

For weeks we hit every store in Philly, Baltimore and D.C. My boy didn't have to want for nothing. He had every Polo outfit the stores got in and I wasn't doing bad either. James hit the jewelry cases for twenty, thirty and forty thousand dollar pieces and I got a break down from everything. I was cool for the moment. It was risky and he got locked up from time to time, but it was nice money for me until I found something new to do.

After hitting Baltimore for fifty thousand dollars in merchandise, the most James and I did while on our missions, I drove to the prison to drop Snoop off something. I was still responsible for him until I officially broke it off.

My phone rang minutes after I took my clothes off and I found myself arguing with Chocolate about messing with Bones. I never imagined them two to be together, but they were and they were tight like crazy glue. He got her a new whip. Some nice diamond jewelry and they had a spot together. She wanted me to accept her and Bones because she remained friends with me after Snoop killed Des but it wasn't the same. After all the months that flew by, we still didn't know for sure if Snoop killed Des but we certainly knew Bones killed Luke. That wasn't a secret. The county boys were our enemies and she knew that. That was too much for me to swallow. I had to be true to Luke, dead or alive. A part of my son was gone and I had to live with that.

The next morning it was chaos in the courthouse. Bones family and friends were there on his behalf and my peoples were there on Luke's behalf. Our sons ran up and down the hallway together not knowing what was going on. Nancy kept telling Lil Luke to hit Lil Bones and he didn't know why. They were having fun and that's all he knew but Bones's son was about to lose him to the system and my boy lost his father to the streets. It was crazy. *When will we stop killing our own?*

The cops tried to calm us down in the hallway but things got out of hand. Shalina stepped to Chocolate about being there for Bones and me and Bones baby mom tore the hallway up. Her weave was all over the floor. She had blood leaking everywhere once Nancy got in it.

Candis took the stand on Bones's behalf to tell about what Luke and RJ was doing to Bones. I sat in tears. I couldn't believe she would do what she did but we all had our reasons for the things we did in life and I guess she had hers. Bones gave her some nice money and she couldn't bring Luke back so why not take his dough. She had to survive too.

Bones ended up getting third degree murder and his family flipped. Jail wasn't good enough for me. I wanted his peoples to feel what I was feeling. I wanted that niggas head but it was in the systems hand so I ate that.

Two months later I walked in the court room at the beginning of the week with my son, Lil Nahum and Nathan prepared for the worst while Snoop sat next to his lawyer waiting to be tried on the drug trafficking, tax evasion and murder charges that he and the YBM were indicted for. He already got ten to fifteen years for the Carol's Hall shooting because Yach was working with the Feds and the car he let Snoop hold that night was wired but they wanted to see him behind bars for life. Fifteen years wasn't good enough for all the dirt he committed.

As we took a seat on the third row Agent Powell and all his associates turned and examined the kids and me like we didn't belong there. They disliked me for being Snoop's girl and I disliked them for hating him and putting him behind bars.

Snoop turned and looked at me with a fake smile and sadness in his tired eyes. Knowing I was still hanging in there gave Snoop hope because everybody else had given up on him. All the babies' mamas and all the chicks he had ever tricked, fronted on him. The money was gone and so was he. Nobody really gave a fuck about their squad anymore. They already counted them out. Whatever they got out of them while they were on the streets was enough. The YBM being in jail could do no one any good. Other niggas were out here getting money now since they were gone. They could now move around freely with the YBM behind bars.

After everything was said and done I went straight to the prison to see Snoop. It took a while for him to come up because of it being a court day, but I waited because I knew he needed to talk to me.

Finally the officer in charge called my name. "Thank God. I couldn't wait another minute," I mumbled as I got up. I walked in and sat down. Snoop walked out with a half grin on his face, dressed in all blue.

"Hey baby," he said, bending over to kiss me.

"Hey! How are you holding up?" I asked him.

"Oh, everything is all right. I can't complain. I'm ready to rumble this case and get it over with. They want me to plead out, but I'm not doin' it. I'm gonna rumble this case. Can you believe that bitch ass Bear is telling," he said.

"You are lyin'!"

"No, I'm not baby. He's tellin' it all. Every since Des got killed those niggas been trippin'. The law really has them believin' me and Butch killed him and they're fallin' for it. They even got my man Yach snitchin' to get his time cut," he said.

"No. Not Yach!" I blurted.

"Yeah. My man Yach. The whole time he was gettin' the cars for me in his name, he was working with the Feds," he said. "And that deal that I thought went bad," he paused.

"Yeah."

"It didn't go bad. That was all a set up to see what I was workin' wit'. Hasan set me up, too, and I looked up to that nigga like he was my dad. I knew him for a long time and he sold me out to get his time cut, too," he said with disappointment.

"I don't believe this."

"Yeah. It looks ugly, but I'm gonna ride it out. I'm goin' out fightin' for mine. You heard me! They know I come from the Terror Dome and I don't give a fuck," he spat.

"Yeah. I hear you. It's whatever. I'm here and I'm ridin' out wit' you. I just can't believe the niggas that were supposed to be so tough is really weak. I can't believe they would go out like that," I said.

"I can't either. I was so shocked when the lawyer told me who was testifin' against me. They got us messed up. They are makin' us out to be the most treacherous niggas that ever walked the streets. They are giving us so many murder cases that it's not even funny. They don't want to see me on the streets. You know they are saying Butch ordered the hit on Wayne because of me," he informed me. I tried to fight the tears but they dropped on the old, dusty carpet. I couldn't believe my ears. It hurt and I could see why Butch would've wanted Wayne dead. Wayne was that dude.

"You are lyin'," I cried.

"No, I'm not. See they really believe I killed Des so they killed Wayne because he's supposed to be my peoples. And you know Butch never liked him because of Romaine and he thought they were still creeping so he wanted him dead for two reasons," he said. See, the trouble makin' *Now and Later* bitches.

"Oh, my God! I knew whoever killed him, killed him out of jealousy. He was a good dude. So what are you going to do now that you know this?" I asked.

"Oh, it's on. Whenever I cross that nigga, I'm gonna see him. If he had beef wit' me, he should've seen me. But he waited til I got here to do what he had to do because he knew if I was on the streets it would've been some shit. Nobody would be walking right now. I'm the real killer. Them niggas can't fuck wit' me! They never lived the life I lived. I come straight from the Terror Dome and they know I'm that motherfucka to watch. So he did it at the right time," he said angrily. Frustration overwhelmed Snoop. Him not having control like he was used to having from behind those walls killed him. Some still listened, but very few cared. Snoop being in jail was better for the niggas on the streets because they felt like they could move around him with him being away. They knew he still could have things done from where he stood, but they had a better chance of maneuvering.

I sat lost for words. I wanted Butch dead for having Wayne killed. I knew it was wrong for me to feel that way but I was being real at the moment. Butch had no authority to do what he did. He destroyed so many families. They all did, to be honest. After kickin' it with Snoop, I left the prison upset but I was still holding on to a lie.

After everything was said and done everybody got time, from the captain, down to the sergeant, down to the first and second lieutenant, along with every soldier that played a part in Butch and Snoop's organization. If anyone got left out, they were very lucky. I knew a few that were overlooked and they needed to thank their lucky stars because they were really blessed. Snoop would never see the streets again. He and Butch had the highest rank so they got life. Snoop's man Tap got life. Josh got life. Karon got life. RayRay got twenty years and the rest of them got anywhere from fifteen to thirty years. Butch's man Greg and his brother DeRock got life. Ramik got life and the rest of his squad got anywhere from fifteen to thirty years. RJ finally got ten to twenty years for his shooting case and he took a twenty-year deal on this case so his lawyer got his time running concurrent. Bee and Gee got some time along with a lot of other people. Their whole squad fell apart after Luke's death. Sometime I wished Luke had got indicted instead of getting killed. I could deal with him being behind bars opposed to being dead although, I knew that would've killed him, too. He never liked jail. Luke always said, he rather be dead than in jail. And Snoop, he chose the hard knock life, now he was reaping the benefits of it. *Our lost soldiers.*

I walked to the elevator with some of the Agents after hearing the sentencing. I hated their presence. I wanted nothing to do with them and they didn't particularly care for me, because of whom I represented so the feelings were mutual. I just wanted to get home and relax.

Snoop used his authority to take the phone from one of the inmates to call me, hours later. He knew it was selfish to ask me to wait for him but he needed me in his corner more than ever and I didn't know if I could stand another month of being tied down. And now he would be going upstate so that was even more heartbreaking. How could I do it? There was no real future with a nigga behind bars for life. I wanted a man that could be there for me and Snoop could never do that. He failed me totally. *Something in My Heart* by Mitchelle came on and I cried myself to sleep. My life was shattered. I had pain on top of pain. *The fast life.*

Three weeks later I found myself riding up a long dirt hill with a bunch of Muslim sistas going to see our husbands. The only difference was, I wasn't Muslim and Snoop wasn't my husband by natural law or Islamic law. We just beared the title.

"I'm not feeling Snoop anymore. I'm just seeing him because I made a promise to him. It's been a whole year since I got down and I'm horny, but I don't want to have sex with him. I'm really pass him right now. I'm tired of the whole jail thing. I want to do something with my life and if I stay tied to him, I won't get anything accomplished because he stresses me out. And money is funny right now. I'm not stealing anymore and I don't hang around anyone who does, so I'm barely making it. I take my state boards next month and I'm banking on a job to survive," I thought inwardly as we passed old beat down houses and farms.

Finally we pulled down another long dirt road surrounded by high grass and my heart sank. I wanted to get in and out. I wanted the visit to be over before it began. I didn't know why I agreed to what he asked of me. I had been through so much with him and I was cutting all ties after this visit. I couldn't do it anymore.

The bus pulled to the front of the prison and let us out, one by one. I stood back and let the Muslim sistas guide me since they knew the routine. We hit the prison bars and a Muslim brother garbed in all white greeted us.

"As-salaam-Alikium sisters."

"Walikium-As-salaam," smiled the sisters. I kept silent. I couldn't be phoney.

"Follow me," he said. We walked down the corridor and a few inmates whistled and moaned.

"Hey y'all beautiful women," hollered one. The Muslim brother smelling fresh like Muslim oil continued to make his way through the prison. I couldn't believe how they had things worked out from inside. He walked us down the stairway through another corridor into a room where another Muslim brother greeted and led us down a couple of stairs where Snoop, who now went by the Muslim name Ahkee, and the other Muslim brothers greeted and hugged us all.

"Hey baby," Snoop smiled, from ear to ear, kissing me in my mouth like he hadn't seen me in years as I pushed away. I wasn't feeling him at all. And I didn't want him touching me. His breath smelled horrible.

"What's wrong?" he asked.

"Are we really supposed to be down here?" I questioned as I looked around at the Islamic pictures, drawings and rugs.

"It's cool. We're gonna have prayer, then we're gonna get it in as soon as it's cool," he informed me. And why did he say that. The thought of doing it to him made me sick to my stomach and he looked like shit. His hair was cut in a jailhouse box but he still looked rough and raggedy. I couldn't imagine his body touching mine without throwing up.

We got on our knees with our shoes off to make prayer. I had to fake it of course because I knew nothing about making sa'lot.

Once the Imam whispered in Snoop's ear, he grabbed my hand and escorted me to the back. Before we got to the door, I noticed one of the Muslim sistas behind the curtain sucking her husband's manhood. I turned my head quickly to the right to find the other Muslim sista bent over letting her hubby have his way from the back. The sistas were just as freaky as the average woman. What made me think they were so modest and didn't have the freak in them too? I guess I misunderstood them being covered. *Shit! They have to go for theirs too and who better to do it with but their husbands. We all have sexual desires and fantasies.*

I got sick again once I got inside the small room. Snoop's body was ashy once he came out his jumper. I didn't want his ashy, pimple dick inside me. The thought of him humping me was disgusting.

As soon as Snoop took two humps, he released every bit of cum inside me. I wanted to scream and he actually hoped for a dick suck like the other brothas since he was doing life, too but I wasn't about to put that monster in my mouth. *Uh, un.* He could suck his own dick.

Snoop was breathing like an old ass man with no stamina and I was so happy when the Imam tapped on the door letting us know our time was up. I couldn't wait to wash every trace of him off of me.

74

Back on the rug we lay and waited for everybody to get their turn. I looked around the room counting inside while I held my breath. Snoop talked but I had very little to say. I just wanted to get home to my boy.

Once everybody finished Snoop grabbed me by my waist and tongued me to death. I cried inwardly. I knew this would be my last time visiting him. I wasn't cut out for the phoney shit. I couldn't be bound by him any longer. He had to be my past. It was no way I could fake the funk anymore. His time was up. I did my bid. I couldn't get down with the system any longer. *Sometimes situations allow certain things but this situation wasn't allowing anything but heartache and grief. It was time for me to move forward. I had other roads to travel, other people to see, and better things to do. Snoop really didn't deserve me anymore anyway. When I was the devoted woman of his dreams, he let sex, money and circumstances stand between us. Now that the system had a hold on his life, I was the best thing that ever happened to him and the only thing that could hurt him too and that, I had to do. I had to hurt him in order to save me. I was gone forever.*

Chapter 2
Who's It Gonna Be?
"Job and Cinnamon"

Summer of 1991. I purchased myself a little 1988 Chevy from the auction with money I got from a lawsuit and a portion of the money I invested in some dope because I was tired of being broke.

For two weeks straight Harold stood on the corner of the deli and moved all of my coke but I wasn't comfortable with what we were doing. I knew I was wrong so the first time coping would be the last. There was no future in selling drugs and I knew it was a *dead end to the game.* Schooling and working was the best thing for me. Hustling was in my blood but not that kind of hustle. I had a boy to raise.

I pulled into the park and parked on the grass. It was almost a year since Luke's death and it seemed like yesterday. Lil Luke stared out the window at all the kids playing with their father's. He wanted his daddy and I could do nothing but love him the best I could.

"Did you bring that salad girl?" asked Donna, creeping up on me with a Heineken in her hand. I cracked my eyes and said, "Yeah. I sat it on the table."

Sherly walked over to me and asked, "Are you goin' to play volleyball with us?"

"Yeah," I smiled. I got up and fixed my spandex jumper, then I slid my feet into my red thong sandals. A group of guys watched as we played. And they watched hard, my butt moving around in that one piece looked enticing. And Sheryl, Donna and Teresa had butt for ten chicks. Guys didn't care how you looked most of the time. As long as you had booty for days, you were good.

After three rounds of volleyball, I took it back to the blanket again. The same guys that watched from afar put their beers down and headed our way. I gave the guy Tank my number because he insisted but I still wanted to be alone until I was totally over all of my heartaches. I wouldn't be any good to anyone in the state I remained in.

As soon as I got home, Tank rang my phone and we kicked it about life. He really gave me something to think about. I never looked at things the way he did. Moving on had to be. Snoop was never getting out. I was lying to myself. I was holding onto false hope. I said it was time to move on a while ago. Why was I playing games with my future?

For weeks Tank and I bonded but I didn't want him physically. He was a good, positive young brotha' but he wasn't for me.

Shalina knocked on my door while I laid in my bed thinking deep.

"Yeah," I said.

"Somebody wants to see you outside," said Shalina as she walked in.

"Who?" I asked. Shalina knew how funny I was. I wasn't about to jump unless she gave me specific details and even then, it wasn't definite that I would respond.

"Bryan from up the hill that hangs with Bud," she said. I thought about it for a moment then I said, "What does he want with me?"

"He wants to talk to you about working in his salon," she said. You would've thought he heard my prayers. I had just taken my state boards because it was time to set things in order legally. I couldn't keep living like I was living. I wanted to own my own shop someday and hustling could get you hurt or jail time. Candis and Chocolate finally got sentenced to seven and a half to ten years in prison for everything they had ever did and I couldn't go out like that.

"Really," I said, now excited. "Where's his shop?"

"On the Ave," she said.

"I don't know about working on the Ave." I said.

"Give it a shot. It can't hurt," she said.

"You're right," I said then I walked outside with Shalina to kick it with Bryan about the job.

Days later I stood in the middle of the shop eating, drinking koolaid and socializing at the grand opening of the salon. It seemed like old times. Everybody back together again from the hood. The Ave. never changed. Everybody came out to play, even Tank. He wouldn't miss being around me. I was his dream girl. He had to have me. He wasn't letting up.

For weeks I put in mad hours at the salon. It was slow because we just opened but the experience was fun. I parked down the street from the salon after work to go to Doctor Frazier's before going home. I had a minor yeast infection from a pair of tight jeans that I knew I needed to give up. I gained a couple pounds back and my jeans knew it.

After getting a prescription from the doctor I walked to my car and an old, blue Nineteen Seventy-one-Monte Carlo with a souped up engine pulled up on me.

"Can I go with you?" asked a caramel complexion guy with chink eyes, a pointed nose, straight white teeth and pretty full lips. I must say he was extremely handsome.

"Go with me where?" I smiled like I tasted Haagan Daz for the first time.

"I just want to get to know you. Do you have a minute?" he said with his sexy tone.

"I guess so."

He jumped out with his long legs and broad shoulders, dressed in a wrinkled purple Polo shirt and wrinkled white Polo shorts, smiling.

"What's your name?" he asked me nicely.

"Cinnamon."

"You look like Cinnamon, too. Your hair. Your complexion. You are cute. Do you have a boyfriend?"

"Yeah. Something like that."

"What do you mean something like that?"

"Well, he's incarcerated."

"And you're waiting for him?"

"Yeah."

"You have so much to offer somebody else. You shouldn't be waiting for him." He sounded just like Tank.

"I know. I hear it all the time."

"Can I take you out later?" he wanted to know.

"I don't know."

"Could I have your number and I'll give you mine?"

"Okay."

I watched his strong fingers move across the piece of paper as he wrote his number down. He handed me the paper, then he wrote my number down on another piece of paper.

"I'll call you later," he smiled.

"Okay. Wait a minute" I paused. "I don't even know your name."

"It's Job," he said, jumping back into his car. I got in my car and drove home.

When I got home Job called to tell me what time he was coming to get me and you would've thought Tank knew what was going on because he wouldn't let me hang up the phone but I had to go with my heart. Tank wasn't my man. We were friends but we weren't on the same page. I had an attraction for this man named Job.

Job beeped his horn outside my window. I stood in shock because I was expecting his blue car but he sat handsomely in a champagne colored 1991 Mercedes 560SEC Coupe.

I fixed my hair and clothes then I ran out the door to meet him. I didn't want him to know how excited I was, so I played it cool.

"You look good baby," he smiled while checking me out.

"Thanks. So do you," I said then he pulled off confident and secure. This nigga knew exactly what he wanted. It was no question about what he had in mind. He wanted me to be his girl. I was the one. He dated a select few but none had the qualities I possessed. I was wifey, baby mama material. He could be happy with me and he knew I wasn't going out with him because of what he had. He pulled up on me in an old beat down squatter with work clothes on and I didn't deny him a conversation so I passed the first test.

Twenty minutes later we pulled up to an exquisite restaurant in *Old City* where two gentlemen opened our doors and took the car, then we walked into the restaurant to be seated.

After hours of conversing, I found out Job knew more about me than I thought. He had a brother named Brent that I met through Sugar in 1988. He also saw me one day at Candis's apartment when he came to see her. They went out for two weeks but that was it. She wasn't his type of girl and I was. Brent said some good things about me and Job didn't want me to go through with marrying Snoop because I was worth more than he could imagine. Snoop would never appreciate me for who I was on the inside. Job knew exactly what it took to make me complete.

Job and Snoop came from two different backgrounds. Job was raised in a two parent home with a working mother and father. His father hustled here and there through the years but they were a tight-knit family that held values and morals. Job believed in marriage and family ties whereas Snoop believed in pimping, spreading his seed all over and never committing. The only reason he was thinking marriage now was because of where his life was going. Snoop didn't have his father around so he knew nothing about that bond. He knew nothing about respecting women. Job learned that early on. He would never hurt the one he loved intentionally. Job liked nice things too but he would never kill, steal or destroy to get them. He worked hard for years and what he was doing now was for the betterment of everybody around him, not for himself. Snoop would kill for what he wanted and think nothing of it.

Dinner with Job was so pleasant. My life felt like it changed instantly. Job pulled his wallet from his Versace jeans to pay the waitress. I looked hard because the jeans showed his print well and I was a little horny too but it was too soon in the game for fucking, besides, I wanted to make crazy love to him with all I had backed up inside me.

A month down the road Job and I became tighter than tight. I had to find a way to break the news to Tank. I didn't want to hurt his feelings but I couldn't be with him because I knew him first. I would be cheating myself. Someway, somehow, I had to find a way to tell Tank I was seeing Job.

Job wanted big things for us. I passed my state boards with a 51 which was great because the passing score for Manicurist was 42 and Job wanted me to quit my job at the salon because it was on the Avenue and now that I was dating him, it would only cause too much attention with his status. He wanted to buy me my own salon and move in together but I wasn't ready for that. I wanted to take it nice and slow but I wasn't going to let the hatin' bitches deter me from what I wanted either. Sugar told Shalina she used to see Job and I was irked. I had to know the deal.

Job stared me in the eyes and gave me a run down of his past. He wanted me to know everything. Sugar could never be his girl because she wasn't his type. First of all she was selfish, materialistic and she had a man. She only wanted Job because he had more money than her man and her uncle put her on Job. They plotted on him together because of his status.

Her uncle and Job had some houses together but once Job found out his history, he cut him off and he still owed Job a lot of money but Job wasn't sweating it. He would get it eventually or her uncle would fall off because he was too slimy. He crossed his own family and a *true hustler* knew what it took to be one so Job was all right.

Job let me know he used to mess with Rose too for different reasons but once she crossed him with a local nigga that didn't like him, he cut her off. Job didn't play when it came to respecting him. If you cross the lines of respect, you were no good to him, no good for nothing.

I was a bit jealous when he told me he was messing with Rose from New York. She was my worst nightmare. I could never forget her sleeping with Luke. I just wanted her to go back to her own city and leave me alone. Everybody fell for somebody, even chicks with long track records lucked up and found a good dude that cared for them but it was my turn and Rose wasn't going to get me again. If Job let her or any woman come between us, I would never trust again.

After I let Bryan know I was eventually leaving the salon, I went home and got dressed and waited for Job to pick me up. Tonight would be the night. He would get all that awaited him, all my love juices.

7:01 p.m. Job drove up quietly with, *Moments in Love* by the Art of Noise playing gently in the background.

"I love this," I said as I got in the car.

"Really. I'm glad," he smiled then he pulled off.

Twenty minutes later Job pulled in front of the *Academy of Music*. I knew from the place that he had class. He was 23 years young but he definitely had the qualities of a mature man that been through and experienced enough to last a lifetime.

The attendant ran over and opened our doors, then Job walked around to my side and grabbed my hand gently. I could only imagine I was embarrassed to hold hands in public because I hadn't done it in so long. The only other that held my hand in public was Luke and that was years ago but Job was more than ready for the public appearances. He was very confident and secure with his moves. I reached down to fix the strap on my suede shoe so Job could let my hand go. He was moving too fast for me and he scared me to some degree. I knew I was a likable individual but Job already discussed moving, children and marriage. Nobody dropped it on me like that before. I had one or the other, maybe two at once but never three in one pop.

I felt closer to Job during the show. He really had it together and he couldn't express himself enough. At his age he felt like he did it all and now was the time to settle down and never look back. Although I wasn't ready for the big things, I decided to give him a sure shot. It was on. I was to show him all my love and affection. I had *hidden treasures*.

Once the show ended, we walked to the car hand and hand. There was no need to play the shoe trick this time. Women would've died to be in my shoes. They would've never been too embarrassed to hold this fine man's, soft, gentle, strong hands. He was incredible and smart. While we drove to Job's spot, he popped *Phyllis Hyman's Greatest Hits* into the cassette player. This young man was very different. Other guys his age was running around listening to hard core rap. Hitting everything not tied down and killing for a dollar. Job enjoyed rap too but he didn't listen to it every day. I listened closely to the words of *The Answer is You*. Job was telling me something through the music.

"Do you like Phyllis Hyman?" he asked me.

"Yeah. I think her music is beautiful," I smiled.

"I love her. She's one of my favorites besides Anita Baker," he smiled.

"Yeah. I love Anita too. Both of them are good," I said then I reclined my chair back. Phyllis Hyman's music was relaxing. I could get a good night sleep listening to her music playing softly in the background.

Finally after fifteen minutes we reached Job's spot. It was different from what I imagined. In fact, I had been around Snoop so long that I didn't know what to imagine. Job's outside was immaculate. The freshly polished cherry wood door stood rich and strong. The entire building did. The face was brown brick with marble steps.

"Come on. Get out," he smiled as he opened my door. I was so amazed at the front of his house that I forgot where I was. The spot wasn't a single home like the one Snoop wanted for me but it cost 200,000 dollars because of the area that it was in. I always liked Queen Village.

Job skipped up the steps and opened the door for me. I was still amazed as I smelled the fresh roses that sprung up beautifully in his front yard. I looked at the intercom and the little camera as it moved around. He was sure to know what was going on around him.

Once I stepped inside, he shut the door behind me. I looked around at the Sandpiper tone walls. I was so glad to finally see a brotha with walls other than white. Why was white everybody's favorite color anyway? I hated white walls. They showed everything.

"Come upstairs," he said. I followed him up twenty-two flights of wood steps, the same wood as his floors. Just from the look of things, I knew someone had just polished his floors. I could even smell the polish.

He briefly showed me around the second floor where he did most of his business, then we climbed ten more steps to the third floor. I was so glad to finally stop climbing. My calves were tight but I needed a break.

"Have a seat," he said, as he directed me to his brown leather sofa that had gold studs outlining it.

"Thanks," I smiled as I approached the sofa. I couldn't believe his spot was so spotless. Either he was a clean freak or he hardly stayed home because

81

I couldn't see a spec of dust lying on the glass table and normally glass collected dust.

"Do you want anything to drink?" he asked as he opened the cherry wood cabinet to pull a Mikasa crystal glass from the shelf.

"Water please," I said as I looked around again. "Can I use your bathroom please?"

"Sure. It's straight back to your left," he said. I passed the bar with brown leather and cherry wood stools straight to the bathroom. I knew this was the night. I was a big girl but I still got nervous when I knew I was about to get a stiff one.

Inside Job's bathroom was the same way. Spotless. This man couldn't be home much with a crib looking so clean. And I wanted to know everything. I pulled his shower curtain back to see how he was living for real because some things couldn't be hidden. I got my answer though. He was as clean as the board of health. He had no rings or scum in the shower. His lowboy didn't even have old pee stains on it. I was so glad to know all brothas' didn't leave three years of build up on their toilet seats. After freshening up, I crept back to the bar where Job was waiting patiently for me.

"Are you okay?" he asked.

"Yes. I'm fine," I smiled.

"Here's your water," he said, handing me the glass.

"Thanks," I said then he grabbed my hand and showed me his deck in the back. The wood deck was freshly polished just like his floors.

"You know my fantasy is to make love to you on the deck in the rain," he gently whispered into my ear. My juices immediately leaked in my panties at the sound of his voice. I wanted so badly to make his fantasy come true but it wasn't raining and I didn't want to seem like a freak. We went out on numerous dates but we hadn't made love yet.

"Oh, really," I smiled.

"Yes," he said as he began to nibble on my earlobe. I wanted to snatch his pants off but my mind kept saying, "not yet. Let him make the first move."

"Well, it's not raining," I said with my corny line, pushing my butt out just enough so he could grind on it.

"I know but we can make our own juices," he said then he pulled my hair back and put his tongue all the way down my throat. I held onto him and seductively kissed him back. I was feeling just what he was at this very moment. I wanted him inside me, every inch of his dick. He popped the buttons off my silk Escada shirt and nibbled on my nipples until I screamed his name then he bent down and unstrapped my shoes.

"What are you doing?" I asked him while I hugged his left shoulder.

"Don't worry about a thing," he said. "I got you." He rested my body against the wood and sucked my toes as if they were *lifesaver lollipops*. I couldn't

82

believe he was doing this to me. He kissed me softly up my thighs and pulled my skirt off with one touch as he gently inserted his twelve inches into my wet and wild jungle that yearned for him. This man had em' beat. None ever made me feel this way. I carved my nails into his deck that's how far gone I was. I was in never-never land and I didn't want to be rescued. I wanted to stay with him forever. He was the ultimate pleasure. I became him and he became me. We were one.

I turned him over finally to give him what he gave me. I licked and kissed all his sweet juices. He was in Cinna-land now, my fantasy island. I propped myself on my toes and rode him like a stallion. I was sure to make him love me.

"Is it good to you?" I asked as sweat began to drip from my forehead. I was getting a workout for certain. He wasn't about to take any shorts. He kept me close with his hands rotating my hips.

"Do you love it? Is it enough for you?" he hollered as he pounded me harder and harder. Mind you, I was on top and supposed to be in control but he was pumping like he was on top. The rhythm was perfect. "Is it enough Huh, huh?"

"Yes, it's all I need. I love every bit of it. It's the best," I screamed.

"Are you my girl?" he screamed while hitting my ass now in short, smooth strokes.

"Yes daddy, I'm yours," I hollered back. He kissed my forehead gently, down to my eye lids, around my nose onto my soft, wet lips and straight down my neck in circular motions. I trembled rapidly on the inside.

"Girl, why are you giving it to me like this? Are you trying to make me a fiend for you?" he moaned as he felt himself getting ready to bust again. I gently placed his fingers in my mouth one by one and sucked them.

"Here comes Little Job," he cried as he released inside me.

"What! What are you saying? I'm not ready for any more kids," I moaned in a sweet, sexy tone. I was feeling him but I wasn't ready for another child just yet.

"Well, I just made a baby," he informed me.

"How do you figure?" I asked him.

"I'm telling you that was a baby," he assured me then we stretched out on the deck.

"I'm not ready for any more kids. Luke has been the only child for five years and I'm not ready for any more kids. I only want one child," I said.

"I'll take care of you," he assured me.

"That's not the point. I don't want any more kids," I said.

He smiled and rubbed my hair.

"I didn't know you had freckles on your face. That's so sexy. Girl, you are sexy on the natural. What are you mixed with?" he asked.

"A little bit of this and a little bit of that," was all I could say. You know everybody's mixed with something these days.

"We'll make a beautiful baby."

"Yeah. Yeah," I said.

"I got you," he smiled as he looked me closer in the eyes.

"What's this?" I questioned as I rubbed his back. Job played no games when it came to certain things. These Muslim brothas' tried to shake him down and he went to war with them by himself. They shot him and he shot them back from the roof of his building. They thought they had him but he had artillery everywhere. When one made a move to cover the other, he shot them and Job didn't go to the hospital about his wounds. He took the bullets out himself that's why they didn't heal correctly. I had a pretty thug this time around with the freak in him. Wow!

I looked up and it was dark. So dark that I could see bright stars shining. I looked over and Job was asleep like he was inside and not on the deck butt naked. We were caught up in the *sweet presence of love*.

"Job," I said, nudging him in the side.

"Yeah," he said as he opened one eye.

"I have to get home," I said.

"Okay. Let me get myself together," he smiled. Moments later we walked into the house and showered then we left out.

Two weeks later I sat patiently near the phone waiting for Job to call and it finally rang but it wasn't Job. It was Tank telling me he got the three-piece leather living room set he promised me. I didn't want to move it into the spot Job and I had gotten together but I took it anyway hoping Job would never find out.

Too many niggas started coming to the shop once they found out who I was and whom I was dating. Job knew this day would come and he was upset. I was taking too long to quit. He had to put his foot down. It was my job or Job. Rose's brother-in-law Raheem was sneaking around trying to find out Job's business from me and Job ran into Tank and his cousin Claude leaving the shop one day and everything hit the fan. Tank cried like a baby but I had to go with my heart.

Although I finally told Tank the deal and he knew from Job, he begged me to go out with him on my birthday and I did while I stood Job up. I was dead wrong but I would catch up with Job later.

It was after nine o'clock and Job couldn't imagine where I was on my birthday. He had dinner reservations for us and gifts for me and I was no where to be found.

At ten o'clock I met Job in the Pathmark parking lot. He sat quietly in his car thinking about him and me while, *You Know How to Love Me*, by Phyllis Hyman played.

As soon as Job saw my car he jumped out and pulled me from my seat.

"Read these cards," he smiled while handing me two envelopes and two bags. I opened one card.

"*I thank God for bringing you into my life. You mean the world to me and I can't live my life without you. When I wake up in the morning, I think of you. During my long and stressful days, I think of the happiness that you have brought into my life and it gives me something to look forward to. I ask that you journey with me and stay close to my heart as I'll stay close to yours,*" he wrote in his own words. Tears dropped on the cards and I stood on my toes to embrace my baby. My savior. My king.

"*I love you, too. You mean the world to me. I thank God every day for you. I never thought I could be happy again, but God sent you at the right time and I know it was for the best. Don't ever leave my side because I'm connected to yours at the hip and if you pull from me, you'll break me and I'll be no good.*" I only wished the parking lot was empty so he could bust my bars wide open but it wasn't so we went to his Grandmom's house to chill.

On Job's grandmother sofa I opened the bags to find two pairs of ostrich cowboy boots that we had saw earlier in the week at Start One Shoes and two Michael Simon sweaters from TIA's Boutique on the Ave. I was so grateful for my gifts and I thanked Job for being him. My man had the wisdom of Solomon and the patience of Job for sure. He and I both knew Sugar and Rose were plotting to break us up but he wasn't going to let it go down like that. They could call his beeper forever. He wasn't about to leave me for them.

Chapter 3
The Chances We Take
"Why Do We Hurt Others?"

Job woke up early in the morning feeling proud, strong and content. He did just what he said. He impregnated me. I was having his first born son. He looked at me for the last time laying peacefully then he turned and jumped in the shower.

As the water hit the bottom of the tub, I rolled over and reached for Job only to realize he was gone. "Job," I hollered. "Job!" At the sound of my voice he turned the shower off and ran in the room.

"What's up?" he said.

"Nothing. I didn't know where you were," I said as I wiped the sleep from my eyes.

"Are you okay? Do you need anything?" he asked, sweeping the back of his hand across my face.

"No, I'm fine," I spoke softly.

He leaned forward, kissed me all over my face, then he reached in his stash and put money on the dresser.

"I have to go out," he said as he reached for his pants.

"Okay," I said, then I turned back over and closed my eyes.

"I'll call you soon," he said as he reached for the door.

Job was like a man on the moon and I was depressed. I loved him but not like he loved me. I wasn't ready to have his child and he wanted a boy that would carry his name, a boy that could keep his legacy going when he died, a boy that he could love the way he thought he wasn't loved. Job wanted to set a strong foundation for his child so he wouldn't have to kill, steal or hustle like others to eat. He just wanted to show him the significance of life. It was so much to be given back and Job wanted the opportunity to share some values with his seed. You only get one real shot at life and having a son was his.

Minutes later Job unlocked the door and ran upstairs to me. Rose spray painted his Benz and put sugar in the tank of the blue car. Job wanted to kill her but they were only vehicles so he had the tow truck tow the Benz to the dealer to get it painted over and the blue car he took as a lost. Those things could be gotten again. He just wanted me to be safe and living in my mom's neighborhood wasn't cool. It was too open and people were too jealous of nothing but that's where I chose to be. I had to find something different though because Job didn't know how much more he could take. He hated coming home every night around the area I grew up in. He was so used to his set but I wasn't.

Two weeks later Job pulled up to the house and parked. He had to meditate before coming in because he didn't know what kind of mood I was going to be in. After sitting for ten minutes Job jumped out the car and opened the door.

He walked into the kitchen to find no food on the stove again. This was becoming routine and he hated it. I spoiled him and snatched everything back like a selfish little girl. He ate at the diner he used to eat at before we met and this was hard for him to accept. He never imagined things to be this way. He thought his first experience having a child would be harmonious and we would see eye to eye, but I showed him differently. I did me.

Inside the room Job looked at the ginger ale soda that sat on the night stand with saltine crackers beside it. This was routine too. Every night he found me eating ice, water ice or crackers. He wasn't used to what he was seeing. I went from a loving, caring, gentle woman to a miserable beast. I couldn't eat during the day and at night he found me sick in bed.

Job walked to the bathroom and showered alone. He couldn't wait for the day to watch me bathe again or soak with me. He felt so lonely and out of place. He wanted his baby back.

After washing every ounce of dirt from his body he walked back into the room quietly. He didn't want to alarm me so I could flip on him again. He was so in love with the thought of me carrying his Prince and his world had to be perfect. It just had to be. It could be no other way. He had to do something to make things work for our family. He couldn't stand another night not making love to me.

Job and Tank became tight since they ran into each other at the salon. It was an awkward situation but I had no control over it.

Job gave me seventy two-hundred dollars for my Chevy to make his runs up NYC and that was double the amount I paid for the car. The Chevy was making him lots of money so that seventy-two hundred was nothing compared to what he was getting.

Once Job dropped Luke and I off and made sure we were straight, I emptied my pocketbook out on the bed. I trashed the unnecessary mail, then I opened up a letter from Snoop that I got from my mom's house.

"*As-salaam-Alikium Cinnamon. I hope this letter finds you in the best of health. As for me, I'm maintaining. You don't write anymore and every time I call your mom's, you're not there, so I'm assuming you moved on. And if you did, I'm not mad. You did what you had to do. I just know I'm not right without you Shorty. I need you in my life and without you, I have nothing.*"

The door unlocked and I knew it was Job.

"Oh my God! It's Job," I whispered, balling the letter up. I threw it under the bed before he reached the bedroom door. He passed me my prenatal vitamins that he forgot to give me then he left back out.

I grabbed the letter and ripped it into pieces. It was nothing I could do for Snoop. I got the phone line disconnected at mom's so I wasn't receiving his calls anymore. I didn't write him and I wasn't about to. He had many babies' mamas to take care of him. I had a family and the money Job provided for me wasn't about to go to Snoop's tired ass. I couldn't hold his weight anymore. I would never jeopardize my life for him. I moved on and I was happy with Job although things were shaky at the moment but the doctor said pregnancy would do that to you.

Although I couldn't ask for a better nigga, I went against God and Job's wishes a week later and killed our baby. I knew I wasn't right but I didn't think I could stand him. The pregnancy had me so twisted that I couldn't think clearly. I was so miserable and mean. I hated Job's scent and sound. Everything about him irked me. He cried and pleaded with me the night before the procedure but I got rid of his first born anyway.

After the procedure cousin Justin drove me to mom's where everybody stood around chilling. They didn't know what I did but I knew and I felt guilty. Our family was supposed to keep producing and multiplying and *I killed one of our own.*

I spoke to my family and brushed by the black on black 300TE that my nephew Nathan was leaning against.

"Aunt Cinnamon take this ride with me," Nathan said. His old head Saleem was tryna' holla at me and Nathan figured he would at least try to hook us up because he wanted to gain points with Saleem. Saleem just came home from jail and he was getting a couple dollars so my young nephew wanted to get money any way he could. He watched Luke and RJ do their thing through the years and although their turnout wasn't so good, he still wanted to hustle. He thought hustling was cute.

I thought about what Nathan said as Job pulled around the corner with a *tootsie pop* in his mouth. That was his trademark. He loved sucking lollipops while driving and he looked sexy doing it too.

"Hold up. Let me speak to Job for a minute," I said to Nathan then I walked to the car slowly. I had to hide my guilt.

"What's up?" I asked, looking to the left of me.

"Nothing. What are you doing?" he asked as he looked at the 300 sitting across the street.

"Nothing. I just got here and Nathan asked me to take a ride with him."

"Are you going?"

"Yeah."

"Okay, I'll be home," he said and he was upset. He needed me and I always seemed to put him last.

"All right. I'll be there shortly."

Job pulled off fuming. He wasn't insecure but he didn't like the fact of me riding with my nephew and a nigga he didn't know while I was carrying his seed. Besides, he remembered Saleem's face in traffic and he never forgot the looks he used to give him. Saleem was a hater.

There was no way I could disrespect Job so I told Nathan to go ahead and I walked to my old room to write Job a letter. *"Job, I don't know where to begin this letter, but I am so sorry for what I did today. I had an abortion without your consent and I went up against everything that I was taught about life. What I did was immorally wrong and I can't begin to express how I'm feeling right now. I know I'm asking a lot when asking you to forgive me because it's no way I should've taken a life, but I did. And now I have to answer to God for what I did and I don't know if I can forgive myself, so if you don't forgive me, I understand. I never knew it was going to hurt me so bad and I guess I never really considered your feelings and I didn't give our baby a chance. It never had a choice. I made the choice for all of us and now I'm paying for it. I can't stop thinking about what I did and believe it or not, I asked the doctor to stop, but it was too late. I even felt you leave me while I was on that table, so if you do, I have to deal with it. I'm not saying it's going to be easy, because it won't, but I will have to ask God for strength to continue on with my life. Please baby, please forgive me and find it in your heart to love me the way you always have. Please don't let this be a reason for you leaving me. You remember when you told me about all the abortions you made those girls have and how hurt they were because they wanted to be a part of you. Well, I'm not justifying what I did, but the way they felt is how you feel and it's all wrong. You shouldn't have made them get abortions because you didn't want them to be a part of you and I should not have gotten an abortion because I thought I wasn't ready for what you wanted. It's all wrong and we both made mistakes that we can't change, so please find it in your heart to forgive me the way that they forgave you. I need you in my life and without you there is no me. I want you and I need you. I'm begging you not to go. Love Cinnamon"*

After God dealt with my emotions, I had to tell Job my secret. I couldn't live another day knowing I killed his seed and he didn't know it. Before taking Luke to school, I passed Job the letter as he sat in the window sill waiting for his man Nigel. Nigel was a 65-year young hustler. He did anything for Job and he was loyal too. Job trusted him with his life. And although he was wiser in some areas, he learned a lot from Job. Job was like the son he never had.

Tears began dropping from Job's eyes as soon as he read the first sentence. It was no way he could forgive me for killing his seed. He wanted so badly to choke me but that wasn't going to bring his baby back so he continued to read as I ran out the door. I hated myself for hurting him. I wanted to beat me. The pain was unbearable. I could cry but seeing a man cry, hurt me so much. Especially Job because he didn't deserve the pain. He deserved to be happy. He was a good man.

Although I betrayed Job and he wanted to leave me, he stayed because he loved me. 'Forever My Lady,' by Jodeci made me cry every time I thought of Job, the baby and me but I couldn't change what I did. I only wanted to try and conceive again.

It was a month later and I still wasn't pregnant. I began to believe I couldn't get pregnant but Job let me know I wouldn't get pregnant unless he wanted me to.

The holidays were here and Job never stayed in the city during Christmas or New Years because he was worth millions and times like these only made niggas hungry so he didn't want to be around for the begging and scrambling. *Out of sight, out of mind.* He was tired of holding all the weight too. He didn't mind giving here and there but he did so much for his family and associates through the years and nobody seemed to appreciate him. He helped his brother Brent get a four hundred and fifty thousand dollar home and Brent still ran his mouth too much about his business. Brent seemed to care more about niggas on the streets than his own blood. And Job's sister Gabbie was as selfish as she wanted to be. Job took care of her before he started hustling when he worked fixing boats with the Colombians who later turned him onto the game. He kept Gabbie laced in Gucci bags and bamboo earrings and that only made her spoiled and not want her own. She was 22 and Job was still taking care of her and her kids while her baby's father was running around robbing, stealing and getting high. His mother was the same way. She didn't mind getting new cars, bank accounts and jewels but she treated him like the stepchild. She loved his brother Brent more than she loved him, so Job thought anyway. She constantly downed Job because he didn't work legally and Brent did. Job's entire family came up off him but he didn't feel the love. He gave everything to them on a silver platter and they couldn't maintain the family business he started. It was time to throw in the towel and let them fetch for themselves because he wanted to start his own family.

I sent Luke to his grandmother's down south and Job and I went to the Poconos to rekindle our relationship. The mountains could only bring us excitement, new love and passion.

Job and I stepped our relationship up in the Poconos. I went against the oral sex rule and gave Job what he gave me and he had intricate details for me to follow from messing with the freakiest chick that had *Kama Sutra* down to a science. I couldn't hate. I wanted to learn. I didn't mind learning from him. He knew what he wanted and I knew Job only wanted me to please him and make our thing tight and Job was right, he had control of me getting pregnant because he wanted me pregnant on the trip and it happened. I was to have his baby boy.

"I'm going to California next week to connect with some different people," Job said while coasting down the turnpike back home.

"Why are you going all the way down there?" I asked. I was so in love and I hated to think of him so far away.

"Because I'm looking for better prices and it's good to keep all your options open. If things are better for me in California, I won't deal with the people in New York," he informed me.

"Do you think that's safe?" I asked.

"Nothing is safe in this game. You just do what you have to," he said.

"I don't want you to go," I said.

"I'll be fine. Me, Nigel and Tank are going. Tank wants to make a move and I need Nigel to help me hold all the money I'm taking."

"That's very risky. Are you sure those people are safe?" I questioned.

"I dealt with them before on business and we have been cool for some time."

"Okay. If you trust them, then I guess it's cool," I didn't feel right with his decision but who was I. He was the man and he was going to do what he wanted to regardless of what I said.

Job stood in the middle of the floor with one small suitcase a week later. "Hold these papers for me. I'll be back in a couple of days," he said, handing me the title to the Benz and the deeds to all the properties he owned.

"Where are you going?" I asked.

"I told you I had to go to California," he reminded me.

"Is that all you're taking?" I asked him.

"Yeah. I'll buy clothes when I get there. I don't want any extra luggage," he said.

"Okay baby. I love you and please be safe. Who's taking you to the airport?" I asked while resting to my feet.

"Basil."

"All right."

A horn beeped outside and Job looked out the window.

"That's Tank," he smiled. It was big business awaiting them. Cali had to bring forth some new fruit.

Job walked downstairs to let Tank in. While they talked, I thought of how crazy it was having the two of them in the living room while I sat upstairs. Tank and I still hadn't come face to face and I could only imagine what it would be like when we finally did.

As their voices faded, I jumped up to watch my baby off. I hated for him to leave me but he was the man and he had moves to make so I had to let him go.

91

At the airport Job, Nigel and Tank boarded flight 589 going straight to San Diego, California. Although Job went over the move with Nigel and Tank he had to make sure they were on point because it was a lot of money involved and Job didn't want anything to go wrong.

By ten o'clock in the evening Job, Nigel and Tank checked into the *Embassy Suites San Diego Bay Hotel*. Job phoned his friend Ortiz as soon as he put his bag down to let him know he was in town. Ortiz in turn told Job where to meet him so Job, Nigel and Tank put the seven hundred thousand dollars of currency around their waists, in their jackets, socks and underwear like Job instructed them to then they caught a cab and got dropped off at Park Blvd. so they could walk to Ortiz's house.

Once they reached Ortiz's door, Job told Nigel and Tank to wait on the side while he knocked. After knocking twice Ortiz came to the door with no shirt on and a cigar in his mouth.

"Come in," he told Job. Job looked inside only to notice a table full of Colombians that spoke no English, only Ortiz. He turned and signaled for Tank and Nigel to come and they walked in together.

Ortiz went to the table and whispered something to one of the men sitting at the table and he looked at Job strange. Job looked at Tank and Tank looked at Job.

"What the fuck is goin' on?" said Tank.

"It's cool. We're gonna get the stuff and roll," Job informed him.

"Is everything ready?" Job asked Ortiz. The same man said something in an unknown tongue then Ortiz said, "It's not here yet. You have to come back tonight."

"What the fuck do you mean tonight? You told me to come over and we spoke about this before I got here and you said everything was set up and ready for me. What the fuck is going on?" Job asked, raising his voice. Shit didn't seem right to him at all. The set wasn't cool. Every man at the table jumped to their feet then Ortiz walked over to Job and said, "Hey look. Be patient and I promise you, it'll be ready tonight."

"Job be cool man. We're around all these motherfuckas that don't speak no English with all this money on us. Lets get the fuck outta here," Tank said, tapping Job on the arm. Job looked as if he wanted to say more, then he thought about it and stepped back. What Tank said made sense, but Job was running things.

"Come on. Let's get the fuck outta here," Job said to Tank and Nigel then he opened the door before Ortiz reached it.

"I'll talk to you later," Ortiz said as he watched the back of Job's head.

"Yeah," Job said as he kept walking. They never looked back. They just kept moving until they were out of sight.

"What's on your mind man? Those motherfuckas know what hotel we're staying in and everything. And you wanna argue with them. Are you crazy?" Tank yelled once they got on 4th Avenue.

"No. I know what I'm doing. We'll wait until tonight and if it doesn't go down right, then we're out," Job said.

"I don't trust those motherfuckas either," said Nigel.

"We'll change hotels when we get back and I'll call them instead of him calling me," Job explained.

They got back and switched hotels immediately. Job waited until he thought the time was right, then he phoned Ortiz.

"Is everything straight?" Job asked him.

"No man. We'll meet tomorrow," said Ortiz.

Job slammed the phone down and said, "They're bullshiting!"

"What did he say?" asked Tank.

"He said tomorrow. We'll wait until then," Job said. Instead of buying clothes to wear, Job, Nigel and Tank stood over the tub and washed their underwear out. It was no time to waste. They would wear the same thing twice.

As soon as Job's head hit the pillow he thought of me. He was so caught up in his business but he missed home. He felt me in his arms. He rolled over and grabbed the phone to dial home quickly.

"Hey baby," he smiled as soon as he heard my voice. I was comfort to him.

"Hi, baby," I said, rubbing my stomach. I wished he was home with me.

"How's everything going over there with you?"

"Alright. Did Luke come home yet?" He asked.

"Yeah, he's here. When are you coming home?" I asked.

"I'll be there tomorrow."

"Okay. I love you."

"I love you too," he assured me.

He hung up and I held the phone close to my ear. I didn't want to let go. I wished tomorrow was then. He was my everything. Finally I drifted off with sweet memories of us. *Love is the greatest gift to have.* Job made my world complete. It was no me without him.

Job rested his head on the pillow then he looked Tank in the eyes and said, "Why don't we go back to the city and have a double wedding?"

"I don't know if I'm ready for that," Tank said. He was with his baby's mama only because things didn't work out with us but he didn't know if he could do the marriage thing. And although he cared for Job, he couldn't see us standing side by side in matrimony. That was a bit much for him at the moment. He still hadn't gotten over some things.

"Well, I'm gonna marry my baby. I love her so much," Job said with confidence. He could care less about what was before. I never slept with

93

Tank so he had nothing to worry about. He knew I loved him and no other. The way I made love to him made him sure of what he felt.

Job woke up with all his senses the next morning. He knew shit wasn't right with Ortiz. He was up to no good. Job figured he had enough money. And if he was going to be set up, it wasn't going to happen in California where he had no family and his body would probably never be found. He couldn't go out like that. He had too much to lose.

Job, Tank and Nigel caught the next flight back home. It was a drought and Job needed to serve the city like he normally did with the best coke and he could trust his New York connect so business it was as usual.

As soon as the cab dropped Job to his car, he and Tank drove up NYC while Nigel fell back to make calls. What could be better than dealing with the people that you dealt with since you got into the game? Job could trust Armeleon with his life. Job was like a son to Armeleon. He looked out for Job. Job was moving so much weight for Armeleon that he gave Job twenty bricks for every ten he got.

"I'll never do that again," Job said to Tank on their way back from NYC. He never had to go outside Armeleon to get kilos. Job just liked doing things differently every now and then. And sometimes it didn't pay. What makes sense to you, could be your downfall.

"What?" Tank asked.

"I'm going to stick with my people no matter what. I trust them and they trust me. I just got beside myself thinking I could do both and it's not worth it. Sometimes slow money, is good money," Job seriously said.

"I feel you, but you act like you don't have enough. What you got here is cool," said Tank.

"Yeah, I know. I just want to have enough for my boy. I want to own cattle and sheep. I don't want the small things. Seriously. I want the gold mines. I want to supply the rich. If I had my own oil, I would be straight for life. It's bigger than this here. This shit is nothing. This is small money, man."

"See man you think too deep sometime," said Tank.

"I just want to get a little more, then quit for good," Job said.

"You have enough money now to quit."

"Never. To get out the ghetto and never come back....you have to be the man behind the scenes. I won't have to make runs or take. I'll make the rules and give," Job said as he thought about his unborn son. Job leaned out the window, paid the toll, then he headed uptown to drop Tank off.

For the next couple of weeks Job supplied everybody in my hood and all the surrounding areas. He had the best coke at the moment and the most and I was afraid of what he was doing because I didn't know how well niggas would adjust to Job coming into our neighborhood taking over. Since the YBM everybody had been doing their own thing and dudes weren't really eating too good. Everybody was really out for self and Job coming into a neighborhood that he didn't grow up in with so much coke was scary. Niggas wouldn't take that on the chin so easily.

Shalina introduced her friend Tafik to Job and although I didn't trust him, Job put him on because he needed to get rid of as much coke as he possibly could and Tafik didn't mind at all. He really wanted to run our neighborhood. He just didn't have the drugs to do so but he had the man power. With Job on his side, he could do big things and Job was the kind that played the back burner anyway so Tafik could act like he was the boss.

Once Job and Tafik parted for the night, Job's phone rang and he thought it was me checking on him. I was evil and treating him unfairly again but I always made sure he was straight before going to bed.
"I'm on my way in," he said.
"It's not your girl. It's me Nadja, Job," said the tired voice on the other end of the phone.
"Yeah," Job said while holding the phone. He hadn't spoken to Nadja in weeks so he couldn't understand what the phone call was about.
"I'm pregnant," she announced. Job dropped his cell phone. Nadja and his girl couldn't be pregnant at the same time. He messed up. It was a huge mistake. How could he explain this to me? How was he going to tell me he fucked somebody one time while we were going through a very stressful time in our relationship and she was pregnant?
"Well, Cinnamon is pregnant too and you can't have a baby by me. I love my girl and I'm gonna marry her," he said.
"Oh, so forget me. Are you telling me I have to get an abortion?" she cried.
"I'm sorry Nadja but I love Cinnamon and I can't do this to her. We both knew it was a mistake. I should've never leaned on you for comfort knowing I wasn't going to leave her. I was confused but she does love me. She really loves me despite her ways and I love her too. I planned for her to have my child. I never planned for you to have my baby. I'm sorry," he said.
"I'll give you twenty thousand to have an abortion."
"Okay. When can I see you?" she asked. She needed the money for college. Why have a baby by a man that didn't want her? She could pay her college tuition and go about her business.
"I'll meet you tomorrow afternoon after I talk to Cinnamon," he said.
"About what?" she asked.
"I have to at least tell her. I owe her that much," he said lastly then they hung up.

In the morning Job begged my evilness to go to lunch with him. The atmosphere made a big difference when discussing problems. He knew telling me about Nadja would be a lot for me to consume but that's what love

95

and trust was all about. If our relationship could stand this test, then we could *conquer the world* together.

   After having lunch at the *Engine 46 Steakhouse*, Job and I cruised the city. He didn't have the balls to break my heart at lunchtime so he would tell me while driving home. He had to or he wouldn't be right.

   I stared out the moon roof while Anita Baker's, *Good Love* played smoothly in the background.

"Do you remember when you were pregnant the first time?" Job asked with one hand grasping the steering wheel. He had an unfamiliar look on his face, a new look, in fact, a look I never witnessed before.

My heart raced and I said, "Yeah, why?"

"Do you remember every time I asked you to sleep with me, you rejected me?" He said, now staring straight through me.

"Yes."

"Well, I slept with this girl that I was seeing before you and she's pregnant," he informed me. My heart dropped to my belly where my baby lay. I wanted to die. "Rose?" I mumbled, looking into his slanted eyes that I loved so deeply.

"No, the Mexican and black girl Nadja."

My heart went out the window with the last breeze I felt. I put my hand on my baby and my blood pressure rose.

"How could you do this to me?" I cried.

"I'm sorry. I didn't mean it. I did it out of hurt. I don't want her or the baby. I want you and our baby," he said, coasting down the street with his right hand on my belly.

"You obviously slept with her without protection, jeopardizing my health. Did you even care about giving me something?" I cried, pulling the handle of the door.

"What are you doing?" he asked as he pulled my door shut.

"Let me the fuck out of here! I wanna get out! Please let me go," I cried, trying to catch my breath. "You hurt me and I hate you for this."

   The red light caught Job and I jumped out and ran. I ran two blocks up without stopping. I thought only of my baby. Job left the car in the middle of the street and chased me. He had to let me know nothing could come between us. Yes, he made a mistake but he was sorry. I had to forgive him with the same love it took him to forgive me after I aborted his first child.

"Cinnamon, please get in the car!" Job hollered as he got near. "I love you. I'm so sorry. I promise she won't have the baby."

"Fuck you Job! You hurt me. I don't have anything to say to you," I said as I turned around to see how close he was.

   At the next block my knees gave in. My brain said, "move" but my body wouldn't let it happen. I spotted a Coke bottle by the curb. I picked it up and broke it. If Job got any closer, I was to cut him with it. I was mentally drained. I couldn't adjust to my hormonal change as it was and now he dropped this on me. My rage was high. I loved him and hated him at this very moment.

Job snuck up on me and grabbed me from the back. I swung and kicked but his strong arms wouldn't let me go.

"Please stop. I promise you she won't have the baby. She's getting an abortion. I already told her you were pregnant and I love you and I didn't want her to have the baby. I made a mistake. I only slept with her that one time and she got pregnant," he pleaded.

I fell in his arms and asked, "How far is she?"

"She's two and a half months."

"So she's going to have her baby before me. I hate you. Put me down," I said, swinging the bottle again. Job carefully took the bottle from my hand and tossed it in the street. It was no way I could get away from him. He carried me to the car and begged me not to jump out again.

"Can we just go home and talk? I'll call her and she can tell you that I told her I only want you and my baby," he said, watching me, the door and the road in front of him.

"I don't want to talk to her. Just take me home please," I cried, staring out the window. "Just take me home. I hate you."

Job slid into the parking space in front of the door while he watched me closely. He watched me so close that he didn't see me take his door key from the console. I opened my door and ran up the steps before Job stepped out the car.

After letting myself in, I locked the big steel door behind me. For thirty minutes Job begged for me to let him in but I refused. I let him knock and plead until he got tired and left then I picked the phone up to call his Grandmom. If anybody knew anything, it was she. They were tight. She handled all Job's business for him aside from his Godmother. They believed in Job. It was nothing they wouldn't do for him. They knew he didn't do everything right but his intentions were good. In fact, his Godmother Vera taught him all about the Real Estate game. He confided in her about all his investments. And his Grandmother was sharp too. She was good with numbers. She held card games at the spot on Friday nights. She taught Job how to play pittie pat so good that he would beat her out of her money some Friday's. But that was nothing. Whatever he took from her on Friday's, she got back triple on Monday's. He paid her to stay home with his nephew that they were raising together. Mom Henryetta didn't have to leave the house for nothing. Job made her retire at an early age and he gave her 1,000 dollars a week. She looked out too. She cooked him whatever he wanted but since I came into the picture her hands got a little break because I was doing most of the cooking for Job and he let Mom Henryetta know I was tight in the kitchen too. I did what some Grandmoms could do. I did the baking, frying and broiling. I had the kitchen thing sowed up.

Mom Henryetta didn't know anything about Nadja being pregnant. Neither did Job's sister Gabbie because Job didn't tell anyone about what he did only his man Nigel and Nigel and I weren't close enough for me to ask him.

I didn't speak to Job for two weeks straight. I put him out and kept his keys so he couldn't get in. I was through with him but he made sure Luke and I had what we needed and the bills were paid. He even ordered me a brand-new seven series BMW and he got me a gold bracelet containing eight carat blue diamonds for Valentines Day with a card saying, "Cinnamon, please forgive me for hurting you. I made a big mistake and I only want you in my life. The way I forgave you, is how I need you to forgive me. Please give me a second chance. You mean the world to me. Please Be Mine and Stay Mine forever. Love Job."

Nadja and Job sat in Ladies Medical aborting Job's baby on a Tuesday morning. Job wanted to make sure he was getting what he was paying for. Twenty thousand dollars wasn't a lot but he couldn't stand to make another mistake. Nadja looked at Job for the last time and said, "Are you sure you want me to do this? I love you Job. I'll do anything to have your baby."
"The money is in the car waiting for you when you're finished. Please don't make this harder on yourself. I told you nobody but Cinnamon is to have my child," he seriously said. Nadja cried in her lap then the receptionist called her name.

An hour later Nadja walked through the doors still in tears. She wished she never agreed to the money. While laying on the table she figured she could have the baby and Job would change his mind but then again, why have a baby for a man that had a family already.

Nadja grabbed Job's hand and he pulled away. He let her know again that what they had was over and he was happy at home.
"The money is in the bag in the back seat. I'll drop you off and please don't call me," he said to Nadja as they approached the car.
"Okay," she cried. Job dropped Nadja off at 8th & Markets Street then he headed straight over the bridge to look at a new house for us.

Once Job came back into the city, he purchased two tickets for the Patti LaBelle show. He knew how much I loved Patti so he wanted to see me smile.

After the show I asked Job to come back home. Luke and I really needed him and I was still bitter to some degree but I was willing to make it work because we were family.

In the morning I got up and went to the BMW dealer and dropped 9,500 dollars on a BMW like the one Luke had. I was being selfish and mean knowing Job wanted me to have a car that was paid for but I didn't care. I liked being difficult. I was a rebellious one that liked doing things my way.

Job came in at the normal hour and slammed the door behind him. I knew from the sound of his feet hitting the steps that he saw the car. I tucked my body all the way under the covers.

"Cinnamon," he nudged me, while I played sleep. "Cinnamon. I know you hear me."

"What?" I whispered.

"Why did you go buy a car?" He asked.

"What are you talking about?" I asked him.

"I saw the tag in the window of the car with your name on it. Is that your car?" He asked, hoping for an honest answer.

"Yeah."

"How did you pay for it?" He had to know.

"I only put ninety five-hundred dollars on it and I have a car note," I said.

"Why would you get a note on a used car when I was gonna buy you a car and pay for it in full? You did that to be smart. You're always trying to hurt me, letting me know you don't need me for anything. I know you don't need me. You didn't have to do that. And you only got that car because that's what Luke had."

"I told you to stop bringing him up. I got that car because my son liked it and I like it," I told him. And I did like the car but it brought back good old memories. I was still living in the past to some degree.

"You're always blaming everything on your son. It's not him. It's you holding on to his father," he let me know.

"Oh, you're saying he doesn't love and miss his father."

"I'm not saying that, but a lot of things you say he wants, is what you want."

"Whatever!"

Job and I became distant again and I was still doing things my way. My nephew Nathan asked if he could stay with me because his mom's boyfriend put him out and I cleaned the back room for him against Job's wishes. Home wouldn't be home anymore with Nathan around. He liked him, but he didn't feel comfortable with the situation because of the company Nathan kept. And I couldn't blame him because it bothered me, too, but he was my nephew and I couldn't see him on the streets.

For weeks Nathan came home with Lil Na's co-defendant Jareem while Lil Na sat still in the Juvenile Facility waiting to come home. Every time Job saw them, he left. He couldn't rest with them around. He was worth too much and he knew Jareem was a sneaky motherfucker. Before he had to kill the young boy, he parted like a man but he was so tired of my foolishness. When was I going to put family first, him anyway?

Na was released from the Juvenile Facility finally and he stepped to Job behind my back telling him he was older than he was and Job put him on too but this would only draw more attention because Na trusted the wrong niggas. Anything he thought was cool to talk about, wasn't. Not only were starving niggas on Job heels, the Feds were too. Somebody from the streets told them all about Tank and Job's drug trafficking and they wanted to bring them down. The only thing was, Job was so smooth. They didn't know which angle to take with him so they tried to play me but I played them for Job. I found out everything I needed to know for him so he could be ten steps ahead of them.

Chapter 4
The Choices We Make
"The End Results"

Spring of 1992. I pulled Job's sparklin' clean Benz in front of Club Dynasty around 11:00 p.m. The attendant ran over and opened the doors for Shalina and me to get out. Job was out of town on business so I took his Benz from his house hoping to get the same spot once the night ended.

Des's cousin Rashon was having his twenty-fifth birthday party and although Rashon was big Luke and Lil Luke's barber and Job's barber now, it made very little difference when it came to me being in the streets. Partying was against Job's wishes for me. His woman place was at home. I knew my limits, but I had to be at the hottest spot in the city for the night. I couldn't let Rashon down. The broads hated me and I had to let them see that things were still going well with me, pregnant and all. Actually I was showing my ass.

Shalina and I jumped out at the same time. Arch Street was packed with cars and people. Everybody came out to play. The last major party was the one Butch had so Rashon was trying to do it big this night, better than anyone before in his circle.

As soon as Shalina and I hit the big glass doors gossiped flowed throughout the club. All the broads wanted to see if I was really carrying Job's seed. They heard but many didn't believe. Sugar and her new clique stood by the bathroom gritting as Shalina and I brushed through the crowd. "Old bitch," Sugar mumbled. I heard her but I laughed it off and kept walking. I was pregnant by the nigga she wanted so badly so that was enough satisfaction for me alone. Rose and Carmen pushed their way through the crowd only to notice the glow on my suntanned face. "Oh, no this bitch ain't," Rose said to Carmen.

"What?" said Carmen.

"The bitch Cinnamon. Look at her. Is she pregnant because I can't tell?" said Rose as she looked at my cream sheer dress with Australian studs lining my belly.

"Yeah, she's pregnant," said Carmen. She knew how the pregnancy game went unlike Rose because she couldn't get pregnant to save her life. Carmen could tell by my glow, my full, long hair and my posture. I had a slight curve in my back. She noticed everything on me even my strong nails as I touched Shalina's shoulder.

"Well, it's not Job's baby anyway," Rose said as she flagged her right hand high. She was in straight denial.

Shalina caught a glimpse of Rose talking shit so she stepped to her and Carmen and let them know if they came, they had better come correct because she wasn't having it this night. She'd come out her shit at a drop of a dime about her sister. She was tired of all their shit.

After Shalina got her shit off, I pulled her to the side so she could cool down. I liked the fact that she wasn't a punk but she could be overly aggressive at times and I wasn't about to get caught up in the club fighting while Job was away. He'd be in my ass about acting ghetto with his seed inside me.

It was time for two rounds now. Shalina was steaming and she had to have her Hennessy straight up on the rocks to get the night started. She came out to have fun and fun it was. The broads weren't about to spoil her night. She refused.

While Shalina drank her Hennessy, she held me by the arm. She had to guard me with her life. If she didn't bring me back home safely, she would never forgive herself.

Sugar stared a hole through my head as I stood by the bar. Either the pregnancy brought out the beauty or I was like fine wine because I was simply gorgeous and my hair was tight. Cousin Carol streaked my hair and it was a pretty sight to see. The streaks just complimented my complexion and skin tone. Sugar missed my friendship too as I missed hers as well.

Job called the spot twice to get no answer. That wasn't like me not to answer so he began to wonder where I could've been. After Rose made me feel so uncomfortable, I asked Shalina to leave. She hated the fact that I let others ruin my night but she had to respect me and besides, she had one too many up in her and it was better that she left anyway because she was about to start something just for GP.

Outside the club Sugar, her girl Mira, Rose and Carmen stood heated as I jumped into Job's car. I had the looks, a real man and the material things to compliment me. They simply hated my guts. They wished death on me as I peeled off into the darkness of the night playing my favorite group from back in the day, *The Sugarhill Gang*. They figured I was going home to the dick they wanted but little did they know, I was going home alone this night while my man was away making the bread for his family.

I slid into the same parking spot around 3:00 a.m., thank God. After taking the alarm off I hit the shower and jumped in bed. The phone rang ten minutes later. I reached over and answered it.
"Hello," I said.
"Hey, baby. Where have you been? I was worried about you" said Job.
"Nowhere. I went to my mother's earlier," I lied.
"I'll be home in a few hours," he said.
"Okay. I love you."
"I love you too," he said.

In the morning Job pulled up and noticed the Benz was moved. I always left the wheel turned toward the street when I took the car. He knew I went out and why did I lie. Job came straight to the room and kissed me on the forehead. He wasn't about to question me again about what I did the night before because I lied to him the first time. I turned over and grabbed him so tight. Every time he left me to handle business I worried. And when he returned I was more than relieved. He threw his clothes on the floor and jumped in bed with me.

Around 1:00 p.m. Job and I pulled up to the travel agency to book a trip to Disney World at the end of the week. It was time for a family vacation. After going over all the packages' Job gave the agent 5,200 for his nephew Blaire, my nephew Nick, Lil Luke, myself and him. Then he gave me 3,000 dollars to buy everybody things for the trip while he headed to his restaurant to check on his workers. They were laying cement around the building and he wanted to make sure everything was right.

After buying the Guess and Polo section out I headed straight to the restaurant to meet Job. I pulled in front of the restaurant where Job stood seriously as he watched his workers finish up. He smiled once he noticed me parked across the street.

"Get out," he said.

"Okay," I said as I turned the ignition off then I walked to meet my baby.

"I got you and the boys some Polo and Guess outfits from the mall."

"I'm gonna stop buying Polo gear."

"Why?" I asked.

"Because it's a lot of rumors floating around about this, that and the third."

"Are you serious?" I asked in amazement. After all the money I spent on certain designers that didn't deserve it, it was time for a change.

"Yeah. And you know I like Polo, but I'm not gonna support the designer if that's true. I can give my money to someone else," he seriously said.

"Yeah, you're right. I wish I had known but you know people lie too."

"Do you like the front?" he said, changing the subject.

"Yeah. They're doing a good job."

"Yeah. I can't wait until everything is finished," he said happily. Job just got a contract for a million dollars so things were really looking up for him with the construction business. He just had his van upgraded. He put his company name on it. His boy Tony was designing jackets, sweats and tee shirts with the company's logo too. JSM stood for Job, Shy and Mark. Job knew Mark for years and Shy did odd jobs with Mark so Job took them under his wing and started the construction business.

"Ride with me to my mom's. She asked about you. She wanted to know if you got any bigger," he said.

"Okay."

Job and I pulled up to his mom's door where she kneeled, scrubbing her steps. Job jumped out smiling from ear to ear. He was feeling good about his many accomplishments and he just wanted her to be happy for him this one time. Everything he did was to please her and she didn't seem to be happy about anything he did legally or not.

"Mom here she is," Job smiled as he opened my door. I stepped out the car happy about Job's happiness.

"Hi, Mrs. Jackie," I smiled.

"Hi, Cinnamon. How are you?" She smiled back.

"I'm fine."

"You're not that big, huh!" she said as she looked at my belly.

"No. Not really."

"How's the pregnancy going?" she asked me.

"Everything's fine."

"Here's a picture of the ultrasound mom," Job said, pulling the picture from his wallet.

"Oh, this looks like a boy from the head."

"That's what I said," Job laughed.

"Yeah. Yeah. He thinks it's a boy," I smirked.

"I know it is," he assured me for the hundredth time.

"Are y'all coming in?" She wanted to know.

"No. I have to get back around the restaurant. Did the guy finish laying the floors' mom?" Job asked.

"Yeah. You didn't see it?"

"No."

"Oh, I thought you came here earlier," she said.

"No. I haven't been here all day."

"Cinnamon come see the floor I got my mom."

We walked inside to see the beautiful marble floors that Job had laid for his mother, then Job dropped me back off to my car.

Job went straight to his jeweler and purchased me, a five-carat diamond bezel, gold Rolex watch for Mother's Day. Although Job didn't care for jewelry too much, he didn't mind giving it to me. His first iced out initial chain and his five-carat diamond ring would be his only and last piece of jewelry that he wouldn't wear again. A nice, conservative watch would be the only piece he would be interested in. He didn't care to be too flashy. He preferred his money to be invested for future funds.

The day before the trip Job came home and gave me the watch then we headed to Ardmore to meet his Godmother. He talked about me so much to her that she couldn't wait to meet me. She was so anxious, happy and proud that Job finally got what he wanted. His God brother beat him to the punch. He had a daughter two years ago. Job was in competition with him. They competed with everything but Job would be the man if he had a son.

Job pulled his car into the driveway of his Godmother's four bedroom single brick home with black iron gates surrounding the property. He jumped out and opened my door then we walked up the cement path hand and hand. Job spoke to the landscapers then he rang the bell.

Inside the house lights flashed repeatedly. Job's Godmother hollered so her husband could get the door.

"Hey Job," smiled Mr. Henry as he unlocked the security door.

"Hi, Mr. Henry this is my girlfriend Cinnamon," Job said as we walked inside.

"Hi Cinnamon. How are you?" he said, shaking my hand.

"I'm fine," I smiled. "How are you?"

"Good. Good," he said. Job's Godmother walked down the silver plush carpeted steps with a warm smile across her pretty round face. She had such a pleasant aura. Before she could reach the bottom step Job walked over and embraced her gently.

"Job. How are you?" she smiled, kissing and hugging him back.

"You must be Cinnamon," she said as she reached for me. "Job told me so much about you. He told me you were pretty and you are as pretty as he said you were."

"Thanks," I smiled as we embraced. I appreciated her realness. She cared for me because I was a part of Job. She was a prime example of love.

"Have a seat. Sit down please," she said. She didn't want us to leave. While Job and his Godmother used sign language, I admired her beautiful home. And the smell of raspberry potpourri gave off such a pleasant aroma. I felt so at peace.

Before Job handed his Godmother the diamond heart pendant he got her for Mother's Day, he asked her to be his child's Godmother too. He wanted his baby to enjoy what he had growing up with her during the summers. Job had so much fun on the beach in Wildwood with his Godmother and her children. Playing football and basketball for their community was so fun too. If he had a son, he was going to play every sport just like him.

Mrs. Vera accepted Job's proposal with honor and grace. She was overly proud that he chose her to be his child's Godmother. After making lunch for everyone, Mrs. Vera and Mr. Henry walked Job and I to the car. Everything was glorious. Job felt complete and I was grateful to be surrounded by all the love and affection, something I didn't get from his own people, only his grandmother and oldest sister. They were the only two real ones in the bunch.

Friday morning Nigel took our family to the airport. After Job gave him specific instructions on whom to meet and see, he left and we boarded flight 777 going straight to Orlando, Florida.

Our flight landed at one o' clock in the afternoon. The temperature was 103 degrees, being pregnant only made me more miserable. Sweat poured from my forehead and between my tits. I couldn't wait to get to the Villas to chill. Job flagged a cab down and he dropped us off in Lake Buena Vista, Florida at the *Disney's Boardwalk Villas.*

The first three days we did everything the boys wanted to do. It was so much to see and do that five days wouldn't be enough. Luke especially liked the *Nickelodeon* Studio. He watched it on cable all the time so that was one place he was sure to visit.

The fourth day Job and I got a sitter for the boys and we went out on the town to do us. I hated being so mean and miserable but Florida was extremely hot and I couldn't help my attitude. I took for granted that Job wasn't going anywhere. He was so patient with me because of our child but he was crying inside. I lost respect for him and he didn't know how much more he could take. He thought the trip would do us some good but it only made matters worse. I flipped out on him about a Cinnamon poptart so you know things were crazy. I was a selfish, mean, inconsiderate individual. I only cared about what I wanted and when I didn't get my way, everybody felt my anger. Everybody.

On the fifth day Job broke everything down to me. He loved me and he wanted me to be the mother of his child more than anything but I had to change my ways. We simply couldn't go on if I continued to be disrespectful with my tongue. I verbally abused him and he wasn't used to all the arguing. He got his way with women and I was giving him a run for his money. He liked the fight in me but when it came to being the ruler of the home, he wanted to be the man. He didn't like me making him feel less than that.

By ten o'clock in the evening we boarded flight 333 going straight back to Philadelphia. The boys had something to remember for the rest of their lives but Job and I were on the outs again. We planned not to speak to each other once we got back home. He would stay at his spot and I would stay at my mom's. I wasn't feeling him at the moment and it was better that we parted instead of staying together on foul terms. My pregnancy was taking over and I cared about nothing anymore. Not even the relationship.

Nigel waited patiently outside the airport for us to exit the plane. Once we got all of our bags, Nigel dropped Luke, Nick and me off at mom's house then he headed downtown to drop Job and his nephew Blaire off at Job's spot.

Job sat in the car with Nigel once Blaire went inside the house. He could talk to Nigel about any and everything. He was stubborn but he hated the fact that we weren't speaking. It was killing him and he didn't know if he could make it long without seeing me because I was carrying his child.

Nigel told Job to make me sweat for a couple days but to eat his pride as a man because of his family. Love was strange like that and Job had to understand my position too. I was carrying an extra load for him and that meant a lot.

Two days later Job sat on his sofa in disbelief. I didn't bother calling once to talk to him. Any other girl would've been calling, begging and pleading to make up but I was surely different all the way around. I was just as stubborn as him. He reached over and picked up the phone. He really missed Luke and me.

"Hello," I said.

"Are we going to be together or what? I don't want my child being raised in a broken home. I want us to be a family," said Job.

"I don't need you. I can raise my baby on my own. I did it once. I can do it again," I said angrily. I was still holding on to the past.

"Everything your son father did to you, you're taking it out on me. You couldn't trust him and he abused you and you're bringing it into our relationship," he said. And he was right. Everything I had gone through in my past, I brought it into our relationship and it wasn't fair to Job. He treated me like a real woman. He never turned his back on me.

"Whatever!" I said. I couldn't be honest so I brushed him off. "Whatever you say!"

"If you don't want me. Let me give you a half a million dollars for my baby," he said. And he meant it. He loved me but he loved his child greater. If we couldn't be together then he was willing to pay for his other half.

"Are you out of your mind? I'm not selling my baby. You can't put a price on him. I love this baby and I'm not carrying him to give him to you. I would never take your money for my child. I can't believe you said that," I said.

"That's how bad I want him. I want to wake up to him every morning. I want him to roll with me every day. I want us to eat, sleep and shit together. I want to give him the life I didn't have," he seriously said and he would do anything to raise his boy. Whatever the price was, he was more than willing to pay it.

"You had your father. He took you everywhere. He took you camping, hiking, swimming. Y'all went to the parks. Y'all had all the cookouts. You and your dad did a lot," I said.

"Yeah, we did and I want to do more with my son. I want to give him what I missed. My dad did those things but he still lacked in some areas and I don't want to lack in any," he assured me.

"You'll be a great father Job. Stop worrying. You're going to be the best father in the world. This baby is going to have the best with you and it goes beyond the money because you are going to love him with all your heart," I said once I came to my senses. I knew Job was a good, well-rounded individual.

"You are right. I will die for him."

"You're going to be the best and I would never keep him from you even if we don't make it. He's going to know you more than he knows me. Believe that," I honestly said.

"I know. When you wake up in the mornings we're gonna be gone. You're gonna look up and say where are they at. We are gonna do everything together," he said while imagining the future.

"Boy you better stop. I know you are happy, but don't go crazy with it. You know they say if you cherish something God will take that very thing you cherish."

"It's not like that. I just can't wait. I have never been this anxious about anything in my life. I always dreamed about this."

"Okay I have to go."

I held out another week and a half, then I called Job to come get me. I missed him so much. I needed him more than anything. I was being a real bitch but deep down inside, I loved him like I loved myself. I would die for him.

Job picked me up and took me to *Azalea* for brunch. It felt so good to be together again. While we waited for our food we reminisced on different events in our relationship, then lust entered our beings. We hadn't made love in a while so we asked the waiter to make our order to go and we left the restaurant to go to Job's spot.

After a night of passionate sex, Job gave me money to buy new clothes so I headed straight to *Toby Lerners* first to get shoes then I went to *Saks* and purchased two *Moschino* jump suits, a few linen outfits and two large rhinestone belts to compliment my outfits. Pregnancy wasn't about to stop me from wearing what I liked.

I pulled my car into the parking space in front of mom's door. I reached in the back and grabbed my bags then I carefully got out the car. It was a whole new era and the young boys had it sowed up around mom's way. They knocked the old hustlers off their game.

I put my bags on the porch then I sat on the sidewalk to let the warm, gentle breeze cut through my silk Moschino jumper. The extra weight was beginning to take its course.

A cream Lexus coupe pulled in front of me and stopped. I wasn't impressed with the cars or the niggas anymore. I'd been there, done that. I really didn't give a hoot. I was happy and secure with mine. The seventeen-year-old young boy raised up and said, "What's going on Shorty?" He was hyped about the streets. Still wet behind the ears and releasing too fast for himself.

"Nothing. I'm just chilling," I said as cool and calm as I could possibly be. I wasn't *new to the game.*

"I like you," he announced. He was corny as hell with that line.

"Yeah," I smiled.

"Yeah, I seen you around a couple times and I wanted to holler at you looking all good in that BM," he said, still corny.

"For real," I laughed.

"Yeah. Can I take you shopping?"

"No."

"Come on girl. Anything you want, I'll buy it. Let's go to New York?" He asked.

"I can't."

"Can you go with me to the Lexus dealer? I wanna cop this four-door sedan," he said. He was getting worst and worst with the verses. He was trying too hard and I couldn't be bought. The material things didn't move me. I had a few and I had a man that could buy me whatever. I wasn't fascinated. I was living life and being true to my man and myself at this point in the game. It was no disrespecting and no game playin'. It was all real and true.

"No."

"Why girl? Why you actin' like that?" he asked, like I was stupid. Little did he know. He was probably coping from my man anyway. He was definitely traveling the wrong route because I wasn't bending for his narrow curves.

"I'm pregnant and I have a man," I said. I had to let him know because he was getting on my nerves.

"I have a girl and she's pregnant, too" he said, coming back at me.

"You're crazy," I laughed.

"No, I'm serious and I don't care about that. Who's your man?" He asked.

"Job."

"Oh, my God!" he said, trying to find himself. "That's my man. You know what?"

"What?" I questioned. "What?"

"He has a good woman. I'm gonna tell him he has a good girl. You take care Shorty," he said, walking away. Yeah, he was definitely biting from the hand that fed him. He was totally out of order but respectful enough to swallow his pride. He respected Job as a man, hustler and a real nigga.

"Okay you, too," I said, cracking up. Job's name said enough and I was glad he was finished.

The young boy told Job what happened before I could. Job was definitely his meal ticket and he didn't want Job to get it twisted. He really didn't know I was Job's girl.

Things were definitely looking up for Na these days. He was pushing two bricks and it hadn't been two months since his release. He was definitely moving up in the world and his peers were jealous because they'd been hustling for years and they were still messing with ounces. They had no cars nor their own spots. Na and Nathan shared an apartment on City Line Ave. that Job dressed up with fifteen thousand dollars in furniture. They weren't doing too badly for young boys and I was still in the dark about Na's connect. I didn't know my man was his supplier.

Job called Na and told him to put his business off for a couple days because he wanted him to take a trip with us to Aruba. Job was generous like that so I thought nothing of it. I knew he liked Na's style therefore I thought he was being an uncle to him and nothing else.

Nigel dropped Job, Na and me off at the airport on Saturday afternoon. While we waited for our flight, I passed Job a black, shiny box.

"What's this?" he asked.

"Just an early Father's Day gift," I smiled. Job opened the box to find a gold Presidential Rolex watch.

"Why did you spend that kind of money on this watch?" he said. He liked it but he could do without, some things he didn't stand for.

"I got it under its cost from James," I said.

"Oh," he smirked. It was no way he could take it back so he tucked it in his luggage and kissed me on the forehead. His favorite spot.

Minutes later Job, Na and I boarded Delta Airways flight 070 going straight to Aruba. I traveled a few places in my younger years but Aruba was a place I dreamed of going to. I heard so much about it through old timers that had been around the world and I couldn't wait to get there to see what the set would add to me and Job's love life.

We landed in Queen Beatrix's Airport around 10:30 p.m. It was late but the night just begun for Job. He was up and ready to explore. After dropping our luggage at the *Hyatt Regency Aruba Resort&Casino*, we headed to the Bonbini Festival.

Job promised never to drink again but he and Na got a few tropical drinks mixed with very little liquor. And how could I be mad? We were vacationing and he deserved it with all the stress he had in his life back at home.

Around 3:30 a.m. Job and I made sure Na made it to his room then we went to our room to wind down and relax. I had a little energy left in my body but Job forgot I was pregnant. He took me to the balcony and made me cry to the ocean. I cried so loud that the waves did back flips. His tongue did miracles this night and my pussy was well pleased so I returned the tongue favor and licked all the important spots that I knew would make him run wild.

Job and I never made it to our king size bed. We slept on the balcony until the sunset. Job was a nature boy growing up and he still liked running naked but I couldn't allow him to do so at home because of Luke so every time we got a chance to be alone, he got buck wild. Mom raised us differently than Job's mom because I had brothers and some things she just didn't tolerate. I still couldn't run around like Jane in the jungle but I got a kick out of my Tarzan.

By ten o'clock a.m. Job and Na hit the casino inside our hotel. Job loved gambling and Na had the same weakness so what could be better than having the luxury at their hands. I fell back while they gambled away thirty thousand dollars together. What could I say? They weren't about to listen to me sound like their mothers. They liked what they did.

Job and Na made a bet after gambling so they took it to the basketball courts to see who would win the five thousand dollars they put in the pot. I was amazed at their childish ways. They had a lot of kid in them. Na was a teenager therefore I expected his mentally but Job, I really got to see the kid in him on this one.

For two hours I watched Job and Na. I couldn't wait until somebody broke the tie because I was ready to hit Oranjestad to shop. That was my weakness. I loved the malls and Job gave me generously so that's what I did with my spare time these days. He didn't want me to work and school I would do once I had the baby so while he took care of business, I shopped all the malls back home.

Finally Job won the five grand so we hit the mall while Na went to his room to chill. After buying souvenirs, T-shirts and other gifts to take back to our family and friends at home, Job suggested we go parasailing but I would just watch because I couldn't get down with going 1200ft above water. It was no way. And I was pregnant too. *Uh,un.*

Once the ship pulled from the dock Job kneeled before me.

"Get up Job," I smiled. "What are you doing?"

"You know I love you right," he smiled as our eyes locked.

"Yes."

"I love you so much and what you stand for. I think you're a beautiful mother to Luke and I know you're gonna be a greater mother to our son," he paused as he reached into his front pocket. Tears formed in my eyes because he was everything to me and more. I knew my baby had a winner for a father. He was everything I didn't get from my dad. "Well, I was hoping you would marry me." I couldn't open my mouth. I had two rings before but nothing ever came of the proposal but this time was different. I knew I was going to die Mrs. Job Heavensbee. I had to. He was definitely my *soul mate.*

"Job I would love to be your wife," I said as I embraced him and cried on his strong shoulders. So much was going on in his life and he wanted to do everything he hadn't done thus far. Rumors were going around about Rose having HIV and although Job got tested after they broke up, he couldn't risk losing what he had now. I took the test and was cool so it was safe to stick with home and never go outside of it. It wasn't worth it. Pussy wasn't worth that much. It wasn't worth his life. Not the best pussy either because he figured he had a prize package.

Job gently put the five-carat blue diamond engagement ring on my size five finger. Thank God he knew to go up half a size because of my pregnancy.

"It's time for us to get out of Philly. I'm going to Miami next week to look at this property."

"I can't go to Florida and leave my family here. All I know is my family. My mom needs me and I need her. What will I do so far away?" I seriously asked him.

"I'm your family, too, and you can visit anytime you want," he assured me. Money was right so I could fly frequently.

"I don't know about that. Can we just buy a house here and relocate later?" I asked.

He looked as if his dreams went out the ship into the ocean and vanished. He wanted me to want what he wanted. I was his life. His child and I were his world. Our happiness was more important than his. It was about us. He wanted us far away from the madness. The city we grew up in was full of people that wanted to hold us back. He wanted a new life where nobody knew us. It was time to get away and start anew. The city was full of backbiting haters.

"Okay. I can deal with that," he answered, knowing he was settling. He loved me and he would do anything to see me smile.

The next morning Na was awakened by Nathan around 11:00 a.m. The Muslim brother Mike and his squad ran up in Na and Nathan's apartment looking for Na and Job. They knew Job was getting money for some time now and they heard about Job looking out generously for Na. It was time for Job to give them money for the Muslim school.

Na came to our room and knocked on the door. He had to let Job know immediately about what was going down in the city. Job opened the door naked.

"Yoo, man," said Na.

"Hold up. Let me get a towel," Job said as he walked back into the bathroom. "What's up?"

"I just hung up with Nathan and he said brother Mike and his boys ran up in the apartment and handcuffed and beat him and his girl looking for us," Na said angrily as he thought about his brother being home alone while he was vacationing. And the bad part about it, Nathan wasn't getting his coke from Job but he suffered anyway.

"Get the fuck! The motherfuckas did that bullshit! I gotta handle mine," he said as he hit the wall. He was sick and tired of the threats. The way he hustled hard for his, is the way the next man should've hustled for theirs. He wasn't about to just give up what he risked his life for. He would go all out for his, like a real man. Brother Mike and whoever took from the next man was nothing but pussies to Job. He had no respect for that kind of hustle. But one sin wasn't greater or worst than the next. That's what went with the territory and Job wasn't about to sleep on this one.

"Yeah man. I can't let him go around making these threats. Something has to be done," said Na. Na was young but he was by no means a sucker. He couldn't be soft in this game. Since he made men choices, he had to handle his business like a man but he was really a kid.

"We need to go back home right now," said Job.

I stood in the floor with my heart in my mules. The thought of losing Job killed me. I couldn't imagine a second without him. I knew shit was crazy anytime the Muslims beat my nephew and they were looking for Na and Job. For the life of me, I couldn't understand their reasoning. How could they be against drugs and violence yet they ran around extorting, kidnaping and killing drug dealers? There was no unity in what they were doing. They took the lives of other children's fathers then they went home to their children like it was nothing and what they did was right. They would have to answer to a higher God. We all would have to stand before God and be judge for what we did on earth. *We all have to answer for our wrongdoings.*

Job gave me the cue and I began packing my things immediately with a heavy heart. I just wished everything to be perfect. And it was in my world but it was a world outside of mine that wasn't fair and I had to eat that. I had to accept the fact that other people would stop at nothing to steal others joy.

The flight home was quiet. Job and Na thought deeply about what they had to do. It wasn't much to talk about. They just had to handle theirs and there wasn't anytime to waste. They had to knock brother Mike out of the picture or he was going to keep harassing anybody close to them until Job paid up. Now was the time to set an example.

As soon as we landed home, Job took me to his spot and left with Na. He cared about my tears but if he didn't handle his, I would shed more than a night of tears. I would shed a lifetime of tears and he wasn't about to put me through that misery. He knew it would be too painful and he loved me too much to leave me so soon.

For hours Job and Na drove around looking for brother Mike. They checked all the bars and after hours spots he hung in but they couldn't put their hands on him. Brother Mike was on top of his game. He knew once he beat Nathan, Job would be looking for him so he would lay low until Job cooled down.

Job dropped Na off then he came home pissed. He felt like brother Mike had a jump start on him and he wasn't about to get beat. It was no way we could stay at his spot anymore. Too many people knew about it. A few of his old female friends and a couple niggas that he called associates and enemies.

In the morning I went apartment shopping to find a temporary spot until Job made a major move. We just needed a quick place to chill at that nobody knew about.

After five long hours I found a Condominium in Montgomery County. It wasn't what Job particularly wanted but he trusted my decision. We would move in two weeks.

After picking Luke up from mom's I drove to Job's house and parked in the driveway. I knew how Job felt about me being out late so I watched around me like he instructed me to. Once I thought the time was right, Luke and I jumped out the car and went into the house.

As soon as I tucked Luke in, Job came walking through the door. Shalina worried him all day about brother Mike and he was tired of hearing his name. He just needed a few hours. We cuddled and caressed until we fell asleep.

Around two o'clock in the morning the phone rang out of control. Only a hand full of people had Job's house number and I couldn't imagine any of them calling at that hour unless it was an emergency. After the thirtieth ring I wobbled into Job's office to answer the phone.

"Hello," I said, while catching my breath.

"Sugar and her girls jumped me at the Seafood Bar," said Shalina.

"Get the fuck outta here!" I said lowly. I was so hurt but I couldn't let Job know what was going on because he had enough to worry about and if he knew, he would only have to keep his eye on me because he knew how I felt about my sister.

"I'll be out west tomorrow and we're gonna ride until we find those bitches," I whispered. I was so tired and sick of the jealousy. I couldn't wait until all the chicks got off my back.

"Alright, I'll see you tomorrow," said Shalina.

"Okay." Shalina and I went to sleep with a plan. We weren't going to rest until we beat Sugar and her girl down.

Early the next morning I jumped into my car as soon as Job pulled out the driveway. I had a new burst of energy and somebody had to feel my frustration.

I jumped off 76 east and headed straight to my mom's. The weather was beautiful and my Bose system rocked, *"Summertime"* by Will Smith. I could only admire his many accomplishments. It was so strange to think back to old times when I graduated from High School.

I pulled into the parking space in front of mom's door and beeped the horn twice to let Shalina know I was outside.

"I'm coming," she hollered from the front bedroom window. I was singing so hard that I didn't hear her.

Minutes later she jumped in the front seat prepared to find our enemies. We drove up and down Ludlow Street. Finally Mira came bouncing out her aunt's door with a big grin across her face.

Before I could get Luke's bat from the trunk, Shalina dropped Mira in the street. It was a knockout but I took it to her back with the bat anyway for all the pain her and Sugar caused my family.

Of course, Sugar was never to be found but everybody family members paid somehow and Job found out about what I did. He checked me for acting ghetto with his seed in me but I had to do what I had to.

The next day I pulled up to Job's restaurant to see the finished product. Mark and Shy were just about finish and Job couldn't wait for me to see what they did.

"Get out," Job said from inside the restaurant. I turned the car off and walked inside to find Tank sitting at the first table. My heart dropped because this was our first time seeing each other face to face. Tank glanced at me for a split second then he turned his head the other way. It had been a year but it seemed like yesterday. *Ain't this some shit!*

"Come upstairs baby," said Job. I walked pass Tank and headed up the steps. I was so glad Job called me.

On the second floor I stood in amazement. I watched Job's building go from a shell to a perfectly laid out restaurant. He spent more than 175,000 dollars building the property up and it was worth every dime. I was so happy to have a man with a mind like him. He truly impressed me every day.

Once I got back downstairs Tank was gone. My presence was too overwhelming. It was no doubt he grew to love Job, but he still couldn't stand being around us as a couple.

"I don't believe he did that," Job said once he noticed Tank gone. "He could've said something."

"He told me to tell you he'd get with you later," said Mark.

"Okay cool," said Job then we left.

The next day a Rolls Royce limo pulled around the corner and stopped in front of mom's house. The chauffeur got out and opened the back door.

"Hey baby," Job smiled as he got out the limo dressed in rust and cream linen with gold Cartier glasses on his face. My baby was looking sexy and handsome.

"Hi," I smirked. Na had just left being sneaky. My girl Cookie that I met while attending S High called me earlier out of nowhere and Job never mentioned us doing anything before I left home so I knew I was in for a surprise.

"Let's get something to eat," Job smiled.

"Okay," I said. "But let me get Luke first."

"Go ahead." I got Luke and we jumped into the limo.

The chauffeur pulled into Adam's Mark lot thirty minutes later. I knew the Marker was inside the hotel but Job was acting too strange just to be getting something to eat. He did unusual things but a limo for dinner was a bit much. I knew something was up.

"I thought we were getting something to eat?" I asked.

"We are. I got a room earlier and we can eat here."

"Okay."

Inside the hotel lobby Job hit the elevator's up button. I knew we weren't getting anything to eat at this point so I waited patiently to see what was next. Once we got on the elevator Job hit the button going to the 9th floor.

The elevator doors opened at the 9th floor and Job escorted me down the hallway to suite 992. Either he had a surprise wedding ceremony awaiting me or I was having a surprise baby shower that I told Shalina I didn't want.

Na told everybody Job and I were on our way up so they had the lights dimmed waiting for me to make my entrance. As soon as Job opened the door everybody screamed and hollered, "surprise." I stood flabbergasted. Job and Shalina went all out for me. He spent more than seven thousand dollars on gifts, caterers, decorations, open bar and photographers. The only thing missing was his family. All of my family was there but his family remained absent and I couldn't understand their absence to save my life. This was Job's first child and they couldn't be present.

Once the night ended, I cried to Job about his family and he let me know that he was all I needed and as long as I had him, I had nothing to worry about. If his family couldn't be happy for us then we didn't need them around and with that, I rested peacefully in his arms.

Chapter 5
The Test
"Jealousy and Envy"

I arrived to the quiet hospital in tears. My cervix was dilated about seven centimeters and it was just a matter of time before my baby made its entrance. I was sure of that. I wasn't about to do fifteen hours of labor like I did with Luke.

I was surprised the emergency room wasn't full with people because something was always going on in the city.

Once Shalina helped me into a wheelchair, Job walked through the sliding doors drenched in sweat. You would've thought he ran six miles the way he looked. I was so glad that he made it and I could go on. It was no need to wait any longer. If the doctor didn't get to me quickly enough, Job would deliver our baby. He was ready to do that anyway.

Inside the room I got undressed then I leaped on the bed and waited for the doctor to come in. The pain was kicking my ass and Job felt every bit of it. I held his hand so tight that his blood stopped circulating.

The doctor came in ten minutes later to monitor the baby. I couldn't stand seatbelts on me and this was even worst. I begged for Job's help. I didn't know if I could go natural again. Luke scared me for life and this would be double life this time.

Within minutes I was ready for the world. My baby was to come and nobody could stop him. Not even the doctor. Before Dr. Snow could check me again, I pushed while Job stood over me in shock. He never experienced such joy. He was watching his other half come into this world. He would never be the same. Anything that ever mattered to him couldn't measure up to the life that he was about to see. He would trade his life for this baby's life if he had to.

Job looked down at his fresh white Nike Air Max's with my blood covering them. He actually had my blood on his sneaks. This was crazy. As much as he wanted to trade places with me, he couldn't. All he could do was hold my hand and rub my face. He just wanted his baby to come so the pain could be over. He would take this memory to his grave. I put my life on the line for him and our child and he would love me with an everlasting love for this. He would kill an entire city for his boy and me.

Seconds later a light-skinned seven pounds, 0.2 ounce baby boy swivelled out of my canal looking just like his father. This baby had eyelashes and eyebrows at birth. He was such a beautiful sight to see. His hair laid dark, silky and straight just like Luke's when he was born.

The nurse that assisted the doctor called all the other nurses on shift into the room. They couldn't believe how gorgeous this baby was. They wondered what we were mixed with.

Before I could push the afterbirth out, Job took his baby in the corner and bonded with him immediately. God gave him one of his final wishes. Getting married would complete his life.

Lil Job slept for ten hours. Something wasn't right and I demanded to know what the problem was. I wasn't used to this. When I had Luke, he stayed in the same room with me and my Lil Job wasn't responding. The doctor kept telling me he had a hard time and he was resting but as a mother, I knew something wasn't right.

Finally Job walked me to the Intensive Care Unit. He didn't know how to tell me something was wrong with my child and they didn't know what. I washed my hands like the nurse told me then Job and I sat with our baby. I took notes on everything so nobody would leave with the baby Job would die for.

Doctor Snow walked to the ICU to speak with Job and me. Our baby was in need of a blood transfusion and we had documents to sign. For the life of me I couldn't understand where I went wrong. I didn't want my baby using blood from strangers but his life depended on it.

Job and I talked for twenty minutes then we signed the papers. We wanted to give our blood but it wasn't possible so we did what we thought was right for our son.

I couldn't rest knowing my baby was laying in an incubator. He was so innocent and why did he have to suffer the way he was suffering. I prayed, begged and pleaded with God to bring my baby through. I knew he could make all his blood cells right. I knew he could line things up in the name of Jesus so I stayed close to my baby's side while God did his work.

Slowly but surely Lil Job began to come around. He woke up at the sound of Job's voice within hours. He knew his father. Job visited the ICU more than me because he wanted me to rest before I broke down. He needed both of us and we were going to pull through for him. We didn't travel the long road we traveled for nothing. He wasn't about to lose what he'd die for.

Job's parents stayed in the ICU with their grand baby for hours. It was no way they could deny Job's child. He had the family trademark. He had the same noise as Job's grandfather.

I was healthy, black and my medical wasn't topnotch so it was time for me to leave the hospital while my baby stayed. I played ill. I fell out. I told my doctor I was hemorrhaging but they still discharged my lying behind and I hated them for separating me from my baby.

Job told me to go home and get some rest while he stayed with our son. For the life of me I didn't want to leave but I knew he wouldn't let anything happen to our boy so I fed him, pumped the remaining milk for him, then I left brokenhearted. I felt like the worst mother that walked the earth. God blessed Job with his wish and I messed up somehow. I did something to cause my baby's illness.

In the middle of the night I heard my baby's cry. I jumped to my feet and drove to the hospital. I knew I wasn't supposed to be out of bed but how could I rest with my baby in the ICU.

Once I reached the ICU unit a nurse was cuddling my baby as if he was her own. I instantly felt cheated. I washed my hands and walked in.

"You should be in bed," she said as she looked me up and down.

"I know but I couldn't rest," I smiled. "Where's his father?"

"He stepped out for a minute," she said. Everybody knew how I felt about canned milk and she was feeding my baby formula.

"Why didn't someone call me and tell me my baby ran out of milk?" I said.

"He can have formula. It's nothing wrong with it," she smiled.

"It's my baby and I don't want him drinking formula," I said as I took my baby from her.

Job walked in minutes later and we talked. The doctor told him our baby was well and he could go home in the morning. I was so excited. God answered our prayers.

Job drove around the city giving out cigars to his associates and a few of his old acquaintances too. If anybody ever doubted his love for me, they knew this day. His son was the boss and everybody better respect Lil Job and the mother that beared him.

Two weeks later Job, the kids and I hit the highway to go to mom's house for a visit. We needed some fresh air and Job needed to handle a couple things around mom's area so we tagged along.

Sugar's heart dropped when she noticed Job's Benz turning quietly into the block. Her aunt already told her our baby looked just like his father and he was handsome. She hated our unit because we were happy and she was miserable because her man was still cheating on her.

While Job unstrapped our baby from his car seat, Sugar got closer to catch a glimpse of him. She wanted to see what everybody else was talking about. She wouldn't believe anything until she saw it with her own eyes.

"What's her problem?" I said as I looked across the street.

"Come on Cinnamon, go in the house," said Job. He didn't want any trouble. He had his family and he could care less about what people were saying. He knew who his boy belonged to. He knew Rose put out rumors about his son being Snoop's because she hated me. It was no way his son belonged to another nigga. As little as he was, his dick curved just like his fathers and that was no coincidence. His son had his smallest imperfections and even if he didn't, he knew he was his. It was no mistaking that.

As soon and Job and I went into the house Nancy walked over to Sugar and asked her what the fuck was her problem. She hated Sugar and she wanted to beat her down. They definitely weren't the same age but Nancy was wild and didn't give a fuck about nothing. She had the mentally of a nigga.

Sugar couldn't contain her tongue. She kept going on and on and before Nancy could swing, her sister jumped in the middle.

"Come on Nancy. Forget her," said Neicy.

"Naw. I'm gonna fuck this bitch up," Nancy said as she pushed her sister to the side. I heard the commotion from inside so I ran out the door and Job followed me.

"Come on Nancy why are you arguing with her?" I asked as I pulled her away.

"She a jealous bitch, that's why. I hate her fuckin' ass," Nancy said, frowning.

"Watch your mouth and come up the street. Forget her," I said.

"Go 'head Cinnamon. You think you got something. You ain't got nothing. You need to worry about what your man is doin'," Sugar spat as she twirled her pumpkin head around.

I stepped up to get a little closer. I couldn't believe she went there.

"First of all bitch! I don't need to worry about anything because you're doing it for me. And if you were happy at home, you wouldn't have time to be concerned with someone that isn't yours. You need to get a life," I spat.

"You just started getting shit since you've been with Job," she spat back.

"No bitch! I been had. I just have more now and I'm not talkin' about material things, because you and I both know I always had that. I'm talking about family, dedication and a strong foundation. I have more of that now with my new addition and that's what you hate the most. See you're the one worryin' about his money. I don't have to worry about it, because he's with me and I got him for whom he is. Not for what he's worth," I said, giving it to her like it was. She got hyped knowing I hit her where it hurt the most so she tried to come back.

"You need to be worryin' about that Puerto Rican girl," she said. My heart dropped. I began to think about what Job and I went through early in my pregnancy.

"You know what Sugar. I'm not worried about her either. Just like he's with me, he could have been with her, you and anyone else for that matter and he's not, so what the fuck do I really care. I know who he loves," I said. As much as Job hated to get involved, he did and I knew I should've waited to snap on him but I had to ask, "what is she screaming about a Puerto Rican girl?"

"What!" he snapped.

"You heard me. She said I need to worry about the Puerto Rican girl that you suppose to mess with," I said.

"She knew about her from when I went out with her before we got together. Sugar you need to grow up. Don't you have a man? Why are you so concerned with us? And by the way, tell your uncle to stop duckin' me. I want the money he owes me and I don't give a fuck about him or his family, okay!" he told her. Sugar's face turned flushed. She huffed and puffed as she reached in her car for her club. She didn't know what Nancy and I were about to do at this point and as badly as I wanted to rip her head off, I grabbed Nancy and we walked away. All three of us. We left Sugar with the dumb look as she watched Job and I hold hands. She couldn't begin to understand our unit.

At the end of the week Brent called to get Job out of the house. Gabbie and her girlfriend Denise planned a baby shower for Job and I wasn't invited. The mother of his child wasn't good enough to attend the shower. Besides, Gabbie wanted to gain points with Job by doing this. She hated the fact that her money was cut and she constantly tried to stir up trouble between Job and me but he knew what she and his mother's motives were. They only cared about where his money was going. They didn't want him to be his own man and take care of home. They felt like they deserved it all and I was nothing but another chick. They hated the way Job felt about us. As soon as Lil Job got his social security number, all the properties were to be changed over to his son and me. He was tired of everybody and their greed.

Job and Brent arrived at Job's house around 4:00 p.m. All of Job's family and friends he grew up with, stood around drinking, eating and socializing. Some were really happy for Job. They loved him and they knew what we meant to him so it was genuine but others were there for all the wrong reasons.

Job handed his Godmother her Godchild for the first time. She couldn't believe this boy was the spitting imagine of his father. And the glow on Job's face filled her heart with joy. She hadn't seen Job that happy since he was a kid when she got him his first bike. Something his mother promised him and Job never got.

Job walked through his house like he was the King. Gabbie knew how to break him. She knew what made him tick. He would do something nice for Gabbie since she made him feel special. Everybody in the family was about to get something new. Whatever their request was, they were about to get it fulfilled.

Job and his old head Barry went to Job's office to kick it while everybody passed the baby around. Job always went to Barry for advice and as much as he wanted Barry to be Lil Job's Godfather, he already asked Tank since they had been rollies for the past year.

"It's time for me to get outta Philly. Shit is getting crazy. It's nothing here for me anymore but Cinnamon doesn't want to leave her family," Job said to Barry as he twirled around in his brown leather office chair.

"Damn. I don't know what to say. I know how you feel," Barry said.

"Armeleon wants to sell me his house in Miami and I want it. I want outta here," he seriously said. "And I don't know why she doesn't want to leave. My boy and Cinnamon are all I have. They're my world. I want better for her and the kids. I don't want my kids raised around this bullshit."

"Maybe you should get it anyway. She'll change her mind eventually," Barry said and he was hoping I would because he knew how Job felt. It was a must that we left Philly.

"Yeah. I'm gonna get the crib anyway," Job said after he thought about Barry's words. Job hugged Barry then they went back to where everybody was at.

For hours Job sat around and made everybody laugh. He was definitely the comedian of the family. He told them about my labor and every event with the baby up until the baby shower. I was only a donor just like Job said because he did everything for our boy. He washed, changed and clothed him. The only thing I did was feed our boy.

Early in the morning Job woke the whole house up to go to the restaurant to see the sign hung high before the Grand Opening party in the evening. Job invited everybody in the city and afar to come to Job's Inn to dine and party. There weren't many black owned restaurants in his neighborhood so his had to be a winner. His grandmother and I would be the cooks. After tasting all of my dishes he was impressed. He still planned to get me my own salon but I did wonders in the kitchen. This would be our focus until he moved us out of the city and his young boy would take over and run the restaurant thereafter.

After we watched the sign go up and ate, Job and I took the kids to Nancy so we could get ready for the Grand Opening Party.

By eight o'clock the Ali Baba limos dropped Job and me off at the restaurant in all black, he rocked one of the two piece suits he got from his favorite spot Couco's and I had on a black sheer dress that he got me from the 17th Street Boutique. You know I was doing it with my sexy hairdo that complimented my dress.

Dad stood at the door of the restaurant grinning. He liked Job because he was a black Entrepreneur but he still searched for a loop hole somewhere. Job had to be doing something illegal but I wasn't about to tell him what my man was into. If he found out, he was gonna find out on his own and besides, who was he. He wasn't perfect. He had his share of illegal activities when he was younger too. He didn't sell drugs but he got caught up one time doing checks and his first bad experience was his last and nobody held it over his head so he wasn't about to take me through it about my husband to be.

All of our family and friends watched Job and me throughout the night. We were really in love. The majority of my family hadn't seen me this happy in years. Job definitely was my soul mate. It was no doubt about it.

"Are you ready to be my wife?" Job asked as we stood in the middle of the floor grinding. "No, seriously. I know I asked you this in Aruba but I want us to start planning now. I know you want a fairytale wedding and all so I want to see you happy."

"Yes, baby yes. I am ready to be your wife," I cried as I buried myself into the depths of his chest.

"I can't wait another day. Did you change your mind about relocating?" he said.

"Not yet. Give me some more time please," I said as I put my arms around his neck then the DJ put on "Electric Slide" and everybody joined. Even our Grandmothers and they had it down to a science because the slide was out way before our time.

In the morning Job got out of bed before Luke woke up like usual. His thing was to never let Luke see him laying around doing nothing. He wanted him to know real men got up every morning to bring the bread home. Only a lazy, trifling nigga would sit around waiting for something to come his way.

"I have to go out of town to handle something, but I'll be back by six o'clock okay," Job said, while changing his boy.

"Okay," I said, kissing him on the lips. "I'll be right here."

Job jumped in his Benz proudly. It was nothing like being loved. He knew he had something to come home to and he was straight. Now he had to do what he thought was right as a man. He couldn't allow me to make the choices for our family. He knew the streets better than me and niggas were heated about his status. Many couldn't accept the fact that he had black owned businesses and he took his thing to the entertainment level as well. He and Tank found a couple artists and they stayed in the studio for the past couple of weeks lacing tracks. Things were looking up all around for them and the ones that didn't have what they had, were jealous.

Six o'clock came and Job hadn't come home nor did he call. It wasn't like him to say something and not do it so I got worried but it was early so I couldn't panic. I bathed the boys and we got in bed early to catch a few shows on cable.

Around twelve o'clock I called Job's phone to get no answer so I paced the floors in tears. Something wasn't right and flutters raced through my abdomen. I was sick from crying. I searched high and low for Tank's number. I hated to have to call him now but he would know Job's moves.

Finally I stumbled over a piece of paper with Tank's pager number on it so I paged him and waited for him to call.

Tank rolled over and looked at his pager. He didn't recognize the number so he ignored the page until I paged him three more times. The phone rang and I snatched it from the hook.

"Hello," I said.

"Did somebody page me?" asked Tank.

"Yeah, it's Cinnamon. Have you seen Job?" I asked, hoping for an answer.

"No," he said. My heart dropped to my feet. I knew something wasn't right.

"You haven't seen him all day," I said.

"I talked to him earlier but that was it," he told me.

"Around what time?" I asked, stumbling over my words.

"Around four this afternoon," he said.

"He hasn't come home yet and I'm worried. He said he was gonna be home by six. I called his cell phone and he won't answer. I paged him and he won't call me back. This isn't like him," I said as my throat began to lock.

"I don't know what to say. If I hear anything, I'll call you," he said. To me, Tank didn't want to be bothered or it was me that he wasn't feeling. I didn't know but he didn't sound very concerned. He seemed a bit cold or bitter. Or maybe it was the hour. I couldn't figure it out and all I wanted was Job. "Please," I begged, holding onto the phone tight. I wished he was Job that I was talking to.

Two thirty a.m. the phone rang. I jumped to my feet hoping it was Job and not Tank with bad news, nobody with bad news for that matter.

"Hello."

"Cinnamon, it's me," whispered Job. My heart felt at ease instantly. My baby was okay.

"Baby, I was so worried. Where are you?" I asked quietly. I didn't want to wake the kids.

"I'm locked up over Jersey. Take all this information down, call my mom and tell her and my dad to come get me," he said.

"Okay. What is it?" I asked.

He told me everything I needed to know, then I called his mom.

"Thanks Cinnamon. Me and his father are on our way to get him," she informed me.

"Okay, thank you Mrs. Jackie."

Before I got up to take Luke to school, Job stepped in the door worn out from not getting any rest in the small holding cell. I looked him in the eyes and said, "What happened?"

"I don't know. I was on the turnpike and a State Trooper flashed his lights on me to stop and I pulled over. He checked the car and found eighty thousand dollars in the trunk. Being as though the car is in your name, I told him you were supposed to have deposited the money in the bank earlier from the businesses and you made it to the bank too late and I took the car out of town, forgetting it was in there," he explained.

"What!" I said.

"Yeah and I had two hundred thousand dollars in the back set under that compartment that they didn't find. They only took me in to run my name through because you're not supposed to have more than ten thousand dollars of currency on you. I'm clean so they had to let me go, but I have to go to court about that money. And I know they're gonna dig up something about me by then. Once they talk to these city cops over here, they're gonna stick me," he seriously said. He knew things were catching up to him. It was just a matter of time. He could feel it in his bones.

"I have to take Luke to school. Watch the baby. I'll be right back," I said as I walked out the room.

I returned home to Job and Lil Job cuddled up closely. I hated to break the moment but I had to know what was going on. Job felt my presence and said, "I'm out the game. Things are getting scarce. And I don't know who to trust. I keep thinking somebody told them I was comin' through the turnpike. How did they know to check the trunk? Why did they pick me out of all people?" He said with deep thought. He began to check everybody in his circle. He couldn't trust somebody and to keep things sensible. He would cut everybody off, especially the closest people to him.

"I don't know," I said.

"I'm not dealin' with nobody anymore. We have enough goin' on right now. And all I want to do is focus on my family. I'm not dealing with your nephew. I already told him I was gonna stop a while ago and he doesn't care. He just keeps putting the pressure on. I found out how old he is," he said.

"You mean to tell me you didn't know," I said.

"No. He told me he was eighteen when I met him," he said.

"He did!" I frowned.

"Yeah, and he owes me fifty thousand dollars and I still gave him some stuff. He takes me for granted because he's your nephew and he knows I'm not gonna do anything to him. So I don't want to deal with him anymore. And Tank is the only person that can hurt me," he explained.

"What do you mean?" I asked.

"We have gotten so close over the months that he knows so much about me. And if anyone can tell on me. It's him," he said. And he was serious. As much as he loved Tank, he couldn't risk his freedom for anything or anybody. He had a family to live for.

"Damn," I said as I nodded my head.

"I'm serious baby. I'm not goin' to NY anymore. I just want to live in peace. Right now if anyone calls for me, I'm not here. I don't want to talk to anyone, not even Tank," he said.

"Okay."

I heard what he said and it crushed me because I knew how close Job, Tank and Na had become, but my man had to do what any smart man would do, leave everybody behind.

For weeks Job laid low. He always did Football Sunday's at home but he didn't go out without me. We stayed in the restaurant together until it was time to go home. We were tighter than tight and the streets didn't see Job. When he met his artist in the studio, the kids and I went with him. The only time we separated is when he did a job with Mark and Shy and I wanted to go then because I wanted to learn the construction business too but Job wouldn't allow me to.

Na and Tank took Job's absence hard. They really couldn't understand what was going on. How could Job show Na the game and leave him dead and dry? Na had to eat. He didn't want to go to Tafik or Nathan's old head Saleem for dope. Job was his man but he made Na bitter toward him because he became so dependant upon Job. Now what was he to do? And Tank felt the same. He was bitter with Job because Job had a better hand and he left him hanging. All Tank wanted was what he worked for and they could go their separate ways for good. He was crushed but what was he to do as well?

Job broke everybody off nicely once he thought about what he wanted to do. He had enough to go around and once he did this, nobody could be mad at him. Everybody could go on with their lives and be happy.

Job sent me to my mom's while he went to Miami on legal business, so he told me. He didn't want me to know what he was doing because I told him how I felt already about relocating.

Armeleon picked Job up from the airport around noon, then they went straight to his house on NE 89th Street. Job visited Armeleon's ten bedroom mansion but he never saw the house that he wanted Job to buy. He just heard how beautiful it was.

Once Job stepped inside the five bedroom house, he knew it was for me. It was the house of my dreams. It had everything I wanted and needed. The master bedroom had a fireplace, dressing room and a patio overlooking the ocean. The vaulted ceilings and skylights had a perfect view of the sky. It was like paradise.

Every room in the house was unique. Job just imagined the kids running through the house making noise but the only thing was, he would never hear them because the house was huge. Everybody could have their own set. The house was more than 6,200 sq. ft.

Armeleon took Job to the back of the house to show him the tikki hut, pool and the Chaparral 2550 boat he was giving Job as a house warming gift. It was no way Job could let this opportunity go by.
"I love you man," Job said as he embraced Armeleon. Armeleon was doing what nobody would do for Job.

"I love you too," Armeleon said. "I knocked off an extra two hundred thousand dollars from the house for your son. Congratulations again." Job stood in amazement. He was getting a 900,000 dollar house for 350,000 dollars. And the boat was worth more than 25,000 dollars. Job didn't have to look at illegal substances anymore. He actually reached his quota. Our boys could go to the best private schools. I could be the doctor I always wanted to be without worrying about grants or loans. We could actually live comfortably without worrying about where our next dollar was coming from. Job had five million dollars in cash, cd's, bonds and businesses. He was worth too much to remain in our city. He was just waiting on me to make my move.

The next evening Job called me on the way home from the airport to let me know he was back. Every time he reached the city he got the jitters.

I waited patiently in the living room for Job to beep his horn outside of mom's. The horn beeped finally. I ran outside with the kids and jumped in the car. The ride home was quiet. Job wanted so badly to tell me about the house but he couldn't. It would be my honeymoon surprise.

"In the morning I need you to take five thousand dollars to the wedding planner," Job said while we sat in the parking lot in front of the Condo.

"Okay," I smiled. I was more than anxious about our wedding.

After taking the money to the wedding planner Job and I dropped the kids off at mom's then we headed to the Theater to catch a play. It had been a while since Job and I had been out on the town.

Once the attendant took the Mercedes Job and I walked hand and hand up the steps of the Theater. Of course I had on a skirt suit that he picked out for me from Cachets and he had on a black and white pinstriped suit from Allures.

Job picked the perfect spot for the night because everybody with money and class was at the Theater. And we felt like a million dollar couple with everybody greeting Job. People acted as if they hadn't seen him in years instead of weeks. It was crazy but I was feeling good with my man by my side.

When Job stopped to talk to Neil from 32nd Street, I got annoyed. Neil used to be cool with Dante and he crossed him for a dollar so I knew he was no good. He stayed talking shit about the next man because he really wanted to be that man he was talking about.

I gave Neil the dirty look while he and Job discussed business. I let him know what I was feeling with my eyes. If eyes could kill, he'd be dead.

Once Job and I walked away, people in the hallway talked, including Neil but what did we care. We had what we wanted. I had Job and he had me so we were complete.

On the ride home I told Job how I felt about Neil and what I knew about him personally then I left it alone because I knew some things men had to experience on their own so with that, I had to let Job be his own man but it was my place as his woman to look out.

After we tucked the kids in bed at home, Job and I chilled by the fireplace. He told me all about his new friend Chantel from 22nd Street. I knew nothing about her so I had to trust my man but I didn't like the fact that he was helping her financially with her new business. She was a hustler so she looked out for Job with all the materials he needed for his businesses but my thing was, he didn't need her. He had enough money to buy his things legally and not hot but Job always looked for ways to cut corners and I couldn't get through to him. He felt comfortable with her and it was nothing I could do about their business.

Job sent me out to buy Christmas gifts for everybody. Our unit was so big that he gave me twenty thousand to start with and he gave me another twenty to pay the taxes on all the businesses.

After paying the taxes and shopping, I picked Luke up from school then I headed home safely. All I could hear were Job's very precise words replaying in my head. I was living like a dude. I stayed on top of my game. I watched everything around me so no one could catch me slipping. It was rough and I had to play my part because rumor had it, they wanted my man.

I phoned Job from outside and asked if he could help with the bags.
"Did you get Lil Job's social security number yet?" Job asked as he reached in the back seat to grab his son.
"Yeah why?" I asked.
"I told you I need to switch the properties in y'all names," he said. "I have to get them out of my peoples names." Things couldn't be put off any longer.

"It's at my mom's house," I said.
"Why is it there?" He asked.
"That's the address they had when I was in the hospital so I asked mom to put it up. I didn't need it for anything," I explained.
"Well, get it as soon as possible," he said.
"Okay. I will."

Once everything was out of the car, Job sat me at the dining room table and gave me 75,000 to put in my stash for bills or whatever that I may need while he was out. I still had ten thousand from the other stash he gave me when we first moved together so now I had eighty-five thousand to tuck away for a rainy day.
"Do you know Tafik gave me all this counterfeit money again?" Job said as he got up from the table.
"Are you serious?" I asked.

"Yeah. I let him go the last time, figuring somebody passed it off to him and I passed it off to my people. But this time he gave me too much of it. And I need my money," he said.

"I thought you weren't dealing anymore," I said.

"I know but a couple people needed me and I looked out," he let me know. The game was addictive

"I don't trust him Job," I said. "I told you I never trusted him."

"Don't worry. As soon as he gives me the fifty he owes me, he's cut," he seriously said.

"Can you tell me one thing?" I asked.

"What?"

"Who else do you deal with up that end?"

"Black Mike and Booker," he said. I really didn't like that. Black Mike was a house thief. He was known for robbing hustlers and his peoples never liked my family and Booker was Sugar's old young love and he robbed people too, with my old friend Darren from back in the day. Neither of them was any good for Job but Job was about his business and what could I do. "That's not good. Those dudes ain't right. They just wanna eat. They aren't shit. And I will never trust them. And don't think they care about you either, because they don't," I let him know.

Job knew niggas didn't care about him like that. Some were around only because of what he could do for them. Others were around because they needed his name then you had the ones that cared a little but not enough to ride or die for him. The game had its own strategy.

In the morning Job got dressed to go to court with his dad while I got dressed to go to Nathan's hearing. Nathan just caught a bullshit case and he wanted me to be there for him and how could I say no. As much as Job stressed to me the night before about not wanting me to go, I went against his wishes and made up my mind to be loyal to people that Job didn't believe, deserved my loyalty. He wanted me to cut all the bad seeds off and be wise and not foolish to the things around me. But I looked at it like going to court for his father was no different from me going to court for my peoples. They both made a mistake and we were doing what we thought was right.

Once Job left Nathan called and told me his hearing was postponed and I didn't have to come down so I jumped on the expressway and headed to the consignment shop to drop off all my old leathers, furs and clothes that I didn't want.

Black Mike and two of his associates waited until they thought I was at Luke's school then they walked up the steps of our building and kicked our door in. For weeks the back door to the building wouldn't lock and maintenance didn't bother fixing it. And the security wasn't worth a dime either because they checked all the cars coming through but these niggas came in on foot. Black Mike followed Job for days and he learned everything about our development before he made his move.

Inside our spot Black Mike hit every hiding spot he could think of. As a drug boy himself, he knew the stash spots and he was on point. They cleaned us out. They took everything that was worth something. They took all of our jewelry and furs. They took the .44 magnum from underneath the mattress that Job gave me for protection. They took my Gucci jewelry case that held all the deeds to Job's properties including our birth certificates, social security cards and my stash. They even took the three hundred and fifty thousand dollars that Job stashed the night before without me knowing. They got us really good.

Job returned home while I was on my way to my mom's. As soon as he reached the door he knew we were got but he prayed the kids and I wasn't inside.

He pushed the door back and looked around. The place was like a tornado. Everything was pulled out and flipped over. Job shook his head and called for me. Once he didn't see any signs of me he called my mom's and I wasn't there so he left a message for me to come home immediately. As sharp as he thought he was, somebody got him anyway but it wasn't a big deal. That money could be replaced but we couldn't so he was glad we weren't there.

While Job waited for me to come home, he called a few people to see where they were then he called his sister Gabbie and told her what happened. She immediately told him it was my nephew Na and I had something to do with it but he wasn't willing to accept I had my hand in that. Why would I? He gave me everything. I was straight. I didn't know about the other money he just stashed and he slept with me for over a year. I wasn't that kind of girl. I wasn't cut from that kind of cloth. I loved him and our circle. I had nothing to gain by getting us robbed. It didn't make sense but everybody was a suspect at this point, everybody, including Job's people. He would just sit back and wait to hear something. He wouldn't tell anybody about how much money was involved. Things would surface one day and in the meantime, he'd be on his grind to get that change back. It was nothing but money. It could be gotten again.

For days things were stressful. Sleeping apart from Job killed me internally but I knew it was for the best. He couldn't risk having me at the Condo with him anymore. He and Brent had to be on post but Black Mike wasn't coming back. Other dudes watched Job bounce back and they wanted to rob him but Black Mike was straight. He had enough to buy what he wanted from Job now. He was coping with Job's money and Job didn't know it. He wondered how Black Mike came up all of a sudden but he wasn't sure.

Job made most of his money back within days and he started taking me to the shooting range with him. It was better that way. If I became as good as Job, we could bust a couple niggas asses legally. Me strapped with a ladies Smith&Wesson 38. revolver and him strapped with his Smith&Wesson 9.

The following week I sat in the Condo gathering receipts to send to the insurance company while Job ran around with Chantel. He told her what happened at the spot and he was buying eighty thousand dollar furs from her for his mom and me so she knew what he was worth. Brother Mike was right. Job was worth millions and he wanted him. Job ignored him one too many times and he didn't know Chantel was Brother Mike's baby mama. Brother Mike was pretty smooth. He put Chantel on Job and Job was in the dark about her. He thought she was cool and she liked him but all along, she was setting him up for her man.

Job and I headed to the *Chart House* for a late dinner. We had so much to talk about. Not only did he buy his mother and me the sables, he bought Denise, Gabbie and I sherlings too, in different colors. I was pissed but Denise held his drugs so what could I say. Job looked out for her like that.

"Even though I made my money back, it bothers me not knowing who ran up in our place. So many different things have been said, but nothing is definite," Job said, while looking at the Aquarium.
"I know. We still don't know. We don't know who to point the finger at," I said as I watched him eat.
"We can't trust anybody," he informed me.
"I feel so uncomfortable around people. Even certain family members sometimes," I said, staring at the view outside. Nothing made sense. We couldn't even enjoy our life. We only wanted what every normal, young couple wanted, and that was to be happy and drama free. We didn't want any trouble. We wanted peace and harmony.
"Me, too."
People said things sometimes not knowing whom they were jeopardizing. Na and Nathan talked about Job's business thinking every body was cool and it was okay to brag but that only made a few people in their circle want to kidnap Job. Tafik told people things about Job too. Not many could hold water. People talked just to talk and somebody sucked Job's business up and took it for what it was worth to them. Some things just couldn't be done in the city. Some people couldn't accept the next man having more than them. Everybody wanted out of the ghetto and you couldn't go around shitting on people. Shining and glistening while others were struggling. It simply couldn't be.

In the morning Job ran around meeting people and collecting money. He made sure he saw everybody including Na and Tank. He really missed them too. Before Job parted from Tank he asked him if he wanted to ride with him and Tank said no. Although Job spilled his heart to Tank, he was still kinda bitter about everything. Tank felt like Job left him hanging. He spent restless nights in the studio with their artist while Job sat back and chilled. But Tank didn't know what Job was going through. He was hustling hard to make a come back. He ran like a chicken with his head chopped off for the last couple of weeks. He was physically drained and he had to watch everybody around him. He wasn't living in peace like he wanted to. Everything around him was crazy and he was living painfully deep down inside and no one ever knew his grief.

Job pulled in front of mom's around eight o'clock in the evening. You could see the stress in his eyes. He stood pounding at the door in his black Marcus Bachanan leather jacket with fringes. His dark-blue Versace jeans hung loose because of the couple pounds he lost in the last couple of days.

I opened the door in shock. I couldn't believe Job and his son were dressed alike and we hadn't planned it. Lil Job had on suede moccasins though instead of ostrich cowboy boots because his feet were still too small for hard soles. My boys looked like they were from the wild, wild west. All they needed was a horse and a whip now.

I grabbed Job's hand and pulled him inside. He took his suede cowboy hat off and placed it on the coffee table then he rested his body on the sofa while I ran upstairs to get my camera. I had to capture this moment. I had my Cowboy and Indian. My Lone Ranger and Tonto.

After taking pictures Nancy walked downstairs. I told Job she was home and he knew what was next. She needed to stay with us and he didn't mind as long as she would help me with the kids while I went to college because he paid my tuition earlier in the day. I would start in the Spring.

Job's eyes began to burn so he let me know he had to get home before he couldn't make it and we'd meet in the morning at the Condo.

The kids and I walked him to the car to see him off. On the sidewalk our family huddled in a small circle giving each other hugs and kisses then Job jumped in his car and turned the key while our eyes stayed locked. I wanted so badly to go with him but I knew he would say *no* so I just watched as the Benz hugged the corner quietly and vanished.

Chapter 6
Emotional
"The Setback"

Inside the lot Job noticed my car coming down the hill so he jumped out his car and waited for me to park, before I turned the ignition off Job grabbed his boy and rushed into the building. He was so happy about being with us again with everything being so scarce and crazy. He knew he couldn't trust anyone and we truly loved him as a unit.

After I cooked Job breakfast we wrapped presents and put them under the Christmas tree while Christmas carols pumped through the Onkyo system then Job, the baby and I took a bath.

Once Job and I got out the tub, he gave Nancy the baby to watch while he talked to me in private.

Inside the room Job ripped my nightie off and arched my back against the wall. He hadn't been that aggressive in a while.

"Is everything okay?" I asked as he gave it to me passionately.

"Yes. I just miss you so much. I can't wait for you to be my wife. Another month is too long," he moaned as he knocked things off the dresser to position me right where he needed me to be. I stretched my legs as wide as they could go while he pushed deeply inside of me. I wanted everything I never got before. If our relationship was missing anything, I wanted it all this day. I loved him for life.

I cried as my body trembled rapidly. Job's rhythm was quiet, smooth and gentle. This was the best love session that I ever experienced with him. My breath left my body and I became closer to his soul. I felt his joy, pain and happiness all at once. Job was actually afraid for once in his life. He was scared of losing his family.

After we released three times each, we lay in each other's arms peacefully. We were all we needed to make it through the day.

"I want you to know that I love you more than anything in this world. I love you for giving me our son. I love you for loving me even when I didn't do right and was hard headed. I love you just for being you. You are a good woman and you deserve happiness. You deserve peace more than anything and I want to be your everything," he cried.

"I love you too honey. What's wrong?" I asked him. "What is it?"

"I've been going through it since we've been separated and I feel like somebody's been watching me," he said.

"Oh, my God," I said as I sat up on the bed.

"Don't worry. Everything is gonna be alright. I have to meet with someone at three o'clock about buying a skating rink on Rich Ferry Avenue," he said, while fixing my dark, perfectly arched eyebrows. He couldn't take his eyes off mine. He appreciated everything I stood for. I was a true gem. The mother of his prince and he'd die for me.

"Really."

"Yeah. Then I'm going with Chantel to get Christmas stuff," he said casually.

"Why are you still messing with her?" I asked with paranoia.

"I told you. It's business," he assured me.

"Well, good luck with the skating rink. Let me know how everything went," I said as I admired everything about him.

"You need to pick up the pictures from the studio today," he reminded me.

"I know," I smiled with such joy.

"As soon as you get them call me and we can meet up for dinner," he said.

"Okay."

"The food should be done. Are you ready to eat?" I questioned, while finding something to throw on.

"Yeah. Can you bring it in here?" He asked.

"Okay."

I walked in the living room to find Lil Job asleep in his Graco swing and Nancy and Luke talking on the sofa.

"Do y'all want something to eat?" I asked them with a big grin across my face. I always felt extra special after getting it in good.

"Yeah," both of them said without hesitating once. I made them a plate, then I made Job his plate.

I opened the door to find Job laying in a daze with his hands behind his head moments later. The room was gloomy. The atmosphere was strange. Something just wasn't right and I didn't know what to do.

Nancy came in and handed Job the baby. He gently put his son on his chest and whispered in his ear like he normally did but this time was different. Tears rolled off his cheeks as he embraced him and Lil Job looked into his eyes like he understood him fully and his wish was granted. I instantly felt left out. I wanted to know their secret but Job wouldn't disclose it to me. It was between his boy and him.

After a moment of silence Job dressed Lil Job then him while I put on items Job picked out for me too. He taught me a few dress tricks.

I watched closely as Job brushed the waves down on his head then he turned and kissed the baby and me on the forehead before leaving out the door.

"Do you want a roast beef sandwich to go since you didn't eat your food?" I asked him.

"I'm cool. I'll grab something if I get hungry," he said then he passed Luke and Nancy a twenty-dollar bill and left. I hollered out the window for Job to wait for us. I wanted us to leave from the development together as a family.

We pulled out the black iron gates together. I followed Job down I95 until we got to exit 5 then I watched the Benz closely until I couldn't see the back lights anymore.

While I shopped the stores, Job stopped by his mom's in between making runs to carry the three five gallons of Great Bear spring water into the kitchen, then he stopped by the restaurant to make sure everything was right with his young boy Kev before meeting Neil to collect a hundred thousand dollars from him.

After Job collected his money from Neil he went to his mom's and stashed it in his old room then he set the alarm, locked the rod iron gate and headed to Basil and Denise's to collect a hundred thousand dollars from them together.

Job left Denise with fifty thousand dollars in coke and Basil with a hundred and fifty dollars in product that he had to deliver to people later in the day then he called Black Mike and Booker to let them know he'd see them later on to collect his money.

Job stashed the hundred thousand dollars in the steering column of his Benz and locked it then he jumped in the little car to pick Chantel up.

Once Job called Chantel and told her he was five minutes away, she called Brother Mike to let him know that everything was going as planned and she'd call him back as soon as she and Job finished handling their business.

Job beeped the horn outside of Chantel's house on Berkley Street five minutes after four o'clock. If everything went as planned she wouldn't have to stay in that beat down house anymore. She and Brother Mike could move to the suburbs with their kids and be comfortable for a while.
"What's up?" Chantel smiled as she jumped in the front seat of the car.
"Nothing. Where are we going to first?" Job asked.
"Lets hit Kay B's for the kids first," she said.

Job and Chantel went down every isle in the toy store. They had a cart a piece and they needed a third cart that's how much stuff they got. Down isle seven Job stumbled into Brent.
"Who are you in here with?" asked Brent.
"I'm with her," Job pointed to Chantel.
Brent looked at Chantel and whispered, "What are you doin' with her man? She's bad business."
"We do business together," Job said.
"What! Are you crazy or something? You don't need her. Do you know she just got out of jail? She's a dyke. She's not to be trusted. I know a lot about her. How do you know she's not tryna' set you up or something?" he frowned.

135

"She's cool. I've been around her for a couple of months now and we've been helping each other out. She's about gettin' money," Job smiled.

"Exactly. She's about gettin' money. And she'll do anything to get money. You better watch yourself. Be careful man. I'll talk to you later," Brent said as he turned to walk away.

"Cool, I'll talk to you," Job said. Chantel looked at Job with a strange face and Job repeatedly rehearsed what Brent said in his mind then he thought about what I said about trusting Chantel too but he had things to get so he kept shopping.

At the register Job ran into Brent again.

"I'm telling you. She's not right," Brent said to Job as he walked away from the counter. Chantel turned so she and Brent couldn't make eye contact but she felt him staring. Everybody in line felt him staring at her. Brent knew Chantel didn't mean his little brother any good but Job was his own man. He listened to Brent when he wanted to and that was very seldom. Chantel wrote fake checks for all the items her and Job had then they left to hit a couple other stores.

Once I picked up our family portraits I wanted so badly to call Job because it was around dinner time and he said we could go out to eat but I knew it was the night before Christmas and he had a lot to take care of so I refrained from doing so.

I kept stopping because the portraits were so heavy and I was lightheaded. Something kept pulling at my spirit and I couldn't figure it out. It scared me a little and something kept telling me to call Job but my fingers wouldn't allow me to do so.

I grabbed Lil Job from Nancy and held him near my heart then Luke, Nancy and I looked at each other. We all saw the same thing. It was strange and no one could explain it.

"Why does he look like that?" Nancy asked as she got closer to the portrait.

"Like what?" I said.

"Like his face is blurred," she said.

"I know. His face does look blurred doesn't," I said as I went across the picture lightly with my finger tips to feel the texture.

"I know mommy," Luke said. "Job's face looks funny."

"This is going to look so nice in the restaurant," I said as I changed the subject. This moment was crazy and I couldn't believe we were all on the same page.

"That's where he's hangin' it?" asked Nancy.

"Yeah. That's why he got this one like this," I said.

"He picked out the frame, too," she said.

"Yeah, he matched it up with the fixtures in the restaurant," I said.

136

While we talked Job pulled up to Chantel's salon and parked, then they walked inside so Job could see how far Mark and Shy got on the first floor. Job walked around admiring his workers skills. They could turn a shack into a palace. Chantel's salon would be the best in the area. Nobody from the bottom had a top notch salon with three levels.

Chantel snuck away and called Brother Mike to let him know they were at the salon and Job would be leaving in a few minutes then she walked back to the front to see Job off.

"So, you'll get with me once you drop the stuff off and see your peoples," Chantel smiled.

"Yeah. I have to take my family to dinner," Job said as he walked toward the door.

"Okay. Hit me up when you finish," Chantel said.

"Cool," Job said then he walked outside and jumped in his car. As soon as he turned the corner Brother Mike and three of his brothers followed Job in an old, beat down 1980 Ford Club van.

On 43rd Street Job sat patiently three cars behind waiting for the light to turn green. One arm Josh hollered in the street at Job to distract him for Brother Mike. Job looked to his left and noticed one arm Josh so he cracked his window and said, "What's up bull?"

"Nothing much. I see you still rollin'," one arm Josh smiled. The black Ford Taurus in back of Job went around him and Brother Mike pulled right behind Job and tapped his car with the van.

"What the fuck!" Job said as he looked in his rearview mirror only to see two dudes that he never saw in his life. Brother Mike fired a bullet through the back side window hitting Job in his upper left shoulder. The pain kicked in immediately and Job couldn't move. Brother Mike and the three Muslim brothers jumped out the van and rushed Job's doors to pull him out. Job pulled his 9 millimeter from underneath his seat and put a hole in Brother Shariff's face.

"Motherfucka," cried Shariff as he fell to the ground. "The pussy shot me."

Brother Mike snatched the keys to the car from the ignition then he and the other two Muslims carried Job around the corner while he fought them. Brother Shariff held his face while jumping in the van then he backed up the block so Brother Mike and the other two could throw Job in the van.

Inside the van Brother Mike handcuffed and gagged Job so he wouldn't make a sound, then they headed down 21st Street to torment Job until his peoples came through with the ransom they wanted.

I pulled into mom's block and parked. Ramina's car was on the other side of the street so I knew we had a house full.

Inside the house Ramina and I went over what we got the family for Christmas while I wrapped the remaining gifts I got for Tank and his children.

Mom's heavy security door opened and somebody knocked hard.

"Who could that be?" I said out loud.

"I'll get it," Ramina said as she walked toward the door. She opened the first door slowly and a man with a very deep voice said, "Is Cinnamon Johnson in?"

An uneasy feeling came over me as I wondered who asked for me.

"Yes. Wait one minute. What's your name?" Ramina asked the stranger.

"Detective Blake," he replied.

I jumped up immediately with a pounding heart. I knew it was about Job. I felt it in my bones. This confirmed what my heart felt on the steps in town. I walked to the door slowly and said, "I'm Cinnamon. What can I do for you?"

"You do own a 1988 Chevy Cavalier don't you?" he asked.

"Yes," I said.

"Did you let anyone use your car today?" He asked.

"Yes, my fiancé has it," I said.

"Well, your car was involved in a crime and it's sitting on the strip. I need you to come with me to identify the car," he said.

My body got numb and all circulation stopped.

"No! No! No! What happened?" I cried. "Where is my fiancé?"

"We don't know yet. We're trying to find out. Someone apparently got shot, but we don't have a body. A witness said four guys carried one guy out the car and took him around the corner," he said.

"Who was the guy?" I sobbed. "Was it Job? Was it him?"

"We don't know," he said. I had no one to call on but God. I couldn't lose Job at a time like this. He was my world, my everything. My kids and I needed him. He couldn't leave us just yet. We were getting ready to get married. I couldn't open my mouth to say a word so I motioned to Ramina to keep an eye on the children and I left with Detective Blake.

Detective Blake pulled on 43rd Street and as soon as I spotted my car in the street with yellow tape surrounding it, I jumped out and ran to the car.

"Please don't touch anything. We have to lift fingerprints," Detective Blake warned. I didn't want to hear his mouth. My car was sitting with a window shot out. My doors were open with the keys to the car laying in the street next to the driver's door and drips of blood led around the corner. Somebody was hurt and I needed to know where Job was. Our son was three months old and it was the night before Christmas. Nobody could imagine my void. Nobody.

"Where is he?" I cried. "Where is Job?"

"Where is who?" an officer replied rudely.

"Where is my fiancé?" I asked, looking for an answer. They knew everything else and the police station was only blocks away, so they could tell me something.

"We don't know. We have a shooting, but we don't have a body. Somebody was shot. It's gun casing around, but we don't have a body," the officer said. I hit the hard, cold concrete and cried to the heaven above.

Detective Blake walked over and pulled me from the ground.

"Please get a hold of yourself," he demanded me. "You can't act like this."

"Don't touch me!" I said, pulling away from him. "Don't tell me what to do. He meant nothing to you, but he means everything to me. Forget y'all." I instantly gave up hope in the system. I was all alone. Nobody out there cared about Job, but me. He was my other half and it was just another job to them. He was a young, black nigga with money. With dirty money as far as they were concerned. Anything legal he did, meant nothing. His name held some meaning to some and they wanted to know what he was made of. As far as I was concerned, the system wanted my man dead.

I got up and followed Job's blood around the corner. I had to investigate the situation for myself. I had to do for him, what he would've done for me, but I wasn't he so the job would be hard. I had half the brain and very little connect.

"Where did they take him? His blood stops here," I sobbed, looking down at the broken cement. I walked up the side streets through the lots looking for him. I searched through abandoned cars and houses crying and screaming his name, "Job where are you at baby? I need you." I walked across the lot through the dirt for the third time and Brent jumped out his Wrangler Jeep and grabbed me quickly.

"Cinnamon get yourself together!" he warned, grippin' me up. "You can't be out here actin' like this. We don't want everybody to know what's goin on."

"What do you mean? I need him. They don't know where he is," I explained. He embraced me and walked me back around the corner where the detectives stood on the job like it was a game.

"Sit here," he said, sitting me on cold, cement steps. "I'll be right back."

While he questioned the Detectives and cops on the scene, I thought of things I should've done. I wished I called him when I started to. I even wished I was with him when all this happened. I wanted and needed an answer.

Minutes later Detective Blake walked over and said, "I need you to come with me to the station to answer some questions."

"Okay," I said as my throat balled up in a knot and locked. I really wanted to throw up.

"I'll be down dad's house. Come down when you're finished," Brent smirked as he walked away.

"Alright."

At the station Detective Blake pissed me off asking me a whole lot of ridiculous questions. My man was missing and nobody knew anything. I didn't feel like his shit. I wanted to find Job and go home to our kids. I was beat down internally and nothing could ease my pain. If he couldn't give me Job back, then he was useless.

"When was the last time you saw Mr. Timbers?" the detective questioned, looking over his glasses, sipping his favorite Dunkin' Donuts coffee.

"This afternoon," I answered softly.

"Where at?" he asked as he looked at the typewriter.

"At our spot in the southeast," I said.

"What was he talking about?" he asked.

"Nothing much," I answered.

"Did he talk about meeting anyone?" he asked, now irking me.

"Yeah," I answered slowly.

"Who?" he said.

"A couple of people," I answered as I looked around the room.

"What was he wearing?" he asked, irking me more with his coffee and cigarette breath.

"A green, blue, red and white Polo sweater, with tan corduroys, argyle socks and tan Dockside shoes," I said as I thought back to him dressing earlier in the day.

"Does he have another girlfriend?" he asked. It was his job to question me but he was going too far with his questioning.

"What! I'm the only one he loves," I blurted with confidence, knowing Job only loved me and his boy. Nobody could tell me otherwise.

"Don't get offended. I was just asking. Sometimes guys like him have several girlfriends. And they go away with them not telling the other girlfriend," he smirked.

"Well, he's not one of those guys. And he's not goin' anywhere without telling me. He would never leave me or his son to go with anyone," I said as I turned toward the door. I couldn't wait to leave. My heart was heavy and he was getting the best of me. He didn't care about my man. All he knew is that, he was a drug dealer and the law could do nothing with him thus far.

"Do you think he would go out of town without telling you?" he asked as he sipped the last bit of his coffee.

"No, I doubt that very seriously. You say someone saw four guys take a guy out of my car putting him in a van didn't you?" I asked.

"Yes," he answered, nodding his huge head.

"Well, there's your answer. Somebody obviously abducted him. Don't you think that makes sense?" I asked sarcastically.

"I don't know. Say it wasn't him," he said. He really wasn't as sharp as he thought he was.

"Who else would it be? No body else had my car. And he hasn't called anyone yet. I know it was him as much as I hate to think about it," I said as the tears began to overflow. I couldn't contain my feelings. My man was missing and I knew it was serious. He was worth something nice to whoever had him.

"Could you give me a number to reach you in case I hear anything?" he asked as he pushed his seat forward.

"Sure. And give me your number, too. I'll call you if he calls me or if I hear anything before you," I said as I stood to my feet.

"Okay," he said as he reached for one of his cards.

"By the way. What are you gonna do with the car?" I asked before I reached for the door.

"We have to keep it for investigation and fingerprints. As soon as we're done with it, I'll call you and you can pick it up," he informed me.

"Alright," I said. We switched numbers, then he took me back to my mom's.

At home I didn't know how to tell my kids what happened to their father. I was lost. I just kept beeping and calling Job but he didn't answer my calls. Job would never ignore me so I knew it was bad.

Finally I called his mother and father to see if they heard anything and they didn't so I left mom's with the children to go to their house like they asked me.

I pulled up to Job's mom house minutes later and my eyes landed on his Benz sitting directly across the street from her house. I knew he must have been there last after seeing the car. Tears dropped from my eyes as I parked. The Benz was a constant reminder of him.

I reached in the back seat and unstrapped Lil Job then I knocked on the door in the heart of a lonely, cold winter, the night before Christmas day.

Job's people never experienced anyone being kidnaped before so they looked in all the wrong places. They thought they could hit me with the bullshit about my nephew being with Job and setting him up but I knew better. I slept with Job every night and Job and I both knew Na would never do anything like that to Job. Somebody in his circle maybe, but not Na and if Na knew anything, he would get Job back or die trying.

I called Na immediately and told him what happened to Job and he begged for me to meet him so I did but Brent had to drive me because he thought he had all the brains.

Brent parked around the corner from Na's brother house while I walked to the house to talk to Na. Na ran down the steps as quickly as he could. He was feeling bad about Job. He knew a couple people mentioned robbing Job and he felt kinda responsible.

"What's up?" I asked as I looked straight into his brown eyes. He pulled a leaf from the tree in front of him and said, "I can think of two people that might have Job."

"Who?" I asked, as if there was some hope. I believed in Na.

"Do you remember me tellin' you about the guy Dip in the summer?"

"Yeah, the one that asked you to set Job up for him," I said, reflecting back to the summer months.

"Yeah," he smirked.

"You did tell Job about him didn't you?" I asked.

"Yeah. You remember. Y'all came up together when I told him," he answered.

"Yeah, I remember vaguely," I said as I nodded my head.

"Well, me and him had a fallin' out because I didn't do what he asked me to. And I know he still wanted to get him but he wasn't gonna say nothing to me about it because he knew if he did, we were gonna go through something," he said.

"Yeah. So do you think he might have him?" I asked.

"If he doesn't. I can think of another person that wanted to do somethin' to him," he said.

"Who? Who is it?" I asked desperately. The more info the better for me.

"Neil," he said.

"Neil from north?" I asked out of shock.

"Yeah," he said.

"I told Job not to trust him. Don't he hang around with those Muslim brothers?" I said.

"Which ones?" Na asked. There were a whole lot of Muslims running around lately. Everybody seemed to be some type of Muslim.

"Brother Mike and them," I said.

"I don't know, but he is Muslim," Na said.

"Alright Na. Thanks for everything. I'll talk to you," I cried as I turned to walk away.

"I'm gonna find out what happened aunt Cinnamon. Trust me. Don't worry about it. I'll call you as soon as I hear somethin'," Na assured me.

"Okay," I said as I walked off the steps feeling emptier than I felt before I got there. Nancy and I walked around the corner and jumped back in the Jeep with Brent.

"What did he say?" Brent asked.

"He said he thinks Dip has him or Neil," I answered.

"What Dip? One arm Josh's brother Dip?" he asked.

"No. Somebody he met in jail that he was doin' business with, in the summer. He saw how big Na was gettin' and he asked him to set up his connect," I said.

"Oh really. Does he know how to get in contact with him?" Brent asked as he put his Jeep into first gear.

"I'm sure he does," I said.

"Well, I need you to call him and get his number from him," he said.

"Okay."

"I know he's not talkin' about Neil from north," he said.

"Yeah," I cried.

"Job and Neil were pretty cool." He was a little confused at this point but he should've known better.

"Yeah, he acted like they were cool. But I never trusted Neil. The only reason he was so cool with Job was because of Job's status. He doesn't really care about Job if you ask me. You know how it goes. People are only cool with you because of what you can do for them. If Job didn't have anything, half of these niggas wouldn't even be around him. He had what they needed and they knew he was genuine. He's the realist dude around. It's no other like him," I said as I gave Brent a reality check.

"I'll get in touch with Neil to find out what he knows," said Brent.

I sat up all night soaking the sheets, listening to Job's beeper beep, hoping he would call back until my eyes got tired and my body gave in. Once the sun came up, I knew it was bad. I hated to accept the worse. I refused to accept what I thought could never happen. I looked at the kids while they slept. I had to figure out what to do next. Getting rob and fearing for our lives was one thing, but Job's disappearance was another. How could I go on without him? I pictured Job and me by the fireplace sipping Hershey's cocoa opening Christmas gifts with the children while he sat in agony and pain. He needed us and we needed him. I had to find Job for our kids. I had to. I couldn't let this happen again. I couldn't. I knew of people getting kidnaped and coming home to their families. Job would return to us. He had to.

In the morning the kids and I got dressed in the outfits Job bought us to wear for Christmas then we headed straight to Job's mom house.

As soon as I pulled into Job's mom block my heart sank. The Benz sat in the same spot untouched. I looked around like Job instructed me to then I took the kids out the car and we knocked on his mother's door.

"Did y'all hear anything?" I asked his Grandmom as soon as I walked in.

"No sweetie. Give me the baby," she said while reaching for her grandson. I gave her the baby, then I walked to the kitchen with Job's mom and dad.

"Nothing yet, huh?" I asked them.

"No," said his dad. He was still trying to be strong but he wanted to break down and cry. He actually felt guilty for what was going on. He could only think if he never kidnaped Orlando, Job wouldn't be in the situation he was in. But no one was to blame for this happening.

"How'd you sleep Cinnamon?" asked his mom.

"I didn't," I said.

"I know. I know," she said, shaking her head.

"Can we make a missing report or something? If it was somebody white or a different situation, the media would've been here. But because he's black and they think it's drug related, they aren't interested. They don't know the situation. And regardless of what they think. He's somebody. And he's important, too. He was abducted. That's a crime. Don't they even care?" I cried.

"Let me make a phone call," suggested his mom. She picked up the phone to call the detectives and the media.

After getting disgusted with their response, she hung up. The detectives couldn't do a missing person's report because of his age. And the media needed okay from the detectives to do anything and they weren't cooperating so Mrs. Jackie decided to hire a private investigator to do the job. She said *fuck the law*.

As soon as Brent came in Mrs. Jackie asked him to move the Benz from in front of the door but he didn't have keys so I gave her my keys so they could do it but before they did anything, I wanted to check inside to see if there were any leads to Job's disappearance.

Outside I held my breath before I opened the car door. I felt strange because of the situation but I had to see what I could find. I unlocked the doors then I moved the seat back before getting in. The trophy I had gotten Job for his birthday sat on the console untouched. Job never moved the trophy. From the day I gave it to him, he proudly displayed it and nobody could move it. I opened the glove compartment to find a box containing a three-carat diamond ring. I had a ring so I could only wonder who it was for. I put it in my pocket and closed the compartment back then I decided not to look anymore. It was nothing in there leading up to his disappearance so it was time to lock up and get out.

Inside the house Mrs. Jackie asked me what I found and I showed her the ring. Her eyes lit up and she grabbed it from me.

"Thanks," she said as she put it in her purse.

"Your welcome," I said. She didn't care whose it was. All she knew is that, it was in her son's car and he wasn't around so it belonged to her. She held her hand out for the keys and I gave them to her then I sat down with my kids. Nothing meant more to me than making them happy. It was Christmas and they were restless. They knew we had gifts to be opened at our place and Job still hadn't shown his face. They were confused.

After sitting a little longer I had to come up with a plan of my own because Job's family huddled in a corner inside the kitchen while I remained in the dark about everything. They didn't want me to know anything. They wanted to keep me in bondage about my fiancé. They wanted me bound, gagged and cripple. I couldn't express myself to them. They wanted me to stay off the streets and not look for him when I know he would've died finding me. I had a lot at stake too. My other half was missing.

Minutes later Brent walked in frustrated. He spoke to everybody then he grabbed Lil Job from his seat and sat down beside me.

"Did you talk to your nephew?" he asked.

"No, but I'll talk to him later. Brent, I can't sit up here not knowing anything. I have to find Job. I'm going back up the strip to talk to some people. I know somebody saw something. The detective said people on the block saw what happened," I said.

"Don't go up there. Let me handle everything. Job wouldn't want you out there like that," he insisted.

"No offense to you, but nobody is doin' anything. If it was you or me, Job wouldn't be sitting here. He would be out there looking for us," I said.

"I know, but we have to play it by ear. Don't leave out the house. They might be watching you," he said.

"I really don't care. If they are, they are. And if they want me they are going to get me one way or another just like they got him. I can't believe he let them get him. He always told me to be careful so how could he let them grab him," I said.

"You know Chantel set it up. She had them waiting for him. I told him not to trust her when I saw them together," he said.

"Oh, you did see them together?" I asked surprisingly.

"Yeah, early yesterday. Here take the baby, I need to speak to Jackie for a minute," he said while passing me the baby.

Mrs. Jackie put all her trust in Brent. She let him call all the shots and I now knew what Job was talking about. I got to see things for myself. It was like he was her boy and Job was the stepchild.

After Brent finished talking to Jackie he walked outside and put his Jeep where the Benz was so he could take it to his spot in Delaware.

I threw my coat on and told Ms. Henryetta that I didn't care what anybody had to say, I was going up the strip to find something out about my man.

"Leave the kids here with Jackie. I'll go with you," she said. We left the kids with Ms. Jackie then we jumped in the car and headed up the strip.

As soon as I hit the block I felt everything that happened to Job the night before. I could picture it clearly in my mind. I parked the car and jumped out. Yellow tape still lay in the middle of the street with glass shattered everywhere. The sun was out so I could see everything clearly, even Job's dried blood in the street. I put my finger in the blood then I walked around the corner to where the trial ended. My inner being let me know Job wasn't dead. I felt him speaking to me.

Ms. Henryetta and I walked the dusty, dirty lots searching for clues. I looked in abandoned cars and trucks for Job but he was laying in a vacant basement down 21st Street, hurt, gagged and handcuffed to an old beat down wood chair that had years of mildew built up on it. He hadn't eaten, drank or moved since the night before and he was weak from losing so much blood. His gunshot wound and the hole in his head from Brother Mike dragging him down the basement steps kept gushing out blood so he was dying internally. If somebody didn't come to his rescue really soon, he was going to go into shock.

"Ms. Henryetta stay right here while I go in. I don't want you going in here with me. It's too much debris and junk in there. And I'm sure it's mice and rodents running around. I'll go in by myself. Just watch around you," I said to Ms. Henryetta after I found an open window on the abandoned school.

"Shit girl! You gotta be crazy. Why you wanna look around in there? It might be crack heads in there," she said, turning her nose up. Even though she feared the worst, she was still comical.

"Say he's in there bleeding. They took him somewhere. I need to find him. I keep picturing him somewhere bleeding, begging for somebody to run across him. I'll be right back," I said as I climbed through the window.

While I searched the nasty, filthy, vacant school that was closed off for years, Brent pulled Job's car up to his fabulous stucco and brick, single home away from the ghetto. He parked the car beside his van, then he searched through it to find the hundred thousand dollars that Job had collected from Basil and Denise. Brent gathered the money together and locked the doors, then he took the money in his house and he stashed it away. He wasn't going to mention it to anyone. Not even his girlfriend. A rat ran across my foot and I knew it was time to go. I ran back to the window in tears and jumped through like I was Wonderwoman.

"What's wrong with you girl?" asked Ms. Henryetta as she puffed on her Salem's light.

"He wasn't in there. I rat chased me outta there. Let's go. I have to find him," I cried. "I can't give up. I can't."

"I know. I know," she said.

We walked back to the strip where a couple of dudes stood on the corner talking. I got my heart together and approached them hoping they knew something.

"Do y'all live around here?" I asked them. They looked at me like I was trippin'.

"I'm just asking because my fiancé was shot out here last night and they can't find him," I explained.

"I don't live around here, but check that house right there," one guy said, pointing to a beat down, raggedy house on the corner.

"Thanks," I smiled as I walked away. We walked up the steps and I knocked on the door of the house. An older man opened the door with liquor on his breath from the night before. "Yeah," he mumbled with his rough edged voice.

"I'm sorry to bother you, but my fiancé was shot out here last night and I wanted to know if you saw anything," I said.

"No, but my girlfriend did," he said.

"Is she home?" I asked.

"No, but she'll be right back," he smiled. Seconds later a thin older lady walked up staggering, with a forty bottle in her hand.

"Baby, this girl wants to know what you saw last night. That was her fiancé that was shot," he said.

"Hi. My name is Cinnamon. Did you see what happened last night?" I asked her.

"No," she said.

"Please Miss, I know people don't like getting involved with other people's business, but I don't know where he is. He got shot out here and they say he was taken away by four men. We have a new baby and I need him. If you help me, I'll give you a reward," I said.

"I saw some guys carry a thin guy away and they put him in a brown van around the corner," she said as she pushed by me.

"Do you know what the guy had on, that they carried away?" I asked.

"I'm not sure. It was dark," she said, walking in the house. She really didn't want to get involved but I needed her.

"Thanks so much. Can I have your number so I can call you? I would like to give you something for talkin' to me," I said. She walked faster and her old man handed me his phone number.

"Thanks so much," I said as I grabbed the paper. This paper would give me some hope eventually, I thought. Maybe she would change her heart and give me what she knew someday.

For days things were mad crazy. Everybody was out for self while Job was being tormented. He wasn't breaking for brother Mike. His threats meant very little. Brother Mike wanted to know where all his money was and when Job didn't tell him, he threatened to kill our son and me but Job knew he didn't mean it. Brother Mike had what he wanted. What did he need with us, too? Job was their key. He was there come up. They already got twenty-five thousand dollars out of his pockets when they abducted him from his car and they wanted a million-dollars ransom. Who could be a better target than him right about now? If they did come for his son and me, who would give the money up for us. Job wasn't going out like a sucker. He was gonna fight until he died on them.

I gave up everything I had of Job's. I couldn't stand his family pressuring me. Job's material possessions meant very little to me. I wanted him and nothing else. I had something of his that no one but God could take from me so they could have all those worldly things.

Mrs. Jackie took Rose with her to Job's spot because she knew some of his stash spots from messing with him and she came up. She took Job's diamond necklace, the ring he never wore and twenty thousand dollars from his freezer. Mrs. Jackie found that money in her house in his old room and Brent and Gabbie got most of Job's money from Basil and they warned him not to give me the rest he was waiting for but Basil came up something nice too. He didn't tell them the truth about how much he had. *That's slime for you.* Nobody cared about Job's wishes for us. All they cared about was what they could get.

I prayed and fasted nights and days for my family because I felt so responsible for Job's disappearance and nobody could help me but God. I had Job's blood all over my hands. He wanted out of Philly and I kept him where he didn't want to be. I had the ball in my court and I did nothing with it. Job would've done anything for me. I made the wrong moves and when I figured it out, it was too late. I was so foolish.

Once my flesh was broken down, I saw things in a different light. I saw things Job's family couldn't see. We couldn't control what was going on. It was better that we stayed on one accord but everybody wanted to do things their way and it wasn't working because they were moving out on the flesh and not the spirit and they didn't have a clue anyway. They kept looking in all the wrong places. Job's family constantly pressured my nephew and me for answers so Na got on his job harder and played the streets.

Na finally caught up to his old associate Dip. Na knew he couldn't trust Dip after talking to him so he gave his number to Brent and Brent messed everything up. Brent told Dip everything Na said word for word so this made Dip want to kill Na and Brent. He didn't care that they only wanted to find Job and they would give up anything for him, he felt betrayed so it was time to do both of them.

Dip agreed to meet Brent but he gave Brent the opposite description of him and then he had the balls to tell Na he was about to kill Brent. Na called and told me so I got on the phone and warned Brent like Na asked me to do.

Brent returned to Mrs. Jackie's house very appreciative for what Na did. He knew he wasn't right about pressuring us and Na saved his ass so Brent came up with another plan. Dip was off limits now. It was time to step to Neil and one arm Josh. The Spectrum was having a show at the end of the week so Brent and Rose were going since she was cool with Neil and Josh too.

After Rose came to Mrs. Jackie's house like she was important and in charge, I got pissed and left. She said she already talked to one arm Josh about Job but I had to talk to him for myself because something wasn't right.

I pulled my car up to the only black and white brick house on the block of 43rd Street. I got out and rang the door bell. An older, dark-skinned lady with silver and black hair opened the door and welcomed me in.
"Hi. My name is Cinnamon. My fiancé was abducted out here a couple nights ago and I'm curious if you saw or know anything, being as though it happened right across the street from you," I smiled.

"I heard the shots, but when I got to the door somebody said four guys already took the one guy out the car and carried him around the corner," said the older lady.

"So you never saw anyone?" I asked.

"No."

Josh walked down the steps quietly. He heard me talking from upstairs and he had to hear what I knew.

"Hey Cinnamon," he said.

"Hey Josh. What's up? Long time no see," I said.

"Yeah, tell me about it. I just been chillin'. These are my peoples," he said, hugging a lady in her twenties, holding a baby.

"Oh, yeah. Is that your baby?" I asked.

"Yeah."

"Nice to meet you. My name is Cinnamon," I said as I extended my hand.

"Hi, I'm Judy," she smiled while extending her hand.

"I know you heard about what happened out here the other night," I said to Josh.

"Yeah, I was here," he said as he thought deeply.

"Did you see anybody grab Job?" I asked.

"No. I saw him before it happened, but I came in the house. By the time I got back outside they already took him," he said.

"For real."

"You know how that goes Cinnamon," he said coldly.

"What do you mean?" I said.

"You know the streets. They took him for ransom. Nobody called you yet?" He said.

"No."

"Not his peoples either?" He said.

"No."

"They'll probably call you soon. They just want some money. You know what's been goin' on in the city. They been grippin' niggas up to get money. And Job was my man. He had change and they want that money. They been wanting him for a long time. You know what he's worth," he said.

"Who? Whose been wanting him?" I asked.

"People, nobody in particular, just people. They know what he was workin' wit," he said.

"I see. Well, here is my number," I said, handing him a piece of paper that I ripped off an envelope from inside my purse. "Call me if you hear anything, please Josh."

"I will. Ay, be strong. I know it's hard for you, but hold your head up. You been through so much. You already lost Luke so I know this is hard for you," he said.

"Yeah. It's really hard. I'm trying to maintain, but it's rough," I smiled.

"You can do it. You always was a survivor. You always stayed on top," he said as he thought about my history.

"Yeah, I guess so, but it's hard. I just want him back. Whatever it takes to get him back, I'll do. If you find out anything let the people know we have the money to give them. Whatever they want, they can get it," I assured him.

"Alright. I'll look out."

"Thanks. It was nice meeting everybody. Thank you all so much." I spoke, facing the door.

"Nice meeting you, too. I hope you find him," said the older lady, walking me out.

"Thank you Miss," I cried. "Thank you."

I couldn't get out the door before the tears fell all over the place. I got in my car confused. I didn't know whose side he was on but it didn't add up.

Once I got back to Mrs. Jackie's house Tank and Claude was there and leaving because they couldn't take Mrs. Jackie's sarcasm. She wanted everybody dead. She couldn't stand Tank, me or a couple other people. She blamed everybody for what her family was going through. She didn't care about anything at this point. She just wanted it to be over with so everybody could leave her alone and get out of her house.

I felt the vibe so I got my kids and belongings and left. I had a little peace at home with my family. I really wanted to be in my own place but mom's was cool for now because I couldn't stand being alone.

Brother Mike had someone following me and I felt it but God wasn't going to allow anyone to take me just yet. He had work for me to do and this wasn't about me. Through all this, He wanted to draw everybody closer to Him. Through all this, souls were to be saved. It was a painful experience but it was nothing God couldn't fix.

Before the show Brent asked me to bring my nephew by because his dad and he came up with something else but I wasn't getting involved anymore. I thought about it and they were tripping. Instead of bothering my young nephew, they should've been putting their faces on and stepping to some grown ass men about their boy. Mr. Bill played gangsta' any other time so now was the time to be gangsta' for real. And Brent knew he wasn't gangsta' so why was he playing like it, nobody knew. Job saved his ass many days.

Rose and Brent kicked it with one arm Josh and Neil at the show, at different times. Everybody was out politicking. Neil told Brent he met up with Job the day he was kidnaped and he gave him a hundred thousand dollars but that was nothing; Brent found that money.

Brent and Rose continued to showcase at the show looking for anyone with info about Job while niggas and girls we all knew from the city stood back with gossip. People knew Rose used to mess with Job and they knew he had me, so they wondered if she was messing with Brent now, and if she wasn't, why was she with him and not me.

A few people let Brent know that they were there for him and Job and some acted like they were glad he was missing. However, Brent had a plan and he knew how the game went. He just wasn't as sharp as Job, in or out the street.

Brent walked the hallway a few times by himself to come up with no clues about his little brother so he located Rose and dropped her off at her house, then he went to his comfort zone, his place of rest, his castle away from the niggas and the city feeling like a loser. He felt like he let his little brother down once again.

At home I tried to come up with something to tell Luke because he kept throwing questions at me but it was no easy way out. I had to tell him the truth and it hurt. He didn't deserve all this pain at six but it was nothing I could do. I could just pray and be the best I could be. I had no other alternatives. I wanted out but I had to be strong the way I knew Job would've wanted me to be.

As soon as I prayed and closed my eyes to find peace, Na pulled up to mom's door and parked. He needed to talk to me. He felt so bad about what I was going through and he wanted to assure me he would find Job. He already made up his mind to go down Dip's set to get inside the scene.

Na stood over my body and whispered but I didn't move. I wanted Job and no one else so I played sleep.

"Big Cinnamon wake up. Wake up," he said quietly, nudging me in the side. He gave me the addition to my name while I was pregnant and he never stopped calling me Big Cinnamon. It wasn't like I didn't love my nephew, I was just drained with everything around me. I had people pulling at my spirit. If I didn't stay at Job's house for one night Gabbie would bring it to me but Mrs. Jackie didn't really want me there so I was stuck between a rock and a hard place. I didn't know what to do and I wanted all this misery to end.

Na finally left and I felt bad so I jumped to my feet to call him back but he couldn't hear me from the window so he pulled off. I fell on the bed and embraced the pillow. I was living a nightmare and it wouldn't fade. Reality couldn't go away.

Love

Love is so beautiful and so true,
especially if you're sharing it with someone that loves,
just like you.
Always there to embrace you, never letting you go,
sharing every moment, as if it's no tomorrow.
Always lifting you up, when you're feeling down,

ever so powerful and strong that nothing can go wrong,
So tight that nothing can break it,
never phony and nothing can erase it.
As bright as the morning stars, love will forever shine,
in your heart and in your mind,
oh, how lovely it is to find.
Love is healthy, it can also hurt
so be willing to let some things go if it doesn't flow
because what you don't have today, you might just get tomorrow.

While I lay in bed tossing and turning Dip picked Na up from his brother Tyree's house and drove him down his way. Normally Tyree's brother and their boy Omar would go with Na but they didn't this night. They let Na ride alone knowing they didn't trust Dip just as much as Dip didn't trust them.

A half and hour later, Na called Tyree and whispered, "If anything happens to me, I'm at a phone booth between 2nd and 3rd Avenue."
"What do you mean if anything happens to you?" asked Tyree.
"Something isn't right. I don't feel right," answered Na as he watched the leaves blow up and down the street.
"Where is Dip and his boy?" asked Tyree.
"They're in a house across the street," said Na as he watched the house from across the street too.
While Na talked on the phone with Tyree, Dip told his Asian boy whose house they were at that he was getting ready to rock Na for snitchin' on him. Na hung up the phone to call his girlfriend fast. Something wasn't right and he had to let her know what he felt, too. He loved her and he tried so hard to get her pregnant for the past month. For some reason he wanted a son just like Job. He was young, but he wanted to be like Job in so many ways. He wanted a boy to leave his mark behind too.
Na told his girlfriend Treasure the same thing he told Tyree, only he told her he loved her and he always would. She questioned what he said at first, then she assured him that she loved him, too.
Before Dip crossed the street Na hung up, but it was too late, Dip already saw him on the phone and it made him madder. He knew Na was crossing him again and it was time to do what he had to do.
"Who was that?" Dip asked angrily.
"My girl," said Na.
"Your girl, huh! Lets take a walk," he rudely said. He hated what Na stood for and if he could've, he would've done him right there on the block.   In front of whomever.
As they walked, Dip's boy stuck his gun in Na's back.

"Keep moving," Joey insisted. They walked Na to a vacant lot behind the River Train apartments on 2nd Avenue then they tussled, threw him down, stripped him and took his Desert Eagle from his waist.

"Oh, you were gonna shoot me?" asked Dip as he held the gun up.

"Naw. I just had it on me to protect myself," said Na.

"Get on your knees," Dip demanded. "Right now."

Na's life flashed before him. Everything my mother taught him about God came to mind and he prayed endlessly to live but God let him know it was time to part from here. The earth was full of hurt and pain and with God, it would be no more. The people Na walked with weren't his friends. They were his enemies and Na was another statistic. The devil cared nothing about him but God did.

Tears fell from Na's eyes. He wondered how his life ended up this way, knowing he was supposed to grow up to be an astronaut or a missionary for God. He thought of the good and bad times with his brothers and sisters. He thought of his mother that he loved dearly. He thought of his father although he wronged him. He thought of his family and friends and how much he was going to miss them. He thought of Job. He knew he was about to part not knowing if Job was alive or dead, like he was getting ready to be. He felt betrayed by the dudes he once walked with, stole with, did business with. He knew he wasn't perfect, but he knew he would've never killed his so-called friend. He was so hurt. He only wished it didn't have to be, but it was.

As Na kneeled, shivering in the 25-degree weather, Dip squeezed the trigger, firing one shot from his own gun into his left hand that he held up to block his face from what he saw coming. As his hand bled, more tears rolled down his face in disbelief. This was his last breath.

Dip fired another shot into Na's right hand then Dip and Joey fired ten shots into Na's head, leaving him in a fetal position. Leaving him the way, he was in his mother's womb. Leaving him cold and lifeless, then his spirit ascended into the arms of the Holy One. Dip and Joey shot Na up with dope so it would look like he was high and somebody robbed and killed him. *What you'd do to your brethren. Another soldier murdered.*

I got up to baggy swollen eyes and a queasy nervous stomach to face another hard day without Job, early in the morning. I could do nothing but get on my knees and pray for my family. I needed an answer. If Job was dead, I had to find his body so I could have closure. If he was alive, I needed him back even if he had any deformities. Nothing could stop the love between us. Nothing.

Inside the homicide unit everything hit the fan. The detectives turned everybody against each other and my family played right into their hands. They told them everything about Job and me. They told them exact figures we were rob for and how much money Job was willing to give me for our son which didn't make sense to me. Our business wasn't theirs. They didn't care about anyone. It was just a job to them.

My sister Ramina left the homicide unit wanting to kill me. She thought I picked Na up and took him to Brent and he killed him but when you're weak, people can pump anything into your head. That's why it's good to have a strong mind of your own and keep yourself surrounded by positive things, this way no one can be ruler over your universe but you.

Mom got home with a weary heart. Her family was falling apart. She loved all her children but one wanted to kill the other so she begged me to stay away until things got better but how could I stay away and I needed them too. Na was my heart. We had a strong history together. We came up like brother and sister instead of aunt and nephew.

After the detectives questioned me I went back to Mrs. Jackie's house hating them because they didn't care about my family either. Everybody was caught up and I was getting blamed on both ends. The dumb detective even wondered if Job's disappearance was a prank and he had Na killed over money he may have owed him or because he robbed us and Job and I both knew that was a lie. I knew Na didn't rob us and Job was really abducted because he would've never hurt our son and me that way.

Once my brother Micah flew in days later to talk to Ramina, she had a change of heart. She didn't want to kill me anymore but she still blamed me for everything but at least I could be around the rest of my family.

Mrs. Jackie wanted to go to our spot to get all Job's things so I went too because I had to get some clothes for the kids and me.

Once we arrived to the Condo I had a change of mind about going in. It was too much for me to consume so I asked Mr. Bill to grab me a few things while I waited in Job's company van.

Mrs. Jackie stepped inside our spot and stopped at the entrance. She knew Job and I had taste but she didn't imagine our spot to look like it did. "I can't believe he had her living like this," Mrs. Jackie turned and said to Mr. Bill with disgust written all over her narrow face.

"Come on. Let's just get the clothes and leave," he said, cutting her off. He was so tired of hearing about material things. He just wanted his boy back. He was there to take care of his boy's business.

"Do you see this shit?" she said as she looked around at the gray leather living room set that sat directly in front of the gray marble fireplace with sterling silver pieces complimenting it. She looked at the white Christmas tree and shook her head.

"I don't believe this shit," she said as she wiped dust from the chrome lamps then she proceeded down the hallway to see the rest of the place.

Inside the room she gasped for air when she noticed the cherry wood bedroom set and the 36-inch Sony television that rested on rose colored carpet.

"What the hell was she thinking of to have light pink carpet with kids," she mumbled while Mr. Bill gathered Job's clothes from the walk in closet.

On the wall was a 16x20 family portrait taken by Clair Pruett. "She won't be living lavishly now," she said as she walked into the master bathroom. Job's scent still lingered in the air. She couldn't take it so she shut the door and walked into Luke's room to see how he was living.

"Oh, he was living better than me too, huh!" she smirked.

"Are you ready?" hollered Mr. Bill. He was finished already and she was still looking around.

"Here I come," she said as she looked around for the last time. She was sure to be back for the things she wanted. I wasn't about to be with another nigga with her son's shit.

The ride back into the city was quiet. Mrs. Jackie wanted to say something to me so badly but she had to wait for the right time.

Before we reached her house she broke the silence and said, "you had a nice place."

"Thanks," I said.

"Well, you can't live like that anymore. You need to think about living conservative now," she coldly said. It was no more lavish living in her eyes. My mouth hit the floor of the van. I couldn't believe she was so blatant.

"You were livin' like a queen with that expensive living room and bedroom set. I know that cost Job a fortune, not to mention the crystal pieces in the breakfront and on the tables. And that dining room set, is beautiful. Job told me he bought that piece of art from the art gallery for twenty thousand dollars. Mr. Bill and I will be back to get it. Job said you had rich taste. You and him like expensive things I see," she said.

"I see where she's going with this but she better get out my face with the bullshit. I had shit before I met Job. Yeah, he took care of home, but I had a lot before him. Some pieces, I got on my own," I sat thinking to myself.

"That's a shame. Maybe if Job treated me better, this wouldn't be happening. He had you livin' like a queen while I'm livin' the way I'm living," she said. I couldn't believe the words that came from her mouth after all Job did for her. He just bought her a sable mink for Christmas. She had a restaurant in her name. A paid for house and car. And she had a big bank account. What more could she ask for? She was really being selfish and he didn't think she deserved all he gave her because of her attitude. I just wished Job could see what was going on but he already knew. He told me how they were before this happened.

The next day I rented an Uhaul truck. Cousin Justin and Micah went back to the Condo with me to get the rest of my things. I wasn't prepared for what I was about to experience but I had to do it or it would never be done.

As soon as I opened the door, a ray of light outlined the entire place. Justin and Micah thought I was crazy. They felt differently but they couldn't even imagine what God was doing in me. He was strengthening me inside out. He was doing a new work in me while he was working in Job too. Nobody could heal our broken hearts and souls and deliver us but Him. I fell to the floor and cried.

"Daughter I love you. You are special in my sight and I will never leave you nor forsake you. I will walk with you till the end. I will be your guide, your protection, your strength. No one or nothing can stop me from loving you. I know this may be hard, but you can make it. Through me you will survive. If no one loves you, I do. If no one has faith and trust in you, I do. I know your heart like no other. And you are caring, loving and special. And no, he is not dead," said God.

Micah and Justin ran over to me and asked at the same time, "Are you okay?" I scared the life out of them. They never saw me like that.

"I'm fine. God is good. Job isn't dead. I knew he wasn't dead. He's alive somewhere. I feel the spirit of God. Can y'all feel him?" I smiled with joy. They looked at me like I spoke an unknown tongue.

I sat on the carpet Indian style and opened the boxes with the Coogi sweaters and Polo corduroys that I had gotten Job. I couldn't wait to see him in them but I didn't know if he was ever going to get his gifts. I looked at the fifty boxes or more and my heart sank into the carpet. Christmas would never be Christmas for our family anymore. No more pillow fights with Na, Luke and Job, no more late nights playing Nintendo eating fried shrimp or watching *Ninja Turtles,* Luke's favorite. I had so many good and bad memories.

I got up and looked in the bathroom that held the last wash cloth Job used. I looked at the baby's tub and remembered Job giving the baby his baths and how he used to steam the bathroom up to make it warm before he brought the baby in to wash him. And how he had me video taping everything, capturing all the special moments in our household.

I took Job's undershirt out the dirty clothes to smell his scent. I needed to smell him. I clinched his undershirt so tight in my hands and held it closely to my nostrils. I had to breathe him one last time.

I walked into our room with his undershirt in my hand. I looked at his cologne that sat perfectly on the dresser along with the baby's things. I sprayed his cologne on my body then I fell to the bed and remembered our last love session and how beautiful it was. I now knew why it was so different the last time. God knew we weren't going to see each other again. Job knew it. He sensed it. Everything started to make sense to me now. Job and I were connected at the heart, soul and mind. We cried internally for each other. He felt what I was feeling while he laid in that basement. He wished he could hold his son one last time but he felt his little presence, his love and spirit. He knew he had a gem. He knew he had a winner. He knew the name he gave him was for a reason. He was the boss and would grow to be a *strong leader*.

"Cinnamon we got most of the stuff out. Are you taking this bedroom set?" Micah asked, waking me out of my trance.

"I don't think you should," said Justin. "It's too much for you to deal with. It's gonna bring back too many memories."

"Yeah, but I'm gonna take it," I said.

The next day I went to the funeral parlor with mom and Shalina. I had to see Na before the funeral and it was heartbreaking. I never experienced seeing anyone I loved opened up and disfigured. I went to funerals after bodies were made up but seeing Na that way killed me. It was so much to consume but I loved him even more. I felt like he was my life and he gave it up for Job and me although God had it all under control and no one was to blame. I just wanted God to punish Dip for what he did to my baby.

While our family sat around making final arrangements for Na's home going service, Mrs. Jackie and Mr. Bill went to the Condo and took televisions, my stereo, my VCR, the painting she wanted and souvenirs we got from Aruba while Na's father did the same. He cleaned Na's apartment out.

I sat directly in front of Na's casket weeping and daydreaming while the pastor preached and people stared at me. They wondered when I was going to crack and break. I sat at my nephew's funeral and my fiancé was missing. They couldn't understand it but I had to hold it together for my children no matter what I was feeling inside. I couldn't make a scene in front of people that didn't understand me and talked wrongly about me. I had to hold it down.

I heard Arabic prayer in the background. I wondered who it was coming from. I looked and looked then I heard mom rebuking Nahum. She was vexed. This was her grandchild's day. God's day. Nahum wasn't going to have his way, this day, uh, un, not this day.

"The devil is a liar. My grandson wasn't Muslim. He was saved by the blood of Jesus. I rebuke you devil," she said boldly. Na's dad couldn't believe his ears. He and the other Muslims tripped, but mom didn't care. That was her grandson. Latina took the microphone and began preaching while mom prayed. Treasure got up and pulled at Na.

"Please Na! I need you," she cried as she fell to her knees, knocking the flowers and plants over. "Please! I need you!"

Ramina sat in her seat in a daze. Her body was there, but her mind wasn't. I felt her grief but I didn't know how to comfort her. I loved her and wished her pain away but there was little I could do.

At the burial site Tyree and Omar walked up to me telling me what happened the night Na went with Dip and how they thought Dip had Job. I listened but I knew they couldn't be trusted either.

Tyree and Omar walked off quickly to get away from me. Their guilt was eating them alive because they knew they planned to rob us too but somebody got us before they could so they didn't feel comfortable in my presence. How could they look me in the eyes knowing all they had done and I was only good to them? How could they? After everyone walked away, I read Na a poem in silence. It was just he, God and I.

NEPHEW

My nephew, my boy, I watched you grow up from riding bikes
and playing with toys,
to telling me about your future and what you had in store.
A mothers' love is ever so great but me being your aunt,
loving you from your head down to your baby toe,
watching you grow,
not being there for you when you were murdered,
hurt me even so.
I know my pain can't compare to your moms,
but a piece of me is gone and I can't get it back, in fact,
I often question why mankind had to hurt us like that.
One thing for sure that they might not have known,
is that your spirit is resting and that's the greatest blessing,
that neither them, you nor me
could ever have done for us human beings can't you see.
So something greater has come of your death,
and no matter how hard it is to deal with,
our love has been put to the test
and we have the Lords spirit that has done more than manifest.
So I thank God on this very day,
remembering you always and never forgetting to pray
because for sure He is the only way.
And in my heart nephew, forever will you stay.
ONE LOVE!

Chapter 7
The Answer
"Job Is Found"

Three weeks later fliers with Job's picture and information on it blew all over the streets in the big *City of Brotherly Love*. In some of the most popular stores and posted on electric poles and trees were more fliers with Job's picture on it, offering a hundred thousand dollar reward for information leading to his abduction. The law wasn't doing their job and the private investigator was doing everything possible to find him but no one would come forth.

One girl named Jessica that lived across the street from the house where Job was knew everything but she was too scared to say anything because she knew how treacherous brother Mike and his crew were. Although she kept picturing my face crying, she couldn't mumble a word because she had a family to raise too and she couldn't get involved. She knew the law wasn't going to protect her. She threw the Neighborhood Weekly in the trash. She looked at the house across the street again, then she walked up her steps and shut the door behind her.

While I prayed to God to put an end to my misery brother Mike phoned Mrs. Jackie to tell her, it was time to meet. He wanted one million dollars in big bills and no cops involved. Mrs. Jackie thought it was another prank so she hung up and called Mr. Bill, Brent and Gabbie to let them know about the call then she put her answering machine on and locked her house up instead of letting someone sit and wait for brother Mike to call with final arrangements. This was the most crucial time of Job's disappearance and Mrs. Jackie took it lightly. She jumped in her car and went to work to carry out her normal duties as a nurse.

I picked Lil Job up to embrace him because he finally said his first word, which was "dada" and Job didn't answer so he flipped out. Job would've wanted to be there but he took his last breath. His strong, healthy heart stopped for good. His soul reached out to heaven and God took him away, leaving his body in the broken down wood chair dampening brother Mike's plan. His body couldn't take anymore. It went into shock from losing so much blood during those twenty-eight long and stressful days. As soon as they decided to make the phone call to get the money for him, he parted from them leaving them with no money and his blood on their hands. Their plan backfired. He died on them.

Brother Mike ran down the basement steps to let Job know they were about to make the deal with his people and Job lay lifeless.
"Get up motherfucka!" brother Mike hollered, nudging Job. "Get the fuck up! We talked to your peoples." With no heartbeat or pulse, brother Mike kicked

the chair over knocking Job and the chair to the floor then he ran upstairs to tell his associates Job was dead.

"Get the fuck outta here!" smirked brother Shariff with a mark on his cheek that would constantly remind him of Job.

"We gotta get rid of him now," demanded brother Mike. "Grab that curtain and two trash bags so we can get rid of him."

They went down the basement to put the trash bags over Job's head so his blood wouldn't leave any traces. With him still handcuffed, they rolled him up in the curtain, carried him out the house, put him back in the van, then they dumped his lifeless body along the railroad tracks on the Avenue, making it look like it was a connection with him and Na's death by them both being left on the Avenue down east, only fourteen blocks away from one another.

Two days later two scavengers picking through debris, stumbled over Job's body.

"Oh, shit," they said to one another. "It's a body. A young man." They ran frantically to the nearest phone booth to call the police about what they saw.

With the description I had given the detectives thirty days earlier and from Job's fingerprints and dental records, they called Mrs. Jackie hours later telling her, they thought they had her son's body. She in turn called all the family to let them know and Brent called me to tell me to meet him at Ms. Henryetta's house. With the sound of his voice, I sensed something wasn't right so I left the kids with mom and headed straight over to Ms. Henryetta's house.

Ms. Henryetta opened the door quietly dressed in her favorite striped housecoat. She was hurt about her first, her only grandson and her favorite. And she definitely didn't know how to tell me my baby was found dead.

Gabbie's cry traveled throughout the house and I knew it was bad news. Ms. Henryetta didn't have to say a word. The remainder of my broken heart, shattered into tiny pieces.

"Go upstairs with Gabbie and Brent," she said softly. I tiptoed by her and as soon as I reached the top of the steps, Brent embraced me tight. I pushed him away and I fell to the floor in disbelief.

"No Brent! No! Don't tell me he's dead," I screamed. "Don't do this to me. Don't tell me that."

"They think they have his body, but we're not sure. We still have to identify him. But more than likely, it's him. They say he fits the description and he has on the clothes that you said he was wearing last," he said.

"Oh my God! God no!" I sobbed. Although God gave me the answer I just prayed about two days earlier, it still hurt. Denial overwhelmed me. I couldn't believe it. And I wasn't about to accept it that easily either. I wanted to but how could I?

Early the next morning I sat in front of the monitor talking to Job at the morgue. He looked the same way he looked when I saw him last but I knew whoever had him wasn't treating him good. Why would they? They took him from us so I knew they weren't about to look out for him and I wanted to kill Chantel. She called Mrs. Jackie's house a week before talking about the kidnapers wanted a million dollars like she had nothing to do with his disappearance but I knew better and I didn't like the fact that Mrs. Jackie and the rest of them kept me in the dark about everything concerning my man.

Two days later Gabbie, Mrs. Jackie and I sat in three different rooms inside the homicide unit. Detective Moore and two other detectives working on Job's case wanted to know every little detail about Job. They wanted to know his connect and everybody he sold the product to. They wanted to know all his enemies, friends and companions if he had any.

I broke down in tears when detective Moore showed me pictures of Job's lifeless body. I couldn't believe how he looked laying in garbage. Job would throw a fit if he knew where he was.

Detective Moore reached for the pictures before I could get to the last ones. It was too much for me to bear but I had to see all of them. I had to know everything that happened to my fiancé.

I pulled back and the picture pierced me deeply. The back of Job's head was disfigured and his left earlobe was gone. Rodents ate at his flesh for the two days he was on the tracks. And this would happen if sinners went to hell too. Their flesh would be eaten away by rodents and worms. They would only have eye sockets and bones and the difference is, where Job couldn't feel them eating at him, sinners would feel everything in hell plus triple. They would be aware of everything happening to them and there will be no getting away. *They'll be tormented eternally.*

Back at Mrs. Jackie's house Mr. Bill stood in the living room floor embracing this beautiful woman, I knew instantly it was Nadja. She had a bronze complexion, dark features, and beautiful black hair hanging to her waist. I was definitely jealous but how could I control who came and went from Mrs. Jackie's house. I sat on the sofa while they finished talking.

"I loved him. Why!" Nadja screamed.

"You'll be okay," Mr. Bill said as he wiped her tears. "Everything will be fine." Job said she was corny and he dressed her and from the looks of things, he was right but all those things didn't matter anymore. You could have all the finest things and not be happy because I sure as hell wasn't happy.

As soon as Nadja left, I asked Mr. Bill who she was.

"A friend of Job's," he said.

"One of his other girlfriends?" I asked sarcastically.

"I don't know about Job having other girlfriends. He loved you and you were his fiancee. That's all that matters. She is just a friend, nothing more." I left it dead knowing I was out of order and it wasn't the time. People were going to come and go and I had to accept that. I even prepared myself for the lies. I knew some would be coming through with fake stories just like they did while he was abducted. *Misery.*

I went upstairs to pick one of Job's suits out to take to the undertaker then I headed to Cachet to get me an outfit with the money Brent had given me that belonged to Job anyway.

Back at the house Gabbie promised to give me the money she had gotten from Basil. She knew what Job wanted for us. He wanted us long gone, tucked away and free from all harm and danger. He didn't want us to be in the city where his life meant very little to some and the world to others. He would've wanted us to start over and be where he wanted us to be in the first place and that was far away from the ghetto.

Two days later the four Ali Baba limos' dropped Job's family, close friends and me off at the three story white church on 12th Street. The church Job got baptized in. I sat amazed at all the cars in the middle of the street, up and down the block. It was incredibly crowded. It was like that of a show or our wedding.

I stepped out the car with my boys and we lined up with the family so we could go inside. Tears fell from everybody's eyes, even Lil Job's. And I could only wonder if he was crying because I was or did he know what was going on.

I heard, *here comes the bride* as I walked down the isle on the plush red carpet in a two-piece black spandex and sheer skirt set, studded out with Australian crystals with black suede Via Spiga shoes with a diamond studded front to match. Suddenly I realized, *It's So Hard to Say Good-Bye to Yesterday* played gently in the background and I was paying my last respects to my fiancé, instead of getting married. I looked nervously at all the people in the church. It was packed. The church couldn't hold another sole. Every seat was full. You couldn't even move freely down the isles or in the hallway. Job knew so many people and they respected him for different reasons. Some respected him because he was a young black business man. Others respected him because of his drug game. Then you had the ones that respected him because of the money they spent with him.

As I approached the front row, a clock made out of roses with the time stopped caught my eyes specifically. I could only wonder who sent them. Out of the two hundred flowers they stood out boldly. Somebody was trying to tell us something.

Armeleon sat in the balcony with his wife and three kids. He had been trying to contact me since he heard about Job's disappearance but Mrs. Jackie, Gabbie and Brent kept that information from me. They told him I didn't want to be bothered by anyone so he gave them the deeds to the boat and house, hoping they would give it to me when I came around.

Rose, Nadja and Sugar sat as close to the front as they possibly could. None of them was going to miss this. Rose and Sugar didn't want Job dead but they were glad that I didn't have him anymore. I wasn't going to be getting any nice gifts or real love with him gone. Nobody was going to want me with two kids with dead fathers.

Mrs. Jackie took her sable fur off and sat between Mr. Bill and Brent. She was going to be the only one shining this day. She took my sable fur and shearlings and hid them. The only thing I had was what I left her house in and that was the swing mink Job had given me to kick around in until he replaced it with the sable fur.

I shook my head once Mrs. Jackie sat down. Job's death wasn't a joke. It was a wake up call for everybody around us and people were still worrying about material things. Everybody there showed off their furs. I was too through with the madness.

I looked around for Tank. I really needed to see his face. I knew what went on between him and Job but Job also told me they settled their differences before he was kidnaped.

I finally spotted both of their artist sitting three rows behind on the left but Tank wasn't with them. I had to respect the fact that some people didn't do funerals and I really hoped that was the case with Tank.

Lil Job had to make himself known. He gurgled, hollered and moaned. He wondered what all these people were doing. He couldn't understand what their cries were for. He needed to see his daddy's face.

"Oh my God! Why is he doing this? He's usually good in church," I mumbled lowly.

"It's his dad's day. Let him cry. Don't worry about it. If people don't like it, so what," said Brent, embracing me tight. I passed Job back and forth, from his great-grandmother to his godmother. Nothing worked, he kept it going looking for his father, then he looked at Luke and laughed with tears. The love for his brother was dear. Luke sat confused too. He wanted Job back but he knew it was the same with his father. No matter how much he cried, looked and prayed, his father never returned and he couldn't accept that again. He wanted Job alive.

I cried harder when the preacher summed up his message. He was right. God makes no mistakes. When we go out the will of God, we open the doors for the enemy. Job or Na had no business in the streets. They were supposed to do the will of the Lord. But because they accepted Christ, they have eternal life. They will live on. And it's our duty to get there. It's easy to fall, but get back up and seek God for the answers. Let him lead and guide you. As long as you have God, you can't go wrong. I thought to myself. After Job's classmate sang a beautiful hymn, Gabbie got up to read Lil Job's poem because I couldn't do it.

SHATTERED DREAMS

Daddy my dreams are shattered right now.
I never imagined things to be this way.
You were my world and I was yours.
From the day I entered mommy's womb, you made plans for me.
You wanted me to see, what you didn't see.
You said you wanted to be loved like no one ever loved you before
and that no one was gonna stop us
because you were my dad and I was your boy.
You called me boss and I thought you were my king
and having me changed your world and the way you used to think.
You no longer cared about the meaningless things of this world
because it was all about us and the people you thought you could trust.
Us two, unstoppable together and the bond we had,
not even death could break and when you left me in the flesh,
I wasn't surprised by all the fakes.
It was you that told me from birth in my little ears
when you washed and clothed me, wiping my little tears,
not knowing your time was near, that there was gonna be a time
when we would have to part but son know this first;
"I'll always love you like I did from the very start."
Yeah, they selfishly took you away from me, mommy
and my brother but know the joy and love we shared,
can no man put asunder.
We'll remember hearing your voice and seeing your smiling face,
knowing all that life meant to you and trust me dear daddy,
no one will ever take your place.
When I look at myself, I'll see a reflection of you
and what will make me happier,
knowing you told me exactly what to do.
"Follow your dreams, be successful, stay strong, and follow God and
nothing can go wrong. And when you're weak and even if you fall. Don't
beat yourself down son, get up, stand strong, push yourself forward and
know with God, you can't go wrong."

Your first born and only child, Job

After the service everybody got back in their cars and headed to the cemetery; even our enemies. Once the limo pulled up to the gate, I realized Luke was buried at the same place and everything sank into my heart even deeper. I now had two kids' fathers in the same cemetery. I now had to bring both children to see their dads.

Everyone grabbed a flower and the pastor said a prayer before Job's body was lowered into the ground. Job was my life. I wanted so badly to be dead with him. He wasn't supposed to be turning into ashes and dust. He was supposed to be a new husband this day. We were supposed to be a happy family celebrating at our reception. When it was my turn to place my flower, Shalina stepped up with me. She felt my thoughts but I wasn't about to give myself to the devil. I knew I had boys to raise. I loved him but little did she know, I wasn't about to commit suicide and Job wouldn't expect that from me. He knew he had a *soldier*. I was his *Queen*. Nothing could stop the fight in me.

After everybody left I went to the limo to get the three doves I had purchased two days before. One was to represent the love that Job and I shared. The second one was for the love Job and his son shared and the third one was for the love Luke and he had between them. He was to know he could never be replaced. We all make mistakes but he was a hell of a young man, no other made my blood pump like him.

Back at the house everyone sat around laughing and talking while the sun shined bright through the window pane of Mrs. Jackie's kitchen.

"When I saw her coming, I said she has too much hair. I'm not doin' all that stuff. It's too thick and long. I got something nice for her," Francis said, twitching his lips. Francis was a friend of Mrs. Jackie's and Gabbie. I heard of him through them but I never let him do my hair until Job's funeral and why did I do that. He set me up something nice. All the hair I grew during my pregnancy that Job loved, he cut but that was nothing, my family had a history of long, full hair, so mine would grow back before he blinked his eyes.

"It's alright. You got that one off, but my hair grows well, so it'll grow back," I spat back at his feminine behind. His lip hit his chin. He didn't know I heard him. I turned away calling him every name in the book. I realized how people really hated, even the older ones when I thought they knew better.

Ebony and Marsha grabbed me once I reached the dining room to give me their condolences. I was really glad to know they cared enough to make it. So many people came out just to be nosey but I knew Ebony and Marsha were sincere. They knew how much Job and I loved each other and they knew this was heartbreaking for me. How could I go through such turmoil again?

Weeks later I sat around tripping off everybody. All the fronting, Sunday dinners and the game parties were over for us. Nobody respected Job's wishes. Everybody was out for self and they did them. All the promises were broken. Tafik, Booker and a couple other fake niggas never gave me Job's money that they promised me. You know the old saying, "when you're dead and gone, somebody else wears your shoes." Whatever Job left on the streets was history and none of his so-called friends were really friends because none of them looked out for his son. Mrs. Jackie, Gabbie and

Brent did what they wanted to do with Job's possessions but I had the best treasure and that was Job's son, something they could never take from me. We were destined to be blessed regardless of our struggle. Mrs. Jackie even hit me with the, "Mama's baby, daddy's maybe," and she knew how Job felt about his son. He never once gave them the indication that he wasn't his seed. He never had any doubts about our son, but that's how it goes and I would keep my promise though. I would try to keep the baby close to his family as long as I could. And that would make them hate me more.

I was marked and some people would never look at me the same. I was a black widow. A bad seed and anything I touched, died. I was thought of as an outcast and slimy but I ate all of that because I knew better and the *3 Men I Chose to Love*, knew better too. Why would I hurt the ones I loved when I was happy? I was complete with my unit. I wasn't desperate, hungry or bitter. I had hope. I was eating and happy. Why would I risk all that for, *A Lifetime of Pain?* I wasn't that crazy and selfish. I had all my senses and it would only hurt me in the end. I would have to die with that guilt and I couldn't live with that.

PART III

Chapter 1
They Can't Break Cinnamon
"I'm a Survivor"

Three months later. I grew to hate the *City of Brotherly Love* where I grew up at. There wasn't any love in the city for me. People ran around worrying about my financial status since they knew my man was handling. They thought he left me with all this dough and property but little did they know I just got a check from the insurance company for one hundred thousand dollars for the things that were stolen from our Condo. They replaced some of the electronics, a small portion of our jewelry but that was nothing, that money wouldn't go far with me not working. Job had plenty but I had very little. His people reaped all his benefits and I had kids to raise.

After getting depressed with the gossip I got up and purchased a brand-new Ninja 500 from the Kawasaki dealer and later I traded my 635 in for a brand new 1994 BMW 325i drop top in my favorite color and it was the year before. I loved fast toys and why did I do that? Niggas hustled late nights and days to survive and they were still driving squatters. My motive wasn't to offend anyone. I was just tired of people doggin' my name. I had to give them something to talk about and yes, "I was being foolish." This really wasn't the time to shine. I had been through enough and it was time to grow up. I should've taken that money and moved my kids away but I didn't have any study income to pay a high mortgage and I was scared to move without Job being around. I never lived with anyone before and I wasn't ready to do it alone either.

Harold pulled me over at the light on the Ave.
"Damn shorty! You did the thing to them. My man just called me telling me the niggas from the strip just saw you fly by and they're heated. They are talkin' about you like they talk about other niggas," he smiled.
"Well, whose fault is that? It certainly isn't mine and they're gonna talk about me until I die, so I'm gonna do me. They can care less about me or mine. They're the same people that'll pass me by if I'm starving. And they're the same people that'll smile in my face and talk about me when I'm not around," I smirked.
"Right. Just be careful shorty," he smiled as he revved the engine on his purple and yellow Suzuki 1100. He had been riding motorcycles since he was eleven and he taught me how to ride my bike. I bought my bike without knowing how to ride but Harold took me out to the park on the first night and we ripped the strip until I mastered my toy and it wasn't long either. I caught on fast. To be said, I was the truth.
"I will," I assured him as I peeled off. I had to get home to take Lil Job to the hospital. Something his father wanted to do but he wasn't around and I

didn't have sufficient funds like him to have Job's hearing deficiency and ear lesions removed but with the money I got, I could do it finally.

Bright and early in the morning the kids, Amil and I hit I95 south to Washington, D.C. Amil was Barry's wife and we'd become close since Job's death. Although Mrs. Jackie cut us off, her friends didn't. They knew how much Job loved us and they could do nothing but love us too. We were a part of Job and they couldn't feel the way Mrs. Jackie felt. They wanted to see Job grow to be a fine young man.

Amil had been getting her hair done in D.C. for the past ten years and since I didn't feel comfortable getting my hair done in our city anymore, she introduced me to all of her family in D.C. and that's where I shopped and got my hair done. I wasn't about to go back to Carol's for anything. I hated the people and the gossip. Some things never changed and it was too much back biting going on in there for me.

I exited off the expressway and drove until I reached 14th Street NW. I loved the way Sherika did my hair. She definitely had it growing back too. It was hanging to the middle of my back. I was loving it. Every time I got the chance I drove by Francis salon so he could see my hair. He hated me too. He hated me mostly because he loved Mrs. Jackie and she didn't do me.

Once I dropped Amil back off at home I drove to Mrs. Jackie's house to try again. She ignored all of my phone calls, messages and cards and I only wanted her to see how her grandchild was growing. I made a promise to Job and I had to keep it.

Gabbie opened the door and let us in. As soon as Mrs. Jackie heard my voice, she came downstairs and said, "hi" then she left. She still didn't want to try to be a family on the strength of her son.

"Why are you still in Philly?" asked Gabbie as she sat next to me on the sofa.

"What do you mean?" I asked her as I looked across the room only to notice my stereo. I hadn't been to Mrs. Jackie's in a while so she brought my stereo from the basement and placed it in her living room like it was her own.

"Why didn't you move yet? I told you to move from here because you don't belong here," she said.

"Move how and for what?" I asked her.

"Because Job didn't want y'all here," she said. I wanted to hold my tongue but I couldn't.

"Well, maybe if I had the money you all took, I could've moved and never had to worry about rent or mortgage. But because I don't have what you all have, I can't do but so much," I said.

"You got insurance money. A new car and bike. Why are you still talking about Job's money? You need to stop worrying about my brother's money," she said coldly. I wanted to smack the shit outta her. She talked about me worrying about his money yet she took his money and she was still collecting the money from his properties while his son and I moved from place to place and we didn't have a place to call our own. I wanted so badly to break her jaw.

"You know what!" I said.

"What!" she said.

"Nothing. I just know now. Job was right," I said as I got up. I grabbed the kids and we jumped in the car that she and her mother envied. Job promised them both convertibles but they didn't get them and I had one when they had all his money. Money could buy some things but they were scared to spend his money because it was drug money but the law didn't care about his money anymore. He was dead so that was enough satisfaction for them alone.

Once I kicked off my shoes and jumped in the hot shower, I began to think about what Gabbie said earlier. I really had no place in the city anymore. I had a little dough, a nice car, a few gadgets, my beautiful kids, but I didn't have Job. I didn't have a good man or anything close to one. I tried so hard to find a replacement, but it wasn't happening. Nothing or no one could replace that hell of a man, nothing. He was something special and nobody could come close to him. At 26, I was still searching for love. Luke's mother lived in Atlanta so the kids and I would move there.

At the end of the week I left my toy at home and Nancy, Luke, the baby and I hit I95 south. I had to do this for myself, the kids and Job. It was time to relocate.

After a week in the hot beaming sun, the kids and I packed up and headed back home. South just wasn't for the kids or me. We hated it. Living in the city all of our lives did something to us because we could see things no other way. We had to be a part of our hometown whether it brought us misery or not.

I pulled down 19th Street with my top dropped and hair flowing. It was my second week at college and I was loving it. I went to the gym in between classes and I did aerobics too so I could keep my body tight.

As soon as I turned into the lot, the same young boys that always stood in front of the Green building, whispered about me. They even made a bet that I would turn them down and act snotty if they said something to me.

I parked my car and broke the ice before they could say a word. They couldn't believe who I was after a few sentences. They instantly fell in love with me. I put a stop to the stereotype. They thought I only dealt with dudes that had cake. And it wasn't like that; I liked whom I liked. From a young girl I always wanted my own. The only thing I wanted from a man was dedication, love and respect. If you had dough, it was all good and if you didn't, it wasn't a big issue because we could put our heads together and

170

come up with a master plan. It had nothing to do with money. I didn't mind contributing to mine.

After I told the boys I had two sons and the oldest was seven, they fell out. They thought I was fresh out of high school. It dawned on me after a while that everybody wasn't against me and I had to accept things for what it was worth. They talked about our Lord and Savior so who was I? I was a nobody compared to him.

I pulled my car from the school lot only to bump into Nathan's old head Saleem.

"Are you still doing nails?" he asked me.

"No. I'm studying to be a doctor," I said.

"Get outta here. That's what's up," he smiled. "Are you working anywhere?"

"No," I said. He was asking a lot of questions that I didn't feel like answering.

"Well, I just opened this salon and I need you to come do nails for me," he said. I really needed the extra cash because the social security checks were nice but not enough.

"Where's your salon?"

"Down 33rd and Belmont." I admired any man that had his own.

"Maybe I'll stop by tomorrow to check it out," I smiled.

"Okay," he said as he pulled off.

"What's the name of the place?" I hollered to him from the window.

"It's Yours," he said. The name was kinda ghetto but it couldn't hurt to drop by and see what he was working with.

After school the next day, I drove straight to *It's Yours* and parked. The three story building was okay from the outside so I jumped out and hit the buzzer. Saleem fixed his mustache and buzzed me in. He couldn't wait to get me inside. He'd been loving me since I was with Job and now that Job was dead, he could come at me directly and not sideways. He was going to have me, one way or another.

I looked around at the bright white walls, black Hampton ceiling fans and recess lights. Saleem didn't have taste like Job but he was doing okay for himself.

"Let me show you upstairs where the nail stations are," he said as he stood to his size ten Nikes.

"Okay," I smiled as I followed. We walked up the spiral steps to the second floor.

"If you don't like this. You can have the third floor to yourself," he said. The third floor was for the barbers' but he would give it to me just to have me work for him.

"This is fine," I said. "I can work wit' this."

After talking about how I had been making it since Job's death, I left with intentions on coming back. I wanted to move from mom's because we weren't getting along too well and with the job, I could pay rent somewhere while I was in school.

For months Saleem stayed on my heels like he was my man. Every night before I left, he was in my ear about some pussy and I hated it. I wasn't about to fuck him because he had a couple dollars. I was still in love with Job and I promised myself and him that I wouldn't love another. Besides, Saleem wasn't my type. He was ten years older than I, bald and I heard he wasn't working with anything between the legs. I simply wasn't attracted to his old ass.

One slow night I stayed at the salon late while everybody left. Saleem wanted a manicure and pedicure and I promised him I would take care of him as soon as I straightened up my station.

After giving Saleem his services he asked me to jerk him off for a thousand dollars. I told him to kiss my yellow ass and walked away. I had to pee so bad and I couldn't wait until I got home. I locked the bathroom door and sat on the toilet. As I got up to pull my dress down, a knock on the door startled me. Saleem knew I was in there so why was he knocking? I washed my hands and the door opened.

"What are you doing?" I asked Saleem as he stood in the floor drooling. "What do you want?"

"You know I want you. I always wanted you," he said while foam formed in the cracks of his mouth. I pushed by him to open the door wider so I could run.

"Get off the door and take your clothes off," he demanded me.

"What? No!" I said. "Get the fuck from in front of me you fuckin' pervert!"

"Don't make me hurt you," he said then he ripped my dress off and threw me to the floor.

"Why are you doing this?" I asked. "You don't have to take it. I'll give it to you."

"For real. Okay," he said as he pulled back but I was taking too long so he ripped my panties off and licked me until my juices leaked in his mouth then he stuck his pencil dick inside me while I scratched his face and neck screaming for help. This instance took me back to Brother Patrick molesting me at the age of four. He was a church friend of my mothers and I hated him for fondling me. Saleem took two good long pumps then he got up and pulled his pants up.

"Did it feel good to you?" he asked with no remorse.

"Fuck you, you fuckin' bastard! I hope somebody blows your brains out, you fuckin' bitch! You're nothing but a pussy," I screamed.

He grabbed me tight and said, "I just want you to be my girl, that's all. If you just jerk my dick, I'll look out. I'll take care of you shorty."

I pulled back from him and said, "I don't like you. I never have and now I hate you."

172

"Are you gonna get me locked up?" he asked.

"I should. Just leave please. Just let me the fuck out!" When he opened the door, I ran out and jumped in my car. I hated to face my kids but I had to.

Inside my two bedroom apartment I washed myself until I bled while the kids slept peacefully with Nancy. I wanted no signs of Saleem on me. I felt like filth and scum. I began to blame myself for everything that happened to me. Then I blamed Job and dad for leaving me. If my dad raised me like he should've, I wouldn't have been going through what I was going through. Men saw the weakness in me. I attracted negativity to me, so I thought in my mind.

I fell asleep in the living room. I couldn't sleep in the bed with my kids after what happened to me. I couldn't let them or anyone know what happened to me. I had to bury the extra burden inside of me.

Early in the morning I got up to face my normal task. I had to act like what happened the night before didn't happen. I wanted to see Saleem behind bars for the pain he caused me, but I didn't feel like everybody in my business. Some would blame me anyway so I chose to ride it out alone. God would take care of him for me.

I dropped the kids off at school then I headed over to the college. I had no plans on going back to the salon. All of my products could stay there and rot. I wasn't about to go back for a thousand dollars worth of OPI nails, glue, acrylic powder, liquid and polish. The other nail technicians could have my things. I was good.

I walked outside after school only to find gasoline on the hood of my car. Why was somebody messing with me? Hadn't I been through enough? I was sick and tired of the haters and manipulators. I just wanted peace.

I got a rag from my trunk and wiped the gas stain away. I couldn't worry myself to death about what the devil was trying to do. I had to hold on and be strong. I had to be the soldier I was. I couldn't let the streets get the best of me. I couldn't. I had too much to live for. I had my boys to raise and God had work for me to do.

God

You will always be special in my sight.
You knew how to love me, even when I wasn't right.
Through my flaws and pain You always remained,
never leaving me abandoned,
never making me feel ashamed.
And when I had no one to turn to,
You embraced me with open arms,
saying, "daughter it's alright, no one can do you any more harm."
You let me know if I only trusted and believed in You
and let You be my guide,

173

that things wouldn't be easy for me,
but I would know how to survive.
And when the storm formed up against me,
I wouldn't fall,
because I had the strength and power of the Lord
and with that,
I had it all.

The following week while the boys and I sat in the AMC theater watching a flick, Rose had her flunkies vandalize my car. I was still holding on since Job's death and she wanted to see me break.

I dropped my car off at the Foreign Car Body shop in West Chester to have the damages repaired the next day. The tab was six thousand dollars because I had to have the top replaced and the whole car painted. I was hurt financially but the insurance company would reimburse most of the money to me so I was cool.

Once my car was done, I took it back to the BMW dealer and traded it in for a 525i station wagon for two reasons; one because it was causing me too much money already and every hater knew whose car it was because I was the only one in the city with one of that color and I had my kids name on a chrome plate in front of the car so it could be pointed out anywhere and two, because Shalina was expecting by one of the youngins from the B squad so we'd be doing a lot together. Her baby's father introduced me to his boy Todd and I kinda liked his style. He was young, about six years younger than I but he was intelligent and smooth. Since everybody that was getting money back in the day was dead or in jail, the B squad took over the entire westside of town and they were rippin' it too. The young boys rode motorcycles and I loved that. They had classic cars with hydraulics. They had a few businesses and properties. They had high maintenance vehicles and nice clothes and jewelry. Todd had a girl but he wouldn't disclose that information to me. I was older, had been through some things and I could teach him something about my world. I could definitely show him something his young mind never experienced.

After a long day of sitting in the courthouse for Dip's hearing about Na, I needed to get out. I hadn't done so in a while, besides, Shalina wanted me to see Todd and the rest of the B squad in full force. They were racing their bikes on Delaware Avenue and we couldn't miss it.

I pulled my shiny white freshly cleaned BMW up to the club, "Bahama Island," and parked with all the other high maintenance vehicles.
"Let's get out," smiled Nancy. She was definitely too young for the club but she could stay outside and watch everybody mingle while Shalina and I stepped away after watching the B squad race.

"Alright," I said as I checked in the mirror one last time. I had to make sure everything was in place, my hair, Gucci sunglasses and clothes. I had on a two-piece white linen pant set with a pair of red ostriches that I purchased from Bottino's for a gee. I had every color the store had. I was still spending foolishly but I was caught up. I stepped away from those things for a minute but I loved clothes and shoes. I had a fetish for shopping. Shalina, Nancy and I stepped out the car at the same time and shut the doors. The weather was simply beautiful. It wasn't too humid or too cool. It was just right.

I opened the back hatch so we could sit and watch as the motorcycles raced. The B squad was so thick that I started to wonder if I wanted to date Todd or not. The boy Gee looked rather nice. He was tall, slim, chocolate and sexy, just like I liked it and Shalina said the girls hollered about his dick and fuck game. She said the skinny nigga was working with a ruler or more. And you know that made me wet but they said Todd was working with something nice too so I couldn't just diss him. I had to give him a chance since he stepped first.

The B squad raced their motorcycles for a half an hour straight. I was really impressed. They wheeled the block without stopping. They had mad tricks and all their bike gear was tight. They had one piece jumpers with leather bike boots. Some even had Harley Davidson attire and not too many people were down with that top notch shit. The young boys had it going on and after seeing what they were made of, it was on. I was going to break the juices for the young nigga. I was going to give him a chance.

I told Todd, Shalina and I were going inside the club and I'd see him later. He smiled, blushed and giggled. He bet Shalina's baby father Dre that he would get me and things were definitely going his way.

Inside the club was nice. I had never been to *Bahama Island.* The set up was like a tropical island. Palm trees, sand and water. Yes, water. The atmosphere was pleasant but it was a lot of haters still around.

"Shalina look," I pointed over to the bar.

"What?" she said.

"Look at Mrs. Jackie and Gabbie."

"Oh, no they're not doing the club together," Shalina smirked. Mrs. Jackie was too old for that set.

"Oh, yes they are," I said, laughing.

"Well, Mrs. Jackie still looks like a young girl," Shalina said.

"I know. In fact, she looks better than her daughter."

"You are so right," Shalina said as she pulled me to the bar. You know her night wouldn't be right without her Hennesey straight up on the rocks with a Heineken to follow. I spoke to Mrs. Jackie and Gabbie then they walked away. They never expected to see me out. They had been doing the party scene for a minute and they never ran into me.

175

After dancing a few records straight, Shalina and I met back up with Nancy outside. Nancy was kicking it with Todd and Dre in the middle of the street. Anybody getting fast money was cool with her. And if her aunts had anybody getting fast money, she was in because they always looked out generously for her too.

I woke up in Todd's arms the next morning. I couldn't believe I fucked him. I actually broke my promise to Job. I did it to somebody else and to be younger than I. He had tricks. He taught me something in bed. After showering Todd drove me to the airport to pick up my mother's sister.

Once mom's sister excited off the plane, I stood speechless. I couldn't believe I was looking at somebody that favored mom so much. It was unbelievable.

On the ride back home aunt Silvia and I talked about our family roots. I couldn't believe the similarity between my mother and her. We lived in two different cities, fifteen hours away from each other but we actually shared identical things. She had a model, singer and artist in her family and so did we. When she popped her son's cd in,"Ain't Gonna Trip" I flipped out. He reminded her so much of me. We had some of the same qualities and I couldn't wait to meet my cuz. I had to see the man that looked so much like Job. Honestly, I wished he wasn't my cousin because he was the closest thing to my Job. They had some of the same qualities as men.

Todd dropped aunt Silvia off at mom's then he took me to my apartment on Spruce Street. As soon as Todd pulled off, Booker and his boy put guns to me and the kids' heads looking for Nathan and Saleem. They did a bank heist together and Nathan and Saleem burnt them of their cut.

Tears fell from my eyes as I watched Booker with his gun to my head. I couldn't believe he had the nerve to disrespect me after all Job did for him and I was angry with Nathan and Saleem too for putting us in that predicament. They were causing me so much pain. And I was to blame too for my kids suffering. Job told me to cut everybody off and I was still allowing my family to interfere with my life. I had no business letting Nathan come to my apartment after he did his dirt, when I was going to learn and put my kids first? When would I seriously wash my hands from the things that hurt me the most? When would I? When would I put God first was the truth?

I packed my things and called a moving company once I laid Nathan out. I couldn't take another day at the spot I called home, that my nephew burnt out. It wasn't home for my kids and me anymore. Everybody knew about my little joint and I had to leave it behind. I put my things in a storage unit with the intentions on trying down south again. I was tired of the drama.

After talking to Todd about my decision I was ready to go. I needed a change away from people that cared nothing about me. I couldn't take the jealousy, envy or greed another day. Gabbie kept throwing smart remarks my way again. She hated the fact that I had a new car and I was seeing someone else but she was the one that told me life went on and if I got with someone and had other kids that it would be okay because it wasn't like I had kids by different men and they were alive. My situation was excusable so she said, now she turned the script back two pages.

Nathan's mom asked to borrow money before I left because Nathan wanted a new car like mine and out of guilt and stupidity, I gave them five thousand dollars from the little car that I finally got rid of. I sold my bike to Harold for his girl and I cleaned my bank account out. I would set up accounts and insurance in Atlanta.

I pulled my BMW station wagon up Glenridge Drive and parked around one o'clock in the afternoon. My girlfriend from High School named Melissah, welcomed me to stay with her until my apartment came through and Luke's mom lived not too far so I had two places that I could stay at. Whenever I got tired of one, I could go to the other.

I phoned Melissah from outside to let her know I was there. Although we kept in touch by phone through the years, I hadn't seen her since High School and I really missed her so much. She was really doing well in Atlanta and she had no plans on ever coming back to the city. Her children were around the same ages as Luke and they stayed in boarding schools while she studied medicine. We had the same dream but she was in Medical school already because she had a lot of support from family members. Her fiancé was a surgeon so she was living good.

Melissah ran outside and embraced me gently. She couldn't believe I actually made it. She'd been trying to convince me to leave the city too and I kept promising her I would come down and never did but I was there in full form.

"Hey girl," I smiled as I stood back. "You look so good. Look at you."

"You look great too. You're still beautiful and in shape," she laughed. I loved her deep dimples and straight white teeth.

"You're the one girl. Where's the rich hubby at?" I asked.

"Oh, he's at work. You know, long days and nights. Besides, he don't stay the night. You know we have to wait until we're married," she laughed as she grabbed the baby. "Look at the beautiful kids."

"Thanks. Where's Megan and Matt?"

"Oh, they didn't come home this month. I'm studying hard so I told them they had to stay," she said. Melissah had the most beautiful kids by a natural born Indian and I couldn't understand for the life of me why she sent them to boarding school. I knew how badly she wanted to become a doctor and I did too but I could never see myself away from my children.

After settling in, Melissah drove me to the Lenox Square Mall to shop my favorite stores. I had to get some new things because I left most of my clothes in the storage unit. We did Macy's for the children then I did my stores of course. I needed new sandals, a pocket book and a few pairs of jeans. I stayed in jeans these days.

Back at home Melissah asked her fiancé Pedro to watch the kids so we could do the club. I really hated leaving my kids with a stranger but I figured he was cool if Melissah was about to marry him. If he was a lunatic, she would've found out by now.

We hit the club *Reach* around eleven o'clock. Anybody that was somebody was there. The set was completely different from back home. It wasn't too much hating going on. Everybody was friendly and they had their own money. They weren't robbing, killing and stealing from the next man. If anything, they helped each other out.

Melissah introduced me to a nice Junior Middleweight boxer from Atlanta. He was average height, not too cute but he was attractive in his own way. It couldn't hurt to have a friend. I needed somebody to connect with. I really needed to change my circle of friends and I needed to start giving other brothas' a chance. The drug boys caused me so much pain.

I sat at the bar all night talking to Larry while Melissah danced with a few of his friends. Although she had a fiancé at home, she didn't mind flirting. She was still the same way she was in High School; quiet but outgoing and flirtatious. Larry and I had so much in common. He wanted to keep in touch but Todd would be visiting back and forth and I couldn't do both of them.

My night ended with a soft kiss from Larry. He really felt something special for me and wanted so badly to meet my boys. He had a five-year-old daughter that he loved dearly so he knew my boys needed their fathers. He wanted to show us a good time in his hometown, another side of living.

In the morning Larry came by Melissah's and picked the boys and me up to take us to Centinnel Olympic Park. He wanted to show them a great time then he would do me later without the children.

After buying everything that he could possibly buy for the children, Larry took me back to the apartment so Melissah could watch the boys while he took me to dinner and a movie. I was really having fun for a change. I hadn't enjoyed myself this much in a while. I cared about Todd but being with someone legal was different. I didn't have to watch over my shoulder or worry about what was going to happen next. I could be anywhere and be comfortable. The only difference was, people ran up to Larry every minute asking for autographs. Although he had only been boxing for two years, he had 18 knock outs under his belt, a very promising future ahead of him.

For the next two weeks Larry showed me the best time in a long time. He sent me on a shopping spree to Lenox Square Mall because he loved how I dressed and he gave me a nice four carat diamond tennis bracelet that he purchased from Tiffany & Co. from Phipps Plaza and I hadn't even fucked him yet. He truly knew how to make me smile but he definitely wanted some and I knew that.

Mom called me and told me my roster came in the mail and I was to start back to college in three days. I couldn't believe I forgot all about college in Philly. I was supposed to straighten all that out before I got to Atlanta but I didn't and Todd kept begging me to come home. He missed me and things just wasn't right with me gone. His girl simply got on his nerves and it was nothing like being in my presence. He needed little old me back.

I told Melissah and Larry that I would be leaving and coming back once the semester in Philly was over. Melissah understood and awaited my return but Larry was heartbroken. He really wanted me to be his girl.

After listening to Larry beg all day, I left the kids with Melissah and went over to his spot to give him a little to hold off until I came back. What Todd didn't know, wouldn't hurt. Besides, he had a girl that he kept saying was just his baby mama. That was the famous excuse and I wasn't stupid. I just couldn't prove it because nobody would snitch on him and he was never seen anywhere with her.

I pulled up to Larry's five bedroom burgundy brick house and parked in the driveway. The area reminded me so much of Federal Way where dad lived. The set up was so similar. I grabbed my Gucci handbag from the passenger seat and got out. I couldn't forget the rubbers. I wasn't about to fuck Larry bareback. I didn't know much about his past. I only knew what I knew from Melissah and him and it wasn't bad but I had to play it safe.

Larry opened his big oak door with a burgundy satin robe loosely draped over him. His definitions and cuts protruded through the opening of the robe. I never had a man cut up like him. Job and Luke were tall, slim and lean. He kissed me on the cheek and welcomed me inside like a real gentleman.

Once he shut the door behind me I got butterflies in my belly. I had a change of heart about doing it to him. I really didn't want to fuck. A movie and dinner would do just fine.

"Are you thirsty?" he asked. I was so glad he said that instead of showing me to his bedroom first.

"Yes," I smiled.

"I only have water," he said.

"No problem. I don't need anything else," I said. I gave up sodas years ago. I only drank water anyway. That's how I kept my weight down. I ate junk but I substituted soda and juice for water so that cut my calories down a lot. Larry passed me the bottled spring water then we sat on his burgundy leather sectional. He loved burgundy and the color combination in his spot was perfect. The burgundy looked rich against the cherry wood floors and gold fixtures.

"Would you like to see the rest of the house?" he casually asked.

"Sure," I said. I put my bag and water down then I followed him through the house. In the back of the house sat a twelve-foot pool shaped like a boxing glove. I smiled when I saw it. I thought the idea was so cute. He definitely loved what he did. Larry dropped his robe to the ground then he grabbed me and threw me in the pool with him. He knew I would have to stay once he did this.

"Why the hell would you do that?" I asked as I held onto him tight. I couldn't swim to save my own life.

"It's okay," he said as he held me gently in his arms. He wasn't about to let me go. He licked and sucked the water running from my body as I watched. I couldn't believe his tongue. It actually felt good against my skin. Larry pulled my skirt up and pushed my panties to the side so he could put his dick in me but it wouldn't get up for some reason so he carried me from the pool into his room.

"Wait. I have to get something," I said as I reached for the door.

"I have some," he smiled. He pulled a Trojan from his night stand and placed it on his three inches. I really didn't want to give him any after seeing his little peter. My boys' had him beat. Larry bent down and sucked my pussy then he stuck his dick inside me. *What the fuck!* I thought to myself as I felt a pinch. Larry drooled and moaned as he moved rapidly. He acted like a wild beast. You would've thought he didn't have good pussy before. I moved back only so he could hurry up and finish. Not because I liked it. I was so disgusted and turned off. I wanted to get my clothes on and leave but they were wet.

Once Larry released he wanted to lean back and cuddle but I had to go so I found my way to the laundry room to dry my clothes. I sat in Larry's guest room while my clothes dried in the dryer.

"What's wrong?" Larry asked as he walked in the room half naked.

"Nothing. I just needed time to think," I said as tears formed in my eyes.

"What is it?" he asked. "Is it the kids?"

"Not really," I said.

"Their father's," he said.

"Yes," I cried. He reached over and embraced me. He had deep feelings for me and I didn't want any parts of him after this. I regretted what I had done. As soon as my clothes were dry, I put them on and Larry walked me to the door.

"Are you gonna keep in touch?" he asked. He knew I wasn't but he had to ask anyway.

"Yeah. I'll be in touch," I said as I walked down his tan marble steps to my car.

I pulled up to Melissah's apartment around nine o'clock in the evening. It was late but if I hit the road right away, I would get to Philly by sometime in the afternoon. Melissah helped me load my things in the car then she watched as I pulled off. I was to call her as soon as I got home.

I arrived back to Philly mid afternoon. My family was outside on the porch so we sat and kicked it about everything that was going on in the city.

Shalina finally told me all about Todd's girlfriend. Nancy knew but she withheld that information from me because Todd was breaking her off and they had that kind of relationship. I cried because I really cared for Todd but I had to break it off with him. I never played second fiddle knowingly and I wasn't about to do it for him. He was no different from the next man. If I didn't take that off of my kids' fathers, I wasn't about to let him get away with it.

I walked in the house and broke it off with Todd immediately. The apartment and furniture he got us, he could keep. I was through.

Once we hung up Todd was pissed. He sent me four thousand dollars while I was in Atlanta. He spent another thirty on the apartment and furniture and I broke up with him. He didn't think so. I wasn't walking away from him just like that. The money wasn't the issue, it was the principal that mattered.

Todd told his young boys, Isiah and Dominique to set my car on fire. I wasn't going to be driving through the city looking pretty without him. If I wanted out, I had to start from rock bottom.

Around 12:00 a.m., I crept in the bed with the kids. I was tired and needed some sleep. Everybody on the block was in except Nancy and our neighbor Slimmey. Isiah and Dominique drove by only to notice Nancy still out so they phoned Todd and told him what the deal was.

"Give it until 2:00 then go back," Todd said. They hung up and waited around until 2:00 then they circled mom's block again and everybody was in except Mrs. Patsy. She sat on her enclosed porch being nosey like usual. She knew everything that happened on the block but she kept some things to herself. She knew what she could and couldn't tell or say.

Isiah and Dominique parked their tinted Celebrity around the corner from mom's then they jumped out with their one piece blue Dickies on and a can of gasoline. They were ready to handle Todd's business. While Isiah made a trail from my car down the street, Dominique held the lighter and waited for him to finish.

Once Isiah finished and stepped away, Dominique set fire to the gasoline then they ran. They didn't have to stick around and watch. They would drive by while everybody else did the looking.

The flames grew out of control. They got so bad that they climbed mom's bricks all the way to the top of the house.

"Cinnamon! Mrs. Johnson! Get the kids and get out the house! The car is on fire and it's climbing your bricks. Your house is gonna catch on fire!"

hollered Mr. Duce from across the street. He feared for our lives and he wanted to rescue us but he knew he couldn't. All he could do is call 911 and watch until they came.

I jumped up to the sound of Mr. Duce's voice. I knew it couldn't be a dream because I smelled the gasoline too good. I looked up and saw flames outside mom's window. It felt like an oven inside the room. The heat was too intense and I had to think fast.

"Mom lets go! Get out the house!" I screamed. "Somebody set the car on fire." I grabbed my kids and Shalina's baby and we all ran out the back of mom's house, barefoot and half naked. We didn't have time to do anything but run.

We stood on the corner of the block and watched the BMW go up in flames. I didn't care about the car. I was grateful that we were alive.

"The rotten dogs. Whoever it was," frowned mom. She could only pray for the person that did this to us.

"I'm glad the house didn't catch on fire," I said. When I looked at my babies in their underwear, I cried. Then I thank God once more because some people weren't fortunate as us. Some lost everything they owned because of things like this and we only lost a BMW, something that could be replaced.

"Mommy fire," said Lil Job.

"Yes baby fire."

Luke stood amazed. When was all this gonna end? He thought. He only wanted to live a normal life. He wanted so much to be a kid, free from all hurt and pain, but it wasn't happening. Somebody wanted to cause us misery. Somebody didn't want to see us rest. Somebody was too jealous of nothing. Somebody was caught up in anguish and misery.

While the fire department came and put the fire out, neighbors stood on their porches gossiping. Some never liked us anyway so it was funny to them. It was just a matter of time for something else to go on in our household. We were entertainment for them but they didn't know what was going to hit their doors.

As I stood and watched, I could only wonder who had it out for me. I had so many enemies that it wasn't even funny. Girls and niggas hated me for different reasons and I only wanted peace. I stayed to myself and didn't tend to other people's business so why did they continue to mind mine? Whatever grim I committed, I would have to answer for it. People didn't have to continue to kick my name around because I didn't do it to them and I had reason to.

PEOPLE

On the outside looking in,
not knowing the pain, I had to sustain.
Not knowing about the nights I was put to the test,
trying to deal with the loses, that was put to rest.
Not knowing about the aching heart, of not being able to touch or feel,
my loved ones, whose lives, were snatched for real.
Not knowing about the tears that I constantly dropped,
trying to accept the fact, of what I could not stop.
Not knowing how it felt to be ridiculed, accused and blamed,
wishing the pain would all stop and no more shame put to my name.
Wishing only to be stronger and dying to live longer.
Wishing all the lies away,
so I constantly prayed, knowing peace was near
and sorrow would someday fade.

"Who does this vehicle belong to?" asked the Fire Marshall.
"Cinnamon," hollered Mr. Duce. "They wanna see you."
I walked up the street to the Fire Marshall.
"Hi," I said to the Fire Marshall.
"Is this your car?" he asked me.
"Yes," I answered.
"Do you know who did this and why?" he asked.
"No."
"Well, they apparently put gasoline on your car and set it on fire," he said.
"Yeah." After he took his report, my family and I sat around talking until the sun came up. The BMW was a beast. It was still standing strong after all it had been through. I took some photos and whatever wasn't burnt from the car then I walked in the house drained.

The following week I went straight to the auction and purchased a 1988 Chevy Celebrity to get around in. I couldn't depend on other people and I was staying as my sister's spot paying rent until I figured out what to do next.

As soon as I pulled the car into the block Todd pulled up.
"I heard about what happened to your car. Are you cool?" he asked.
"Yeah. I'm fine," I said.
"Can I see you later?" he asked.
"I'm chillin'," I said as I reached in the back to unfasten Lil Job from his new car seat.
"Do you need anything?" he said.
"No."
"Nothing. Let me take your car and get it detailed," he said.

"Okay." Todd parked his car in my space then he sped off in my squatter. I couldn't let that offer go. The inside of my squatter was horrible. It smelled like old wet dogs, the steering wheel was coated with backed up dirt from years and the seats were worn down. I knew Todd was gonna hook my car up.

Once Todd got back with my squatter I was finished cooking dinner. He asked if he could stay to eat some of my roast chicken with cornbread stuffing, macaroni and cheese, fresh string beans and candied yams and apples; one of my favorites and I said, "yes."

I kindly made Todd a plate then we sat and talked our relationship over. I was kinda lonely but I wasn't about to play his games.

After eating desert Todd walked me to my room. The kids were sound asleep so he could stay for a little while but he had to be up and out before they got up in the morning.

After undressing Todd and I jumped in the shower together. Something I hadn't done often, if at all. After caressing each other I jumped out first. I had a change of heart.

Before I could reach my room Todd fell before me, sucking my pussy in the middle of the floor. I couldn't believe this young boy. He was trying to turn me out so I could stay. He really wanted me. I leaned against the wall until he finished. My legs were crippled. I couldn't move. I was a part of the wall. Todd grabbed my hand and put me gently in bed then we made love until I came three times.

Early the next morning I got up and called the insurance adjuster about my car.

"Hi, Mr. Cummings. This is Cinnamon. I haven't received anything from you concerning my claim," I said.

"If it was a ten thousand-dollar car Ms. Johnson things would be different. But we're talking about a fifty thousand-dollar car here. My car doesn't even cost more than ten thousand dollars. This isn't a regular claim. First of all, it's arson. And we have to see if you set your own car on fire," he said.

"That's bullshit! Why would I set my own car on fire? I'm not in debt. I just got the car. The car wasn't a month old. I loved my car. Why would I want to set it on fire to collect the money? I didn't have to pay for it if I didn't want it. This is crazy," I said, hysterically.

"Another thing Ms. Johnson, this took place in a high risk area and you were supposed to be living in Atlanta and this happened here," he said.

I couldn't believe this motherfucker of a different race. He definitely sounded bias to me.

"I don't care where it happened. I'm insured and I did move to Atlanta with intentions to stay. I just had unfinished business up here that I had to take care of. And besides, my family lives here so I can come and go as I please. You can't tell me what to do."

"I'm not saying that but you don't have your own address in Atlanta. You have your friends address and your kids aren't enrolled in school down there."

"I just got there. Things take time. And school wasn't in session for them. I see where you're going with this and I'm not gonna debate with you any longer. You are looking at my race, my financial status and the area that I come from and where this all took place, so I'll have my attorney talk to you. I wish to discuss this no further," I said angrily then I banged in his ear. "Old fucker! He's just mad because he has a cheap car and I don't. People in the work place are just as bad as people on the streets. They look at all the material substances instead of the issue at hand."

"Do you need my lawyer?" Todd asked.

"No. I'm straight. I have an attorney." I called my attorney of twelve years.

"Mr. Barringer please," I said to the secretary.

"Hold on. Is this Shalina or Cinnamon?" said his secretary.

After all these years she still can't tell us apart.

"It's Cinnamon."

"Hi, Cinnamon. Hold on."

"Hey sweetie," he said, picking up on line one.

"Hi, Mr. Barringer."

"Whatcha' have for me?" He asked.

"My car was burned and my insurance company doesn't want to pay," I said.

"Your car was burned. You're fuckin kidding!" he said, all emotional. He knew me all too well and he loved my family and me.

"No, I'm not. Somebody set it on fire in front of my mom's. I just got back in town and while I was sleep somebody put gasoline on it and set it on fire."

"Oh, sweetie I feel so bad for you. How are the kids?" he asked.

"They're fine."

"And mom?" He said.

"She's fine, too."

"And the rest of the family?"

"Everyone is fine."

"You have been having so much bad luck," he said, reflecting back to all that I had been through since he'd known me. I held no secrets from him. He was one of us.

"I know and that's why I moved. I just came back because I had to take care of a few things, and the insurance adjuster acts like I wasn't supposed to be here. And he said because it's a fifty thousand-dollar car and arson is involved, they have to investigate further because I might have done it."

185

"That's bullshit honey. Don't worry about it. Come see me first thing in the morning. You know these insurance companies are such rip offs. Come see me. I'll take care of it. Bring me your policy, all your paperwork to the car and pictures, if you have any."

"Thanks so much."

After the continuous phone calls, letters and arguments to the insurance company; Mr. Barringer decided to take it to court. The insurance company simply didn't want to pay and they wanted my yellow ass in jail for arson and fraud. I had no one to turn to but God.

I joined the neighborhood church where Shanee from down the street from mom's was the assistant Pastor and Tammi that went to school with my brother Micah was the Pastor. Mom had left our family church to join Pastor Tammi's church since her girlfriend was going there. She heard they were doing good things in the name of the Lord but Micah didn't like either one of them. He thought Tammi was after our money and he didn't trust her and he knew Shanee was full of shit. She was nothing but a manipulator. She's the one that gave Micah his first dick suck and mom knew nothing about it and she taught me how to smoke when I was only eleven while giving me dance lessons in her basement. She wasn't right at all.

For weeks I learned plenty under Pastor Tammi's ministry even though they weren't right but God could fix the worst person and make them new. Reading Gods word gave me intellect and I could only thank Him for my new family. They warfare and prayed with me about my car situation. And I moved out willingly on Gods word. Paying my tithes was a must. Giving a love offering when God put it in my heart was done. Whatever God said, I did, especially when it came to the pastor. She got my last, if need be. She got the sunglasses off my face, if she wanted them. She got whatever. She wasn't like the other pastor at Mighty Works Ministry. She showed me love, but she couldn't replace the pastor from our home church whom I loved dearly. We knew him from early childhood and I would always consider his church, my home church. A man after Gods heart is truly what he was.

Once Pastor Tammi saw the teaching ability in me, she asked me to teach bible study and I accepted gracefully. It gave me so much insight. I learned more about myself and God through this experience. I now understood why the young always clung to me.

After Sunday service I called Mrs. Jackie again to see if she had a change of heart about my son and nothing changed. She still didn't want to be a part of his life so I gave up the good fight. I tried to uphold my promise to Job but I had to let go. God told me to. He also told me if I wanted to do right and continue to teach his word, I had to give Todd up too because I was living in sin. I was committing fornication and I couldn't teach his children and I wasn't living right.

I dialed Todd's number to let him know I had to cut things off with him again and this time for good. I wasn't about to go to hell for him.

"What! How are you gonna cut me off?" Todd said, angrily on the other end of the phone.

"I have to," I said. "You can come get your things or I'll give them to Nancy to give to you."

"Don't give my things to nobody. I'll come get them. I'll continue to give the church money too. I know I'm not living right so this is my way of paying God back for all my wrong," he said.

As I walked the floors singing my Christian hymns, Todd pulled up on his Kawasaki Ninja 900 and tooted the horn. I knew he wasn't coming to get his things on his bike. He came to see if he could persuade me to stay with him and I wasn't bending. I wasn't about to break my promise to God.

I walked on the porch with dazzie duke Gap jean shorts on, a demin waist shirt and silver Gucci clogs. God was still dealing with me and my dress attire. I hadn't given it all up yet. I was committed, but I still wore revealing clothing at times.

"What's up Shorty?" he said, smiling through his helmet.

"Nothing. What's going on?" I asked. "Are you here to get your things?"

"Not yet," he said.

"Well, I need to go to the bank. Can you give me a ride?"

"Sure. Hop on," he said while passing me his helmet. I put the helmet on and jumped on with him. Todd revved his engine then we pulled off. Todd got two blocks up and a car pulled out of the parking spot on 74th Street and made a u turn our way. I closed my eyes and prayed. I could do nothing but brace myself from what I saw coming.

God sent my angels down to camp around me. The devil wanted Todd and me dead but because I was a child of God, doing His will, He couldn't let it be. I belonged to Him and it wasn't my time yet. The car smacked us and sent us twenty-five feet high then we hit the ground.

Todd and I landed in the oncoming traffic lane six feet apart busted up, bleeding and unconscious but I could hear voices around me talking, I just couldn't respond. I even heard the tow man Willie that I knew from the neighborhood but I couldn't say a word to him. He cried because he didn't think I was going to make. He got on his phone to see if somebody could get a message to my family.

Most of my hair was wrapped around the front tire of Todd's bike and some of it laid not far from my body. I had road rash, cuts and bruises all over my body while Todd bled internally.

Finally the ambulance came and the paramedics put braces around our necks, then they put us in the back, side by side and sped off to the nearest hospital.

At the hospital hours later my family, pastor, church friends and a few neighbors surrounded me with prayers, thanking God for my life. They didn't know how they were going to tell me Todd didn't make it once I came through.

Once the clock struck twelve, I woke up to my family. My boys' eyes were so swollen that I didn't know who they were. Mom smiled with joy after seeing my eyes open again. She didn't care what I looked like. I was her daughter and she loved me the same.

"Todd didn't make it," she said, while rubbing my fingers. I closed my eyes and blacked out again. I didn't want to deal with the pain of losing another friend. I couldn't take anymore. Why me? I had enough pain already.

Out of the hospital days later, but scarred physically and mentally. I put antibiotic ointment on my scars, I bandaged them up, then I limped outside to face reality. I had to or it was gonna hurt me in the worst way. I was a big girl. I was strong. I couldn't hide from the truth. It was, what it was and I couldn't change it.

After seeing motorcycles and cars drive through the block, I left a puddle of tears on the steps and went inside. I couldn't get away from what hurt me the most. I sat on the sofa to read the word of the Lord, my bread for the day, my refuge and strength, my rock.

The phone rang and I answered it slowly.

"Hello," I said.

"How are you baby?" asked Larry.

How did he find out? "I'm fine," I said.

"No, seriously. I heard about your accident," he said.

"From who?" I asked.

"One of your mom's church friends called Melissah's grandmother for prayer and Melissah told me," he said.

"Oh. I'm doing okay."

"I'll be in Philly this weekend. I have a fight," he said.

"Really," I said.

"Yeah. Do you feel up to coming?" he asked.

"I'll come."

"Okay. I'll call you when I get there okay," he said then we hung up.

Chapter 2
Falling Short
"Cinnamon and Daniel"

The end of 1995, one month later. I sat outside enjoying life. The insurance company finally gave up the money they owed me for my car but I lost big time in lawyer fees. I ended up with twenty gees plus another twenty thousand from the motorcycle accident that Todd and I had. I wasn't at Pastor Tammi's church anymore. Micah was right, she drained me for a lot of cash because I was faithful in giving. Some saints were no different from some sinners. It was a whole lot of back biting, jealousy, envy, and greed, going on in the sanctuary. I was accused of things I didn't do. I was judged because of what I wore. I was simply the talk of the church. I couldn't take it anymore.

A CBR pulled up and stopped in front of me. I really couldn't stand motorcycles anymore after what happened to me so I turned my head the other way. From the corner of my eyes I could see brown, strong hands removing the helmet slowly so I turned my head back their way. Beautiful hazel eyes stared straight through me. I could do nothing but hold my breath. The man was gorgeous. His skin was the color of fine cocoa. His smile was soft and warm. He had deep dimples too and I loved dimples. "Can you take my number and call me?" he asked, passing me a paper from his fresh Guess jeans. I looked him up and down only to find a white sock covering one of his fresh Timberlands.

"He's cute," I thought, chuckling to myself. "I don't know. I might give you a call."

He smiled and said, "What's your name?"

"Cinnamon."

"That's cute. Please try to call me," he smiled, looking like a lost puppy wanting food. He revved his engine and pulled off, popping a wheelie on the block.

"You see that mommy," smiled Job.

"That was decent. I like that bike," laughed Luke.

"Yeah. Me too," I said then we walked in the house to help mom rearrange her furniture. Something she often did.

After helping mom I sat on the sofa and pulled the paper from my pocket. I didn't even know his name.

"Oh, Daniel" I said as I looked at the paper closely. I could only think about how it felt to be in love again. It had been three years since Job's death and I was still in love with him. I had relations with Todd and Larry but I didn't love them. I was really missing something in my life. Nobody could replace my Job and I had to accept that.

A week later I drove to the King of Prussia mall in my new 1996 Honda to buy Christmas gifts for the boys. The mall was flooded with shoppers so I would do Macy's for them for a few outfits then I would return on another day when it wouldn't be so busy.

After charging my Macy's card to the limit, I ran into the guy Daniel at the exit and he was happy and disappointed at the same time. Happy to see me again but disappointed that I didn't bother to call him so he gave me his number again and we parted.

On the way home I really felt good for a number of reasons; I wasn't driving that beat down squatter anymore, I was doing extremely well in college with a 3.75 GPA and I had a little bit of money to hold me off until I graduated. I was doing my thing and God was blessing me tremendously. My professors loved me and they would give high recommendations to the Medical school for me. I had so much to be proud of.

At home I unpacked my bags, fed the kids, then I reached in my purse and pulled Daniel's number out and beeped him. Five minutes later the phone rang.

"Did somebody beep Daniel?" he asked.

"Yes I did. It's the girl from the mall," I smiled through the phone line.

"What's up baby?" he smiled, from ear to ear now. He didn't think he was gonna hear from me.

"Nothing," I said, laying across the sofa with a koolaid smile myself.

"Do you have a boyfriend?" he asked, getting straight to the point. He watched me through the years when he was just a little young boy on the steps when Des and his youngins hugged the block around his way. And he knew Luke too. When I used to drive through his side of town to pick Luke up, he just wished he was a little older because he dreamed of a girl like me. Someday Luke would be out the picture and he would get me. He was young but he was willing to go all out for his.

"No. Why?"

"I just wanted to know," he said with a bigger grin now. He finally had an opportunity to get me.

"I'm sure you have a girlfriend," I said, twirling the phone cord between my fingers.

"I do, but we're not together right now," he said. His girl lived two blocks from me and they dated for six years and I never saw him a day in my life. And if I did, I didn't recognize him. His girl was his age so we definitely weren't from the same era but she knew who I was very well. In fact, she knew my entire history. While I was ripping the streets doing my thing with my girls, she was still in private school and couldn't go far from home. Her dream was to grow up to be like me.

"What do you mean? Either you're together or you're not," I said.

190

"No, we're not, I guess," he said. His girl took him through so much. He looked out for her generously while she was away in college and he was just an average working guy but she wanted it all. She wanted things only a hustler could buy her and he wasn't a hustler. He hustled off and on but it wasn't much. He wasn't getting any real money. He was just getting enough to make ends meet and to make sure she was straight while away. He didn't want to be too big and hustling wasn't his forte. He loved his job at the Morgue and his family was financially stable so he didn't have to make hustling his main priority. He did it just to do it. He was tired of being looked at as a mama's boy. He wanted some people to think he worked hard for his when he actually got help from his loved ones.

"How old are you?" I asked.

"I'm twenty-two."

Damn! "You're young," I said.

"I'm not too young for you," he assured me.

"Yes you are," I said. What was I to do with another young boy? Todd and I weren't on the same level although the young boy had it going on in bed so I knew Daniel had to have the same energy. They say the young boys could fuck til you dropped and I didn't mind that. I had a whole lot of energy too and I hadn't had any in a while.

"How old are you?" He asked.

"I'm twenty-eight."

"I've dealt with older women than you," he said.

"Oh, really."

"Yeah, you can teach me something," he said

"What can I possibly teach you?" I asked.

"You're older so I know you can teach me something," he said and he was sure. He watched how I had the niggas I dated twisted. He knew Luke, Wayne and Job loved me and he heard Todd say I had the bomb pussy so he knew I had tricks.

"You can probably teach me something," I laughed as I thought about the nights I had with Todd's young ass. I really missed him too. *May all my peoples rest in peace.*

"Can I take you out?" he asked.

"I don't know. I'm really not supposed to be talkin' to you."

"Why not?" he wanted to know.

"I'm just not. I'm saved and I'm not supposed to talk about doing anything ungodly," I said. Although I wasn't going to Pastor Tammi's church anymore, I was still practicing living right and I visited my home church often.

"I just want to take you out. That's all. I don't want anything else. I'm not talkin' about sleeping with you or anything," he assured me.

191

"Yeah, I know. But one thing leads to another. And I saw you with your kufi on. Are you Muslim?" I had to know because if he was, we were definitely on opposite pages. We would be unequally yoked.

"Yeah. My aunt's boyfriend is one and he has me practicing the religion," he said.

"Well, that's even worst," I said with disappointment.

"Why?" He asked.

"Because it's only one God and we could never date because we are unequally yoked," I let him know and besides, I had a thing against Muslims because of what they did to my Job. Although brother Mike and his brothers escaped the law and none was charged with Job's death, I knew they were responsible and they would pay someday. God would definitely punish them for their sins if they didn't repent.

"It's not that serious. We can still be friends," he assured me.

"No doubt. We are gonna be friends and you can visit my church sometimes," I said.

"Okay. I don't have a problem with that," he smiled and he was sincere. He'd do anything for sweet me.

1996. Daniel and I became inseparable once he put his thing down. I wasn't going to mess with him once Stella interrupted one of our phone conversations but when she called me out of my name, I had to give her a taste of her own medicine. It was a woman's thing and she had to deal with what she dished out.

We had one of the biggest snow storms since the eighties and it was lovely. The kids, Daniel and I were trapped inside his apartment having the most fun. Daniel played Nintendo with the kids while I cooked and while they slept, we made passionate love and I got pregnant with his seed, something I wasn't ready for. It was too soon in the relationship but Daniel wanted me to be his BM so badly. No other had a baby for him. Stella claimed she was pregnant and miscarried while in school but he never knew the truth. Now twenty-two years young and expecting his first child was something to be glad about. In fact, he hoped it happened. From the first day he made love to me, he knew he wanted me forever. He always loved me but I had bomb pussy. I could cook my ass off. I knew how to treat a young nigga and I wasn't with him because of his money because he had very little. He was an average working man working at the morgue and he didn't hustle. Something I was proud of. I loved him for him and we could definitely build together because I had my own; my own car, credit and a couple dollars because I told him so and I was generous when giving when we went out. With Stella, he had to pay for everything, down to her double mint chewing gum that's how petty she was, but with me, what he didn't have, I picked up the tab or I would simply let him pocket his money and pay.

Two weeks into my pregnancy I chose to have an abortion because I couldn't take Stella or the sickness anymore. It was too much for me to deal with at once. Stella tried everything to get Daniel back and although he loved, supported and wasn't leaving me for her, he felt bad about hurting her so some things he didn't know how to deal with but Daniel did tell her I was opposite from what she said I was. I was the sweetest, most lovable person in the world with beautiful children that loved him and he was going to die one day so why not die with the woman of his dreams and she flipped out and tried to commit suicide. She could dish it out, but it was hard to consume.

Daniel cried, begged and pleaded with me not to have an abortion. He even asked to marry me and would convert from being a Muslim to a Christian so the baby wouldn't be confused because I told him that we were unequally yoked, but I still refused to have his child. I was tired and my mind was made up.

I pulled up to Luke's school at 8:45 a.m. to drop him off only to notice Daniel pulling up, too. *Damn! There he goes. I have to duck him. I can't let him see me.* While he got stuck in traffic, I dropped Luke off at the entrance then I pulled off quickly to get away from him. If he could plead with me one last time, it would be no abortion for me. I needed one last tear. Daniel didn't catch me so I headed straight to the bank and withdrew three hundred dollars out for the procedure then I drove to the clinic in guilt.

Although I was in the same clinic, I aborted Job's baby in, I was nervous and scared. I really couldn't fathom me or my decisions. How did I get so comfortable with abortions? I never even considered abortions when Luke was living.

Daniel called every abortion clinic in Philly and finally found out where I was so he came down to beg me once again not to kill his baby and when I refused to see him, he threatened to blow the clinic up.

I couldn't wait for the doctor to call me back because Daniel was making the situation harder on me. I really couldn't block his anger out and I wanted to back down but I was stubborn. I really thought I was through with him.

Once the procedure was over, I ran out the clinic in tears. I wanted my baby back but it was too late. I felt worse than what I felt when I aborted Job's baby because I promised I'd never do that again and I did.

I listened to *Yolanda Adams* tape the entire ride home. I didn't know how I was going to look into Daniel's face again but I knew I had to because he wasn't going to walk away without an answer. He pleaded with me and I totally disregarded his and my baby's feelings but thank God our baby was in God's care just like the other children I lost and aborted.

Later in the evening I tried to sleep but it wasn't happening. Daniel was hurt. I was hurt and only God could fix it because Daniel didn't know if he could ever forgive me for allowing the doctor to suck my baby into a machine. My baby cried while its tiny bones were being broken and its skull was being crushed. My baby only wondered what it did to deserve such pain and not be given a chance at life but it would have no more worries once in heaven.

A month later Daniel and I tried to work our differences out but things weren't the same. He was confused. He didn't know if he wanted Stella or me.

Daniel left me home while he drove six hours to see Stella at college. Once he got there he found out she was cheating all along with a bunch of different dudes but because of what he did with me, they accepted each others past with plans on starting over.

Once Daniel hit the highway to come back home, he realized he couldn't just leave me so he planned to keep both of us. He would deal with me on an everyday basis and Stella whenever she came home to visit.

I sat outside enjoying the warm breeze weeks later. Things definitely changed with Daniel and me again regardless of our talk. He gave me my VCR back and he did it to me the night before like it was our last love session. He put it on me so decent like he wanted me to have something to remember him by. I had to know what was going on.

I picked up the cordless phone and dialed his place. Stella answered on the first ring laughing and my heart dropped. I got the shock of my life. *Oh, no she didn't.* "What are you doing there?" I asked her.
"Who's this?" she smiled through the phone. She knew my voice as well.
"It's Cinnamon. You know who it is. Can you put Daniel on?" I asked.
"Daniel get the phone," she hollered into the bathroom.
"Who is it?" he asked.
"It's Cinnamon. Just get the phone."
"I'm in the shower. Tell her I'll call her back," he said.
They must have just got finished fucking.
"He said he'll call you back," she giggled.
"Can you tell me one thing?" I asked her.
"What is it?" she said.
"What are you doing there with him?" I asked.
"I been here."
"Since when, I just left him earlier. I stayed with him last night. I know we had our problems and I hurt him, trying to spare your feelings, but what's going on between y'all?" I said.
"I know about everything y'all have been through and I don't care. I'm back now and he's my man," she said with all the confidence in the world. She knew how to get what she wanted.
"Oh, really," I said, holding the phone in disbelief. Accepting him with her wasn't happening. It just couldn't be.
"Yes."

"Okay. When I hear it from him, then I'll believe it," I said.

She put the phone down and walked to the bathroom. He was gonna tell me something as far as she was concerned. She ran that relationship. He came to the phone lost for words. He didn't know where to start.

"Are you back with Stella, Daniel?" I asked.

He held the phone in silence.

"Are you back with her? Just tell me so I can go on," I demanding to know. He owed me that much.

"Yeah."

My heart dropped to the floor. I wanted an answer, but I couldn't stand the truth. He played me. He got me back really good. Yes, I hurt him, but I thought I had enough reason to do what I did and I was wrong. I thought they deserved each other and really I wasn't ready to let go. I was trippin' all along. I was in denial. He was for me.

I hung up the phone and called Daniel's cousin Tee. She and Daniel were tight and she knew everything about him.

"Hello," she said.

"Why didn't you tell me Stella and Daniel was back together?" I said.

"What!"

"I called him and she answered. I just left him this morning. I stayed there last night. He had been acting funny since I got the abortion and I kept asking him and he wouldn't tell me until she answered the phone today," I whined.

"I don't care about her. I blame her for starting all this trouble between you and him. I feel like if it wasn't for her, you would still be pregnant. She wasn't paying him no mind until she found out about you and then she wanted him so bad. She been doing her thing. And he told me he found out she been cheatin' on him. I can't believe him. I'm gonna lay him out," she said and she was serious. She couldn't stand what Stella stood for. She was a gold diggin' whore who wanted to drain her cousin mentally and financially.

"It's cool. Don't say nothing. I did it to myself. I should have never killed my baby for nobody or no reason. They're meant to be together," I said.

"No, they are not. She doesn't care about my cousin. She means him no good. He never started paying his bills until he met you because she always wanted something. And she never cooked for him. She always wanted to eat out. She only wants to spend his money. She can care less about him. And she used to hang with his girlfriend before her. Did you know that?" she said.

"What!"

"Yeah. That's why I don't like her. She talked about you knew about her when I know you didn't. Daniel did that to be smart, but she used to hang with Vicky and then she started messing with him behind her back. So even

195

if you did know, she's getting back what she did. And she's always talking about somebody is ugly. She calls all his girlfriends ugly. She tried to call you ugly and I told her she was trippin'," she said.

"She said that. And I think she's cute. I give credit where it's due," I said, being honest.

"But she doesn't. And I have seen my cousin do wrong. He was still in love with Vicky when he started messing Stella and she was so sweet. She hung in there til the end because she loved him so much. He was in love with both of them at the same time, but Stella wouldn't let go either. That's why you were crazy to let him go for her. She wouldn't have done it for you," she said.

"I know."

"And don't give up now. That's what she wants. She's just up here to be smart. She knows he loves you. And if you give up, she's gonna get the last laugh," she said.

"Well, I'm too old to play games and he told me out his own mouth. That was enough for me."

"She was probably threatening him or something," she said.

"I don't care. I'm through. I'll talk to you," I said. I was hurt and needed to sit back and think.

"Alright."

I got up and walked down the street to the corner store. I had to do something to keep myself busy or I was gonna lose it. Job got a bag of Herrs' chips, a Nantucket and a pack of juicy fruit gum, then we headed back up the street with me thinking about Daniel and Stella every step of the way. A black Pathfinder slowly pulled up to catch my attention.

"Oh, my God," said a deep voice from the Jeep. I looked closely. The voice sounded familiar, but I wasn't sure. Tank jumped out the Pathfinder slowly with a koolaid smile.

"Is that little Job?" he asked, pointing to Job. "I know it has to be, looking just like his father. He has his square head, his nose and eyes."

"Yeah, that's him. Job look. That's your long lost godfather," I pointed. He looked at Tank and smiled. They connected immediately. Job's cousin Claude jumped out the passenger side with a big grin. He had to make his presence known, too, because he was family so that stood for something special.

"What's up Cinnamon?" he asked me.

"What's goin' on?" I smiled. Seeing them at a time like this, took my mind off Daniel momentarily.

"Look at little Job man. Don't he look just like his dad?" said Tank, hitting Claude on the arm.

"No doubt. What's up bull?" said Claude.

"Job that's your cousin Claude. He's your dad's first cousin," I explained. Job looked at Claude with warmth, then he smiled to let him know it was all good.

"Damn girl! You still look good," smiled Tank as he looked from my hair to my feet.

"Yeah, right," I smirked, brushing him off.

"No, I'm serious," he smiled harder.

"It's been three and a half years since I saw you last. Why did you disappear like that?" I asked out of concern, knowing we had a lot to discuss. It was pieces missing to the puzzle and I had to know some things. I just had to know. For years things remained blank. Now was the time to put things in order.

"It was so much going on. I'll talk to you about it. Where are you staying?" he asked.

"Right here."

"Can I call you sometimes?" He said.

"Sure."

"Do you have a man?" he asked quietly, hoping Claude wouldn't hear.

"Not really, I guess I had a friend, but he's back with his ex now," I said.

"Don't sweat it. You can have anybody you want."

"It's one thing to get anybody and it's another thing to be with the person you want to be with," I said.

"I feel you, but you can do better if a nigga doesn't want to be with you," he let me know.

He got acquainted with Job then we exchanged numbers and they left. Tank still had a way of making me feel like somebody. I knew from what he said that I should not let what went on between Daniel and me, affect my life. If he didn't want me, then it was time to move on, but could I let go was the question.

Tank was definitely back. For days he walked me through the pain of getting over Daniel. And all the hurt of losing Job resurfaced, too. We never had the chance to talk about Job and we made up for lost time. The fact that he did get married hurt me because Job and I weren't able to do what we wanted to. I was actually jealous to some degree but Tank's marriage came to an abrupt end so he was pushing back up on me and I couldn't do it. We didn't do it before Job and now that he was gone, the same thing applied. I still had the utmost respect for Job and I knew he wouldn't want me to see his friend, but Tank felt differently. He felt like he could treat me better than anybody out there and Job would want me with him opposed to anybody else because he would know how to treat me and it was better for me to see his friend than some other cat.

I talked to different people about the situation and everybody had their own opinion. My family felt like me. "It was a no, no, with no questions

197

asked." But the car dealer, which was a good friend of mine, who sold me both of my BMW's, felt like Tank.

He said, "When I die, I want my best friend with my wife, because he will know exactly how to treat her and I rather her with my good friend than anyone else."

That just didn't sit well with me, although I knew Tank would treat me good. I could never cross that line.

Although I kept turning Tank down, he was a man and trying to get me couldn't hurt. That didn't mean he didn't respect me because he had mad respect for me and I had respect for him, as well, but he couldn't live with himself if he didn't try again. And Daniel didn't like the thought of Tank coming back around. Job was almost four and Daniel never saw Tank until now so it was jealousy between everybody. We were all stuck.

Tank called waking me from my sleep on a Friday night. R. Kelly's cd was playing in the background and he was so on point. Eating, sleeping and thinking was an issue for me. I knew it was time to move forward but I couldn't go on without Daniel. It was crazy to be in a love triangle and I had to break it because nobody was going to look out for me but me.

Kenny Latimore, Tank's artist and a couple other artists from Philly were performing downtown and Tank wanted me on his hip. The night would simply be perfect for him to show me what he was made of. He certainly changed through the years and now was the time to get me back.

Tank picked me up at eight o'clock and we headed straight to the club. Inside the club all eyes were on us. Everybody greeted Tank and me like we were a couple. And we did the all black thing; he did the black slacks with a black shirt and I did a black skirt with a matching shirt and a pair of black patent leather and silver studded cut out heels that made my legs look sexy and my calves look tight.

Tank spotted his female artist at the bar with her friend who sang, too, so we joined them. After a few drinks, we danced. After a few dances, we sat down to enjoy the rest of the night. Tank couldn't believe he actually had me out dancing, drinking and having fun. He never saw that side of me. He was feeling me even more this night. I had all the ingredients he wanted in a woman. He looked me straight in the eyes and said, "You know I never took nobody I liked to a club with me."

"Oh, really," I smiled.

"Naw and it's pretty cool. I'm really feeling this. You look real sexy," he said, looking me up and down, licking his full, juicy lips.

"Thank you. You look handsome yourself," I said as I looked into his brown pretty eyes. I never noticed how pretty they were before. Tank really got fine with time. His whole attitude toned down a bit. He was never loud but he was so quiet, smooth and gentle.

"Thanks," he smiled. "Are you ready to go?"

"Yeah."

Tank and I said goodnight to everyone, then we left the club tipsy. Outside he opened my door first and I got in the Jeep, then he climbed in his seat. I leaned back to chill and he leaned over, putting his tongue in my mouth.

"What was that all about?" I asked in shock. He let the liquor pump him. If he was sober that wouldn't have happened. He never had the heart to make that move.

"I always wanted to do that and I never had the chance. You know you cheated me before," he smiled, while looking deep into my eyes. Tank asked me to drive but I wasn't in a position to drive either so he suggested we go to the Guest Quarters to chill until the morning. What could be a better outlet?

Inside the room Tank told me about the days and nights he spent thinking only of me but I could never see making love to him. It was no way.

Tank convinced me to share the king size bed with him. He made his move once again and I checked him for the last time. My devotion was to Job and Tank couldn't come between that. I loved Tank as a friend and I wanted it to stay that way. Besides, I was in love with Daniel too.

I walked around Daniel's apartment cleaning and cooking for him with his 31 Pacers Jersey on butt ass naked. We were back together again because Daniel thought about everything fully. I had more to offer him at the present time. I was older, maturer. I had money and he needed some of it because he wanted to hustle again so I gave him fifteen grand to do his thing.

I looked at my wrist later in the evening. *I forgot to put on my Rolex after I showered.* I called Daniel to tell him to put my watch up because I knew his boys would be dropping by through the course of the night.

"Hello," said Stella.

My heart dropped. *Oh, no she's not.* "What are you doing there?" I asked politely.

"Who's this?" she asked, knowing who I was.

"You know who it is. Where is Daniel?" I asked her.

"Daniel get the phone," she said, throwing the Sony phone I just purchased him on the floor.

"What's up?" he asked.

"What is she doin' there?" I said, fuming.

"She just came to get something," he said.

"Get what!" I said hysterically.

"Motherfuckeer don't play with me. Bitch, I'm gonna fuck you up," said Stella in the background.

"Tell her I'm on my way," I spat.

"Don't come up here. I'll handle it," he assured me.

"Okay," I said then I slammed the phone down and paced the floor. I couldn't wait for him to call me back. Five minutes later the phone rang. I jumped and said, "Yes."

"I'm sick of your shit, bitch," said Stella.

"Look. I'm not gonna feed into your bullshit. And you don't want me to come up there," I said.

"Come on you dirty bitch," she spat.

"No, you didn't go there. Dirty," I said. "Please!"

"Come on mam. You have to leave. He wants you out so you have to go," said security to Stella.

"I'm not going nowhere. I'm not leaving," cried Stella.

Daniel picked up the phone and said, "Cinnamon, security is here. Let me make sure this dumb bitch gets out because she's fighting them. She won't leave. I called my mom and she's on her way."

"Okay."

I walked back and forth and forth and back. *Hurry up Daniel, call back or I'm coming up there.* "Old stupid bitch," I shouted aloud.

I waited for fifteen minutes and when Daniel didn't call back, I snatched my keys off the dresser and went to his place. I was stooping to Stella's level and Daniel thought I was the maturer one.

In the back of Daniel's complex Stella and I exchanged words but she never came down and I didn't go up. We just said what we had to say while Daniel stood in between. He wasn't about to let us fight.

Back at home I waited for Daniel to call and finally the phone rang.

"What is it?" I asked, thinking it was Daniel.

"You know she tore up everything in here. She broke the new phone you just got me. She broke all my china. I had to hit the bitch. She tried to cut me and everything," he said.

"Oh, yeah. Why are you putting up with all this? What is it? Don't tell me you still feel sorry for her," I said.

"I do, but I want to be with you. We been together for six years. It's not easy for her to let go," he said.

"And you either, right?" I asked.

"I moved on already. But she keeps making it hard," he explained.

"No. You're making it hard because if you don't want to be with her, you would just cut her off. She can't make you do anything," I said.

"She'll be leaving to go back to school in one week. Can you just bear with me until then?" he begged.

"Are you asking me to accept her? I thought she was finished school," I said.

"She is. She just has to go down there to take one class," he said.

"Sure. I'm not going for it. It's either her or me," I said then I slammed the phone down and he called back five minutes later.

"You are so understanding. She is trippin'," he said.

"Where are you going with this?" I asked. I needed to know.

"She just called me trippin'."

"She said she's gonna kill herself again right?" I asked sarcastically.

"Can you call her and talk to her?" he had the nerve to ask me.

"Are you serious?" I asked.

"Just talk to her so she can leave us alone. If she thinks you don't want me, she'll stop trippin'," he said.

"So the hell with me and compromise with her, huh! Oh, spare her feelings and forget mine. You are crazy," I said.

"You are the bigger one here. And we're gonna be together. I just don't want no trouble from her."

"Alright. Give me her number," I said, finally. He gave me the number and I called her.

"Look Stella. You can have Daniel. I'm tired of the games and I don't want to be bothered anymore, okay."

"I can have him! I can have him! Bitch! I already have him! He's my man. He don't care about you. Why would he want a black widow?" she spat.

"Is that the only thing you can say about me?" I asked her.

"Oh, don't go there bitch," she said.

"No. You are the only bitch. And since you want to be smart, it's on. I thought about it. I'm not giving him to you. In fact, I never left him alone. I was doing him and you a favor, but I'm not anymore. I'm not gonna give up on him like I did before. It's me and him baby," I let her know. She hung up furiously. She wanted so badly to kick my ass, but instead she wrote on all the cards that I gave Daniel and she walked them to my house and stuck them in the doorway for me to read whenever they were to be found.

For the week Stella stayed home she gave us hell. While Daniel and I hit the mall buying him Susan Picadi shoes, Versace slacks and a shirt for the comedy show and me Gucci knee boots, the bag to match and a black dress, Stella came through his window and got him for thirteen thousand dollars before she hit the highway to go back to school. "He's gonna pay for what he did to me. He wanna fuck with that bitch. Okay, now who's gonna have the last laugh," she thought, putting the money in her favorite Coach bag.

When we got back to Daniel's place he didn't want to accept the fact that Stella got him and that made me pissed even more because I knew better. I was so tired of his blindness and stupidity. Even if he thought she did it, he wasn't about to let me know.

Daniel pulled our brand new Limited Jeep Grand Jerokee with all the luxuries into Fridays parking lot. Things couldn't be better for us. The kids and I officially moved into his spot and Stella was gone. Everything was harmonious but I knew I couldn't trust her as far as I could see her because women were shiesty. They'd break up a home in a minute and men were no different. They didn't mind wrecking homes either. We're selfish beings at times. We may not want something but we don't want anyone else to have it either.

Stella's girlfriends noticed Daniel and me by the bar so they walked over to start a conversation up about Stella. They hated us. We were simply the talk of the town at the moment. I was the black widow in most people's eyes, but Daniel didn't care. He checked whomever he had to when it came to someone saying something about me.

"Yeah girl, Stella is so happy with her new man. He just got a new contract with the Portland Trailblazers. I'm so glad she left that loser. Life couldn't be better for her right now," said one while sipping on the cheapest drink Fridays had to offer.

"Who you tellin'," laughed another.

Daniel's face dropped a bit after hearing what they had to say. The reality was, they both cared about what each other was doing and her girlfriends were losers. They had nothing better to do, but worry about Stella, Daniel and me, instead of focusing on their own lives. They were straight air heads.

Although Daniel had no control over what they did or said, I was pissed. I hated the fact that these bitches were in my business. I wanted so badly to say something, but I couldn't. I wasn't about to feed into their hands. They were miserable, wicked bitches with no lives. They looked for trouble. *I had their girls man.*

Two weeks later Stella was back home to pull at Daniel again. She couldn't accept the fact that we moved together, we had a new Jeep and we were in love. She couldn't understand how he could throw everything they had away for me. She was young, in college with no kids and I was old, with kids and my life was over with as far as she was concerned.

Stella ran up and down Daniel's mom block naked begging him to take her back but he was happy with his new family. He acquired so much with me that it wasn't worth going back to Stella but he did sympathize with her. She made him feel bad but he couldn't keep hurting me either. He was so confused. As long as Stella was gone, he was cool.

Early in the morning I jumped in the tub to wash all my pain and tears away. I wanted to forget about Stella and Daniel. I wanted to think about Daniel and me.

I sat in the tub soaking in warm water and Victoria's Secret Pear bubble bath. As I washed, tears fell again. I tried to keep silent, but Daniel heard me so he walked in.

"What's wrong?" he asked silently.

"I keep thinking you're gonna go back to her," I sobbed. He picked up my wash cloth and washed my back as I wept.

"I'm not leaving you. We're gonna be together," he promised me. The phone rang interrupting the mood. He dropped the wash cloth and said, "I'll be right back."

He walked back into the bathroom moments later and said, "Stella wants to know if she can come over to talk to us."

"Sure."

He walked back out to talk to her. I rinsed off and got out the tub. I waited and I waited in the bedroom. I could only think about what she wanted to talk about.

Finally the doorbell rang and Daniel let her in. Daniel and Stella sat in the living room and she gave him pictures of them that they took at her graduation. After they talked and agreed to their break up, she knocked on the bedroom door to make peace with me.

"You can come in," I said as I finished straightening up. She opened the door, she took a couple of steps in, then she stopped. Her heart sank into the plush beige carpet as she looked around at all of our pictures and how I put my touch into the place. Daniel's bachelor spot looked like home for a change. She knew it was over for her and Daniel. His place was never home for him and her. What he and I had was different and something special. We had a family, something she could only imagine.

"I sat up all night thinking, I'm going to let go. I won't bother you and Daniel anymore. I care, but I know it's over between us. We'll never get back together," she said, holding the tears back.

"Never say never. I said the same thing. Who knows how this is gonna end up. I know I'm tired, just like you," I said.

"I'm serious. We've been having problems for a long time now. And I'm letting go," she said. I held my tears back knowing it was hard for both of us. We both loved him. We both wanted to be with him, but we didn't want to share him. And I knew he loved both of us too.

Stella and I talked a little longer, then she left out the room. She gave Daniel a big old bear hug at the door then she walked away from their six-year relationship. She knew it was best for her to let go but she really wasn't prepared for the outcome. She never imagined him to let her go for somebody like me. She hated what I stood for. Through the years not only did I maintain, I managed to take her man and she really couldn't hate because she messed with married men, dudes with girls, but she kept Daniel on a leash and the black widow got him. *Haha*!

I got the kids together, then we jumped in the Jeep to go to Great Adventures. Daniel's favorite place. He loved roller coasters.

As we pulled out the driveway, Stella pulled out, too, staring at us.

203

"He must really care about her and her children for real," she thought as she rolled her window down to let a little air in.

"I feel bad for her, but she had her turn. I want him and it's my turn now," I thought as I blasted the air condition and off we went into the sunset.

Chapter 3
Trials and Tribulations
"Surviving the Game"

Daniel pulled the Cherokee into the lot and paid the parking attendant ten dollars. Keith Sweat was performing at the Spectrum and Daniel wanted everybody in the city to know we were tight and I was definitely happy again with my family.

I couldn't believe the crowd once we walked through. Everybody in the city was out, old and young. Tank and Claude stood by the concession stand with their clique talking about how Lil Job stayed right under Daniel's wings and they had the nerve to be dressed alike, Daniel, Job and Luke. They rocked Polo sweat suits in different colors.

Tank and Claude didn't like the situation, but what could they do. Job was gone and my life had to move on whether they liked it or not. Other people that knew us had something to say, too. People talked about our family unit. Some couldn't believe the match. Either he was too young for me or I was too much for him. Or why was he with the black widow came from the girls who wanted him and hated me. Even some low life niggas said, stupid shit like, I was bad luck or a widow or I didn't deserve to be happy. Some niggas that wanted me that I brushed off was simply mad that I was with a young, handsome nigga that they didn't think had enough for me. They thought their possessions meant more and seeing me with an average, working dude with just enough to make it, made them wonder. *Stereotyping a person is a mother. People expect too much sometimes when it's not that serious. Money or possessions don't make love go around. Love does.*

We took our seats three rows from the front of the stage. In minutes Keith had everybody up singing and dancing. I pressed my butt up against Daniel while the show went on. Keith was all our favorite, down to Lil Job. Job knew most of his songs from listening to Daniel and I pump his cd's regularly.

At intermission Daniel and Nancy walked the hallway to get something to eat and drink and just to see what was what. They had to see what was going on. While Nancy kicked it with a few niggas that she knew, Spice and Chocolate stopped Daniel at different times to kick it with him and simply to be nosey. They both liked Daniel and they wanted to know more about me and his relationship. They wanted to know if we were really as tight as things looked. Chocolate was just released from the Women's Correctional Institution in Delaware County and Candis would be home in a matter of months.

Rose and Chocolate were tight these days and Rose put her two cents in the conversation about me. Everybody had something to say. Chocolate and Spice were indirect with their shit, but Rose was straight forward and Daniel laid her out. He let her know she wasn't shit so she had no room to talk about me just because Job chose me over her and from his knowledge, it wasn't any choosing. Job simply didn't take her seriously. And it was a completely different story with me. He wanted me and he had a family with me and that's how that went so she needed to get over it and let it go because he was gone and life went on.

Daniel walked away loving me even more. Little did people know that what they were saying and doing just made Daniel and me closer.

After the show we took pictures in the hallway with everybody looking on. I even had to laugh at what I saw. Nobody had changed. People were still doing the same things in our city, hating, gossiping, fronting for the next person and back biting.

The following week, fight night to be exact. Daniel and I sat over his boy Ja's house drinking Cristal, watching the fight on his 72inch screen tv with their other boys. It was so strange to be sitting amongst Des and Greg's young boys. I actually watched them grow. They went from flunkies to running around trying to emulate the YBM but their money wasn't that long. Their cars were leased in different girls names and they were paying fifteen hundred dollar car notes to keep up with the fad. They spent their cop money to look good for one night. They were getting a little paper but their shit was raggedy. They were so slimy. They would sell their souls and kill their own for a dollar. Times were really hard for these young black men. They had no loyalty to each other. It was sad. The fight went twelve rounds and everybody parted, going separate ways.

For weeks Daniel took lost after lost. Things just weren't going right with his hustle. Some days he went to the casinos to get back what simply couldn't be gotten. He lost more there, than on the streets.

Finally Daniel got frustrated with hustling so he decided to just chill. Nothing was working for him. His job would be his main focus. He'd put in mad hours to get a decent check. He had to make ends meet. The family had to eat.

Week after week things got tight. Working with no extra money coming in was hard, but we managed for the most part. I still had all my bills and Daniel had his and we had bills together. Spending my stash with no income coming in on my part, took away from me, but it was all good. I knew how to maintain and I wasn't trippin'.

It was my birthday and Daniel wanted to do something special for me. He knew I adored Maxwell so he got us two tickets to see him at the arena in Camden. After getting the tickets Daniel called me on the burn outs he had gotten us and told me to be ready by six thirty so we could roll out.

Luke was with Ramina's kids so I took Lil Job with me to my new hairstylist ReRe. ReRe was Katima's stylist so she turned me onto her and I started going there even though the other stylist in the salon she worked at didn't like me because of BigLuke. They talked trash like all the other haters about my past and the *men I chose to love* but ReRe would get her own shop soon so I would eat the gossip until then.

After ReRe gave me a regular, I hit the highway to go to the mall. I didn't like asking Daniel for much these days because things were tight. He still gave me hair money and small change if I needed it but I held most of my own weight. I figured I could boost me an outfit like old times. I still had my duct tapped Gap bag in the trunk hidden. I could never let Daniel see that bag because he would trip. He never knew about that part of my past. He knew I was saved so he never imagined me to steal.

Inside the department store I looked at the selection then I took what I wanted to the dressing room and began stuffing. I wasn't that comfortable with the store because I didn't know it too well, it had been a while since I got down and I had my baby with me so I was very nervous. I knew I was out of order but the devil told me I could get away with it after I thought about putting the things back a few times.

I grabbed Job's hand and walked toward the door only to notice store security on my heels. I was caught. They knew what I had but I wasn't about to let them grab me with my baby. I had to get away.

I picked Job up and ran to the car. After throwing the bag in the back and him in the front, I sped out the lot with the under covers on my back. They were bound to get my black ass. I came to their county with that ghetto bullshit. They didn't think so.

Once I saw the marked county police pull to the light looking for me, I panicked. I went over the median, through the light and was out. I did 70mph in a 35mph zone. I had to get rid of the evidence.

"Job throw the bag out the window," I asked my boy and he was only five. He didn't know why I wanted him to get rid of the bag that I pulled from the back seat that he'd seen in my hands inside the store earlier.

"No," he said.

"Job please. Please take the bag and throw it out for mommy," I begged.

"No," he said, leaning back in his seat. The sirens roared out of control. They were on my ass and I still wasn't about to stop. I was going to make it out of their county safely. I drove like a mad woman through the county. I didn't know anything about where I was. Had that been my area, I would've been out of there but it wasn't so I was lost without a clue. I had three county police on me within ten minutes. They were bound to catch me. I had twelve hundred dollars in stolen merchandise, I ignored their request to stop and I had them on a high speed chase tearing up cars while in pursuit. They were gonna get me one way or another.

I cried and prayed as I drove. I was so guilty of what I had done. I had my boy on a mission and his life was at stake. How could I ever forgive myself of such a horrific act? I knew better. My boy didn't deserve this. I knew I was never locked up before and I didn't want my boy to see me cuffed either. I was in a state of confusion. I had the good and evil speaking to me.

Finally after another five minutes I realized it was nowhere to go. I got caught in traffic, I hit two other cars trying to bump my way through and the cops had the road blocked ahead waiting for me. I slowed down and drove. Once I reached the road block I noticed the cops with their guns pointing toward me.

"Stop the car!" they hollered. "Stop the fuckin' car!" I pulled into the lot on the side and turned my engine off. You would've thought I killed someone or robbed a bank for a hundred gees or so. They rushed my car and searched it to find the bag of clothes. Thank God they didn't find Daniel's gun under the seat that I didn't even know about. He left it there the night before.

"We have to take your boy too," they said, before cuffing me.

"No. Please don't take my boy. Please don't let him see you cuff me. Can I call someone to come get him before you take me and cuff me?" I begged.

"No. You can call someone to come get him as soon as we take you to the station," the officer said.

"Baby. It's okay. Everything is gonna be fine. I'm gonna call aunt Ramina to come get you when they take us to the station because the bad girl gave mommy the bag and it was things in there that didn't belong to me," I said. Job looked at me and knew better. He wasn't dumb by far. My baby had plenty of sense and he'd never forget what I did. He would take it to his grave and he would even tell some people only because he was a kid.

"What about the hamsters mommy?" he asked with tears in his eyes. We had the hamsters with us that we had just got food for in the morning. Luke and Job took their hamsters everywhere we went.

At the station the officer hand cuffed me to the metal chair after I called Ramina. They gave Job sodas and writing material to keep him occupied until Ramina came. I wanted to beat my ass so badly. It was seven o'clock and Daniel was pacing the apartment floor wondering where I was. He knew something wasn't right because I wasn't answering my phone, it was my birthday, he knew I loved Maxwell and I was never late. I was an on time person.

Ramina arrived to the police station around seven forty with Luke and Nancy. I cried and told her everything I did. She couldn't believe I went out like that on my birthday just because I didn't have money to buy what I wanted to wear to the show. My boosting days were over and I never really knew how to or had to so she didn't understand why but she loved me so she would only be in my corner.

At home Ramina called Daniel and told him what happened then he came to her house and they called Ramina's lawyer friend. He was a well known respectable Muslim lawyer so Daniel loved that. He felt better with him than anyone else.

I sat in the cold cell pissed. I heard stories about jail before but I had never been. I was hoping no one else would come through and have to share the cell with me because it was one hard, iron bench and one toilet. I would never show my ass for a stranger.

Thankfully I had the cell to myself. It wasn't much going on in the county so only one other person got locked up that night and it was a man so he had his own cell next to mine. I couldn't sleep in the cold, lonely cell. I cried and cried because I had never been separated from Daniel and the kids since we moved together and I was sleeping in a cold cell on a hard bench all by myself while Daniel and the kids cried for me too. I never went to the bathroom either. I held my pee the entire night.

I watched the sun come up. One officer named Hook came to my cell and slid a McDonald's pork bacon, egg and cheese on an English muffin with an orange juice in my cell. First of all, I didn't do pork, it was too cold for orange juice and I just wanted to go home. I didn't want any food. I wanted my kids and my man. I sat uncomfortably for twelve hours. I wanted to leave.

"Do you know what time I'm gonna see the judge?" I asked the officer through the bars.

"Soon. Pretty soon," he said as he walked away.

"What did you do?" a voice said from next door.

"I stole something?" I said. "What did you do?"

"Oh, I was drunk and beat up my wife," he answered back.

"Oh," I said then I walked back to the bench while he kept talking. I didn't want to keep discussing my business. I wanted to leave.

Finally I saw the judge, my bail was paid, then I walked to the front to meet up with Ramina, Daniel, the kids and the lawyer, Mr. Muhammad. Everybody was up bright and early to see about me. Nobody could rest. Job and Luke had swollen eyes but they were so happy to embrace me. They hugged me so tight. We hadn't seen too many jail houses where I was the criminal. Daniel looked at me and shook his head. He had mixed emotions. He was so upset because of what I did but he loved me and he knew he wasn't going anywhere. And he was glad they didn't find his gun.

Mr. Muhammad charged me seven thousand dollars for the case because he thought Daniel was a drug boy but he was a working man. And he promised me no jail time because of my clean record. The most I would get was two years probation and the least I would get was ARD, where I would do community service, counseling, and pay restitution.

At work one of Daniel's co-workers stepped to him and turned him on to something sweet. Daniel rejected at first, then he thought about my lawyers' fees, things he wanted us to have and how good it felt to spend and not worry about where the next dime was going to come from so he accepted the offer and they put their money together to cop some coke from his co-worker's people up New York City. It was all good and what could possibly go wrong. Whatever they bought to the table, the people would match it. It was an opportunity for both of them.

Trip, after trip, after trip, up the big city paid off something nice. Daniel and his co-worker Brandon were doing it big and Ja got jealous instantly because his money was messed up and it was an insult to him to have to cop from Daniel. He always wanted to be the one on top out of their clique. Nobody could out shine him so he had a plan for Daniel. He called Daniel and asked him to meet him out of town at one of his girl's houses to sell a brick to two dudes up there. It was a way for him to make money off them and to get Daniel, too. Daniel asked me to take the ride with him because he didn't trust the situation and he had nobody that he could trust to ride with him so I agreed because I didn't trust Ja anyway.

We took the two-hour drive on the turnpike to meet Ja and Braheem upstate around five o'clock in the evening. I stressed my concerns the entire ride and I begged Daniel not to deal with Ja after this. His little money was not important. This dude cared about nobody, but himself. He was a cold-hearted man with no remorse. Killing, stealing and destroying is something he thrived off. He lost no sleep after he did his dirt. He could smile at you like he did no wrong. He could kill your brethren and you would never know it. He put the s in snake. This nigga wasn't to be trusted. They say he killed his own dad to get insurance money so I knew what he would do to Daniel.

We pulled the Jeep next to Ja's Benz coupe in the driveway then we went straight in through his girl's two car garage. Daniel told me to stay put in the family room while he and Ja took care of business upstairs.

After staring at the white walls for twenty minutes, a disagreement broke out above me. I tuned in, but I couldn't hear the details of the argument so I waited for Daniel to come downstairs and say something.

Seconds later Daniel walked downstairs fuming. He passed me a plastic bag and said, "Here. Hold this bag. Don't give it to nobody. I'll be back."

I closed the bag containing twenty-six thousand dollars and sat back nervously, praying and asking God to let us get out of there in one piece because I knew something wasn't right. My gut never lied.

Ten minutes passed by and no Daniel. I looked around at the big screen tv, the stereo system playing Tupac and the sliding glass doors. I looked back at the steps that Daniel had come down.

"Something isn't right. He better hurry up. God what am I doing? I'm so sorry. I know better. I said I wasn't gettin' involved in this lifestyle again. If they come down here, I'm running out the back," I thought to myself.

Braheem came downstairs and flopped on the mint green leather sofa across from me while Ja and Daniel remained upstairs. Ja actually told Braheem to bound and gag me while he took care of Daniel but God wouldn't allow Braheem to touch me. I looked at him and turned away.

Tussling went back and forth across the floor above me. I looked at Braheem again.

"What's goin' on up there?" I asked, expecting an answer.

"They're trippin'," he said, like it meant nothing to him.

"Aren't you gonna see what's goin' on?" I said. He looked at me and didn't move an inch. I grabbed the bag tight and ran upstairs.

I walked through the kitchen and burst through the door to find Daniel with a twenty two pistol in his right hand.

"You tried to shoot me with this little gun motherfucker! I could have killed you if I wanted to," Daniel said to Ja in disbelief while the corner of his eyes landed on me. "My girl had to see all this. Yo' man. You ain't shit! You did this over a couple dollars. That's fucked up."

"You shouldn't of had her here, then she wouldn't of seen this," he said coldly.

"No. I'm glad I had her here because if she wasn't, I would probably be dead. I didn't trust the whole thing, but I didn't think you would try to shoot me," he said, then he threw the gun on the bed. "Come on baby, we're out."

"You ain't shit Ja," I said walking quickly behind Daniel while watching his back. Daniel opened the door and I followed him out slamming it as hard as I could behind me.

We jumped in the Jeep and the tires kicked up the dirt and rocks quickly. We never bothered looking back once.

"I told you not to trust him," I said while looking at the road and him.

"I know," he said. "I know."

"What happened?" I asked.

"He tried to burn me out that money. The boys he had there to cop was nuts, so he thought he could get them and he did. I let him keep the extra money from that, then he tried to get more and I took it. That's when I tossed you the bag and when I went upstairs to get my keys, the nigga pulled the girl's gun from the drawer and tried to shoot me. But he can't beat me. I took it from him. If I wanted to, I could have killed him, but we grew up together," he explained as if that meant something.

"Yeah, but he didn't care about that. He was gonna shoot you," I said.

"I know. That's because he don't care about me the way I care about him," he sadly said. He really loved Ja and Ja only cared about Ja.

"That's what I've been telling you."

We pulled up to the front of the complex hours later. The sun was down and the street lights were shining bright. Daniel parked with Ja on his mind. He still couldn't believe he crossed him and they grew up together. He knew he wasn't shit, but he never tried him before.

Daniel turned the engine off and we ran up the steps quickly to get inside. Daniel unlocked the door. I took everything off in the living room but my white Gucci knee boots. I had the black and white ones and I loved them. They made me feel like a sexy beast. Daniel dressed down to his Polo briefs. His thighs were tight and muscular so he could do the briefs. A skinny nigga couldn't pull that off though. They would look like JayJay from Good Times.

Daniel and I blessed the entire apartment. We went from room to room with our game. We just appreciated each other because of what Ja pulled. The situation actually made us tighter and Daniel's sperm met my egg. Another life was conceived.

Four days later Daniel parked the Jeep in the back of the complex after coming from the super market. We gathered all the groceries and took them inside.

As I stood in the kitchen preparing dinner minutes later, the doorbell rang.

I yelled, "Daniel get the door! I have chicken in my hands."

"I'm in the bathroom!" he hollered back.

I put the chicken down, washed my hands quickly, then I walked to the door and looked out the peephole.

"It's some guys. I don't know who they are," I hollered back to Daniel. He walked behind me, looked out the peephole then he opened the door.

"Did somebody drop a beeper?" said a boy no older than thirteen, holding a Motorola beeper up for us to see.

"No," said Daniel.

One guy ran down the steps, another one ran up the steps and all three of them rushed the door. Daniel, Lil Luke and I pushed the door forward in shock. Danger lingered in the air and we felt death. These fools were not playing. If we didn't get the door shut, it was over for us. The bandit that ran down the steps stuck a machine gun between the door to stop it from closing and they burst in.

Two of the bandits chased Daniel straight to the room with guns to his head telling him to give up the stash and the one guy stuck a gun to Luke's head while I begged them to leave us alone. It was nothing we could do, but pray. They had us and we were unprepared.

As I lay on the carpet, I unfastened my Rolex watch, I took my diamond rings and bracelets off and threw them under the sofa along with my Gucci shoulder bag. It was no way I could unfasten my diamond pendent without him noticing so I left it on. I couldn't let them get everything we had. If they wanted it, I wasn't gonna fight for it, but if it could be hidden that was good, too.

While the bandit that ran the show stayed in the room with Daniel, the other one came out and put his gun to my head. He noticed my six carats diamond pendent around my neck so he grabbed it and I choked from the stress of the pull. It wasn't about to pop easily.

"Please leave us alone. Y'all can have the money," I cried.

"Leave us alone. Don't kill my step dad. Don't kill us," Luke cried. They could care less about our cries so Luke knocked the gun away from his head making them madder.

"Shoot them!" said the masked bandit, holding me. "Shoot the motherfuckers! Fuck them!"

All prayers went up. I saw my life flash before me. I couldn't believe any of this. I couldn't believe they had us and it was nothing we could do. I only wondered what was going on in the other room. I couldn't hear Daniel and I didn't know where my baby Job was. He was silent through all this. I could only imagine the worst and hope for the best.

God heard our prayers and sent angels down to protect us once again. It wasn't our time yet. He was the only one that could stop Satan's attack. These people were working for the enemy.

"God please don't let them kill my children, none of us, but not them. Don't let them die because of my mistakes. God please," I prayed then the third bandit ran out the room with the money finally.

"Let's go," said the guy holding me to the other guy holding Luke.

"Wait. Let me shoot them," he said, pointing the gun back and forth, from me to Luke.

"Come on. We got the money," he said. They ran out the front and Luke ran in the room crying, "Daniel. Daniel. Are you dead?"

Daniel ran out the room in tears. He was more upset that he couldn't do anything. The money wasn't an issue. He just wished he could've put his hand on his gun, but they pushed him in the dark closet so he had no win. *Our own, taking from each other.*

"Are y'all okay?" he asked with tears rolling down his face.

"Yes. Where's Job?" I asked. I wanted to know where my baby was.

"He's in here mom," hollered Luke. I walked in the room to find Job playing the game like nothing happened.

"Are you okay baby?" I asked, picking him up. I kissed his cheeks so hard. I was so grateful that God allowed all of us to escape death.

"Yeah," he answered.

"He doesn't know what happened," said Luke.

"Yes I do. I seen them faggots. They had guns. They tried to shoot Daniel," Job smirked.

"Oh my God! My baby knows. I have to get myself together. These kids have seen enough. I have to change my life. I can't keep exposing them to this kind of danger. It isn't right," I thought to myself.

"I found the money just in time. They were gonna kill all of us. I couldn't see in that dark closet," cried Daniel. "Yeah and I couldn't find it at first. As soon as he pulled the trigger, I found it."

"Did he say anything to you when y'all were back here?" I asked.

"No, why?" he said.

"Because he didn't say anything when he ran out either. The other two said something, but he didn't. It was Ja or somebody you know or Braheem. They didn't want us to hear their voice for a reason," I said.

"You're right," he agreed.

We packed our clothes and headed over to Daniel's mom's house. She said we could stay with her until we got another spot. Daniel's place wasn't safe anymore. It was a slight chance that they would be back, but we couldn't risk our lives. We had to get away. That apartment wasn't home anymore.

We were at Daniel's mom's for two nights and he was staying out late. I knew he was grown but I worried about him so I checked his messages. Daniel gave me his code when Stella was tripping and although I never used it, I never forgot it either. "Hi, baby. It's Tanya. I was on my way to bed and I was thinking about you. I can't believe what happened to you the other night. I was worried. I wanted to make sure you were okay. Call me if you want to see me," a sweet and calm voice said.

My heart fluttered. *This nigga is cheating.* The other line beeped.

"Hello."

"Is Daniel there?" asked a male with a soft voice.

"No, who's this?" I asked.

"It's Ja."

"No!" I said and banged in his ear. I couldn't believe he was calling Daniel's mom for Daniel after what he did. I waited for a minute to calm down.

"Oh, dirty motherfucka'. He's cheatin' on me," I mumbled out loud then I called his beeper back.

"Yo' man. It's cool. Your girl is home. You can get with sis," said Ja.

I got butterflies in my belly. Somebody was gonna tell me something so I called Ja's house.

"Tell Daniel he can get with sis, huh!" I said to Ja.

"What!" he said stupidly.

"You heard me," I said and banged in Ja's ear for the second time to beep Daniel. Fives minutes later and no call back from Daniel so I checked his beeper again.

"Yo' man. Don't do it. Your girl knows," said Ja's dumb ass. He couldn't figure it out. Didn't he know I was listening to Daniel's messages? I called Daniel's beeper to leave a message this time.

"You have the nerve to be out there cheating after all we've been through. You are a rotten motherfucka'. I'm on my way to the apartment to get my things. You don't have to say anything to me. I'm through. And I thought you weren't speaking to Ja after what he did. I can't believe you. You are being stupid."

I took Daniel's mom car and drove through the deserted streets to the apartment in tears, minutes later. I was through. If Daniel wanted to befriend Ja and if he was cheating, he didn't need me in his life. I had enough. I was taking more than I had to.

Five minutes later I pulled into the complex. I turned the engine off in the middle of the street and put the blinkers on. I looked up at the apartment window only to find all the lights out. I got out with the keys in my hand ready to unlock the door. I skipped up the steps lightly, I listened first, then I turned the locks, and pushed the door wide open to stick my head in enough to see and hear anything. After a moment of silence, I stepped in.

"If I get killed coming up in here. I'll never forgive him," I said to myself while looking around the apartment to find the light switch. I found trash bags in the kitchen. I packed all of the kids and my clothes, then I walked back and forth to the car, throwing the bags in quickly.

Daniel pulled up and jumped out the Jeep, stopping me in my tracks.

"Why are you up here by yourself? And why are you taking your stuff at a time like this?" he asked.

"I heard your messages. Who the hell is Tanya and why does she know what happened to us?" I said angrily. I wanted an answer.

"She's just a friend," he said, pulling the bags out the trunk.

"A friend isn't gonna talk about she was thinking about you before she went to sleep and she was worried. I know the difference. And you were supposed to be doing something with a girl. I heard Ja's message too. I thought you weren't speaking to him," I said, putting the bags back in the trunk.

"First of all, I was skating with Tom over Jersey and I can speak to Ja if I want," he let me know.

"Yeah, you can. I'm not saying hold a grudge but use wisdom. You don't have to deal with him. He doesn't care about you. And if he tried to hurt you once, he'll do it again," I said.

"I'm not worried about him," he said. They both had motives. Ja's was to make sure Daniel didn't get too big and find out his connect. And Daniel's

215

was to keep his enemy close. He knew if he played Ja at a distance he wouldn't know what was going on, and besides, Daniel really had a forgiving heart. He had a soft spot for Ja's lying, dishonest, knavish ass.

"Fine! Do what you want. I'm tired," I said, throwing my hands in the air. I had enough. I was through with the whole thing.

"Take the clothes and go to my mom's. I'll follow you."

Five days later everybody crowded the big church on 61st Street. A friend of Daniel and Ja's got killed; which was Greg's nephew Shawn. Shawn was in his second year at Virginia State University, a place Ja and Daniel frequented often. Ja had girls all over. The city was still crazy and we were still killing our own over nothing. Not every black man did dirt. Some just got caught up in the streets and Shawn was one of them. He got killed over a crap game. *Another young soldier.*

Shawn's turnout was nice. His family put him away very well but people still did the same things. They acted like his funeral was a party. Girls stood around plotting on my man talking dirty about me and guys stood around trying to catch new pussy. Some things would never change but I was cool with my baby. He was enough for me. *It's one thing to cheat, another to take a side chick personal. And that's what happens a lot of times. Instead of dudes just cheating, they catch feelings for the chicks then it becomes a problem because they have two people they're caught between then and that can be dangerous. Keep your main girl or dude where they belong and keep the side kicks on the side and in their places. Me preferably, I like to keep it simple. I never liked sharing, especially not willingly.*

After the funeral Daniel and Ja dropped Sharon and me off to go sightseeing. Ja had to take Daniel to see some other chicks. He was never satisfied no matter what. He liked drama and he wanted the chicks to see how he and his boys played. He was nothing but a big front.

While I sat home waiting for Daniel, I listened to his messages. I was simply looking for something now. Worrying was one thing, but being nosey was another. I was now prying into his business. I was asking for trouble.

"Your next motherfuckeer! Ja and Braheem will be carrying your ass out the funeral home next. You stupid motherfuckeer! And the next time that bitch is gonna have you robbed for more money than that. I hate you. I hope somebody blows your brains out," said Stella.

I beeped Daniel and waited for him to call back. I was heated about Stella knowing anything that happened in our home. Daniel called back immediately.

"I heard Stella's message. So you're still talking to her," I said.

"She called me talking about she wanted to see if I was okay because she heard about Shawn. And then she asked me for money to get her hair done and I told her later because I was doing something," he said.

"And."

216

"And I told her what happened at the apartment."

"She doesn't know it was our money."

"She knows we're a team. That's why she's trippin'. And I was gonna give her the money for her hair because it was nothing but forty dollars. She's always talkin' shit, but she's the one beggin' all the time. She's still wearing those old Timberlands I bought her last year," he said.

"So you saw her" I said, picking my heart up from the floor.

"Yeah, I did. But it was nothing. I don't want her. And I'm not giving her nothing now," he said.

"Yeah well, check your friend," I said then I hung up upset. I wanted so badly to call and curse her out. In fact, I was mad at the whole situation. They were still kicking it from time to time and he thought I was stupid but I couldn't control what he did. I only wondered when she was gonna get tired and give up totally.

I was two and a half months pregnant and bleeding. Something wasn't right so I called the doctor then Daniel at work. I had to stay off my feet to save my baby. I was already taking medication to keep my food down and that wasn't working, now I was threatening a miscarriage. Life couldn't be more complicated and I wanted Daniel's baby more than anything. I wanted something Stella didn't have and my plan was working.

Daniel rushed home from work with Roger to see about me. Why was he hanging with Roger, I didn't know? Roger was a liar and manipulator. He was nothing but a back biting trouble maker. He dick rode niggas for anything and Daniel didn't need any new friends. He couldn't trust the ones he already had.

At the hospital I had all kinds of tests ran because my blood count was extremely high. I was pregnant with twins, triplets or not pregnant at all but I knew that was a lie because I was certainly pregnant.

After an ultrasound it was revealed that I was pregnant with twins but one didn't make it. I was sad and grateful at the same time, sad because I lost a baby but grateful that God hopefully blessed me with the little girl of my dreams.

Weeks later Daniel surprised me with a new place that he got in Roger's name. I hated the situation, but he did what was convenient at the time.

While I lay back on the sofa watching the kids play on a boring chilly night, Stella went down Daniel's job trippin' again. She got pregnant by a dude around the corner from Daniel's moms to spite him and once Daniel let her know again that I was his girl and he was happy with my sons, his unborn child and me, she smacked him in the face and threw things at him but he let it go because she was pregnant and he wasn't about to play into her hands like he always did. He laughed and left her by the curb crying. He realized she hadn't changed regardless of the time that passed by and she never would. She would always be crazy ass Stella to him.

217

Four months' pregnant. I sat in mom's room waiting for Daniel to call so I could get half the money for the bills and finally the phone rang.

"Hello."

"What's up?" Daniel asked.

"What took you so long to call?" I asked him.

"My uncle just left here talkin' about you," he said.

"About me?" I asked. I wanted to know what he had to say about me. *We're not the same age. Here comes the bullshit.*

"Yeah, he said his daughter told him that Luke and Job's fathers were dead. And you were bad luck. And how I shouldn't be messin' wit' you. He's not your age. I shouldn't have to hear about you in his conversation," he said, now irritated.

My heart sank into floor. I got pumped up and frustrated. My past would not let me live. People just wouldn't let me be happy. I couldn't fathom anybody around me. I served no purpose in others eyes. I was simply put here to be tormented. I was to be punished for the rest of my life because of what happened around me. I couldn't take anymore.

"He is sixty something years old, isn't he?" I asked, now pissed.

"Yeah."

"Why would he be worrying about me?" I wanted to know.

"I don't know, but I'm tired of the bullshit," he said.

"What are you trying to say Daniel?" I asked. "What the fuck are you saying?"

"Go head wit' that. I don't feel like it."

"You act like I did something to you. They started this argument. You knew I was gonna trip about you saying this to me. You know what I've been through. I don't know your uncle or his daughter. Every time I turn around somebody in your family has something negative to say, instead of being happy for us and furthermore, why the fuck is he in my kids' fathers business? What happened to them is none of his concern. I'm so tired of people blaming me for their deaths. Fuck your family. They don't have to worry about my child. If they don't want anything to do with us, then fuck them! We'll be cool," I spat then I slammed the phone down. I got up and jumped in the Jeep.

On the side streets I did 50 mph to get to his job to get the money and to get the load off my chest. It wasn't over until I said it was over. I was tired of everybody, including him. It was nothing but drama as long as other people intervened in our relationship.

I parked the Jeep in front of Daniel's job and held my breath for sixty seconds while the engine cooled down. I fastened my Gucci belt together to hold my Calvin Klein jeans up, then I jumped out and strutted into the sliding doors to page him to come to the front.

Minutes later Daniel hopped in the waiting area smiling, as if nothing ever happened.

"Let's walk outside," I suggested. We walked out by the phone then we began arguing about the same thing we had argued about minutes ago. Things got heated and we both lost our tempers. Daniel's mom walked out to calm us down, but we kept going.

"Well, maybe you did have something to do with all that happened to you," he said out of frustration. He hit me where it hurt. I tried to block out what I heard, but I only got flashbacks and I lashed back at him.

"You are no better than me, you drug dealer," I spat. He balled his fist in a tight knot and punched me in my right eye, knocking me to my knees. My Gucci sunglasses flew in the street and stars and darkness flashed before me. My eye swelled immediately. I put my left hand over my eye and my belly hit the cement.

"My baby! My baby! I don't believe you. You hit me! You hit me in my eye. I can't see. I can't see," I cried as I turned over with my right hand embracing my belly.

"You said that in front of my supervisor. You didn't have to do that," he said angrily. My hand felt the lump as it grew. I couldn't believe the man I was pregnant for.

Daniel and his mom stood over me like I was wrong. They didn't even care about their seed inside me. Tears fell even more after seeing this. I felt alone, out numbered and abandoned. I was all by myself with no one to turn to.

"I can't believe you. How can I go home like this? I can't get my kids with my eye like this," I sobbed. Daniel walked away and I scrapped the cement with my knees to get up. I looked at his mom inhaling her Newport 100's as if she didn't care. And if she did, she didn't act like it. He was her boy and I was nothing this night. She had to stick by her son. Whatever he did was right.

"You know that wasn't right. Are y'all happy now?" I cried, moving my hand from my eye so she could see what her baby did to me. I had to let her see what she was covering up. A lady with scrubs on walked over to me, "Are you okay? I called the cops for you. Let me help you up," she said, holding her hand out.

"No, I'm fine. I'll be okay," I said as I moved back. I was humiliated. Everybody on the job knew who I was. They saw me come and go. I ate lunch with Daniel. I picked him up and dropped him off most of the time. They thought we were such a cute couple and he did this to me. I was so embarrassed and hurt amongst anything.

Daniel's mom and his supervisor heard the lady so they grabbed my hands and dragged me across the ground to pull me to my feet before the cops came. Everything inside my purse, including a pocket knife I carried for protection, fell out and Daniel's mom picked it up. The cops pulled up and told them to back away.

"Are you okay mam?" asked the lady officer.

"Yes. I'm fine," I said.

"Who did this to you?" she asked as she looked around at all the nosey people standing outside gossiping. It was like I was the villain.

"I just want to know if my baby is okay," I cried.

"She came down here arguing with my son, then she pulled this knife out to cut him and he smacked her in the face," said Daniel's mom, puffing her cigarette, holding the knife up.

I looked at her and shook my head in disbelief. *Old lying bitch.* How could she?

"Do you own that knife mam?" asked the male officer.

"No, she doesn't own the knife," said Daniel, walking out the door.

"If you own that knife, we can arrest you," he said.

"That's not true," Daniel said, verifying the statement again.

"Do you want him locked up?" asked the lady officer.

"No. He didn't hit me," I lied. The officers helped me to the steps, then they questioned me over and over again while Daniel, his mom and his co-workers watched.

"I'm locking him up," the female officer said to her partner. She didn't stand for women abuse. Her husband beat her ass before she became a police officer so she didn't like the thought of a man hitting a woman.

"No, don't lock him up please. It was a big disagreement, that's all," I tried to explain.

"I can't let him walk away and your eye is swelled and bruised up like that. I can't," she said then she walked away with her partner following her. They cuffed Daniel and took him away with his mother cursing and carrying on. The other patrol car drove me to the hospital where they monitored the baby.

While I laid in the hospital crying for Daniel and my baby, he did the same in the small holding cell. We both could've prevented this but it was too late and I had to learn to change the things I could and accept the things I simply couldn't because some people would never change and accept me for whom I was.

Once the doctor told me I could go home, I called Tank and asked him to come get me. It was unfair for him to want me to lose my baby but he was hoping that was the case once I called because he still wanted me and when he found out differently, he was sad but he had to accept the truth. I was having Daniel's baby.

Tank and I had a heart to heart conversation on the way to Daniel's job to pick up the Jeep. He didn't agree with Daniel but he knew how women could get at times because his ex took him there a few times with her mouth and he knocked her to her knees even though he didn't want to. *It's natural to provoke someone and dangerous.*

Before I got out of Tank's van he wanted to know why I took what I took off Daniel and whom I actually loved more between Luke, Job and Daniel. I told him I loved the three of them differently but if I had a choice, I would've been married to Job because he was different from the other two. Job never put his hands on me and he never hurt me verbally whereas Luke and Daniel hit me more than once and they verbally abused me and that I couldn't take. Abuse took so much energy to consume and I didn't need that in my life but they were the *3 Men I chose to Love* so I dealt with a lot.

Back at mom's I stood in the mirror looking at what Daniel did to me. I had to come up with something to tell the children but I didn't know what.

I washed my face and jumped in the tub to soak my pain away. After drying off I slid into bed with the kids with my Gucci shades on. "I'll tell them I fell. No, I'll tell them I hit a pole running from a dog down Daniel's job. They know I went to his job. No, I'll tell them I hit my eye on the steering wheel when somebody tapped me from behind," I thought. After scrambling with my emotions, I closed my eyes lightly so I wouldn't put pressure on the bruised one. I rubbed my stomach, then I thought about Daniel in the cell again. Lord bless him.

The sun shined bright through the window pane, hours later. The alarm clock beeped and I jumped to my feet before anybody could question me wearing shades to bed. I ran to the bathroom to run warm water to wipe my eye. I stared in the mirror in disbelief, then I replayed everything that happened the night before as the water hit the bottom of the sink, along with a few tears. The bathroom door opened and I scrambled for my shades.
"Mom what happened? Who hit you?" Luke asked, standing in the doorway with tears in his wide, bright eyes. He couldn't believe what he just saw. It hurt him more than it hurt me.
"Nobody," I cried.
"Did Daniel do that to you?" he asked.
"No."
"Did he?" he demanded an answer.
"No Luke."
"I'm gonna kill him! I know he did that to you. I hate him!" he said, standing firm.
I messed up again. Whatever love he had for Daniel, I let my foolishness come between it. "It wasn't his fault. I started it Luke."
He turned to walk away. He didn't want to hear anything from me. I grabbed him by his arm and said, "Luke listen to me. Daniel loves you and your brother. He never meant to hurt me. It was a mistake. He didn't mean to

221

hurt me. We had a disagreement and I turned to walk away from him and I hit a pole."

"I don't believe you," he hollered.

"Please believe me. I ran into a pole. Daniel would never hurt mommy," I said.

Job walked in the bathroom and asked, "What happened to your eye mommy?"

"Mommy hit it."

"That hurts. Who hurt you?" asked Job.

"The bad pole hurt mommy."

I grabbed the two of them with a strong but gentle hold, then I squeezed them really tight, hoping they would forget what they saw. Hoping they would forget the nightmare.

I picked up the phone to call Daniel's mom again to see if they got him out and she acted nonchalant because I humiliated her and her son on the job.

Katima called to invite me to her boyfriend's party and I told her what happened but she insisted I be there because it was going to be nice and she needed her family to represent her.

Later in the evening I arrived to the party with my family and Ebony. Nobody noticed my black eye behind my dark Gucci shades or my belly. The dawgs were on my heels.

Terrance and Katima came over to our table holding hands.

"How's everything?" he asked Ebony, Shalina, Micah and me.

"Fine," said everybody at the same time.

Micah shook Terrance's hand.

"Get whatever y'all want. The bar is free. And it's plenty of food in the back," he said with Katima's head resting on his chest. Everybody thanked him, then they walked away to greet the rest of their guest. Terrance was a big willie up the north side of town. He had two bars and one insurance agency. He never dealt drugs but he did everything else illegally and he took good care of Katima.

"Are you okay?" asked Ebony, tapping my shoulder.

"Yeah, I'm fine."

"I can't believe Daniel," said Shalina.

"Oh, don't go there. What about the times you got smacked up?" I asked, defending Daniel although I knew he wasn't right.

"I'm not saying I didn't. I just can't believe him. How could he do that to you while you're pregnant?" she said.

"I provoked him. You know you can provoke a person to do things," I explained.

"Yeah."

"Is it that bad?" asked Ebony.

"Yeah, I don't even want to show you," I said. "Where's a phone?"

"It's one over there by the door," said Shalina.

I got up and walked to the phone.

"Hello," said Ms. Cathy in an irritating tone. She was tired of her phone ringing about nothing.

"Ms. Cathy, did Daniel call yet?" I screamed over the loud music.

"No."

"Okay, I'll call you in a little while."

I hung up and went back to my seat.

"Do you want anything to eat?" said Ebony.

"Not really."

"The jerk chicken is all that."

"Really. I'll have some of that," I said. Jerk chicken was one of my favorites. I walked to the back and got a plate. I sat back down thinking about Daniel as I ate. I left my food and went to the phone again for Ms. Cathy to tell me the same thing. I let an hour pass by, then I called for the third time.

"Ms. Cathy, I don't mean to bother you, but did he call?" I asked.

"No and it seems like you're having fun. Go 'head and party. Don't worry about him. Have you a good time while he's in a jail cell," she said sarcastically.

"In fact, I'm not having fun. I'm sorry this whole thing happened. I can't rest with him in there. I'll call you later," I said with tears rolling down my face. I slammed the phone down and walked back to the table to find everybody on the dark dance floor. I wallowed in my tears alone, picturing Daniel and me out there cuddled up. I always managed to do something wrong and everybody knew my business. I talked too much sometimes. What went on between him and me was nobody's business. I should've said forget the party and everything else until I resolved my own issues at home. My place wasn't there. Katima thought me being out was important. She wanted all of her family at Terrance's party, but it wasn't important to me. I should've sat this one out. My watch read 1:55. Shalina, Ebony and Micah walked back to the table tore up.

"Are you ready Cinnamon?" asked Ebony and Shalina at the same time.

"Yes."

The next day Daniel was released from jail but his family didn't want him seeing me anymore. They thought it was better for us to part but I couldn't accept that. I was having his baby. I needed him. What did they know about our bond and how could they be so selfish? We were old enough to work our problems through without everybody in our business. That's what got us where we were in the first place. If I could forgive him for fracturing my eye, then he could forgive me for him being in jail.

Inside our apartment it was cold and dim. Nobody had been there in days. The kids were so happy to be home that they ran straight to their room to play with their toys while I sat on the sofa and cried. I didn't know how I was gonna make it without Daniel but I knew I had to. I was a survivor and nobody could keep me down, not even the devil himself.

Hours later Daniel opened the front door quietly. How could he listen to his family and stay away from me when I was carrying something they could never give him? He tiptoed back to the room to check on me, he peeped in the boys room, then he jumped in the shower. I was so happy to hear water hit the bottom of the tub and Daniel singing Jigga's verses over and over.

Inside the room Daniel cried when he saw my eye. He really didn't know the depth of his blow. He knew he hurt me but he didn't know how bad and he felt like shit because not only did he hurt me, he hurt the children too and he promised to never do that again. We were his world and nothing should've come between us. He made up big time.

Weeks later things went back to normal, thank God. Daniel and Nancy traveled up to the big city, two to three times a week to cop coke. They opened different shops in their neighborhoods and money was pouring through nicely but jealousy had become stronger and deeper. With the game, came more money and more problems. *More money, more girls, and more problems.* He came home stressed more than he ever did before. He had a baby on the way. He had his job to maintain and he had the streets to worry about. He had to fight with his workers and the people that owed him money for what they bought. It was one thing after another, but he had a goal to reach. He wanted big money. He wanted a big house on a hill for the kids and me, another wheel and plenty of money in the bank for him and his baby. That was the *hood dream*. That was the goal they all wanted to reach and I hated the fact of my niece being involved in the street life, but she wouldn't listen to me. She and Daniel were close. They did everything together. Besides business, they partied, hung out all day and night, except the nights Daniel worked and on those nights, she was right there waiting for him and they'd come home together. I got jealous at times, but what could I do. They were tight and she and I had always been tight, so whatever we did as a family she was right there with us.

After three court hearings and no me, the prosecutor dropped the charges against Daniel for hitting me outside his job but that wasn't it. Some of his family members, his so-called friends, co-workers and a few girl associates, fed his head with a whole lot of bullshit, making him bitter toward me all over again. We had gotten over our hump and it was two months later and we were back to square one. They made him feel like he should've been mad at me for wasting money on an Attorney for the case and for having him locked up period. And I felt like I should've been mad at him instead. If I forgave him, why couldn't he forgive me? How could he let people on the outside influence how he felt about me?

I arrived to the courthouse for the third time by myself. The first two times Daniel was by my side but that changed with everything going on in our relationship. I stood with Mr. Muhammad and waited for my sentence.

By three o'clock I got my answer. Mr. Muhammad was a beast. He got me ARD. I would do community service at a boarding school for all girls. I would pay my restitution and fines. I would go to parenting counseling until the therapist thought I was well enough to stop and my record would be expunged in two years.

I left the courthouse grateful. God really showed me favor after what I had done. I learned my lesson if never before. I was never going to steal another thing. It wasn't worth it. Clothes would get old and I probably wouldn't wear them after the first two times anyway so it wasn't worth my freedom. What I couldn't afford, I wouldn't have.

I walked into the apartment to Daniel watching Bene Hinn. He was so guilty for not going to court with me and he gave his life to God secretly. He was touched like never before. He knew Bene Hinn was real and what he saw wasn't a joke. He healed the sick and crippled.

I got up with a new attitude early the following morning. With an, I don't give a fuck attitude. I washed my hair with Aveda shampoo and conditioner and I pulled it into a ponytail, then I told the kids to get dressed. I threw on a two-piece linen outfit, a pair of fresh white Keds, then I wobbled my fat ass out the door, leaving Daniel stuck in the house alone. I was tired of the bullshit.

"Fuck him! He better get out the best way he can. I'm tired of sitting in the house, crying and eating all day long," I mumbled to myself.

The boys and I jumped in the Jeep, we let all the windows down, then I opened the sunroof to let the warm, spring air and the smell of fresh flowers in. Luke popped in Biggie's new double CD, then we sped off into the sunset.

I hit the bank first to withdraw some money, then the kids and I hit the stores. I purchased Luke and Job a couple of short sleeved Coogi sweaters, two pairs of Jordans a piece, then I hit Saks Fifth Avenue to buy a pair of Gucci clogs to fit my fat feet, a new pair of Gucci sunglasses to match, and two linen pants outfits to fit my fat ass. Then we headed to mom's to catch the view.

Once the sun went down, I drove home only to find Daniel gone and the apartment organized neatly. Something Daniel hadn't done in a while so I knew something was up. I picked up the phone and pushed redial.

"You've reached Tanya. Leave a message or punch in your number."

My heart skipped a beat and I paused for a moment to catch my breath then I clicked the phone off. *Oh, he fucked up. Tanya. That's the same bitch that he said was just a friend.* I pushed redial again in tears.

"Tanya this is Cinnamon. Daniel's girlfriend. You can reach me at 700-6547. We need to talk."

I hung up and paged Daniel.

"You are a rotten motherfucka'. I came in and pushed redial on the phone and you had the nerve to be talking to a bitch from my phone. I thought you said Tanya was a friend. But I see you keep sweatin' her and who the fuck was you frontin' for? We haven't had that centerpiece on the table in months, now you wanna put in on the table for your company. I hope you didn't have a bitch up in here," I blurted quickly before the beep cut me off.

I stood in the kitchen floor fuming, waiting for Tanya or Daniel to call back. I was so mad that the black ceramic tiles could've broken. I opened the black Kenmore refrigerator and pulled chicken breast from the third shelf, then I slammed the refrigerator door shut.

"They might be together. That's probably why neither one of them called yet. He probably called her to tell her he was on his way to her house or something. I'm gonna fuck her up, if I ever see her. I know she knows about me. I swear. Bitches don't even care. They have no respect," I thought to myself. I cleaned the chicken, then I put it in the oven smothered with gravy. I boiled water for rice. Then I cut up some broccoli and threw it on the stove.

Finally the phone rang and I picked it up fast.

"Hello."

"Hi. This is Tanya."

"Hi Tanya. I came in and pushed redial and apparently you are the last person Daniel talked to. I questioned him about you months ago when you left a message on his beeper and he said y'all were just friends."

"Yeah, we are," she said.

"Did you know he had a girlfriend and I'm pregnant?" I said.

"I didn't at first," she said. "I met Daniel through Ja. Ja's girlfriend Sharon is a good friend of mine."

"Oh, really," I said. Sharon smiled in my face and introduced her girl to my man. *That's hoes for you, trickin', suckin' and backbitin'. Damn!*

"Yeah. She was the one that told me about you. Then I asked Daniel and he said you were his girl. We're just friends."

"Did you and Daniel ever sleep together?" I asked.

"No. He's just cool with me and my family. He stops by every now and then. I saw a picture of you in his Jeep. I told him he had a pretty girlfriend," she said.

"Oh, he comes to your house?"

"Sometimes," she said.

226

"And he had you in our Jeep?" I asked her.

"Yeah, but it was nothing. He said he can't wait until you have the baby. He loves you and your boys a lot. And he said you can cook really good. He's just upset with you right now because you had him locked up," she said.

She knew too much of my business. She was more than a friend to Daniel. *They were fucking friends.*

Tears rolled down my face and I said, "He told you I had him locked up?"

"Yeah. He said that's why y'all aren't getting along right now. He said he loves you, but he can't forgive you for having him locked up."

"Well, he didn't tell you the whole story. We had a disagreement and he hit me in front of his job. The police district is right around the corner and somebody else called. I didn't want him locked up, but they had to arrest him because my eye was black and I was pregnant. They couldn't let him walk away that easily. I begged them not to arrest him," I cried.

"It'll be okay. Don't cry," she said softly.

"No, you don't understand. He is obviously holding this against me. And it isn't right. I can't believe he really hates me for what happened."

"Well, don't worry about me. I won't mess with him anymore. I can tell you really love him. And I don't want to be the cause of y'all going through it."

She confused me.

"I thought you said y'all were friends."

"Yeah, we are. I meant, I won't call him anymore," she lied.

Her line clicked and she said, "Hold on a minute."

"Sure."

I fumbled with the phone cord while I waited. Seconds later she clicked back over.

"That was him again," she said.

"Who?" I asked.

"Daniel."

"Oh, he called you before you called me? He told you what to say to me," I said.

"No. I called him when I got your message and he told me to go ahead and call you, so you wouldn't be upset. He just told me to tell you we weren't messing around."

She just contradicted herself. They messed around before or still do. "I have to go. My food is ready. And if you talk to him again, which I'm sure you will, tell him it's cool."

"Alright. Take care," she said.

"I will. You do the same."

I hung up furiously. They played me, so I thought. I made the kids' plates. We said our prayers, then we ate.

Hours later Daniel hopped in the door with Nancy, high off weed like usual. He waited for me to say something about Tanya but I made them a plate and waited for him to say something first.

"What's wrong?" he asked, putting the fork to his mouth as he watched me closely.

"Why did you lie to me about Tanya?" I asked, looking into his reddish-brown eyes that could never lie.

"I didn't lie to you," he said. The white parts of his eyes were red as fire.

"Well, why did you tell her what to say to me?" I said.

"I didn't. She told me you called and I told her to call you back to let you know we weren't messing around," he said.

"She told me in so many words, y'all were or y'all used to," I cried. "And you had her in the Jeep before."

"I went down to see her mom about something because she is a cop. She leaned in the Jeep. She was never in it," he lied.

"Whatever! It's cool. I just wish you would respect me, that's all."

"She knows about you. Everybody knows about you," he said.

"Yeah and everybody knows I had you locked up, too, right. You told her I had you locked up. I never had you locked up," I sobbed.

"Look. Why don't you chill out? It's nothing between her and me. We are just friends. And we are gonna be friends, nothing more. I don't want her. She has a boyfriend. She doesn't care about me. She messes with one of the Nice boys," he said.

"And."

"I know dude. I'm not tryna' go through nothing with him, over her. I'm cool. You just don't know how she rides. She has a new dude every month," he said.

"And you wanna be one of them."

"It's not that deep. I don't want her for my women. She's just cool to kick it with. We talk about our problems. She tells me about dude and I tell her about you," he said. The truth is, they were friends but had fucked before and it wasn't worth losing me so he cut that part of the relationship off. Shit! He was young, handsome and didn't mind trying new pussy every now and then. He strapped up faithfully so he wasn't hurting anybody.

"Whatever!"

"See. That's your problem. You're gonna believe what you wanna believe," he said.

"Did you have a bitch in here earlier?" I said.

"No. My cousin Ronda picked me up earlier."

He knows I don't fuck with her like that. She is the main one starting shit between me and him.

"You straightened up for Ronda! She doesn't like me and I don't care for her too much either," I said.

"Look, that's on y'all. She came here to get me and that's it. That's my cousin," he said. He was tired of the people he loved feuding. Life is short. We had very little time to hate each other. We didn't know our hour.

"You're right and you know they don't care for me."

"I'm tired of all the bullshit. Why don't you chill?" he said.

"Yeah, I am."

I woke up to an empty cold bed, the next morning. I walked into the living room to find Daniel and Nancy stretched out on the sofa and love seat with the television running, cups on the floor, chip bags beside them, and an empty whoppers box thrown on the side. *Trifling*, I thought as I picked up the trash quietly. *I'm tired of cleaning up behind them every time they come in here with the munchies.* I walked in the kitchen, I threw everything in the trash, then I made, fried fish, grits, cheese eggs and corn muffins.

Daniel and Nancy jumped up once they smelled the food and I wasn't about to be rude, I fed everybody.

Chapter 4
Love, Laughter & Pain
"Baby Girl"

I rolled over, glancing at Daniel for the third time. After watching the episode on *New York Undercover* about a young man with a newborn getting killed on his girl's steps and earlier watching three body bags come out the Condos across from us and we didn't see or hear a sound, Daniel was stressed. Death hit home again.

He watched young boys and men come through the morgue on a daily basis between the ages of 14 to 29 and he refused to put his mother through that grief. After two more months in the games, he was done for good. He'd have close to three hundred thousand by then. The family would be straight and he'd have no reason to hustle anymore.

"Come on. Get up," said Daniel patting me on the back softly, early the next morning.

"What time is it?" I asked, rolling over.

"It's nine o'clock. Get dressed. We're going to Great Adventures."

"With who?" I asked.

"Me, you, the kids, Nancy, Frank and one of his girls."

"Frank! Um. I thought y'all didn't hang out anymore," I said.

"We're still cool."

"I haven't seen him since I told you what he said."

"Yeah, well he denied it, so I'm not gonna hold it over his head. I guess he feels uncomfortable around you since I confronted him about it," he said.

"Yeah, yeah. Niggas' ain't shit. And I can't believe you believed him over me," I said nastily. Frank was getting money down 15th Street. He and Daniel did business together so they became pretty tight but Frank cracked on me while I was four months pregnant in our living room while Daniel was counting money in the bedroom. I didn't want to tell Daniel because I had been in a situation like that before and niggas believed their friends first but I didn't know how Frank played so I figured I should tell. Daniel didn't believe me like I thought. He believed Frank's lying ass and I couldn't respect him for lying. He didn't have to start shit in my household.

"Are we goin' back to that? I don't want to hear it. Lets just go and have some fun," he said.

"Alright."

We hit the highway with Daniel and Frank racing until Daniel realized the Jeep couldn't keep up with Frank's convertible 5.0 Mustang and I was about due with his baby and the kids were in the back. He slowed down and cruised the highway.

We drove until we saw exit 7a, then we got off. As soon as we hit the park Daniel, Nancy and the boys left me behind to go on the Batman ride.

I sat on the bench in front of the food court only to have the sun beam on my forehead.

"What's up girl?" said Frank, taking a seat next to me.

"Nothing," I spoke quickly and turned away. I really didn't want to be bothered with him for lying on me.

"Is my man still treating you bad?" he asked me.

"What do you mean by that?" I questioned, trying to keep my cool.

"You know. Are y'all still goin' through it?" he said.

"Look, everything is fine between us right now, but if he starts acting up, I know what to do. It's all about the kids right now. I have to focus on my children. I can't worry about what he's doing," I let him know.

"I feel you. Like I told you before, you deserve to be treated like a queen," he smiled while flossing his new Presidential Rolex.

"I hear you."

"No, I'm serious. You don't need to take no shit off nobody. You got what it takes. I told my man. I admire your strength. You deserve the world girl. And if you were mine, I would treat you right," he said giving me that look, then he walked away giving me something to think about.

"It doesn't make sense to say anything to Daniel because it's gonna start an argument like before and I wouldn't have Frank, so what's the purpose," I thought while I looked around to spot my family. Moments later Daniel, Nancy and the boys walked up laughing and smiling.

"Did y'all have fun?" I asked the boys.

"Yeah, mom. The Batman ride was all that," said Luke.

"Can we take a picture next to the Batman car mom?" said Job.

"Yeah, come on."

We took pictures in front of the Batman car, then we toured the entire park until it got dark.

After giving the kids a bath I found Daniel browsing through porn's on the internet. I flipped because he stopped touching me months ago. No matter what I did, he wouldn't make love to me and I needed some.

"Oh, you can sit here and watch porno's, but you can't fuck me!" I yelled.

"What!"

"You heard me! You are a fuckin' pervert! You can watch bitches on a screen to get your dick hard, but you can't do it to me!" I spat.

"I don't feel like it. Don't start no shit!" he begged.

"Yeah, I am! Anytime I have a man and he can't do it to me, I am gonna start some shit. I feel some type of way about this whole thing. I have been horny for months and you won't do it to me, but you will come in here and look at some bitches on a screen in my face! I'm tired of this. You just expect me to get my shit off myself. I'm tired of playing with my own pussy," I said. I played with my pussy on a regular to get off and my fingers did wonders but it was nothing like the real thing. I needed a rock hard dick

231

inside me. I needed something my pussy could latch onto and Daniel's shit was like that. I was turned out.

"Stop trippin' girl and go to sleep. You always wanna argue," he said, flagging me. Dick and pussy can be very powerful tools at times.

"I'm not arguing. I'm fuckin' horny! I want some dick!" I screamed.

He shut the computer down and walked in the livingroom.

"Fuck you, too!" I blurted aloud, then I slammed the door and climbed into bed. I thought about what Frank said, then I jumped up and walked into the living room to give it Daniel. Although I checked Frank myself, I had to let Daniel have it.

"How far are the contractions?" the doctor asked me. I was having my third child.

"Every minute."

"Come right back," he said. Daniel and the boys pushed me back in the wheel chair.

"Where do you want her?" asked Daniel. He was familiar with hospital procedures because of his experience.

"We're going to put her on this table right here," said the doctor, pointing to the roll away bed.

"How are we gonna lift her?" asked Daniel, participating in every part of what was going on with his baby and me. Daniel and the doctor lift me from the wheel chair to the bed, leaving the boys outside the room, then he examined me immediately. "She's ready," said the doctor, smiling at Daniel and alarming the nurses. The doctor got up for a moment, then he sat before me with the light directly on my pussy and Daniel right beside him, watching closely.

"You can help dad," said the doctor, giving Daniel assurance.

"Take a deep breath, then push," said the doctor.

The door opened and the boys walked in to partake in the birth of their baby. They nurtured it for all these months, so they were not about to be left out. They had just as much right as anyone else in the room. They stepped up and took their places beside the bed, next to me. I inhaled, exhaled, then I pushed. I inhaled, exhaled, then I pushed again really hard.

"I see something," said Daniel.

"Push again," said the doctor. I pushed one last, hard time.

"I see a head full of hair," cried Daniel. Out came a little life full of black, straight hair covered in blood with blue skin, fighting to survive. Fighting to catch her breath, while we all looked on patiently, praying for the best.

"Why is she blue?" asked Luke in fear.

"I don't know. It'll be okay," I tried to assure him. The doctor took her in the corner immediately with Daniel by his side.

Moments later Daniel walked back over to me and put her on my breast. She had all of her father's features and body parts. She didn't have anything like me. The boys were amazed at what they saw. They finally got a sister. They finally got the chance to see the little life they had been waiting to see for so long. The little life they helped take care of for nine long months, the one that survived through losing its twin, the one that finally made it into this cruel, cruel world.

"Congratulations," said the doctor, shaking my hand. "You did a good job. In at 8:00 and you birthed her at 8:31. You have a beautiful baby girl. She weighs 6lbs 12ounces."

"Thanks," I smiled. Luke weighed 4 ounces less than my baby girl at birth.

The next morning Daniel went to the tattoo parlor and had Danielle's name written across his entire back. He was so proud of his little darling and he'd kill for her.

Daniel came home the following week with two pit bulls, one for Job and one for Luke. Luke named his tan friend Versace and he had hazel eyes just like Daniel's and Job named his pretty white friend Diamond. She had beautiful blue eyes just like a precious blue stone. The boys were so grateful. Daniel did anything to make them happy.

After taking Job and Luke to the pet store to get cages, food, bowls, brushes and shampoo, Daniel went down 62nd Street to set up shop with a couple new young boys named Kalif and Tim, and his old, but faithful young boy, Nas.

A month later Daniel walked into the bedroom with three boxes for Danielle and me. One box had four carat diamond hoop earrings for me. The other box had a two-carat diamond bagel bracelet with Danielle's birth date inscribed inside of it and the other one had a "Daddy's Little Girl" diamond pendant. The gifts were lovely but I wanted Daniel to stop hustling. He had a good job and a family that cared about him. He didn't have to hustle. We could make ends meet with what we had. I had two more years to go in college and I was willing to work once the baby turned one. Daniel didn't have to do what he was doing but he wanted the best for our daughter. He didn't want her to have to ask another man for anything. He wanted to be her everything.

Daniel stepping his game up to the highest level only made people jealous, especially Roger. Daniel did anything for him but that wasn't enough. He stole Daniel's gun and put the Nice boys on him so they could rob him blind but Tanya overheard everything and she gave Daniel a heads up but he couldn't tell me what was going on because he knew what I was going to say so he just packed us up and moved us while Roger had the locks changed anyway by maintenance. He wondered how Daniel knew what he was thinking. He was pissed that his plan didn't work but at least he had a half-furnished apartment because we left what we didn't want and he used it like the bum he was.

Daniel went to his shop with Versace to check on his squad. They'd been messing up a whole lot of money and Daniel was getting frustrated. Every time he turned around they had a story to tell.

Daniel walked into a room full of niggas; smoking blunts.

"What's goin' on?" he asked Kalif while looking around at the youngins'.

"Nothing. We was just chillin'," he answered, exhaling smoke with his feet up on the coffee table.

"Well, it's not that type of party. You know what you're suppose to be doin'. It's all work and no play nigga. You messed up a lot of money," said Daniel with a straight face. He was tired of the games. Kalif looked at him like he was tired of the bullshit, too. He didn't feel like taking orders from Daniel anymore. He wanted to run his own shit.

"Alright," he spat aloud then he got up and put everybody out that didn't belong there.

"Here. Take your hat," Kalif said, smacking one of the young boys in his head.

"Nas, I need you to clean Versace up for me. I'll pay you in the morning," said Daniel.

"Okay. I got you," said the faithful Nas. He loved Daniel because Daniel wasn't your average hustler. He clothed, fed and gave them extra money if they did small things. He looked out generously for them and never threw it in their faces.

"In fact, I'll take y'all shopping in the morning," Daniel said to Kalif, Nas and Tim.

"Good lookin' Daniel. I'll see you in the morning," Nas smiled.

In the morning Daniel took Danielle out on a date before he picked his gang up to go shopping. Daniel and Danielle always did outings together, just the two of them.

Kalif was getting madder and madder with Daniel. He busted his butt selling dope for him and although Daniel treated him good Daniel didn't take any shit either. When he messed his money up, Daniel smacked him around and he was one of the reasons Daniel just purchased a brand new Suzuki GXSR 1100, the bike of his dreams and a brand-new Grand National. Whom did Daniel think he was?

Kalif's sister boyfriend Ty was home after doing ten years in the penitentiary. He was the perfect one for Daniel. He didn't have anything to lose. Kalif would tell him all about Daniel so they could take him out the picture.

While Daniel and I sat in *Ruth's Chris* having dinner, Kalif called Daniel and told him some guy just stuck him up for all his dope, money and gun. Daniel told him it was cool but he had to work triple shifts to get that money back. Kalif wasn't going for that because he had extra money now. The joke was on Daniel.

"I want you to know that I love you and I always will. I hate us living apart, but I'm afraid for us to be together sometimes," Daniel said, while staring me in the eyes. It was no way he could risk our lives at the moment. He had us staying at mom's until he found a securer place to tuck us away at.

"Why?" I asked.

"I just am."

"You have been saying this for a while," I said.

"I know. Things just don't feel right. I'm happy about us. I am so happy about our daughter. I love her so much. If anything ever separated us, I would die. She means everything to me. I love you and my mom, but I love her more," he said.

"I understand. She's your everything and I'm happy for you and her. I'm glad she has you. I'm glad Job and Luke has you, too. They love you so much and I know how much you love them. You took on a big responsibility being a stepfather to them at such a young age. I commend you for that. I am just so happy that Danielle has you for a father. Look at you and me. We both grew up without our fathers. I am so glad she has you. I'm glad she has something I never had. Do you know it still affects me that my father wasn't around sometimes?"

"I can believe that. And if anything happens to me, I don't want my dad at my funeral," he said.

"Why would you say that?" I asked him.

"I just don't. He never did anything for me. My mom and my aunt took care of me. They made sure I had what I needed. And my uncles took me under their wings and showed me things that my dad was supposed to show me. They took out time with me," he said with the glare of the candle bouncing off his tears. Daniel's father wasn't there for him but it was always two sides to every story. Daniel's mother moved him away from his father and didn't tell him where they were but she was all Daniel ever knew growing up so he loved her more than anything. His father meant very little to him.

"At least you had them. I didn't have anyone to fill that void. My mom struggled alone, but we made it. And my boys didn't have anyone. Everybody had their own families, so no one had time to do things with my boys that men do with their sons. It wasn't until you came along, they experienced doing certain things. I did the games with them and other little things, but moms can only do but so much. I appreciate what you have given us. I really do. I love you for making things complete. I know we had our trials and tribulations, but I'm not mad. That's what life is all about. It's all about ups and downs, ins and outs. I love you Daniel."

"I love you, too."

Daniel sat in the conference room with the rest of his family members while their cousin Steve, the spokesperson for the family did all the talking, on Friday.

"I knew it! I don't believe this shit! I'm out," mumbled Daniel, pushing his body out the seat.

"Hold up. You're not leaving are you?" asked Steve.

"Yeah."

"Well, I'm not finished yet," his cousin said.

"What I can't understand is, why do y'all keep talkin' about Cinnamon like she has me doing what I'm doing. Did anybody blame Faith Evans when her husband, the man she loved, Biggie Smalls, died? What happened to him, happened. And she had nothing to do with it. It was beyond her control. It was bigger than Faith. I love Cinnamon. I love my daughter. I love my stepsons. They're my family. I love them. She was there for me when some of my own so-called friends and family members weren't. She stuck by me through thick and thin. She took a lot off me. And I have been through a lot with her. I know she isn't perfect, like none of us in here or outside of here are, but I love her and I'm tired of people looking at her funny. I am tired of them blaming her for what happened in her life. No one goes around blaming anyone else for anything. She had nothing to do with what her kid's fathers did. And she has nothing to do with what I do. I do what I do because I want to," he let him know.

"But you don't have to do what you do," said Steve.

"I know what I'm doing. I have a good job. My daughter and I have good medical coverage. I have a woman that loves me. I'm not happy about everything in my life and I hope it gets better, but I'm not gonna sit here and listen to y'all dog me like I'm the only one in here doing wrong. It's other people in here doing things and I don't hear you talking about that," he said.

"Well, this meeting wasn't supposed to be about that. We actually came here to discuss the funds for the younger children in this generation and your children are a part of this generation," said Steve.

"Yeah, but the discussion went elsewhere by mistake, huh! Look. I love all of you. I have always looked up to you and I wish I could be in your position, but I'm not. I didn't make it through college like you. I'm not in an executive office like you, making big money. I wish I was, but we are all here to do different things and I want to own my own someday. I have a bigger picture. I don't want to work for somebody else all my life. I want my daughter to go to the best of schools. I don't want her to look at nobody in the streets for anything. I don't want Cinnamon to struggle to raise our kids. She had it hard enough and I want to make her happy. She deserves to be happy. If something happens to me, I don't want her to go from place to place with my daughter. I want her to be stable. I'm tired of people worrying about what we are doing. I'm tired of them trying to come between me and my family. I just want to be happy. And I want her and the kids to be safe," he said.

"I feel you Daniel. And believe me, I do understand. I see the best men go under every day, even doing what I do. It's not easy out here in the

236

business world either. It's not. I know," he said seriously. He knew all too well and it was a struggle where he was too. Just not an illegal struggle but everybody fought for a position while some got it easy for different reasons. Daniel hugged everybody, then he left. He didn't want to hear the bullshit or excuses anymore.

Two weeks later Ty drove through Daniel's set all day, hoping to bump into him while Daniel paced the floors at work. Everything turned personal. Ty felt like he knew Daniel already. It was about more than just money now. It was jealousy, envy, greed and revenge. Daniel had what Ty didn't, and he was upset. Ty sitting in the penitentiary for years made him more than bitter and Kalif was just a troubled child that didn't care about anything or anybody. School wasn't even on his agenda. Daniel talked to him so much about going to school, but he let it go in one ear and out the other. All he wanted to do was hustle and take from other people. He even hated Daniel now to death and Ty wanted to take over Daniel's spot and his workers. Tim and Nas didn't like what Kalif was doing, but they were caught in between. They loved Daniel, but they were intimidated by Ty.

It was the night before Christmas. Daniel wanted everybody at his mom's house for Christmas day. I packed my Christion Dior bag with everything I needed then we headed over to Ms. Cathy's house for the night.

As soon as we pulled up to the house the kids got excited. Ms. Cathy's house was decorated so beautifully. She had bright lights, a snowman in the front yard. Her door was wrapped so neatly. Christmas at her house was warm and pleasant. They went all out for the kids and they couldn't wait for Christmas day.

After getting settled in Daniel zipped up his butter soft, Marcus Buchanan black leather jacket, then he hopped out the door to take care of business. His beeper had been beeping off the hook and he promised to come right back in.

Before coming in the house Ty stepped to Daniel again but this time Daniel couldn't threaten him because he didn't know where we were in the house so he just played it cool and ran. He didn't care what Ty thought about him. He had a family to live for.

After Daniel told me what Ty did, I was petrified. Shit was getting crazier and crazier by the moment. I didn't know what to do.

Daniel got out of his bed early in the morning and left us behind. It was a must that he got a gun permit. He wanted to be licensed when trouble came his way again. He was tired of the games. He had never been convicted of a crime and his life was in danger. He had to be well prepared for whatever. Rumor had it. Ty wanted his head.

After filling out the application for the gun permit, Daniel took the test to be a firefighter. Daniel's life had made an abrupt turn and he was destined to be in control of it. He had a better plan that the streets couldn't offer him. Everything had to be legal from this point on. He had to be a living example for the boys and his daughter. He was the man of the house. If anybody was to do right, it was he and saving others lives would only pay back for some of the wrong he had done in his life.

After Daniel finished taking care of business, we hit the mall to buy something to wear for the comedy show. He purchased a pair of brown corduroy Versace pants with a Versace sweater to compliment the pants. A pair of brown suede Versace three quarter length boots from the Versace shop and a tan three quarter length wool coat from Bernini's. I purchased a matching brown Versace dress, a pair of brown Versace stiletto heels and a brown and tan, wool swing coat to compliment my outfit from Neiman Marcus. Luke picked Nancy something up to wear too then we got her and headed over to Daniel's place to get dressed.

We arrived at the Tower twenty minutes late to find everybody lingering in the hallway. Sugar stood on the side with John taking pictures.
"They're still together. Look at John's fat ass," laughed Nancy.
"Shut up girl, you are always talkin' about somebody," I laughed back.

While we waited in the hallway to take pictures too, Nancy talked about everybody that came and went with no regrets. I stood back and watched Sugar. I could only remember the days when she and I did the same thing at the shows. Seeing Sugar again made me remember the good and bad times we had together but I wasn't bitter with her anymore. What happened, happened and I was happy with my family while she was still going through the baby mama drama and to top it off, she and John were turned out on coke but Sugar held things down. Her tan suede dress complimented her dark skin. She wasn't about to let the streets see her slipping while she covered John's addiction but everybody in the city knew he was snorted out. You could see it.

Daniel, Nancy and I took our flicks minutes later, then we walked into the dark auditorium to find everybody laughing at Jammie Foxx. The usher flashed her light on our tickets, then she escorted us to our seats. I felt good with my man right by my side. After seeing all the old people from my past, it felt good to still be holding on.

After the show everybody crammed the hallway of the theater. Ms. Cathy came from the balcony with her co-worker Muggy that liked Daniel. She looked at Daniel and me and rolled her eyes.
"What's her problem?" I asked Daniel.
"What?"
"Your mom's girlfriend," I said. "What's her problem?"
"Oh, she's nobody. Don't worry about her," he said.

"No. I will punch her in her face if she rolls her eyes again," I said.

"Yeah, she don't know. She'll get beat down," said Nancy, sucking her teeth.

"You have more class than that," he said, bringing me back to reality.

"Yeah, you're right. But I'm not stupid. I know she likes you," I said.

How is Ms. Cathy playing? "Did you enjoy the show Ms. Cathy?" I asked while gritting on Muggy.

"Yeah, it was good," she smiled. Daniel grabbed my hand to let Muggy know that I was all he needed and they followed behind us to get to Ms. Cathy's car.

"Look at this shit. They are dressed alike. How cute, old bitch," said Muggy inwardly as she watched every step Daniel and I made. I turned around and cut my eyes at Muggy to let her know she couldn't have Daniel even if she danced ass naked in front of him. He was mine. She couldn't change that. She was just a trick bitch that fucked everybody on the job, including all of Daniel's friends. It was time to turn her cards in because her time was definitely up. All the head she gave couldn't make Daniel leave me. She really didn't know that my game was tight. I lacked in some things, but I held shit down too.

Daniel showed his mom to her car, then we jumped in our Jeep and headed to Fridays for appetizers and drinks. We had to get there before the clock struck twelve so we could bring the New Years in with a special toast. And later, wet kisses, sensual sucks, intense sexual encounters between the warm silk sheets, on the cold wood floor, in the hot shower, on the slippery counter top, wherever Daniel wanted it.

Chapter 5
DENIAL
"Holding On"

Two weeks later Brent's 6'3" sturdy frame walked down the bright hallway of the Justice Center dressed in a two-piece black Armani suit with a pair of black leather Cole Haan shoes on looking serious but pleasant.

"Here comes your uncle Job," I smiled.

"Where?" he asked, looking around.

"Coming down the hallway," I pointed. He stopped and planted his feet right in front of Daniel, Danielle, Job and me.

"What's going on Cinnamon?" he smiled.

"How have you been Brent? This is Daniel," I said, introducing him to Daniel.

"Hi, how are you, man?" smiled Brent, grabbing Daniel's hand.

"It's nice to meet you. I'm well," said Daniel, shaking Brent's hand.

"This is our daughter, Danielle," I said, holding Danielle up.

"She is a doll baby. Hey man, come give me a hug," Brent said to Job. Job jumped in Brent's lap and threw his little arms around his strong neck.

"I missed you man," he said to Job. "How have you been doing?"

"Fine," Job smiled. Daniel walked back into the courtroom with Ramina, Nancy and the rest of my family members so Brent and I could talk. A lot of time came between us so he knew we had some catching up to do.

"He seems to be a nice guy," Brent said as the courtroom door shut behind Daniel.

"Yeah, he is."

"What does he do for a living?" he asked out of concern for us and to be really nosey at the same time. Knowing everybody's business was Brent's thing.

"He works at the morgue," I said, proudly.

"That's good. He's younger than you, too," Brent smiled.

"Yeah. How did you know?" I asked.

"I just knew. But it's okay. That's nothing. You know Cinnamon, age, status and other things don't matter sometimes, especially when someone makes you happy. If he makes you happy, then everything is all good. And if my nephew is happy, than I'm happy. You don't need a hustler or a dude that isn't or can't treat you right or make you happy. Look at my situation. I never wanted kids or a wife, but I have a kid and a wife now. Job always wanted a family. He wanted to be married with kids. I used to tell him he was crazy for wanting to be settled down, because I wanted to run the streets. I didn't want to be tied down and I still don't. But Job was right. Being settled with a family is what we need sometimes. The streets don't owe us anything and who can we really trust," Brent smiled.

"Tell me about it," I smiled back.

The big wooden doors opened. The detectives handling Na's case walked out and said to Brent, "The prosecutor needs you inside."

"Okay," he said as he turned to walk away. "Oh, yeah. The girl Chantel is upstate doing ten to twenty years and she's talking about brother Mike kidnaped Job and she is willing to testify to get her time cut because he crossed her. He sent naked pictures of her through the jail. Now she wants to talk but because of her record, her word will be mud in court so we'll play it by ear. Brother Mike played her and she thought having a baby by him meant something."

"I told Job. That snake," I cried.

"I'll talk to you when I come back out," he said. I paced the shiny hallway floors for hours while my family members cried inside the courtroom from seeing pictures of Na's lifeless body for the second time. I kept replaying what Brent said to me over and over in my mind. I was so hurt.

The doors opened finally. Everybody started coming out, one by one. "Cinnamon here's my number. Call me so I can get Lil Job sometimes," Brent said, passing me his number on a small piece of paper.

"Okay, I will," I smiled. Although we talked, he still didn't trust me to some degree because all he gave was a beeper number. *I tell you. Some things will never change.* I knew how that went because I was the same way about certain people. Everybody couldn't get my house number either.

"I'll see you later, man," Brent said to Job, shaking his hand. Job smiled, then he followed him down the hallway.

"Come back, boo," I hollered to Job.

After two days of testimony the Jury reached a verdict. Joey and Dip got first degree murder for killing Na.

On the quiet elevator going down Daniel turned and asked me if Brent knew who killed Job. I cried knowing we finally found out after all these years, but no one had been charged for his death. And knowing that, I still hadn't told my child how his father was brutally tormented because of his tender age, the thought of him growing up knowing no one was charged with his father's death, hurt me more than anything. Something I fought with for all these years. A mystery unknown. A secret unfolded finally, an unsolved death. We still didn't know the full truth. It was all hearsay and speculation.

Daniel kissed and hugged me tight, then the elevator doors slid open letting me know it was hope on the other side no matter how things looked. "The system might not have them, but they will pay. God promised. So I'm not mad," I thought looking through the crowd of people scrambling to get on and off the elevator. Daniel walked hand and hand with me through the doors. He knew God was good after all this and he had a strong woman.

241

Early the next morning Daniel went to my jewelers to purchase himself a Cartier watch and me a diamond engagement ring. He wasn't going anywhere so it was time to step up to the plate. He wanted to give me what no other man ever had.

After leaving the jewelry store Daniel walked into 1st Common Bank proud to open an account up for his baby girl. Everything he hustled hard for was finally paying off. He had to put things in order now.

Stella's mother spotted Daniel from her desk so she ran over to him. "Hey Daniel. How are you?" she smiled.

"I'm fine," he smiled back. Knowing all his business and everything about every transaction that Daniel made with the bank, she offered her assistance.

"What can I do for you today?" she asked him.

"I wanna open an account for my daughter," he proudly said.

"Fine. I can help you with that, have a seat at my desk," she said. Daniel took a seat at her desk holding pictures of him and Stella on her prom and at her graduation. She still loved Daniel and she was living in the past. When was she gonna let go? When was she gonna accept Daniel moving on?

"Okay. What type of account would you like to set up for your daughter and how much are you putting in today?" she asked him.

"Fifty thousand dollars," he said.

Her heart dropped to the floor. She wasn't expecting him to say that type of money.

"That's a lot of money," she smirked.

"Yeah, but it's for a good cause. And my baby deserves the best. Here's a picture of my sweetie," he said, reaching for his Gucci leather wallet. She glanced at the picture like Danielle was nothing. She didn't want to accept his daughter. She was in a state of denial. Her and her daughter.

"What are you doing these days? I know you're still working because you just had a deposit from work," she said, changing the subject.

"And," he said rudely.

"Nothing," she said.

"What are you asking or what do you want to know?" he asked blatantly. He wasn't pulling any punches with her. He wanted her to come clean and direct.

"Nothing Daniel," she said, brushing him off.

"I have a check here from my lawyer and the rest is cash. And I want Cinnamon as the trustee on the account. Here's her social security card," he said.

Oh no he isn't. That bitch is not gonna be on this account if I have anything to do with it. "It can only be in your daughter's name," she lied, fearing I would benefit if something happened to Daniel and simply because she

242

didn't like me or my daughter because her daughter didn't like us. "You can be the trustee since you're opening the account."

"Okay," he said, trusting her. She took Danielle's social security card along with the other necessary information that she needed, then she set up the account for Danielle the way she wanted it to be set up.

I left the kids with Daniel and drove the trolley tracks over to Bishop Hightower's for my weekly counseling. The director of the ARD program said I didn't have to go to the therapist of their choice. I could go to any counselor as long as it could be documented so I chose Bishop Hightower because he was highly recommended through the church. He was close to us and it was better for me to go to Christian counseling opposed to seeking counseling from somebody I knew nothing about that could teach me nothing about being spiritually grounded. My first interview with a therapist that was set up through the system was horrible. The lady talked left field and I knew she had her own issues so how was she going to help me with mine. She had liquor on her breath. Her eyes were dark as the streets and she didn't have kids or a husband so how was she going to help me with my family problems.

I reached bishop Hightower's gate with a sense of relief. Part of my burden was lifted immediately knowing I was about to discuss my fears that only he seemed to understand about me. He unlocked the gate and let me in.

"God bless you sister,"he said with a pleasant smile while embracing me.

"God bless you," I greeted him in return.

"Do you have your homework assignments finished that I gave you to do last week?" he asked.

"Yes," I said as I followed him inside the church.

I sat down at the round table to prepare myself for the week session.

"How's everything going with you and Daniel?" he asked me.

"Everything is about the same. We have our good days and we still have our bad ones," I said as I thought of all that Daniel and I was going through. Our relationship was really being tested. Although he gave me a ring, we weren't getting along so well.

"I understand," he said attentively. "You know. God is working it out. It may not seem like it, but he is. I told you before that it is not God that hasn't forgiven you of your mistakes. It's you. Even the strongest Christians aren't perfect. I'm not perfect and neither are you. You have to stop being so hard on yourself when you make a mistake," he said.

"But I get so upset that I flip out. I promised myself that I would not lose it and I still do," I said.

"That's understandable," he smiled.

"But I know I'm not supposed to curse and sin and I do sometimes," I honestly said.

243

"That's not abnormal. It's practicing sin that is wrong. As long as you don't practice sin, than you are forgiven," he let me know.

"Well, Daniel and I are supposed to get married, so we won't be living in sin anymore," I said.

"Are you sure that's what God wants you to do?" he asked me.

"Well, I don't want to go to hell for having sex out of marriage," I said.

"Yeah, but you want to make sure you are marrying the man that God sent for you," he let me know.

"Well, I don't want to be with anyone else. I want to marry the man I have kids with. Besides, who else is gonna want me? Who else is going to deal with all my flaws?" I asked.

"God will give you someone that will love you for you. Don't worry about your flaws. Who's perfect? We all have flaws," he said.

"Yeah, but nobody else is gonna love me like him," I said.

"You can't say that. God will give you someone that will love you and your children. You are beautiful and you have beautiful children. Are you still planning on doing your book that you talked to me about?" he asked.

"Yes. That's my dream. I've been sleeping on it for years and it's time. I really want to do it. How is your new novel coming along?" I asked him.

"Good. I'm blessed. God has been moving and I am excited," he smiled.

"Praise God. I'm happy for you," I cried.

"It's okay. Let God have his way and he'll work it out. Trust and believe," he said.

"Amen."

Bishop Hightower counseled me, giving me the best advice, then I went back to Daniel with a new attitude, with a new heart.

I laid in bed exhausted. Daniel took the kids and me to Dave and Busters for Valentine's Day and they wore us out. My phone rang repeatedly and finally I answered it.

"What were you doing?" said Daniel, waking me from my nod.

"Sleeping," I yawned.

"I need to talk. I can't sleep," he said.

"What's wrong?" I asked.

"I haven't been able to sleep lately. I hate staying here by myself at night," he said.

"You'll be okay. Do you want me to drive over there?" I asked.

"Are the kids sleep?" he said.

"Yeah. They went to sleep early," I said.

"I should have told you to meet me here after work," he said

"I know. You sure should have."

"You know that dude Ty is still riding around asking people about me," he said.

"Are you serious?" I said.

"Yeah."

"What does he look like?" I asked.

"Do you remember that day when that Maxima pulled up beside me and I walked in the street to talk to that guy?" he asked.

"Yeah."

"Well, that was him," he let me know.

"I thought that was somebody you were all right with," I said.

"No. That was Ty. I'm gonna go to sleep. I'll talk to you in the morning," he said.

"Alright."

"Cinnamon," he paused.

"Yes," I listened closely.

"Don't get upset but I found out who robbed us at the apartment," he said.

"Who?"

"Ja sent Braheem in to do it. You were right. You are always right. I love you," he said.

"I love you too. I knew it. People are vicious but they'll pay in the end," I said.

"Good night baby," he said lastly.

"Good night boo."

The following night I put the kids to sleep, then I put on my workout clothes to go to the gym, something I had just started back doing.

I stepped out into the cold night air. I hit the alarm on the Jeep, then I got in and pushed track 11, "All My Life" on K-Ci & JoJo's cd. I cried like a baby driving through the desolated streets thinking about Daniel.

Daniel phoned the house to get no answer from me. He needed his daughter and me desperately. Something just wasn't right.

"Why isn't she answering the phone?" he asked aloud. He hung up the phone and pushed track 13, "Soon" on Christion's Ghetto Cyrano cd and tears fell from his eyes. He thought of his life. He thought about his daughter that he loved and cherished with all his heart. He thought of her pretty face and smile. He thought of how precious she was and how lucky he was to have such a beautiful daughter, then he thought of me. The mother of his child, who he loved, too. He wanted so much to be with us. The boys crossed his mind and he fell to his knees to pray. Something he hadn't done in a while. The game wasn't a game anymore. He wanted nothing to do with the game. It was causing him too many problems. All he wanted was a good life and a happy family. People hating on him because of a couple of dollars was getting the best of him. The lies, the competition, everything that came with the game, he envied now. Daniel picked up the phone to call me once again before he hit the sack. He got no answer.

The next morning Daniel woke up early from his restless night. He picked the phone up to dial me again.

"Hello," I answered lowly.

"I was calling you all night. I need to see my daughter," he said.

"Okay. We're here."

He rose from his bed fast, he showered, then he put on the red Polo hooded sweatshirt, the dark Guess jeans and Tims that the kids got him for Christmas that he never touched. He looked in his full length mirror, he brushed his waves down on his head, he grabbed his keys off the tv, then he hopped on the elevator and pushed the button going straight to the lobby floor.

On the first floor Daniel checked his mailbox, then he hit the bridge to see his baby girl. She was the only thing that gave him something to look forward to.

He parked his car and I met him at the door with his little angel.

"Hey sweetie," he smiled. Danielle jumped in his arms and his heart was at peace. We sat at the dining room table while the rest of the family stayed in bed. An uneasy presence filled the room and Daniel sat spaced out.

"What's wrong? Is something on your mind?" I asked him. He kept his mouth shut, knowing he wanted to spill his guts to me then tears filled his eyes momentarily.

"What's wrong Daniel?" I asked, rubbing his hand. "Tell me what's wrong."

"I couldn't sleep all night. I sat up and cried all night," he said.

"For what?" I asked him.

"I called you and got no answer," he said.

"I went to the gym."

"I didn't know where you were," he said.

"Now you know how I used to feel when I couldn't find you sometimes. But I didn't do it on purpose. You know I go to the gym some nights," I explained.

"I know, but I needed y'all last night. I really needed y'all. I just wanted to hear you and my baby's voice. It's so hard sleeping without y'all at night," he sobbed.

"But we are there most nights. We are there more than we are here," I said.

"I know, but it's not like sleeping together every night," he said.

"But you wanted it to be this way. And the house should be coming through soon," I said.

"I only wanted it to be like this because of everything that's going on, but it's hard and I need y'all."

"But we are right here."

"I know. I sat up and listened to Christion's cd and cried like a baby. I dedicated it to my daughter," he sobbed more as tears flooded mom's glass dining table.

"What track?" I asked, quietly.

"Track 13. I want you to listen to it, okay," he said.

246

"Okay," I cried then I reached over and hugged him tight. I could feel something different. He was really worried. This wasn't a game. It was serious.

"It's okay, boo. We're right here. And we love you," I assured him. Danielle leaned forward and planted a kiss on his lips.

"Oh baby. Daddy loves you. You gotta date with daddy again, okay," he smiled.

"Where are y'all going?" I asked.

"I'm taking her to the mall, then we're going to my spot to chill. I just wanna chill with my baby girl," he said. I said a prayer for Daniel and my baby then I watched them off.

Job, Luke and I hit the Aquarium not far from Daniel's while Daniel and Danielle enjoyed their date alone. By seven o'clock we were back at home chilling.

Danielle woke up in Daniel's arms wanting milk by eight. He got up and checked the amount in her bottle. She had no more milk so he hit the bridge back to Philly. He headed his mom's way coming off the bridge so she could see Danielle, then he remembered she had no milk so he came my way.

Daniel walked up with Danielle and a hand full of bags from the mall.

"Here. Grab her," he said. I sat on the sofa to feed my boo, boo while he unpacked the bags to show me what they got from the mall for everybody.

"That was so sweet," I smiled. "You and daddy shopped for everybody."

"I have to take care of something okay," Daniel said to me.

"Where are you going?" I asked him.

"I'll be back for y'all. You are staying with me, aren't you?" he asked.

"Yeah. Of course," I smiled. I loved it when we spent the night together.

"I have to meet my man. I gotta stop pass my mom's first to grab some change, then I'm coming right back to get y'all," he assured me.

"How long do you think that's gonna be so we can be ready?" I asked him.

"About an hour," he smiled.

"Okay, cool."

He turned to the door, he put his hand on the knob, then he paused for a moment and said, "Oh, yeah. Get me that thing that I gave you a couple of weeks ago."

"What thing?" I asked.

"That Sigsaur," he said.

"No! For what? What do you need that for?" I asked.

"For protection, that's all," he said.

"Say you get stopped by the police or something. You don't need it. No," I said.

"Alright. I'm taking the Jeep," he said. He unlocked the door, then he looked back for the last time.

"I love y'all," he smiled.

"We love you, too. We'll see you in a minute," I said.

I got our clothes together for the week and we waited for Daniel's return. The boys asked for something to eat so I got up and threw four Murray's chicken patties in the oven, then I sat on the sofa to write while I waited for them to cook. I thought of bishop Hightower. "I forgot to call him back," I mumbled to myself as I grabbed the cordless phone off the table. We talked even when I didn't have sessions. We became close friends. He even said he might be the husband I had been waiting on. I couldn't see that in the cards though. I knew God would give me somebody I liked and not somebody that just liked me. The feelings had to be mutual. I knew some feelings came with time, but I couldn't see this one. He just wasn't my type.

"Praise the Lord," he answered.

"Praise God. Are you busy?" I asked.

"No. No, I'm not. I'm never too busy for you," he said.

"Thank God."

"How are you feeling?" he asked me.

"I'm fine."

"Is something wrong?" he said.

"No, I was just writing down some thoughts on a paper for my book and I wanted to ask you some questions," I said.

"Go right ahead."

While I asked bishop Hightower a series of questions, Daniel talked to his mom briefly, then he grabbed his money from his stash. Before leaving out the door, Daniel looked around the house that he grew up in then he told his mom he loved her and he'd be back.

Daniel made a u turn in front of his mom's door, then he headed up the Blvd. Ty had just pulled from Daniel's moms not long before Daniel had pulled up.

Daniel proceeded down the strip.

"Yoo, Daniel!" hollered Kalif as he stood in front of the Jamaican store. Daniel pushed the automatic button to see the person calling him. The tinted window slid down slowly. Kalif let off six rounds, shooting Daniel in the head. Daniel's foot continued to press the gas while he held onto life. A passerby saw what happened. He reached in the window to coast the Jeep down the street while Daniel gasped for air. Daniel's head leaned in the passenger's seat and he let go, milliseconds later. The man jumped out the way and the Jeep crashed into the metal fenced gate, a half a block away.

Word traveled fast throughout the city because everybody knew Daniel and his peoples. Once Daniel's cousin Tee called Nancy, she clicked in on the other line to tell me.

"Can you hold on bishop Hightower?" I asked. "Hello."

"Cinnamon, Daniel just got shot in the head," Nancy screamed through the phone. I lost contact with the world. All my hopes and dreams flew out the window.

"No, he didn't. He just left here not too long ago and he said he was coming right back. Stop playing with me. I don't feel like this," I shouted in disbelief. I was in a state of denial. Nobody could tell me my Daniel got shot.

"I'm not playing. I wouldn't lie to you. Tina just called me and said he got shot in the head," she cried.

"No, he didn't! He didn't get shot! I'm not tryna' hear that one. Don't call me with the lies. He didn't get shot! I know he didn't. He promised us he would be back. He promised. He just dropped Danielle off and he said he was coming back," I cried, wishing it wasn't true.

"I'm coming to get you," she said.

"No, you're not! He didn't get shot!" I kept saying then I threw the phone down and ran upstairs to my room to get away from the truth. I wasn't about to accept that one. They were lying to me. It couldn't be true. It couldn't.

It took minutes for reality to sink in and once Nick came in my room hollering, I knew it wasn't a lie because they knew what I'd been through and they wouldn't play with my emotions like that.

Inside the waiting area Daniel's family waited for an answer. I felt so out of place once Daniel's cousin April gave me that look. She still hated the sight of me but I was a part of Daniel and nobody could change that.

Once Ms. Cathy saw Daniel she came back into the waiting room and grabbed the baby from me. She was the closest thing to Daniel. Everybody knew how he felt about his baby girl. She definitely represented him.

Ms. Cathy gave Danielle back and told me to go see him. He needed to hear our voices. If he knew we were there, maybe he would come through.

In the back I cried and begged Daniel to get up but he didn't move. He wanted to but he couldn't. He was dealing with God at the moment. It was nothing he could say. He could hear our cries but he couldn't respond.

I wiped the blood that trickled from his head and nose. I moved his fingers and toes and he still didn't wake up. Danielle kissed and hugged him and he didn't move at the sound of her voice. Nancy pleaded with him to come through because she knew what it would do to us and she knew how he felt about his girl but he still didn't mumble a word. He lay peacefully. It was time to go. He couldn't fight anymore. He already made peace with God. As much as he begged Him for one more time, God said, "not your will, but my will."

I went across his waves with my hand. I blamed me for not giving him his gun then the doctor walked over and asked if I was his wife because they needed to move Daniel upstairs for more testing.

Ms. Cathy and I watched as they rolled Daniel to the elevator. We were so crushed.

"Daniel please pull through for Danielle and me. Daniel please," cried Ms. Cathy then the nurse said, "It's a family room upstairs that you all can wait in. Anyone in the family that wants to come up is welcomed." Ms. Cathy nodded her head to let the nurse know it was okay, then she and I looked at Daniel lying still, once again. The doctor took Daniel up on the elevator while Ms. Cathy gathered everybody together to go up to wait for the results of her baby boy.

I walked in the hallway to find Stella and her girlfriends crying with April. The nurse held the elevator used for deliveries so everybody could go up all at once. Stella and her girlfriends stepped on first with a few family members.

"Oh, no they didn't. They could have let the family members get on first," I thought inwardly then I crammed the kids and me on and the door shut in my face. I was his baby's mother and fiancee. They were not about to play me this day.

I looked up at the numbers to block the phobia surrounding me. Number four lit up and the doors slid open slowly. I stepped off the elevator and my spirit ascended from my body. I walked down the hallway with bright lights leading me. I felt like I was somewhere else. Nothing seemed real. It was like I was in another zone just watching everybody around me.

"What is she doing here?" asked Tee, tapping me from behind on my shoulder. "What the fuck is Stella and her fuckin' girlfriends doing? I can't believe April would invite them up here. She didn't care about my cousin. She just wished him dead not too long ago. Her or her girlfriends can care less. They don't even like you or your kids."

She was right, but what could I do. Daniel's life was more important at the moment. Those groupies were not about to make me look bad. I wasn't going to lose my cool for them. They could get off this day. It didn't matter much.

I walked into the dark family room only to get cold chills. I looked around at everybody, then I slumped in the seat and cried to God.

"Come on Cinnamon. You have to get yourself together. You can't let the kids see you like this. If you're not strong, everybody else is gonna get weak," said Tee.

"I can't help it. He is my everything. Look at our baby. She loves and needs her father. What are we gonna do without him? Who's gonna be there for us? Who's gonna take care of us?" I said.

"You are stronger than this. You can make it. It's gonna be alright. Be strong for him, okay," she said. I looked at the kids and my body got strength to move, but my inner being remained distraught and weak. Danielle looked at me from across the room with her innocence. I got up and grabbed my baby to feel her daddy. Two women dressed in black dress pants and blue shirts opened the door. My heart sank, knowing it was about Daniel. God please don't let it be. I can't hear it right now.

"We need the mother and the wife," said one. Ms. Cathy, aunt Marge and I jumped quickly to our feet and walked outside the room with the doctors.

"Please have a seat," said the blonde haired one. We all sat down slowly.

"If Daniel doesn't make it, would you all consider donating his organs?" she said. Ms. Cathy looked at her sister Marge.

"No," they both said at the same time.

"Are you sure? He's very healthy and we're not sure he is gonna make it," she said.

"No. If he wanted to donate his organs, he would've told us so," said Ms. Cathy.

"Yeah, he would have put it on his license if he wanted to be an organ donor. Are you saying he's not going to make it?" I asked. Although I volunteered to be an organ donor, I couldn't be upset with others decisions. My organs would do me no good dead. If they could help someone else, then that's what I wanted. My body was nothing but a living temple. My spirit would ascend to my Father anyway. I wouldn't get a fair shot at life either, being a donor.

"His brain is swelled and we aren't getting any activity from it," said the dark-haired doctor.

"What about his heart? Is his heart beating?" I cried, holding on to hope, knowing God was a miracle worker. Knowing God could do what he wanted. Knowing God could raise the dead. Knowing God was omniscient.

"Yes. It's beating, but right now the respirator is helping him breath," she said.

"We'll give you all time to think everything over, then we'll come back," said the blonde haired doctor standing to her feet.

"Okay," said aunt Marge.

I walked back into the family room to call bishop Hightower while aunt Marge and Ms. Cathy discussed the welfare of Daniel.

"Praise God," said bishop Hightower.

"Praise the Lord," I cried.

"What's wrong?" he asked softly.

"Do you remember when I was on the phone with you earlier and the line beeped?" I paused.

"Yes."

"Well, it was my niece telling me my daughter's father got shot in the head," I sobbed.

"Oh Jesus. How is he?" he asked as he began to pray inwardly.

"Well, he's on a respirator to help him breath. They say his brain swelled up a lot, but I'm not giving up. I know God can work a miracle," I said.

"Yes he can. Let's pray," he said. The bishop prayed with me while everyone in the room looked on in silence. I didn't care about what they thought. Daniel's life was on the line. It didn't matter if I was misunderstood or thought of as crazy. They weren't feeling me anyway.

While we prayed in the spirit, everybody really looked at me like I was a nut. Some knew what speaking in tongues were and others were simply ignorant to it. We cried and begged God for Daniel's soul, then I saw Daniel's mom break down outside the door and I knew he didn't make it. *I would never forget the cry of a mother that lost her child.*

"Bishop, I have to go," I said as I reached for the door.

"Is everything okay?" he asked.

"Yes, but Daniel's mom just fell out. I don't think it's good. I'll call you right back," I said then I slammed the phone down and ran out the door.

"Daniel, no! My baby! God please! I spent nine months and sixteen hours of labor for nothing. I did all that for nothing! I carried him and went through all that pain to lose him," Ms. Cathy cried in her lap. She wanted to physically die with her baby. She had another, but Daniel was her everything. He knew her better than herself. He was her strength. He kept her moving. He made her feel more like a sister than a mother.

"He's not dead, is he? Is he dead?" I sobbed, hitting the floor. I tried to prepare myself for the worst, but reality hit me hard. It was no preparing for this. Nancy ran down the hallway with Luke and Job to get away from the truth. She couldn't accept losing her best friend. One of Stella's girlfriends walked over to me and said, "I'm sorry. I'm so sorry. Please be strong for the kids." I looked at her spaced out and nodded my head gently, giving her my thanks, then I fell to my knees. The doctors walked over to us and said, "We are gonna disconnect the respirator and clean him up, then you all can go back and be with him."

Ms. Cathy ran back before they could get back to him to find him already disconnected from the respirator. "They already unplugged the machine. Why did they say they were gonna unplug it, then clean him up? They didn't give us a chance to say anything. They did what they wanted to do," she screamed. And that, they did. They already ruled out the possibility of life. They didn't care about my prayers. They didn't care that God was a miracle worker. They didn't ask for our permission first. When they asked about his organs, they already decided for him. They already counted his organs as theirs. Once we denied giving them what they wanted, what did they really

252

care. Another black man, a statistic to them, that's all. *Our crazy, confused, mixed up world.*

Daniel's spirit looked down on us as we wept. It was nothing he could do now but look. He wanted to tell us he loved us and there was a better place after death. He wanted so badly to say, "hell is real and if you don't repent of your sins, you will not make it to heaven. You will be tormented by Satan day and night when all you have to do is say, 'yes' to Jesus and you will spend eternity in heaven where sorrow and pain is no more. If you love me and want to see me again, just say 'yes' to Jesus, if not, Satan will be your Father and his Kingdom will be your home. Please my family, say 'yes.'"

I picked up the phone to dial bishop Hightower.

"Praise God," he said.

"He didn't make it," I cried.

"Oh, Cinnamon. God is with you. My prayers are with you and the family. I have been praying since I talked to you," he said. He really felt my void. He prayed deeply for me to be strong.

"Thanks."

"Cinnamon," he paused.

"Yes."

"Do you remember what you were talkin' to me about when your niece called?" he asked.

"Yes."

"Well, you know you have to write that book. It's meant to be. It is written," he said.

"I know. I was trying to figure out how to end the book after Job's death and Daniel got shot as we were speaking on the phone. This is unbelievable. God knew it wasn't time then. I had more to experience and write about. I guess that's why I hadn't done it then. Now I have to do it," I said.

"Yes you do. It has to be done," he assured me.

"It's written. I'll talk to you later," I said.

"Believe God. He may not have answered your prayers the way you wanted Him to, but He knows best. He is God," he said lastly.

"I know. Thank you so much. I can't understand it now, but I know it will come clearer later. I'll talk to you," I said then I walked in the bathroom to wash my face and hands.

Stella stood at the sink crying while her girlfriends comforted her. None of us knew the hour so it was time for us to get it right. We fought over *titles, love and money* and God wanted us to put Him first. He was the key to our happiness.

Two days later. While the earth revolved around me, I became a prisoner of my surroundings. I hadn't left Ms. Cathy's room. I hadn't eaten, slept or moved out the door. It was nothing outside for me. My world remained at a stand still. It was nothing out there that could make me whole. I talked to bishop Hightower around the clock to make sense of my nightmare. I talked to him about my fears, guilt, pain and grief. He understood me, God understood me, but I didn't understand me. I didn't understand myself or anything around me. I constantly asked God if I was the reason for Daniel's death, if I was bad luck, if I was cursed. He said I was not, but I didn't believe him.

The next day Ms. Cathy asked me to go with her to Daniel's place to get his things. That was hard for me to do although it wasn't my first time doing it.

I walked inside Daniel's place to find everything the way we left it last. The food Daniel prepared for us nights before, spoiled on the stove. The glass he drank from last, sat on the counter top untouched. I looked at the pool table and the screen t.v. then I walked over to the window to catch the view of the bridge that we watched so often together talking about our future and accomplishments.

"Mom can we play the game?" said Luke, catching my attention.

"Sure. Go ahead."

I sat Danielle down on the floor to play with her toys. She pulled everything from the closet and laid it out like Daniel normally did for her to play. She looked at her Little Tykes kitchen set, then she pulled the plastic pots out the oven.

"Dada," she smiled, beating on the stove top. She knew where she was. This was her spot. It was her resting place. She had so many memories there. She and Daniel bonded even more the past few weeks. Tears dropped from my eyes and I walked into the bedroom to gather my belongings. I couldn't think any deeper.

Ms. Cathy pulled boxes from the closets.

"One thousand, two thousand, three thousand," she counted, looking into one of Danielle's boxes from Christmas. "I'm gonna put this with the rest of Danielle's money."

I nodded my head and said, "I'll give you the account number so you can make the deposit."

"It isn't in the bank anymore," she said.

"What do you mean?" I asked.

"Stella's mother came by and gave me a check for the money," she let me know. Ms. Thang went against the law and regulations of the bank and withdrew my baby's money and Ms. Cathy trusted her so much but she got her for six thousand. She believed she and her daughter deserved that. *See, when you try to be slick, you get out slicked.*

"What right did she have, doing that? Who does she think she is?" I asked her.

"She said she didn't want anybody to be able to get a hold of her money," she said.

254

"Who is anybody? She was talking about me. I am the only one that could have gotten my daughter's money. In other words, she's saying she knows what is best for my daughter. She's saying it's okay to take things into her own hands. When were you gonna tell me?" I asked her.

"I was gonna mention it," she said.

"Her money should have stayed where Daniel left it. He put it there for a reason. Why is everybody worried about what plans he had? Why is everyone so concerned with what they think he wanted or what they think is best? Who said he wanted, what they want? I'm not saying I do either, but I know what he wanted for me and his daughter. I know what we talked about for our family. I know what plans we made. Stella has a baby, a life, a baby's father and her and her mother needs to be concerned with that. Best believe you couldn't even have an opinion when it comes to that child. So how could you let them have anything to do with Daniel and his daughter?" I asked angrily.

"I didn't mind her bringing the check over anyway because I needed the money to bury him. My insurance check won't come until after his funeral. It takes time," she said.

"I have no problem with that. But when it comes to anything else, it seems like I'm not to be trusted and I'm Danielle's mother. Daniel and I knew what was best for our daughter. He wanted me to be the trustee on the account for a reason. Now everybody wants control over something that isn't theirs. I hate selfish, nosey, inconsiderate people. I am so tired of people minding my business. Thinking they know what's best for me. Thinking they know what's best for my daughter. No one has to take care of her, but me. I can care less about the money, but it was wrong. It was wrong to go against Daniel's wishes," I said.

"Her money is going back in the bank. I didn't want it in that bank anyway. As far as I'm concerned, she might have taken some of the money," she said.

I turned to the window to catch my breath and swallow my words. The nonsense just wouldn't stop. People still remained in our business and he was dead. She looked under his mattress to find his Hechler&Koch 40.caliber gun. She took it and put it with the rest of his things, then she pulled everything out, piece by piece.

"Did he keep any money here?" she asked.

"In that compartment right there," I pointed to the wall. She pulled the door off the compartment and I walked to the kitchen to get a trash bag to put my things in.

Seconds later I walked back to the room to find Ms. Cathy looking through the items I gathered together.

"She doesn't trust me or something. Why is she looking through my things? I don't have anything that doesn't belong to me. I don't believe her. I would

255

never take anything that doesn't belong to me. If I found anything, I would give it to her, hoping she would do the right thing," I thought as I stood in the doorway waiting for Ms. Cathy to finish searching through my things. After finding nothing other than what belonged to me, Ms. Cathy finished gathering Daniel's things together.

"Are you okay Ms. Cathy?" I asked as I walked into the room

"Yeah, I'm fine. Do you want these pictures?" She asked.

"You can have them if you want them. I have enough already," I said. I stumbled over a Visa Card with a Brittney Smith's name on it and my heart sank.

"Do you know anyone named Brittney Smith?" I asked Ms. Cathy.

"No," answered Ms. Cathy.

"Well, here's her credit card. I guess Daniel had her here and she forgot it," I said.

"I doubt it."

"Well, it didn't get here by itself. How and when did he have time to have someone here?" I wondered.

"I don't know."

"Well, anything is possible. I guess he managed to cheat somehow or another, just like everyone else," I said, then I walked into the bathroom looking for evidence now. I searched the medicine cabinets for proof of another woman even though he was dead. I was trippin'. I looked on the floor and in the shower for hair. I found a few strands but Luke said they were mine and Danielle's so I gave up the search. It was nothing I could do anyway. I couldn't go to him and fight about it. He was dead.   Inside the hallway closet Daniel had another stash and I kindly gave it to Ms. Cathy then we hauled everything out and put it in the Uhaul truck.

The next day Nancy and Ms. Cathy went back to Daniel's to open the compartment in his wall. Nancy claim Daniel was holding ten thousand dollars of hers and he had that much at the apartment but I didn't know if she was telling the truth or not and Ms. Cathy wasn't about to give her the money she found anyway. Daniel wasn't here to say what was what, so that was that.

I got myself together and went to mom's to get clean clothes for the kids and me. I stepped up in my room hating the sight of it. I pulled out the purple Cashmere sweater, the purple Chanel suede boots, a pair of Gap stonewash jeans and the Chanel belt that Daniel purchased me as gifts. I stood in the mirror and put on piece by piece slowly.

"Damn! I miss you Daniel. You just don't know how hard it is to be without you. You don't know how badly we miss you," I sobbed as I dressed. I sat on the bed to zip my boots up only to notice a brown large envelope staring me in the face. I picked it up slowly and opened it up.

"We were supposed to pick up Daniel's income tax check," I spoke aloud as I looked at the documents from H&R block. I picked up the phone and called the lady that prepared Daniel's refund and to my surprise, she said I could get the check and I needed it for multiple reasons.

I pulled Daniel's mom car directly in front of the door only to find myself looking for Daniel and the Jeep. I still hadn't gotten used to the situation. "He's not here. What am I thinking?" I asked myself as I got out the car slowly.

"I know she isn't," I blurted.

"What!" said Luke.

"Stella."

"What about her?" he said, looking around. "Oh, she's in the house."

"I hope not. If she is, I'm out and I'm not coming back," I said.

I walked into Ms. Cathy's house to find Ms. Cathy holding Stella's baby and Stella smiling on the sofa reminiscing about her and Daniel. She made sure I heard her say she talked to Daniel the night before he got murdered. I was hurt but I couldn't let her know. I went straight to Ms. Cathy's room to write a tribute for Daniel from his daughter.

Daddy My Love

Daddy my love, Daddy my friend.
Daddy I never thought that this life would end.
Through it all, you said you would be here,
now all I have are memories to share.
You were a gift from heaven above,
and God sent you here to share your tender love.
When it was close for you to part,
I was thought of through the heart.
I was created through the love that you and mommy shared,
and it was a must that I would be here,
to blossom like a flower of your tender love.
None knows the pain that mommy and I feel
because it happened so fast that it doesn't feel real.
Your touch, your love will never be forgotten,
because you were the love of my life and I was your angel,
your love and friend;
Therefore, I'll hold our love close till the end.
Mommy, my brothers and I will never be the same
because everything was incomplete until you came.
We never imagined it to be this way.
We always told you never to go away.
Now that this has happened, we must go on
and be strong the way you would if it were one of us.

Daddy, my love, Daddy my friend,
I'll always love you until the end.
We had precious moments together that no one knows about but you
and I and I know I'll look back on those memories some days,
and I'll cry not knowing why you had to say goodbye.
Daddy, my love, Daddy my friend,
God will truly give me the strength to endure this pain til the end.
Daddy, you spelled my name like this for a reason.

D-arling I'll never forget the love, laughter and joy of the day
     that you came.
A-lways and forever will our love remain.
N-ow thanking God once again for giving us a chance to love
     and know each other from the very start.
I-nside opening my eyes to yours, will never leave my heart.
E-arly mornings hearing your voice in the air,
L-oving everything about you, up to your precious hair.
L-ord knows the connect that we share.
E-verday and always will I thank him for giving you to me
     and me to you and for blessing mommy with the Danielle
     that she longed for.
     I'll love you forever and always my love,
      you mean the world to me.
     You are my life, my joy, my morning star.
     And trust me love, I won't be far.

Hours later I walked downstairs to get my baby only to find Ms. Cathy sitting on the sofa with her co-worker Muggy and her daughter. I grabbed Danielle from her walker and walked to the kitchen only to hear Muggy cries, "I loved him so much. I haven't been able to sleep since his death." I peeped out the kitchen to make sure I heard correctly. How was Ms. Cathy playing? Ms. Cathy looked at me and turned her head.
"I don't believe this. I am so tired of hearing everybody talk about how much they loved Daniel. I know he was a loving person, but they are really trying to get under my skin. She better hope I don't trip on her," I mumbled, trying to keep my composure. I wanted to check the shiesty bitch. She knew I was his girl but that's the way things went. Some women would never change. I couldn't wait for Muggy to leave so I could question Ms. Cathy about her. I couldn't understand her position. I didn't know if she was trying to be smart or what.

An hour later Muggy got up and looked at me once again. She wanted me to believe that Daniel cared about her and I knew better. I knew he never cheated on me with her and if he did, she was the only fool because she knew how he felt about me. All the bitches on his job knew for that matter. I had no reason to hate them because they hated me for having what they wanted so badly. They didn't have anything I needed.

I held onto the chair so I wouldn't haul off and hit her out of respect for Ms. Cathy, then she pranced her crater face out the door. She was so glad I didn't make bigger holes in her mug. She knew I was about to go off on her.

"Was Daniel messing with Muggy?" I asked Ms. Cathy.

"No," she replied.

"Well, what was she talking about? And what did she mean by she was so in love with him and she don't know how she is going to make it without him now that he's gone?" I said.

"She was in love with him, but he wasn't in love with her," she finally admitted.

"What do you mean? Was he messing with her?" I asked.

"He didn't like her like that. I know she was trying to see him, but I don't think he did anything with her. She bothered him at work every day. You know that night after y'all left the comedy show," she paused.

"Yeah."

"She came here with me and waited for him all night," she let me know now that he was gone.

"What! How did you let her wait for him knowing he had a family? Knowing we were together," I cried.

"I told her she wasn't right. Daniel did come in for a minute that night," she said. My heart sank into the vinyl floors as I listened closely. I couldn't believe what I just heard.

"He did?" I asked.

"Yeah. She cried and begged him to stay. She pulled on his legs and he pushed her away and told her he loved his family then he left. She said she is still in love with him. She said she can't do anything without him. She hasn't been back to work since his death. She really loves him. Marcy was in love with him, too. But he didn't pay any of the girls on the job any mind. She flirted with him all the time. She would ask him to bring her lunch or dinner to the job whenever she saw him," she went on and on. *Now she's telling me all this. She knew they liked him all along. That's why they couldn't stand me and they treated me funny for no reason. She let them sit in her house and around me knowing what they were up to.*

"Yeah. I couldn't believe half of them. You know how we are sometimes. We want what we can't have," she said lastly. I stared at the ceiling in disbelief. I cried silently to myself. She hurt my feelings on purpose. I grabbed by baby. My boo. My pride and joy. A part of Daniel that those chicks didn't have and went to my hiding place to cry alone, to cry to Daniel. That's all I could do is weep alone because I couldn't bring him from the grave and check him about all the things he did wrong in our relationship. I wasn't perfect either.

After seeing Daniel at the funeral home, I went back to Ms. Cathy's to find her sitting with Ja and my heart ached more. I could take no more phoniness. I was tired of all the fakes and he irked me with his leprechaun looking ass.

"What's up Cinnamon?" he asked. I could see straight through him. He was glad he had no real competition around. Braheem was nothing but a loser and couldn't keep a dollar so Ja could have all the shine with Daniel gone.

"Nothing," I answered rudely.

"If I can do anything for you, let me know," he said.

"If you can't give me Daniel, then you can't do nothing for me," I blurted, standing strong and firm. I had to hide my weakness and pain. I couldn't let him know what I was feeling. He hurt me once before and I wasn't about to let him see me sweat. He was to know. I was a big girl. He was to know, I was solid as a rock and nothing could break my spirits. He was to know that. I turned my back and went upstairs to get away from his presence fast.

Ms. Cathy asked Ja to be a pallbearer because he and Daniel grew up together. She simply forget about how he crossed Daniel or she forgave him, but the *Soul Train Awards* was more important to him and a couple of Daniel's other so called friends. His real friends stayed behind. They even lost the money they spent on airfare, tickets to the awards and hotel reservations. Daniel was their dawg. The awards would come again, but saying good-bye to him wouldn't.

The limos pulled up to the church full of people standing around crying and comforting one another. People kindly made a path for the family to make an entrance. We stepped out the limos' one by one with butterflies in our bellies.

At the door my sisters, brothers, nieces and nephews grabbed me to give me their condolences once again and words of encouragement to make it through the service.

I stepped in quietly with the family and we all sat down directly in front of Daniel's bronze casket surrounded by beautiful flowers and a pure white spray.

Stella's scream for Daniel caught my attention. I tuned in immediately then I noticed her body bent over the casket, and her feet pounding the floor upset everybody in the church.

"Why Daniel! Why! Why did you do this to me?" she cried. *Old bitch please! You just spoke death on him.* Stella's mother got up to comfort her then she guided her to her seat across from me. You would've thought someone told Stella what colors' Daniel, the kids and I were gonna wear.

She had on a brown, two piece skirt suit similar to mine with brown two inch leather heels to boost her little ass. We were both, short, petite and nice looking but Stella knew she was the shit while I was very humble and low key. I shook my head and put it in my lap. *Why me?* Tanya sat on the same row as Stella with Ja's girlfriend Sharon and Daniel's first girl Vicky. Some things couldn't be changed.

After everyone made their entrance the pastor began speaking, then Daniel's cousin Steve did the remarks. No one could describe Daniel better than Steve. Daniel's cousin Brady sang a beautiful song, then the pastor asked the family to come up once again to view Daniel.

Stella raced to the front with the family to block my entrance. She was to make sure my kids and I couldn't get through.

"Excuse me," I whispered. "Excuse me." Stella's body stood firm. She didn't budge a bit. She totally ignored me so I kindly put my hand in her side and pushed her back a few feet and made an entrance for the kids and me to form a circle with the family. She needed to stand where her place was. I was his present. She was his past. It was all good, if she meant well, but she was trippin' this day. She showed no respect to me and mine. I wasn't having that.

Everyone broke down before Daniel. Ms. Cathy begged for Daniel's life once again. Danielle stared, not fully understanding. Luke flipped out begging for Daniel to come back. Job's tears fell silently. I knew I had to accept his death, but my conscious wouldn't allow me to. The state of denial dwelled inside my very being.

After everyone saw Daniel for the last time, Ms. Cathy placed the white cloth gently over her baby boy's face, the funeral director closed the casket, then we all made our way into the basement of the church to feast.

At the entrance of the church Daniel's father, his wife, his brothers and sisters stopped the funeral director to see Daniel as they were carrying Daniel's body out the church.

"That's my boy in there," he said. The director had little knowledge of whom he was and besides, the funeral was over and the family was downstairs eating.

Mr. Daniel made an entrance into the basement very distraught about not being able to see his boy. He wanted so badly to lay Ms. Cathy out. He thought she could give him permission to see his boy and she didn't on purpose.

Ms. Cathy sat in her chair and rolled her eyes at Mr. Daniel. She gave him the information, but like always, he failed her and her boy and Daniel got his wish whether he meant it or not. *Hurt and bitterness will make you say some things.*

Mr. Daniel gave everybody the cold shoulder, then he burst out the back entrance of the church with his family. He wanted nothing to do with anyone after this. His intentions were to never turn back. His boy was gone so there was no need for him to come our way again. He thought he was gonna be a part of his granddaughter's life, but without Daniel, he thought it was impossible. He just knew Ms. Cathy was in control of that situation, too. There was no place for him in our city anymore. The country held his family and happiness.

I had the Jeep repaired and gave it to Katima because Ms. Cathy didn't want to see it again and I didn't know how much I could take either. I felt so alone. I tried to understand Ms. Cathy's grief but she seemed a little bitter toward me about wanting to keep the Jeep but I didn't have another vehicle and I only had a couple dollars in my savings and three kids to raise on my own. Things were really rough and I had to come up with something for my kids and me. It was time to start over again.

Chapter 6
ACCEPTANCE
"Letting Go"

Three months since Daniel's death. Ms. Cathy gave me ten thousand dollars to find a place and sent me on my way. She needed her space. It was time for me to start living again but little did she know, I really needed her. She was the last reminder of my Daniel. Without her, I had very little. I considered her a friend and I felt like she abandoned me too.

I ran back and forth to Home Depot with my contractor to get materials to redo my kitchen, bathroom, the two bedrooms and to make minor adjustments to the rest of the place that my kids and I would now call home.

After spending close to twenty thousand dollars on redoing the place and some new pieces of furniture for the kids and me, I felt a little better that I had something to offer my babies, not everything or the best, but something. Being left with a couple of dollars in my pocket meant little, knowing my babies had a suitable place to live in.

Dad flew in from out of town ten days later. He helped me move a lot of things into my spot from the storage unit and mom's house. I glanced at him every now and then only to think of why or how he did what he did to me. I thought I forgave him, but this instance would remind me of the hard times in my life without him. Tears rolled down my face, but I continued to do what needed to be done and when the sunset, I drove dad back to his dad's house.

I woke up in my new queen-sized Broyhill bed surrounded by throw pillows and my babies at the end of the week. I looked up at the newly painted ceiling only to realize Daniel, Job and Luke would not spend Father's Day with their children. I looked at each of their seeds and smiled. I was so grateful to have three remainders of my past that would never die. The flesh would always go but the memories wouldn't. I had a part of the *3 Men I Chose to Love* and I was so at peace with that alone. The phone rang. Luke jumped up to answer it.

"Hello," he said.

"Hi Luke. Can I speak to your mom?" asked Ebony.

"Here mom, it's Ebony."

"Hey girl, what's up?" I said.

"How are you doin'?" she asked me.

"I'm fine," I said.

"What are you doin' today?" she asked.

"Nothing much, why?" I asked.

"Do you remember the guy I wanted you to meet, months ago?" she said.

"The one you called me about when Daniel was living and I told you I couldn't go out with y'all because it was against what I stood for," I said.

"Yeah."

"What about him?" I asked her.

"Well, he asked me about you again. And I thought since Daniel wasn't here anymore that maybe you would go out with him now," she said.

"I don't know about that one. Daniel isn't here in the flesh, but I still love him. And I don't know if I am ready to see anyone right now," I said.

"Well, you don't have to see him, but can I give him your phone number because he wants to meet you badly. I think y'all are perfect for each other," she smiled.

"Why do you think that?" I asked.

"He reminds me of Job," she said.

"How?" I asked.

"They have some of the same characteristics. Their style is similar. I think Job was a smoother dude and nobody can compare to him, but I think you and Whitey would be good for each other," she said.

"Oh yeah," I smiled as I thought of Job.

"Yeah, y'all would be good together. Y'all would make a nice couple. He's nice looking. You're pretty. Y'all both have class. I just think y'all would fit together nicely," she said.

I sat on the other end of the phone imagining what it would be like to have someone similar to Job. I knew no one could ever take his place, but the thought of having someone close to his character, made my heart beat fast. *Ebony has class and good taste. I can trust her judgement. She never steered me wrong.*

"Does he have a girlfriend?" I asked. That was one of the first things a sista needed to know. I never liked stepping on anyone's toes. I didn't stand for that because I didn't like it when it was done to me.

"I know he has twin boys, but him and his boys mother isn't together. He used to mess with a girl I know, but he said they don't mess around anymore. He said he is trying to find him a good girl and I thought of you again. I think y'all would work out. I really do. Let me give him the number," she insisted. What could it hurt? If I don't feel his conversation, I won't talk to him again that's all. "Okay. Give him the number," I said then we hung up and Ebony called Whitey right away to give him my number. Not only did she want to hook us up, she went out with his friend so she wanted to keep it in the family.

Day and night Whitey and I sat on the phone getting to know each other. He told me of the times he saw me years back when I had my drop top BM and he had his 750 BMW. And how one day his boy's mom smacked him in the face for looking at me at the gas station and I fell out because I never knew about it until this day. He told me about the days he sat back hoping to get the opportunity to see me again. He assured me I would recognize him when I saw him. He explained his situation about two girls that fought over him recently, but he had no interest in either of them. He expressed his feelings about him and his boys' mother. I felt his pain of not being able to wake up to his family anymore because I myself, was feeling the same emptiness. He shared his emotions, his thoughts, strengths and weaknesses. He said he only wanted to love my kids and me regardless of what anyone had to say about the situation. He only wanted to be what Danielle didn't have. He knew he couldn't replace her father, but knowing what little angels required, he was destined to fulfill that need. A daughter was something he didn't have and somewhere in his heart, he wanted a daughter or a little girl that he could feel like a father to.

With all that I was impressed with Whitey because he knew how to make a sista feel good but I was afraid of the feeling deep within so I tried to cut the connection between us off. I was afraid to get attached and hurt all over again but I wanted to be a part of something special and loved, too, at the same time so I promised myself to take it nice and slow. I promised to keep him at a distant in the flesh and close to the heart until the right time for me, and especially the children. I knew they loved Daniel deeply and they only wanted him and no one else. I knew they didn't and wasn't ready for me to be with anyone, aside from him. Night and day they stressed their feelings about me being with someone else and they wanted no parts of a new man. If it wasn't Daniel, it was no one.

After weeks of talking to Whitey on the phone I agreed to a night out with him. I didn't know what he looked like, but I had to take my chances, besides, how could I go wrong. We already connected mentally so from there it would be all physical.

Once Whitey pulled up in his F250, I was impressed. He had light curly hair, big round eyes, a narrow nose that laid perfectly against his smooth soft, bronze skin. His lips were full and luscious. I was satisfied and he looked like he was once I got into the truck with him because he kept looking over at me every now and then to check what he had beside him.

We crossed the bridge to go to *Benihanas* with very little to say. He sparked up different conversations, but with little feedback from me, he kept it to a minimum. I was right, he thought, I didn't talk much in person.

Whitey swerved into the crowded lot full of phat cars, minutes later. "Have you ever been here before?" he asked me. Benihanas was one of his favorite spots. He loved their food.

"No," I answered quickly. He smiled and jumped out, then he came around and opened my door for me. His eyes watched close as my legs stepped out of the truck. He had a thing for legs.

"Here, let me help you," he said, grabbing my hand to help me to the ground. I landed on the ground, thirteen inches below him. I looked up at his eyes only to realize he had something else that attracted me. *Okay. He has to be every bit of 6'2".*

"How tall are you?"I asked.

"Six two," he smiled.

"I thought so."

I looked him up and down to check out what he was working with. *Sizing a nigga up, is important.*

"Wait a minute. I have something for you and my baby in the back," he said, then he reached in the back to pull out two dozen red roses.

"These are for you," he smiled. I inhaled the fresh scent of the roses only to sense how sweet he was.

"This is for baby girl," he said, handing me two big boxes. "Open it up to see if she can fit the stuff."

I opened both boxes full of clothes to check for sizes.

"She can fit everything. You have good taste," I said. And he took time to pick out the right colors and sizes. I didn't shop at Children's Place for my Danielle but the items Whitey selected were nice.

"I try."

As I watched Whitey walk, I realized he had a combination of my Luke, Job and Daniel put together. I found some of all the men I loved in this one man.

We got a little more acquainted while we waited for the cook to prepare our food before us. We already knew each other from weeks of talking on the phone and the turnout was no disappointment. I was what he wanted and he was what I wanted too, being in each other's company just made the feelings stronger. We ended the night with a long walk by Penn's Landing.

As soon as I put the kids to bed, my phone rang and it was Whitey talking dirty to me. I didn't know what it was about him, but we were definitely on the same page.

After we had phone sex, Whitey came by my house and gave me money to buy something seductive for our date the next day. He loved the way I looked and he wanted to see me in something appealing that I picked out exclusively for him.

I hit Toby Lerners the next day to purchase a seductive dress that I thought would entice Whitey the way he wanted. My goal was to please him although I was scared of the challenge. The thought of doing something different, interested me. The words he quoted to me about "trying new things," entered my mind and I knew it was time to step up my game. I was a big girl now.

I paid my girl Wednesday for the shoes and dress, then I walked to the car and headed up east to get my hair done for the night. Cousin Carol just opened her new salon so I didn't have to deal with the hating bitches anymore. Most couldn't afford her new prices so I left ReRe's and was back home. I could get the real treatment unlike some of the ghetto girls in town that talked about me. I didn't have to go to the chinks to get my nails, toes, and eyebrows done then somewhere else for a hair do. I could get everything in one whop at my cousin Carol's joint; *The Best is Blessed, Phase III.*

The Honda screeched to a stop, JADAKISS pumped through the system loud and hard, making me think of Daniel like usual, although Jada was Whitey's boy too.

I pulled up to Carol's lot and parked, minutes later.

"Hey girl," I spoke to my cousin, my hairdresser of umpteen years.

"What's up girl?" she smiled.

"Nothing much," I grinned back.

"How's everything going with you and your new friend?" she asked me.

"It's cool. I like him. He loves Danielle. They get along great. He really admires her," I let her know.

"Who wouldn't love that chocolate, pretty baby? She is the best. Where is my baby anyway? You know you can't come here without her," she laughed.

"She's with her grandmother," I said.

"Well, bring her back by to see me later," she said.

"Okay."

I sat at the bowl and my cell phone rang.

"Hello."

"What's up baby?" said Whitey.

"Hey," I smiled as I closed my surroundings off.

"Whatcha' doin'?" he asked.

"I'm getting my hair done. What's up?" I said as my panties got moist.

"I was just checking."

"Oh."

"Call me when you're finished," he said.

My cousin hooked my hair up something decent. She put a few streaks in my hair to give me a change, then I rushed home to get dressed for my date with Whitey.

We arrived to *Planet Hollywood* restaurant two hours later. Whitey ordered steak and vegetables and I ordered salmon. I sat and watched him through my shades as he ate. It was something about him that I couldn't put my hands on. His phone rang interrupting our dinner.

"Yeah. I don't wanna hear that shit!" he hollered into his cell phone then he closed it hard.

"That was my son's mom calling with that bullshit," he smirked.

I sat speechlessly. What could I say? She knew how to push his buttons. His phone rang again.

"Yeah. I told you I'm not in the mood for that. I'm sure you have him around your friends, now you wanna trip because he told you he was around my friend. Look, call me later," he said, rudely. *Oh she's trippin' about another woman. It must be serious for her to act like that and he's taking it pretty serious, too. Either he was lying about seeing somebody or it is something I don't know about.*

"Are you okay?" he asked me.

"Yeah, I'm fine," I smiled with a half grin. I knew it was something now.

Weeks later. Whitey finally took me to his spot to show me around. We were past point A. It was time for point B now. As he drove up the hill to his house, he looked around with a puzzled face. Something wasn't right. He was sure he locked all the windows but the side one was open.

"What's wrong?" I asked him.

"Nothing. Wait here," he said as he got out the car. I knew from Ebony that Whitey hustled but I didn't know to what extent or if he had any enemies because I knew nothing about him. I had never even heard of him until Ebony mentioned him and I was locked down for some years and talked to no gossiping girls so I wasn't updated with all the new hustlers in every area. I knew of some local ones but not all of them.

Whitey was very young when he hung around the old head Bizzy from the same area B squad was from. Bizzy never let Whitey hustle. He just kept him under his wing and gave him anything he wanted to keep him from hustling. But when Gee from the B squad mirked Bizzy over a drug quarrel, Whitey had all his drugs and money. He took over the game at a very early age and because he was young and testified against Gee, he had to be very low key because he was marked but he figured because he was only fifteen when he testified, that he would grow older and people would forget but some didn't.

Whitey called Cee to make sure he was safe then he checked the spot. After realizing the rain and wind pushed the screen through, he came back to the car to get me to go inside.

"Come on baby," he smiled.

"Is everything okay?" I asked as I calmed myself down. I really thought something bad happened to him. I was so shook inside. I got out the car and followed Whitey up the long concrete steps. His Townhouse was set up differently than the ones I had been to. He had so many steps leading to his.

I walked into the plush, bright Townhouse with white leather furniture, a smoked marble fireplace, a big screen tv, and a built in fish tank in the wall. I felt uneasy and afraid with it being our first time alone behind closed doors.

Whitey showed me around the nicely laid out joint, then we walked upstairs to his room.

"Sit down. Get comfortable," he suggested. I sat on the bed slowly while looking around the room.

"Nice taste," I thought looking at his charcoal gray, leather headboard. He dimmed the recess lights low, then he pushed the cd player on.

"Do you wanna listen to some music or watch a movie?" he asked as he reached for the remote.

"It doesn't matter," I smiled. He took his basketball sneaks off and leaned against the back of the bed.

"Come here. Come close to me," he said. I moved back to get a little closer to the man that came in and captured my heart.

All the talk over the phone about making love went out the window. The feelings were too overwhelming. Whitey's dick was limp.

I sat back wondering what the problem was. *I hope this nigga dick isn't little. Why can't he get it up?* I reached over to size him up again to make sure I didn't make a mistake. *I can't really tell. It's not hard. But how larger can it get? What the fuck! I just hope he knows how to work with what he has. A big dick is nice, but if it's not and it's satisfying, then that's okay. I can work with that. I can't rule a nigga out that quick. I already have feelings for him.*

"I'm sorry. I'm too excited right now," he grinned.

"It's okay. I'm not going anywhere. We have all the time in the world," I assured him.

I woke up in Whitey's arms and rushed home quickly. I had a party to attend. It was Daniel and Danielle's first birthday party and his family went all out just like Daniel would've. They had catered food, pony's, clowns, Mini, Mickey, Barney and a few other characters along with a DJ, a pool and a garden full of family and friends.

Back at mom's house Whitey pulled up and handed Danielle one carat heart diamond stud earrings for her birthday to replace the ones Danielle had lost. Then he pulled a silver bag from the back seat and handed it to me. I looked in the bag to find a box wrapped nicely with a silver satin bow. I opened it up to find a pair of silver Gucci sunglasses.

"Thank you so much," I smiled.

"You're welcomed. Where are the boys?" he asked.

"They are on their way," I said.

"I'm ready to meet them," he assured me.

"I think my oldest son may be cool with it, but I don't know about the other one," I said.

"Let me handle it."

Moments later the boys pulled up. Luke stepped out the car first and gritted on Whitey.

269

"What's up man?" said Whitey.

"Nothing," said Luke with an uneasy feeling. Job stepped out the car and looked Whitey up and down suspiciously. He twisted his lips tight and tears filled his slanted eyes.

"Who are you?" he asked Whitey. "Who is he mom?"

"His name is Whitey," I said.

"Is he your boyfriend?" he smirked. I stood in shock at his words but that was him. He was a grown man stuck in a little boy's body.

"You said you would never have another boyfriend as long as you lived. You said you only loved Daniel. You promised you would never have nobody else," he cried.

"Job please don't do this," I begged.

"Let me handle this. Is it okay if I take him for a walk alone?" asked Whitey.

"Sure. Go ahead."

Whitey picked Job up and they walked around the corner alone while I waited patiently for their return. I had to figure out how I was going to please everybody. I made a promise to them and their fathers but I was lonely and feeling Whitey too.

Thirty minutes later Whitey and Job walked up smiling.

"What did you say to him?" I asked. I couldn't believe the change in Job's attitude. He was actually acting different.

"I told him I didn't want to do you all any harm. I only want to be a friend. I asked him how would he feel if I disliked him without getting to know him first. I asked him how he would feel if Allen Iverson passed him by and talked to all the other kids," he said.

"Oh yeah. What else did y'all talk about?" I asked.

"I can't tell you everything, but he's gonna be alright. Can I take Luke and his cousin to play a game of basketball? I wanna see what your son is workin' wit'," he smiled.

"Sure."

Luke, his cousin, Job and Whitey went to Tustin's playground to shoot some ball while Danielle and I sat on the porch to chill with mom. Whitey knew Tustin's courts all too well because he coached his summer leagues there.

An hour later the boys returned with water bottles and sodas in their hands.

"What happened?" I asked.

"Oh, he has game. He can play alright," said Whitey.

"I told you my boy had game," I smiled. Whitey shook the boy's hand, then he kissed Danielle on the cheek goodnight. He knew he just broke the ice with the boys so he chose not to touch me. He could wait for tomorrow.

"Call me when you get home," he said to me.

"I will," I smiled.

The next evening Whitey got a suite at *The End of the Dove* with intentions on doing whatever necessary to make me feel him deeply. Things were gonna go down as planned this time around. He was to fuck the shit outta me and make me fall in *love*.

We walked into the room with him ready and anxious about what he wanted to do to me while I feared doing it to somebody new and starting all over again. Knowing my kids' fathers loved me with all my flaws bothered me like always and the thought of another man seeing me naked made me nervous and shame.

"Take your stuff off," he smiled while looking at me with lust.

"Huh?" I said.

"Come here," he said. I walked up to him slowly and stopped. He gently untied my Versace halter top. *Oh my God! Not my tits. Milk is gonna come out.* "Whitey you know I breast-feed Danielle," I alarmed him.

"I don't care about that. I love her and I'm feeling you. Be quiet. Let me do this," he softly said. He unzipped my leather Versace pants very carefully then he pulled my Victoria's Secret sheer thongs down my legs slowly. He came back up and unsnapped my half bra, then he put my hard nipples gently in his mouth while caressing my firm tits in a circular motion. The sweet milk that belonged to Danielle slid down his throat slowly and he moaned with such pleasure.

"Is it good?" I laughed while caressing his shoulders. I couldn't believe him. He never lied about feeling me. He was telling the truth. He wanted all of me. He sucked and slurped like I breast-fed him for months.

"It's good," he said, now looking straight into my eyes while playing in my fine pubic hairs. He pulled back momentarily and cupped my breast together and while the milk ran down my belly onto my pussy, he made sure he licked and sucked every bit of it until he got to my jungle. He opened my forest and tickled me silly with his tongue movements while inserting his middle finger deeply inside me. This moment felt so good that I couldn't wait to have all of him. This was our first intimate moment together and he was going all out. I couldn't believe him. I threw my head back and held on tight then he let me taste my juices.

"Did you know you tasted so good?" he asked while opening my legs far and wide so he could position himself just the way he wanted.

"No," I moaned while grabbing his strong back, wiggling my toes. He went back inside the forest to search for any hidden treasures. Although his eat game wasn't the best, I was still impressed by what I felt. I knew if he even took time to explore the depths of me, he was worth all of my treats so once he finished licking and sucking, I took every bit of him in and swallowed him up in my forest. Once my juices rained on every part of his dick, it would be no turning back. He'd want me every night and he'd die to find anything he thought he'd missed.

271

Chapter 7
OBSESSION & CONTROLLING
"A Recurrence"

For the next couple of weeks were the obsession and controlling. Whitey's feelings began to take control over the entire situation. What I was to do, wear, think or feel, had to be controlled by Whitey. His insecurities became my life. Whatever he wanted or thought, had to be fulfilled by me. I had to prove myself and love to Whitey or else he didn't feel wanted or needed. Showing and broadcasting my feelings toward him, had to be known. He wanted the world to know I loved him. Marking my body was a must. It made Whitey feel special. Doing things I never did, was a must for him. It was to make him know he was loved more than any man I ever loved. His place was first place or no place, sex anywhere, at any given time. Home cooked meals that he fell in love with by me were to be done at his request. Loyalty, promptness and attention were the rulers of his universe. Everything had to be right and consistent or else there was a problem.

I lay on my amethyst colored leather sofa that Whitey had purchased me from Jonne's furniture in Baltimore. I finally got rid of the set Tank had given me. I passed it on to mom although she didn't need it so she put it in her recreation room for the grand kids. Whitey also gave me eight thousand dollars for additional repairs to my spot and with the change, I purchased platinum and amethyst colored bar stools for the bar. He didn't mind helping a sista that helped herself.

As I got up to put a DVD into the changer, I realized I hadn't seen or talked to Whitey since the morning so I leaned over and picked up the phone to call the block to see if any of his boys spoke to him.

"Hello," said a female on the other end trying to sound sexy and sweet. The voice sounded familiar, but I didn't want to jump to conclusions.

"Can I speak to Whitey please?" I kindly asked her.

"Is this Cinnamon?" she asked me. The familiar became perfectly remembered instantly. My past came back to haunt me.

"Yes," I said.

"Why are you calling here for Whitey?" asked Candis.

My heart dropped to my size six feet. I couldn't believe this shit. *Don't tell me he is messing with this bitch.* "Excuse me," I said.

"You heard me Cinnamon. What do you want with Whitey?" she kindly asked. She feared the worst, just like me. If any woman in the world could break her, it was me. Whitey knew how to hurt Candis for all the slimy, underhanded things she did to him. Even though he was still fucking her back out, making her do all kinds of foul things for him, he waited for the day to get her back. He knew what would hurt her the most, and it was me. I was the perfect get back.

"Is he there?" I said.

"No, he isn't here right now. He is locked up. Are you messin' with him?" she asked.

"Yes and I consider it more than messing with him. We are rather serious about each other," I said.

"How long have y'all been seeing each other?" she asked as her voice began to crack and tears fluttered her eyes.

"For a good little while now, why?" I asked.

"Because we are supposed to be seeing each other," she said.

"Is that so?" I smirked.

"Yeah."

"Well, he never mentioned you. And nobody has ever mentioned you for that matter. He takes me everywhere with him. If you were his girl, why would he take me out in public knowing everybody knows you and me and the word would get back? I know he has twins and wait a minute. I hope you aren't one of the girls that he said was fighting over him months ago," I said.

"What me and Fall?" she said.

"Yeah, I guess so. Ebony told me about her, but she said they weren't messing around anymore and she was messing with his young boy now, but nobody mentioned you," I said.

"Yeah, we got into something over him. She was fuckin' wit' him first, then he met me and he bought me a house. She saw me and him together one day and she tripped out. But he took her home and he came back for me. He blacked my eye and I blacked his. It was a back and forth thing for a little while. But she is out of the picture now. I'm not gonna act like him and I are on good terms either, because we aren't, but he never told me that we weren't together. We've been going through some things and I haven't been seeing him that much lately. I asked him if it was another girl and he said no. But I guessed it was because he had been acting funny for months now. Did you sleep with him?" she asked. That was the only other thing that could hurt her because she knew what I was working with from Luke, Wayne, Job and she heard while in prison how I had the young boys Todd and Daniel tossed.

"Yes."

"I guess that's why he hasn't been sleeping wit' me. Did he tell you he loved you?" she said.

"Yes he did," I said proudly.

"Do you believe him?" she asked.

"Yes I do," I said.

"Are you gonna continue to mess with him now that you know about me?" she said.

"I don't know about that one. What I do know is, if he wants to mess with you and he tells me it is over between us, then it is over," I let her know.

"Well, I love him and I'm not gonna let go that easy. We have so much together. We have a house. A family. I love his boys like my own. I'm not goin' nowhere," she let me know in return. She simply let me know it was war between us and she was gearing herself up for the battle field. She was going to war for hers.

Yeah you acted like you loved my son when his father was alive. Please bitch. I know better. "Oh, you and his twins are close," I said.

"Yeah. Me, his boys and his mom. Whitey's mom stays with us," she said.

"Are you tellin' me, y'all live together?" I said.

"Like I said. We haven't been gettin' along for the past months, but he is all I want. I love him. I been through so much with him. That's why I am here right now. I know everything about him. He couldn't call you to come here to wait for his phone call because you probably don't even know his real name," she laughed. "I know all his aliases. He called me when he got locked up. He asked me to come down there and he kissed me and told me he loved me before I left. He begged me to wait here for him until he called so I could bail him out. He didn't have to tell me he loved me," she cried.

I sat in disbelief. *I don't believe this shit. Not again. I be damn if I go through something with this girl again. Ten years later and she is back in my life. I went through too much with her and Luke. I am not about to go through nothing with her over Whitey. I refuse.* "I understand how you feel. I just need to talk to him," I said.

"Okay."

We both hung up fucked up.

Candis thought long and hard about what she had to do to get Whitey back and keep him. The time Whitey and I spent together was a threat to her and she didn't know what route to take. She mastered the fuck game. She knew every trick in the book from way back when she was a young girl, but she knew it was a whole new era and she didn't know how I was playing these days. She didn't know if I stepped up the game since my last experience and she knew Whitey was the man and he had it going on so she wasn't about to throw in the towel for me. Whatever it took to save what little she thought she had. She was destined to do it. Little old Cinnamon couldn't step on her toes and steal her man. She was that girl, the badest bitch when it came to suckin' and fuckin'. If I already put my thing down in the bedroom, which she doubted and had very little worry of, she was ten steps ahead of me with everything. The things I had that she knew the niggas loved about me were, class, sex appeal, dedication, loyalty, a strong mind and I was the truth and she knew she couldn't fuck with that but she

274

had a hell of a street game. She learned the streets early on, different from me. I had my share of things but she wrote the game when it came to out slicking niggas, so she thought. All her years on the streets and all her years in the system, still couldn't fuck with what I had tied up in this one little, sweet package, so I buried in my mind and Candis feared that. Candis would ride or die for a nigga, but I was ride or die. I earned my stripes honestly. My devotion had been proven many times before to the world. My devotion lied deep within. My devotion was my life, my all, my everything and Candis knew that from getting to know me years before, so the competition begun. It was on. It was do or die baby, all for this one selfish, arrogant fuck.

I lay in deep thought for hours to come up with a solution. I tried to find an answer for myself. I wondered how I got myself in this mess and how I was gonna get out or if I was gonna get out at all.

The phone rang hours later at Whitey's chill spot.

"Hello," said Candis, laying across Whitey's bed sucking her fingers.

"Where is my brother?" Whitey asked on the other end from the jail house.

"He's in the other room," she said.

"Well, put him on," Whitey demanded.

"Okay."

Candis got Whitey's brother and they talked briefly while he looked at her with disgust because he heard her annoying me for hours about Whitey. After he finished talking to Whitey he slammed the door behind him. *Stupid bitch! I don't know what was on Whitey's mind, fuckin' with her.* Candis jumped up from the bed to open the door.

"Where are you goin'?" she asked him.

"I'm goin' to get my brother, why?" he said coldly.

"I'm goin'."

Whitey's brother didn't want to get ruder so he let her ride.

At the prison Bee and Candis paid Whitey's bail, then they jumped back on the expressway. Being mischievous, hateful, jealous and mean, Candis wanted to see if she still had it. She knew her and Whitey wasn't together for real, but her pride wasn't about to let me have him without trying to wheel him back in. Whether she wanted him or not, the thought of him fucking her knowing he was supposed to be my man, was all she cared about. Hurting me became her number one priority again.

With no mention of our conversation, Candis sucked Whitey's dick in the back of the car for the forty-five minutes that it took them to get back to the block and she sucked it good. She sucked it so good that the nigga got a charley horse and she had lockjaw. How did he keep letting her win?

While I sat home wondering if Whitey got my messages, Candis took Whitey in the house and let him have his way. She had all kinds of treats lined up for him. She had her girlfriend with her. She had all kinds of sex toys. She gave Whitey ass shots because he loved that the most; it made him feel like the President.

After Candis finished with Whitey, she listened to his messages then she had Roxy call Shalina so she could tell me Whitey was home and he was laid up with her.

While Levert's-Love & Consequences cd track 2 played, I cried. I couldn't fathom Whitey's selfish ass after all I had given him. I gave him my heart, my all, everything I said I wouldn't. I promised Job and Daniel that I would never love another and I actually fell for this two-time fake. He gave me a reason to have a relapse. He gave me a reason to call out to God again.

After crying my eyes out I was ready to rumble. I couldn't let Candis win. It was time to get her back for all the pain she caused me. I really didn't want Whitey like that at this point, but it was time to be vindictive.

Candis walked back into the room where Whitey lay on the bed thinking about me and what he'd just done. He was actually a freak himself and didn't mind Candis being a lesbian but he knew I was a different kind of girl. He wanted and needed me in his life. I was the good in him. I showed him life wasn't only about freaking, sex and money. Life had plenty meaning. Life was beautiful especially when shared with someone honest and loving. Life didn't have to be miserable and corrupt. Life could be whatever you wanted it to be, if you wanted life to be peaceful and glorious. It could be that. If you wanted it to be dysfunctional and dead, it could be that too. Life was whatever you made it.

"Why didn't you tell me you were seeing Cinnamon when I asked you if it was another woman?" she asked as she stood in the doorway of Whitey's room.

"What!" he said as he looked her up and down.

"I talked to her while you were locked up," she said, surprising him. He sat up on the bed ass naked to make sure he heard right.

"You talked to her?" he asked her.

"Yeah. She kept calling here. She rang this phone off the hook," she lied.

"What did you say to her?" he asked.

"I told her we were together, but we were having problems lately. She told me all the things you did for her and her daughter. Did you know she was a lesbian and she and I partied dudes back in the day?" she lied again, hoping he would get turned off and not want to mess with me. "She had her kids' father's set up. She isn't to be trusted. She'll get you setup. You are gonna die fuckin' with her. Don't you know she is bad luck? You knew the connection with us and you messed with her to be smart didn't you? You tried to hurt me for all the things I did. You did this because of what I did to you. I told you I was sorry for what I did. I never meant to cheat on you. I never meant to do the things I did. I stole your credit cards and charged

276

them because I was hurt about you and Fall. I never meant to hurt you. But all you do is try to hurt me. You knew what it would do to me if you messed with Cinnamon. Out of all the girls in the city, why would you choose the one and only woman that could break me? Why would you hurt me like this? You could mess with anybody, but her. I could accept anybody else, but Cinnamon. I hate her. I guess you think she is a goody two shoe, huh? I guess you think she is innocent or something. I guess you think she wouldn't cross you. I guess you think she is loyal to you. She is sneaky and slimy just like the rest of us. She is a whore just like every other whore out here. She is just discrete with her shit. She is quiet and she does her shit on the down low, whereas I don't care about what a motherfucka' thinks about me. I can care less about what I do. I am straight forward with my shit. Either you like me for me or you don't. I don't hide shit. Cinnamon is a sneaky little bitch. Don't get it twisted. You just will never find out about her shit. That's the only difference between us. I can say the bitch is good. She uses motherfuckas, too. Her shit just looks good. She is after a niggas money just like me. Don't think I want you for your money and she doesn't," she said lastly.

Whitey got away from Candis to listen to his messages. My words cut through him like a sword. He knew he had to get his shit right before he called me.

He put Candis out his place fast, he thought long and hard, then he called me like nothing happened. And when I did question him about Candis, he assured me she was lying and all he wanted was me.

Whitey walked outside to find Candis on his porch crying and begging him to be with her but he didn't care about her tears. He wanted me more because I was new and challenging and her game was getting weak.

For days Candis annoyed me. How she got my number, I didn't know but I was tired of her already. She wanted to see me at my mothers so we could talk so I put on my size zero Gap jeans, my Dolce halter top, my Gucci belt and glasses Whitey bought me. I threw on my Manolo Blahnik sandals that gave me three inches, then I jumped in Whitey's convertible that he left in my garage.

I pulled up to Luke's aunt house to pick Lil Luke up first and Teresa jumped in the street to give me the 411. Candis let them know Whitey was her man and I was sneaking with him behind her back and she was going to see me and Ebony for hooking us up.

I laughed at Teresa and peeled off. I wasn't worried about Candis like that anymore. It wasn't the eighties and whatever she wanted to see me about. I wasn't afraid. I was good and ready for her ass this time.

I pulled up to mom's house and parked. I stepped out the car to talk to Shalina before going in the house.

"So what happened with you and Candis?" she asked me.

"Girl, it's a big old mess. She called me again and I just saw Teresa and she told her all this stuff. I don't know what to do," I said.

"Well, how do you feel about him?" she asked.

"I love him. I don't know if I believe everything he said or she said, but I have to do something. I know she isn't going to let up easily. She already said she wasn't gonna turn and walk away after all this time," I said.

"There goes Candis right there," Shalina nodded her head toward the street. I turned around slowly and said, "Oh, God. I am tired of her already."

Candis parked her car and got out. "Damn girl! Look at your tits. They got all big. I haven't seen you in so long. You are so skinny. I see why Whitey likes you. He loves big tits," she laughed.

"Well, they are extra big these days and look at you. Your hair is so long and healthy," I smiled.

"I couldn't do nothing to my hair up there, but braid it up. I couldn't get perms or nothing. I kept it braided all the time while my girls rolled theirs with tissue," she smiled.

"I heard you turned Muslim, huh?" I laughed.

"Well, I still am. I'm just not into it as much because the dude I was in love with and about to marry, left me broken hearted and he had me practicing the religion hard," she said.

"You just got home Candis?" asked Shalina.

"No. I've been home for a while now," she said.

"You gained a lot of weight," I said but she still looked okay.

"Yeah. I came down a lot because I was bigger than this when I first came home. You know niggas know how to stress you out. I had my feelings wrapped up into my ex and that failed, now I'm going through this with Whitey," she said. She was another one that thought looks were everything but she had to realize looks couldn't substitute for some things. All men weren't pressed about a pretty face and blank mind. Some preferred a strong-minded woman over a pretty face.

"I can't believe you and my sister are going through something again over a nigga," Shalina said.

"Girl, who are you tellin," she said.

"I just hope y'all don't let him play y'all. And I hope y'all don't fall out over him either. It's not worth it," Shalina said.

"I know. Did you talk to him yet?" she asked me.

"No," I said.

"Well, I just called up the block and he wouldn't accept my phone calls. Can you call him and ask him what's up?" she said.

"I don't think that's a good idea. I know he wouldn't like me calling him with you around," I said.

"Please. Can you do it for me? I need to know," she begged.

"What do you need to know?" I asked.

"I need to know if he wants you or me," she said.

"Girl, why would you let him make the decision? If things isn't right, why would you let him choose?" I asked. The conversation went on and on. She finally convinced me to call him.

"Hey baby. What's goin' on?" I asked him.

"Nothing. Do you know that crazy bitch has been calling here acting like you?" Whitey said. I turned and looked at Candis.

"Oh, really."

"Yeah. She has been calling and calling. I told my boys I didn't want to talk to nobody, but you. I guess she got the message and she started acting like you to get me on the phone," he said.

Candis grabbed the phone from my hand and said, "What's up Whitey? Why didn't?" The phone went dead before she could finish. "I don't believe this motherfucker. Let's ride up his house."

"I'm not riding up his house," I let her know.

"Why not?" she asked.

"Why should I?" I said.

"Because I think we should confront him together," she said.

"Let me call him back," I said, then I dialed his number again.

"Hello."

"I can't believe you would call me with that dumb bitch right there! What is wrong wit' you? Why would you feed into her hands? How could you call me with her right there without tellin' me? Whose side are you on?" he asked me. I held the phone with nothing to say. He made me feel like an idiot, then he hung up in my ear.

"What happened?" Candis asked. "Are we goin' up there?"

"No. I'm not going up there," I said. Tears fell from her eyes. She asked me everything she could possibly think of about Whitey and me. She begged to see the mark on my body that represented him. I pulled my shirt up and showed her Whitey's name inside bars with a deadbolt and a broken key inserted inside the bolt.

"What does that represent?" she asked. She knew her unstable mind could not take the truth.

"It represents what we stand for. I belong to Whitey and Whitey only. No other key can fit inside the lock. He's my only King and no other can take his place so he broke the key so no other can get inside of my mind or body and unlock my treasure. I am his precious jewel and I belong to him only."

"Damn. I didn't know y'all were that deep. He wanted me to get a tattoo with his name but I never did," she sobbed. Finally after feeling bad about the entire situation she convinced me to do something I knew would turn him off completely. *What man wants to be confronted about anything he does?*

Candis jumped in Shalina's tinted automobile so no one could see her and I jumped in my car. Fifteen minutes later I walked on the porch of Whitey's chill spot while Shalina and Candis laid low up the street. I knocked on the door once. Nobody answered so I rang the door bell. His brother opened the door and I said, "Hey Bee, is Whitey in?"

"No. He just left," he said.

"Okay."

I stepped off the porch and jumped in the car. Shalina pulled down the street.

"Was he there?" asked Candis, leaning all the way back in the seat.

"No."

"He's in there. He didn't leave that fast. I just called while we were around the corner and I heard him in the background. I'm knocking on the door," she said then she jumped out and ran up the steps. Bee came to the door again and said, "My brother isn't here. Didn't he tell you to leave him alone? What are you up to now with your sneaky ass?"

"Nothing," she laughed. "I just want to see him."

"Well, he's not here and he won't be here for a while, so don't come back," he said, slamming the door in her face. She stepped off the porch then she and Shalina went around the corner to meet me.

"He's in there," Candis insisted. "Let's stay around for a while. He has to come out."

"I'm not stalking him. I'm leaving," I said.

"See. You are a punk. I can't believe you. You are still soft as cotton," she smirked.

"Call it what you want. I don't have time for this mess. We are gonna be together or we're not," I said. I pulled down the block and jumped on the highway with a lot to think about. The thought of me going to Whitey's house with Candis irked him even more. Whitey, his brother or his gang didn't sleep on that one. They figured it all out. Just like we knew what we were doing, so did they.

For days things were mad crazy. I was confused. Candis was hurt and deranged. And Whitey was stuck in the middle. He was definitely feeling me but Candis wouldn't go away. I didn't want to play dirty to get points from Whitey but it was whatever with Candis and Whitey got tired of me being so soft. Candis did everything to assassinate my character and I not once said anything disrespectful about her so Whitey told me Candis didn't give a fuck about me so I better fight for him because she damn sure was going to.

The fact that Candis knew so much dirt about Whitey and his clique made Whitey befriend Candis again and space came between us. Candis began doing things I did for Whitey and his boys. She cooked for them. She made sure the spot was loaded with things that they needed. She walked around butt ass naked but Whitey wasn't turned on anymore. He really missed me. I was new and different. The attraction was fresh and his dick got hard every time he thought about my sex appeal. The way I walked, the way I laughed, smelled, even the way my hair and body flowed when I put that shit on made Whitey get chills all over. He wasn't about to leave my little ass for good. He just had to figure a way outta his mess or it was gonna cause him something nice. Candis would go to the law about him if she had to so Whitey had to break away slowly.

Whitey came home to me every night but he was sneaking around with Candis too on the side every now and then. She was doing things to him that I wasn't doing yet. And every time I left Whitey messages, she listened to them and used them to fuck with me so I began to distrust Whitey even more. We were playing a very foul game and somebody was going to lose in the end.

While Whitey slept peacefully in the bed, I took his phone and figured out his code too. If Candis knew everything I was leaving him on his voice mail, I had to know everything she was leaving him too. I was tired and sick of her shit. I had to know if Whitey was lying to me. I felt it in my heart but I didn't have the proof. He was so dumb too. His code was the last four digits of his beeper number. Such an idiot. It didn't take a genius to find that one out.

As soon as Whitey stayed out all night I listened to his messages and surely he was meeting up with Candis. And not only did his messages give him up, he gave his cell phone to his boy in case I called and his boy slipped up and told on him too. It was on now. I knew I was being stupid because I didn't have to share, but I didn't like the fact that Candis thought she could win. She wasn't about to win this time around. I was going to get the last laugh regardless of the turnout.

Candis tried to hit me with a big one. She had Whitey's father fix his Benz coupe without him knowing and she drove the city to make sure everybody saw her. She stole the spare key and the car was parked in her garage for months because Whitey was in the process of getting rid of it and with everything going on, he simply forgot about it because he wasn't impressed with a new car anymore, new, fancy cars only brought more heat to a baller and he didn't need that. He had too much to lose to get caught up in fancy vehicles. He loved pushing his squatters because they didn't draw a lot of attention but the law or niggas weren't dumb, Whitey already made himself hot by messing with a bunch of women who ran their mouths about his financial status. Besides, he had top notch jewelry worth a couple hundred thousand, a few buildings and a bar that was extremely hot. All the drug boys hung there and that drew a lot of attention alone.

I was so humiliated after all my peoples called me about Candis so I beeped Whitey back to back and finally the phone rang.

"What is Candis doing with your car?" I shouted before Whitey could say anything.

"What are you talking about?" he asked me.

"You let her hold your car, didn't you?" I asked.

"I'm in Kings Dominion with my sons, my bull and his son. What are you talkin' about? I'm not even in the city," he let me know.

"Well, she is touring the city with your car," I informed him.

"What car? Which one?" he asked.

"The Benz."

"I haven't seen that car in weeks. That car has been parked and I haven't touched it in so long. Look. I'll talk to you when I get home. I can't believe you keep letting this bitch come between us," he said.

"I'm not letting her come between us. You know I'm gonna trip if I hear anything. And the fact that she's riding in my neighborhood so my peoples can see her, is treacherous. She is really trying to hurt me. She is tryna' make my life miserable. And it's working. She is really getting on my nerves. I am gonna snap in a minute. She is tryna humiliate me," I said.

"Why don't you calm down. I'll see you in a little while," he assured me.

"Okay."

For weeks Whitey went back and forth; when he'd get tired of Candis, he'd come running home to me. When he'd get mad because I wouldn't give him oral sex, he'd go running back to Candis and as soon as he stayed out all night again, I threw that shit on and Katima and I hit Delaware Ave. to check out the party scene. I knew exactly what to do to make Whitey come running home to me.

Whitey's boys spotted Katima and me from a distance in front of the club. Katima's bottle-shaped figure couldn't be missed in those fitted Versace jeans. They called Whitey to let him know his girl was in the streets.

When my cell phone rang, I got scared. I knew it was nobody but Whitey because the kids were sleep and who else would call me at such an hour.

Once I answered my phone Whitey told me to leave and meet him at Katima's house and I did.

Whitey looked me up and down as soon as I jumped in his car. He hated me in revealing tops. He didn't mind seeing them on other women in the clubs but not his girl. It was cool when we first met but I represented him now . He didn't want other men looking at me.

"That's what I'm talkin' about. Remember that. I represent you just like you represent me," I said, giving him a reality check.

"Cinnamon. I never said I was perfect. I make mistakes too. I'm human just like you. I never did anything to intentionally hurt you. Things happen, but that doesn't mean I don't love you. I do love you. Don't you understand that? I want you to listen to something," he said as he turned the cd changer to Mya track 13, "Movin' On Remix Featuring Silkk the Shocker."

I sat and listened attentively. I made sure to get the full meaning of what he was saying and thinking. While he sang Silkk the Shocker's verse over and over again, I could only feel him. He made it clear that he had flaws and Silkk couldn't put it any better for Whitey. He summed it up perfectly. He knew by looking in my eyes that I wasn't happy. Just like Silkk said, "imagine him with no flaws, a parkin' lot with no cars, a cell block with no bars, a world with no wars, LA with no stars." Whitey could hear my broken heart and he was going through it himself. He was stuck. He was caught up in the streets. His job wasn't easy. He had so much to deal with. He had the women coming from all angles because of his status. He had the jealous niggas on his heels. He had the beggin' niggas. He had the system and everything that came with the game that he had to master. He only wanted peace. He only wanted security himself.

I dropped a few tears, then I embraced Whitey tight. I let him know I'd love him regardless of what went down. I knew he wronged me and his attitude was funky at times but I knew he was a good, sensitive man too, with a heart, he was just caught up and I respected that to some degree. He needed a special kind of woman to deal with all he had to offer because he was a confused man and I loved him. The entire picture became clearer. We developed something new this night.

While I was supposed to be enjoying Wildwood's beach, I called home every minute to talk to Whitey only to hear his sarcasm. He couldn't take it when the shoe was on the other foot. He hated the fact that I up and left just because we had a minor disagreement again. I was beginning to not listen to his demands and he didn't like that. As long as I stayed put and listened to him, he was cool with that.

I stood on the balcony of the motel crying about Whitey's attitude toward me. I was so sick of him. He was sending me through an emotional roller coaster. One minute everything was great and the next it was horrible.

Tank walked up on me and embraced me from behind. He only wanted the kids and me to enjoy ourselves and I brought my problems with me instead of living them back home.

"How can you let that cat stress you out like that? I can't believe you went all out for a good for nothing nigga. He don't deserve you. Fuck him. I can't believe you keep letting these other cats into your life and you would never give me the chance. I would never make you hurt. You would never go through this but I see you like the drama," he said.

"What?" I said.

"Yeah. You don't realize it but you like the drama. If it wasn't action going on in the relationship, you would be bored. You like that shit," he smirked.

"Whatever Tank!" I said then we walked away to take a dive in the pool. Although Tank put things in position, I still wanted Whitey. I wasn't about to be vindictive but I didn't know how much more I could take from Whitey's arrogant ass either. He became a real beast.

Once I returned back to the city, Whitey was off to Virginia Beach with his friends. I hadn't done the Greek weekend in Virginia since Sugar, Chocolate and I had gone. I wasn't fascinated with the *bling-bling and the ching-ching*. I was cool but Whitey loved the Greek weekend because he could fuck whatever he wanted because of his status. You only needed a couple dollars to get laid.

Chapter 8
Back and Forth-Forth And Back
"How Much Can a Girl Take?"

A few days later I drove down to the college and parked in the dim crowded lot. I grabbed my Louis Vuitton back pack from the back seat that Whitey purchased me for school then I strutted into the building knowing what I had to do for myself. I was grateful Whitey had paid my tuition, but I couldn't take his abuse anymore. I no longer wanted to be controlled by him.

A month into the semester Whitey gained interest in me again. He was so confused but I had to give him another chance because I thought I was in love and Whitey realized he never stopped loving me. When he listened to Nas's new cd, it reminded him of him and me for some reason. He had to get things right before he lost me totally. Wherever his games were, he wanted me to be. I sat either in the car or on the bench studying for exams while Whitey coached his football team. I wanted to believe he changed for the better and from Candis messages I knew she was the one holding on to Whitey and not him holding on to her. I knew how hard it was for people to break away. I understood that, so I gave Whitey the benefit of the doubt. I just hoped Candis would give up one day.

Patience working for me couldn't have come at a better time. Whitey had no one to lean on but me, so he thought. He called me up to make arrangements for us to live together permanently. He no longer wanted to reside at his place. Circumstances would not allow him to live comfortably at home. Too many people found out where he laid his head at and he no longer wanted to stay where Candis could come freely.

I left Whitey messages on purpose so Candis would know we were officially back together and shacking. Whatever her plans were, she needed to alter them because Whitey was my live in companion. I wasn't going anywhere.

After listening to my messages Candis burst through the door of the chill spot like a mad woman. Whitey's boys turned around and looked at her like she was stupid. She walked by them without speaking and ran straight into the kitchen where Whitey stood on his gray marble floors, making phone calls.

"So you are still fuckin' wit' that bitch, huh?" she screamed, swinging at Whitey. Whitey grabbed her hand and threw her up against the marble counter.

"Bitch, don't make me hurt you!" he spat.

"Fuck you pussy! You ain't shit!" she screamed. She unraveled her body from his and hit him with a Mikasa plate from the counter and Whitey punched her in the nose, busting it wide open. Once the blood trickled down her lip, she went off throwing things around his kitchen. His brother walked in and threw her out the door.

"Stupid bitch!" Whitey mumbled as he fixed his fresh Mitchell&Ness Jersey. "I wish she would just leave me the fuck alone!"

I sat in front of the computer typing up letters to the family when the phone rang. It was mom telling me to call Mrs. Jackie. After wondering what Mrs. Jackie wanted with me, I finally called her back and she told me Mr. Bill got killed the night before. How was I to tell Lil Job his grandfather got killed six years after his father? He now had no one to do fatherly things with him although Mr. Bill didn't follow through with his promises anyway. He loved Mrs. Jackie so much that he allowed her to control his relationship with his grandchild and now he would never be able to make up for what he didn't do.

Although Mrs. Jackie never understood me, I went to her rescue after I dropped the kids off at school and we cried together. She never understood my pain until now. She lost a child but never a mate and I lost three. Now that was something to consume.

After comforting Mrs. Jackie, I got the kids and went straight to mom's to see if I had any mail there. All my jailhouse friends still sent mail there every now and then. I still used her address too.

I had two letters waiting for me on mom's coffee table, one from Snoop, the other from RJ. Snoop's read,

Greetings in the name of Allah. I've been missing you through the years but I understand your plight. Things hasn't been easy for me here but I'm maintaining. I knew you were a survivor and I'm proud that you're still standing strong. I knew nobody could break you Shorty. You remained a superstar. You are a beautiful woman and don't let those niggas fool you. You're still a black Queen and don't settle for anything less. I never stopped lovin' you. I'll still kill a nation for you. Your friend forever, Ahkee a.k.a. Snoop.

RJ's read,

I know its been a decade but I had to write and apologize for being a boy back then and not a man. I never understood your position until I fathered my own like you said I would someday and then had to lose so much and come here. You were a hell of a woman and still are and I was a real idiot. I was jealous of your devotion to my man and I can't express how sorry I am to have put you though so much pain. I heard my man's son is big and I'm just concerned about him growing up out there. It's rough and I just don't want him to get caught up like his dad and me. I'll be home soon and hopefully I can be a positive role model for him. Despite what you think, I loved his dad like a brother. I was young then so don't hold me accountable for all the bad mistakes I made. It was a learning experience. I'll be in touch and feel free to

*write me some times. **Enclosed are some shots of me now. ONE,
Ramon Jenkins.***

He didn't use his street name anymore. People said he put that name
behind him years ago because that was the old him and now he used his
real handle.

I looked at the pictures and was impressed. Jail changed some people.
I just hoped RJ wasn't talking jail talk. I hope he meant every word he said
because he made me shed tears just because he wrote and apologized
after all these years. I had to respect him for that alone. It took a real man
to do what he did because he would've never done that on the streets when
he was younger. I was so glad that he made peace with himself.

I finally got enough heart to tell Job about his grandfather. Big Job was
right. Orlando killed his father six years later for kidnaping him. Job paying
him off for what his father did was just a little compensation for his
inconvenience. Orlando still had to do what he thought was necessary to
earn some stripes. He was tired of being a victim. He needed to victimize
other people.

A week after Christmas I ran around buying Whitey gifts for his birthday.
I packed helium balloons in the car. I picked up his cake from the Exotic
cake factory that I knew would have him cracking up, then I went home to
set up a fantasy that would leave a mark on him forever. I had to keep the
fire burning or he'd get bored.

I dimmed the lights. Lit candles around the house, including the
bathroom. I ran hot water in the tub along with cherry vitamin oil to soothe
and relax Whitey's body. I laid rose peddles everywhere, from the vestibule
all the way to the bedroom. I planted citrus fruit all around to give the place
a little zest. Whitey loved fruit. I placed exotic oils in every spot that I would
need them. I broke out the Cristal and placed it on the table along with an
exquisite dinner I hooked up straight from the heart. Stuffed red snapper,
Chilean sea bass, and chicken Marsala in case his taste buds didn't know
where to go. Steamed broccoli and asparagus with cheese, baked potatoes
with sour cream and butter, just the way Whitey loved it. I placed chocolate-
covered strawberries with cream on a dessert plate.

I placed a piece of poetry on the night table next to rich, white and dark
chocolate edible dicks, pussies and tit lollipops for us to feed each other.
Then I dressed down in a black sheer nightie from Freds of Hollywood with
a pair of sexy satin pumps exclusively for Whitey. He loved my legs in
heels. Then I threw on a blonde wig to add a touch of excitement to the
fantasy.

I lay on the sofa to listen to a little jazz so I could hear Whitey turn the
locks on the doors. The first door opened ten minutes later and I jumped up
to surprise him. I turned the knob, blind folded and undressed him from
head to toe then I escorted Whitey to the bathroom where I soaked him in

287

the cherry oil for a moment. I pulled him out the tub soak and wet and licked the juices running from his body. I laid him on the bed and massaged his feet with Victoria's Secret cherry message oil all the way up to his neck, then I placed a chocolate pussy in his mouth to see him go to work. I took the blind fold off so he could watch me suck, lick and eat up, the chocolate edible dick, just like he wanted me to do him but it wasn't time yet. I just teased him to make him want me more.

After dancing around the room for Whitey, climbing my bed poll, crawling and purring like a wild cat, I inserted Whitey's dick into my mouth aggressively and sucked like I was a pro. He couldn't believe my rhythm. He grabbed my hair and begged for more.

"Damn girl! I didn't know your game was tight like this. You are sucking the shit outta my dick. Don't stop baby. Please don't stop! I want you to treat daddy like this all the time okay. I don't want to fight wit' you mommy. I want you to love daddy. Forget them bitches. Just keep suckin' daddy just like this. Okay. Alright," he moaned. I giggled with his dick in my mouth. I didn't want to let up and say anything to fuck up the rhythm so I kept it going until he came then I looked him in the eyes and said, "come on. I have something else for you."

I grabbed his hand and escorted him to the dining room where I fed him dinner like he was my child. I gently put the food down his mouth and wiped in between. The red snapper wasn't good enough. Whitey's dick was hard as a rock and he wanted my red snapper right there and then. He couldn't wait another minute because he was about to explode so I gave it to him with cream on top.

While the candles captured the glow of his face and the twinkle in my eye, Whitey melted in me like hot wax. He gave me every bit of him like I was the only one he loved and wanted to love. I was sure to make him forget about all the others.

We poured chocolate syrup on each other's bodies and ate that for dessert. We played the fantasy a little while longer, then he made a couple of thug passions to keep the fire going. Thug passions brought the beast out in him. After I made him cum and scream my name like a little girl, he stretched across the bed and went to sleep ass naked.

In the morning Whitey got up, he showered, then he kissed me good-bye and I doze back off to sleep for a moment only to realize the kids had to go to school.

Luke's aunt pulled me over in front of the school.

"Hi you doin'?" she asked me.

"Fine."

"What's goin' on with you and Candis?" she said.

"What do you mean?" I asked.

288

"She was at my house all morning looking for you. She said she was waiting to catch you take the kids to school," she said.

"Oh, really."

"She said you called her house last night from your cell phone," she said.

"I couldn't have called her. I don't even have my cell phone. Whitey has it," I said.

"Well, she said you called her. I don't trust her Cinnamon. Watch yourself," she warned me.

"What do you mean watch myself? I haven't done anything to her," I said.

"Well, you know she is crazy and she has been actin' crazy over that man," she said.

"Well, that's something she has to deal with. I can't help it if he wants me."

"I don't know what's goin' on. I know she said he is her man even though I don't think he wants her. I think she can't accept him not wanting her. It is hard for her to accept him wanting you over her. You know she thinks she can have anybody. She feels like she took Luke from you so she can take Whitey from you, too," she said.

"Well, I have to go. Thanks for telling me this."

"Okay," she smiled. Luke begged me to keep him home but I took him inside the school anyway. I didn't want him involved.

I checked my messages from mom's before going home.

"I hope this isn't whose voice I think it is and if it is, I'm gonna kill you bitch! I'm gonna fuck you and your man up! I don't know why you called my house, but it's on. Cinnamon, you and Whitey are gonna wish y'all didn't fuck with me when I finish with y'all. I'm gonna kill you, then I'm gonna kill him. Do you hear me bitch! And tell your man I am his worst nightmare," said Candis in a fit of rage.

I called my cell phone to question Whitey about Candis to get no answer. I called his pager and left messages, then I returned home.

Minutes into my nap, somebody kicked my door in and I didn't know what to do. Whoever it was could have all Whitey's money and jewels, I just had to make sure my Danielle was safe or Daniel was going to come back from the grave and kill me.

I slowly walked into the living room where Candis stood outraged and out of control in the middle of the floor.

"Is Whitey here?" she asked with her hands in the pockets of her three quarter length, black leather jacket.

She has something in her pockets. "No, he isn't here. Is everything okay?" I answered softly so I wouldn't upset her dysfunctional mind anymore.

"No, everything isn't okay! I need to speak to him. He is gonna tell me something," she demanded.

"I called him a couple times after I got your messages and he hasn't called me back. Let me beep him again," I said as calmly as I possibly could. Danielle felt something in the air and she began to cry for me.

"I'll be right back Candis," I said as I walked away slowly. I knew I had to come up with what I should or shouldn't do. I feared the welfare of my little angel.

I walked in my bedroom and Candis followed right behind me. She looked around at all the balloons, cards and whatever else left over from me and Whitey's last night of pleasure, then she looked at my bedroom set and asked, "Oh, you got Whitey the balloons for his birthday?"

"Yes."

"That was cute. He told me he wasn't doing nothing for his birthday. Was he here with you all night?" she asked.

"Yes. This is where he stays," I said.

"Yeah, you lay up in an expensive canopy bed like you are a princess and he's your prince or like you're a queen and he's the king. You like treatin' him like a king, don't you? I can't believe his ass. He has you livin' good and I'm living from place to place. Sleeping on peoples floors and shit. He told me to give him some time to find me another spot and he never had intentions on getting me a spot. He doesn't want me. This is where he wants to be, huh! I guess you think it's sweet," she smirked as her face got redder.

"Candis, Whitey doesn't have me living like a queen. I had this bedroom set before we got together. Besides, it didn't cost a fortune," I said nicely.

"Six, seven, eight thousand, something like that. It cost a couple of dollars," she said.

"Yeah, my money, not his, I am sorry about y'all situation. You hustle. You get money. Why are you waiting for him to make a move for you? I wouldn't be sleepin' on nobodies' floors," I said.

"I been through so much shit wit him. He owes me. He owes me a lot," she said as she looked around again, then she looked at Danielle and me with hatred in her eyes. She hated the way Whitey treated us. She wanted me dead.

Before Candis said good-bye, she snuck me and we tore my room into pieces. Shit flew everywhere. She reached and reached in her pocket for her razor but I wouldn't let her get it. She wasn't about to have my blood on her razor. I didn't think so.

When Danielle screamed louder, Candis put her hand over her mouth to shut her up but Ms. Cathy heard her from outside. I forgot she was supposed to be picking Danielle up so that was right on time.

Ms. Cathy and her boyfriend rushed into my spot and while Ms. Cathy picked Danielle up, her boyfriend separated us. "I loved you Cinnamon and this is how you do me," cried Candis, standing in the doorway with her hair standing on top of her head. Ms. Cathy, Bobby and I stood in shock. *She loved me.* "How could you love me and you want me dead? You can care less about me and mine. All you care about is yourself and your feelings. Candis is all that matters to you," I said.

"I can't believe you would do me like this," she cried.

"Bitch! You came here to hurt me in front of my daughter! Get the fuck out!" I screamed then I reached in my drawer to pull out the Smith&Wesson Job had given me and Candis ran out the house and jumped in Roxy's truck and Roxy sped off.

I ran behind her after I thought about what she had the nerve to do. I knew this day how slimy they all were. Roxy actually was friends with me before she met Candis. She stepped to Candis back in the day for me about Luke. She hated the way Candis came between Luke and me and she played a part in my party but we were distant nowadays.

"What happened to you? You have a big ass bald spot in your head. Look at your face. Did you handle your business?" laughed Roxy. She really didn't care about either of us. She still held jealousy in her heart toward Candis for messing with her she-man and she straight up didn't like me because of Larry. When Larry came to Philly to fight after Todd had gotten killed, Roxy and a bunch of other groupies from Philly were on his heels but Roxy got a chance to kick it with him because her brother was an amateur boxer and he knew Larry personally. Roxy fucked him, sucked him, I mean, went all out for him on the first night once she realized how deeply in love he was with me but nothing became of their one night stand because Larry regretted her, the way I did him, so she blamed me and never liked me since. She simply couldn't understand my style like a lot of the other fake broads in our city but that was her problem and I couldn't understand my sister befriended her. That was the one girl I couldn't understand Shalina being friends with because normally we didn't do broads that didn't like one of us but they had a connection and Shalina believed Roxy when she said she didn't hate me, she just admired my style and wanted to be like me.

"Whitey wasn't in there. I'm gonna kill that bitch, if it's the last thing I do," screamed Candis as she pulled her hair back into a ponytail.

For weeks Whitey, the kids and I stayed side by side. Whitey couldn't wait to catch Candis. He wasn't gonna look for her, but he couldn't wait to catch her slippin' either. She tore up at least ten of his cars, she stalked him and every time he ran up on her, she ran. She always had a getaway car. Somebody always helped her do her dirt. She did nothing alone and I have to admit, she was a bad bitch.

Candis ran up on the kids and me one morning and got a rude awakening. She saw big Luke in my son when my boy jumped out the car to chase her with an iron pipe. He wasn't playing games with her anymore. If she wanted to run around stalking us, he was going to beat her silly. He

291

didn't care whose mother she was because she didn't care whose mother I was. It was tit for tat.

Candis drove straight to Whitey's chill spot while he and his boys were out handling business. She climbed through the window that she knew so well and stole his platinum Rolex watch, his platinum bracelet, five thousand dollars and his platinum credit card with a ten thousand-dollar limit on it.

She drove away cracking up. She got more than what she bargained for. She pulled up to her young boy down north and passed him the bracelet. Then she went to the jeweler and sold him the watch. She set her money aside, then shopped the malls with Whitey's credit card like she was his wife. Because of the code that was put on the card by Whitey's father because of the last stunt Candis pulled on him, the last store clerk called it in and the NY State police came and took Candis away but she'd be out soon because she was under an alias.

Candis just wouldn't rest. She was out and up to her dirt again. Whitey beat her down in the street for cutting him in the face with the same razor she tried to cut me with and she went to his bar the next day and vandalized my car but that only made Whitey buy me a pretty red convertible Benz and Candis got sick. She got so sick that she planned to hibernate for a while. She had to sit back and think about what her next moves were gonna be.

As soon as I reached the garage and pulled my car in, my phone rang. I reached in my Louis Vuitton handbag to answer it.

"Hello," I said.

"Hey baby," cried Whitey.

"What's wrong? Baby what's wrong?" I said. Whitey was silent as he cried. I knew it was something because for the entire time I had been with Whitey, I never saw him cry.

"My mom died," he sobbed.

"No Whitey! No, she didn't! Baby, please tell me she didn't," I said as I began to cry. I knew what this would do to him. Whitey loved his mother and this would only make him bitter at the world. He would never be the same with his mother gone. Whitey and his mother had the same relationship Daniel and his mother had. And I didn't know which was worst. Losing your child, or losing your mother then I remembered the words that were once said to me. "The pain is greater when you lose your own child. When you lose your mother, it hurts but you manage to make it but when you lose your child, a part of you is gone and you'll die with that burden."

"Yeah, she did. I need you here with me baby," he sobbed more.

"I'm on my way up there okay baby," I spoke softly into his ear.

"Okay, hurry up. I need you," he cried. I backed the car from the garage and hit the expressway to see about my baby.

For days I stayed by Whitey's side. I could only imagine his void. His mom's death only made us closer. I helped him pick out her dress and he let me do the rest. I got her shoes, underclothes, stockings, wig and jewelry for her home going service.

At the church everyone took their places and filled the seats, giving all respect to Whitey, his family, especially his mother. Candis walked into the church late crying and screaming, looking for attention. She made an extra seat in the aisle next to the family. One of Whitey's cousins looked over and gave Candis a nasty look. A look like, "I'm gonna fuck you up when it's over" look.

While the preacher preached, Candis fell out. Whitey's uncle rushed over to help her from the aisle. He sat her back in the chair and rested her body on his. The same girl that wished Whitey's mother dead, sat in the church actin' a fool but Whitey stayed focus. He was not about to look over at Candis like she wanted him to. He could hear her and that was enough.

Outside the church after the service, everyone stood around greeting Whitey and his family. I stood side by side with my man. All Whitey's ex-girlfriends walked up and greeted him, some of which wanted to be in my shoes. Candis stood adjacent to Whitey and me with jealousy, envy and hatred in her heart. *I hate that bitch. Look at them. He really loves her. She really got him. How did she win him over me? I am not gonna rest. I know I need to let go and I'm gonna try, but I wish them the worst. How can I wish them happiness and I'm miserable?*

Candis hated to accept us together, especially at his mother's funeral where everybody would see us hand and hand. The truth smacked her in the face in front of hundreds of people. All that talk about she was his woman and I was the chick on the side, went out the window. Everyone knew this day who his woman was if they didn't know or believe it before.

Candis hid behind her dark Gucci glasses upset at the world. She thought her being there performing was gonna make Whitey feel sorry for her. The only thing she failed to realize is, this day was about Whitey's mother and his family, nobody else. People showing up to pay their respects were appreciated, but Whitey's load was heavy and Candis was nothing but a burden to him also. He wished her away.

Whitey and I kissed each other good-bye for the moment. He hired caters to cater food at his grandfather's house, but my food was a must at his house. I had to leave to have the food I had prepared, transported to his house in time for his guest.

Candis got furious when Whitey and I touched, but she was so glad that I was leaving. She wanted the opportunity to speak to Whitey alone.

I strutted away in my all black sheer Prada dress that showed no panty print because my sheer black thongs wouldn't reveal themselves. My niece Nichole watched my back as we walked away. She came to support me because she was pretty cool with Whitey too and she knew Candis would be there so she had to watch her. She knew how Candis played and she didn't trust her as far as she could see her. I jumped in my Benz without a care in the world. Candis presence didn't threaten me. My trust stayed with my man.

At home I changed into a pair of black Betsy Johnson jeans with a tee shirt to match and Bottega Veneta sandals complimented my American manicured toes. I was ready to serve my guest. I got my help and we packed everything in the car tight so it would be no spills.

An hour later I arrived to Whitey's spot to unload the food. I put everything on the burners inside the kitchen. Strangers and Whitey's friends rushed in to taste my food. I had a reputation for my cooking. Whitey definitely praised me when it came to the kitchen and the bedroom. The nigga had me on my game. I upped my thing by three.

I walked on the porch to sit with my baby after I cleaned up. Candis sat on the porch down the street with a few of Whitey's family members. She watched and she stared up the street at us. Every time I looked over, she stood watching us. She just couldn't let it go.

"I'm going in," I said as I reached for the door.

"For what?" asked Whitey.

"I can't stand Candis lookin' in my face."

"Forget her. She ain't comin' up here wit' that bullshit. She knows my people only let her come up here because of my mom. If it wasn't my mom's funeral, she wouldn't be up here. She can sit down there with them, but she isn't allowed up here with us. She knows she can't come up here. Get the baby jacket out the car. It's gettin' cool," he said.

As soon as Candis peeped me alone, she came to talk to me about Whitey. She really didn't want any trouble anymore after what she saw this day. It wasn't my fault that Whitey didn't want her. She let me know it was over between us and she wished us the best but I knew how she was. She could be cool one minute and off the next, so I would still keep my guard up because I was nobody's fool anymore. I trusted her one too many times before and it wasn't happening again.

Weeks later. Whitey needed a vacation after all he'd been going through. He couldn't find peace in the city. He had to change the atmosphere around him and the party was in Cancun.

He went to the safe and took out three hundred thousand dollars to buy himself some new jewelry, then he went to his man down the row to purchase a few things.

Inside the jewelry store Whitey purchased a new platinum Rolex watch to replace the one Candis stole. He purchased a platinum and diamond chain and bracelet, then he sent me to Saks and Bloomingdales to pick out a few Polo short sets for his trip while he purchased all the Louis Vuitton luggage from the Louis Vuitton store to carry his items in.

At seven a.m., I watched Whitey and his boy Mack board American Airlines flight 929, going straight to Cancun. No stops. No delays. *I know he does things with his friends all the time, but this one doesn't feel right. If it's not them with him, it's me. Everybody and their mothers are gonna be in Cancun. I hate him going without me, but I have to trust him. I have to trust the fact that he is gonna be good like he said he was.*

"As soon as I hit Cancun, I'll call okay," he said, turning around one last time to say good-bye. "I love you."

"I love you, too," I assured him. I watched as Whitey walked his strong legs across the ramp then I turned around to face people waiting to board other flights.

I rushed through the crowd to get back to my car. I could only think about how many people were gonna be in Cancun. *Whatever's gonna happen, is gonna happen. I can't worry about what he is gonna do. I have to stay focused.*

"Picture us married girl, just you and me," replayed in my mind as I swerved out the airport's parking lot. The thought of being married sent chills through my spine, the thought of Whitey mentioning marriage made my heart beat rapidly. I knew he wanted that bond but he was afraid of committing. Shacking was good enough for him at the moment. He had all the time in the world for marriage. Why not enjoy what he had without the papers? Mom always said, "be careful with whom you choose and watch what you pray for. Wait on God and he will send your mate. Don't be fast to move. Take your time and wait." So with that, I had a lot to think about. I would have an unstable marriage with Whitey because he was so iffy and I wasn't in love with him anyway, I was just caught up in the *now.*

Whitey was asleep when his flight landed at the Cancun airport. He was glad to finally get some shut eye. For the past four weeks, he couldn't rest. Whitey got up and stretched his long legs, then he walked off the airplane with his boy. He couldn't wait to eat. He was so hungry.

After taking their bags to *The Royal Caribbean Villas*, Whitey went to grab a snack while he waited for Mack to finish his phone conversation with his girl. Once Mack finished him and Whitey ate inside the hotel then they went sightseeing to see what was popping.

Day and night Whitey called from Cancun. Aside from missing me, the guilt played a big factor in him calling so much. He wanted to be sure I was being good while he was being what he thought, was a man.

The weather was blazing on the third day. Everybody was out. People from all over were in Cancun doing their thing, from Philly, NYC, Baltimore, Virginia, Washington, D.C. Atlanta, you name a city, somebody from there was in Cancun. The single and committed were mingling. Everybody was having a good time. Nobody wanted to go home. Like Mase said, "what happens in Cancun, stays in Cancun" and everybody was following that.

The ones in serious relationships and the ones that were married were doing them. Not to say that they weren't in love with their mates because they were, they just wanted to have fun like everyone else.

Whitey got up from a long night of drinking and smoking. Weed wasn't his twist, but it was whatever for the time being. He was doing him. His friends convinced him to go all out. His mom just passed away. He'd been stressed. What else could go wrong? Living for the moment made sense.

Whitey and Mack threw on their Polo swim gear and hit the beach to look at all the naked, pretty women.

At the beach the atmosphere was right. The water was beautiful and bluish. The sun was shining. There were so many beings to choose from. Everybody lost control. Nobody stayed focused, not even Whitey.

Particular about what he wanted, his eyes landed on a girl looking similar to what he left home. She stood firm on the beach with her French manicured toes planted in the sand with her girlfriends surrounding her, laughing. She tried to pay Whitey no mind, but she couldn't help herself. He was just her type, too. She glanced through the crowd every now and then only to find herself looking straight at him. She sized him up. She looked at his jewelry carefully. "Yeah, just my type. He looks like he has class. His jewelry is worth a nice amount of money. He doesn't look like the type that would wear somebody else's things. I hope he doesn't have a girlfriend," she thought inwardly.

"She's nice. She has the long hair. The tight body. The look and she looks intelligent, too," Whitey thought to himself.

"Isn't that the girl from the party last night?" asked Whitey's homey, pointing in the crowd full of women.

"Which one?" asked Whitey.

"Over there," he said.

"Yeah. I like her girlfriend," Whitey said.

"Well, I'm gonna push up on sis'. Are you comin'?" he said.

Whitey stood still for a moment then he finally said, "yeah."

They walked over to the girls with their chest stuck out.

"What's up?" said Whitey's homey Mack.

Whitey stood back smiling.

"Nothing," said the girls at the same time.

"This is my man Whitey and my name is Mack," he introduced them.

"Nice meeting y'all. I'm Meena. This is April and that's Mahogany," said Meena smiling from ear to ear, hoping Mack didn't want her.

"What are y'all getting into tonight?" said Mack.

"Anything. What do y'all have planned?" asked Mahogany.

"I want to be with you," said Mack, getting turned on by Mahogany's boldness.

"That sounds good to me," said Mahogany.

Whitey and Meena's eyes stayed locked, but the conversation went nowhere.

"Are you having fun down here?" Whitey asked Meena.

"Yeah," she smiled.

"Do you come down here every year?" he asked her.

"This is my second year here," she said.

"Do you have a man?" he asked.

"No."

That is all I needed to know. "Where are y'all staying or where can I meet up with you tonight?" Whitey asked.

"Do you have a girl?" Meena asked. She had to know that first before she made a move.

"I have a situation, but no girl," he said.

"Take my number down and call me. We can hook up tonight," said Meena. She had a studious but sexy look. Whitey got Meena's number and Mack got the same number for her girlfriend, then they walked away only to meet back up by the bar, minutes later. They had drink, after drink, after drink, until Whitey suggested they go to his room.

Mahogany and Mack laid in one room while Meena and Whitey laid in his room chilling. After a short, but serious conversation, Meena and Whitey felt like they came to Cancun for a good cause. They found something they longed for. Meena hadn't been seeing anyone in a year and Whitey had someone, but what could it hurt to have someone around that didn't live in the city where his girl lived. Meena coming to the city every weekend couldn't hurt. He'd keep her tucked away at his bachelor spot and he'd have me at our spot.

Meena and Whitey got it in. They tore the suite up with no mercy. The liquor set in, the mood was right. What did they have to lose? They came to Cancun to have fun and fun it was. Whitey actually got turned on by Meena's boldness. Meena put her thing down in the bedroom. Meena met the dude she longed for, so it was whatever with her. Whitey had all the qualities Meena wanted in a man and the fact that Whitey told her he didn't have a girl, made her happy. She became Whitey's girl this night. Love at first sight couldn't describe it better. Going all out for him couldn't hurt, in fact, it was well worth it. Whitey laid back in the bed mesmerized. Meena was a combination of something old and new. Meena reminded him of me when we first met, so having that newness sparked his plugs again.

The day came for Whitey to check out of his hotel and head back home, but Meena and her clique weren't leaving. She suggested he stay another night to have some more fun. The thought of making what they had together last longer, intrigued him so he picked up the phone to tell me he'd be home in one more day.

Whitey took Meena to Senor Frog's for BBQ chicken tacos and drinks and after eleven, they partied until 2:00 a.m. then they took it back to Whitey's suite to do it again. This was the first time in a long time that both of them fucked around the clock and it felt wonderful.

In the morning Whitey and Meena went deep sea fishing, sky diving, snorkeling, bike riding then they hit the mall. Whitey bought Meena and me platinum anklets but she thought mine was for his cousin, for a graduation gift.

After shopping Meena picked up some oils to soothe, relax and heal Whitey's wounded heart. He told her about his mother and all he'd been going through lately. He really felt close to her. He never believed in love at first sight until this moment. He really cared about Meena. They were so alike. He loved everything about her; her mannerisms, her touch, her looks, her scent, she was a beautiful person, so similar to me but I was getting bored to him now after all we had been through.

The next day. Whitey and those that stayed in Cancun for an extra day boarded the plane to come back to the city.

Whitey thought about Meena, the entire flight. She thought about him, as well, staring through the clouds waiting for her flight to land in Baltimore. They couldn't wait for the weekend to come so Meena could come to the city to stay with Whitey.

Whitey's flight landed at two o'clock p.m. Reality sank in quickly. Whitey had to face Danielle and me as soon as he excited off the plane. This was serious drama. Whitey actually started a new relationship while he had a committed relationship already. He didn't know how he was gonna pull it off with us two, but he had to. He needed us.

Whitey glanced out the window at the runway, then he unfastened his seat belt slowly.

"Come on Whitey get up," said my back up hairstylist ReRe, waking him from his train of thought.

"Come on dawg. We're home," said his boys from behind.

"I'm sorry, scrap," he said to them then he got up and grabbed his Louis Vuitton Sac Cabourg from the overhead compartment while everyone else grabbed their things. Exhaustion kicked in when he walked off the plane. He was actually tired and worn out from all the fucking and sucking.

"Damn! I'm really tired. I can't wait to get in my bed," he mumbled to himself.

I stood at the front waiting to see Whitey's face walk toward me. I searched and looked through the crowd of people until I saw his 6'2" suntanned frame walk my way.

"Here comes Whitey, Danielle."

298

Danielle smiled and her eyes grew bright. Whitey stepped up to us and grabbed us tight.

"Hey baby," he laughed, kissing Danielle's soft, smooth chocolate skin. "Y'all missed me."

"Yes. We missed you, baby," I laughed.

"Come on. I have to get my luggage," he said. We walked down the ramp holding hands like a happy family.

"Hey girl," said my old stylist from behind.

I turned around and said, "Hey girl. I didn't know you were goin' to Cancun."

"It wasn't planned. It was last minute," she smiled.

"Okay. Okay."

While everybody stood around waiting for the conveyor belt to stop their luggage in front of them, ReRe and I picked up where we left off and Whitey stepped away to talk to his boys'.

"Girl, I didn't know you and Whitey were seeing each other," she smiled.

"Yeah. We've been together for a year now," I smiled proudly.

"He's good peoples. I've been knowing him for years," she said. She wanted to tell me about Meena and Whitey, but she didn't know how to do it. If I ever called, she would break my heart.

"Really. I didn't know that," I said.

"Give me a call. We haven't talked in a while," she said.

"I will."

A month later. Whitey's pattern changed completely. *Men don't know how to cheat right. Women wrote the mack game and played it viciously.* Whitey was a dead give away. He stayed with me from Sunday night to Friday night and every other weekend and from Friday morning to Sunday morning I wouldn't see him anymore. We'd talk but he'd act like he was too caught up doing something to be with me. I wasn't dumb though. I knew him all too well. I knew something wasn't right and I had to find out.

On a lonely Saturday morning after getting no rest, I woke up tearily eyed with a plan. I was going to spy on Whitey. If he was cheating, I needed to know.

I got up and threw on a tee shirt and a pair of Sergio jeans, then Danielle and I left out the door. I planned everything out on the ride up to Whitey's house.

After sitting and waiting for an hour straight, Whitey came out alone but something still wasn't right so I called the block to pick him. He played right into my hands. He said he was just waking up from a long night in A.C. and I know what I saw. He was hiding something from me. Whatever the case was, he cursed me out for spying on him. If I couldn't take his word, it was no need for us to be together.

Meena showered up inside the Condo without a care in the world. She and Whitey had a nice night out the night before with expensive drinks and good food with all his friends at the new club in Manayunk. Whitey's friends thought he was the shit because he had two bad girls in different cities that looked so much alike. It was crazy but he had the best of both worlds.

Whitey and I got up early in the morning to go out. I got a babysitter, then he, his man Arn and his girlfriend Anirah and I went to Dave and Busters to eat, drink and have fun. Arn just came home from doing seven years with the state. He called my house faithfully for Whitey while he was away so we were pretty tight already. He knew how much Whitey loved me but he could see the change in Whitey too. But that was Whitey for you. The nigga changed on you, like he changed his underwear. And that was every day. Maybe two times a day and sometimes not for a couple days. And that's how he rolled too. He could be cool with you for a couple days, then flip. Or cool with you one minute and change on you in a blink of an eye. You had to be some kind of special dealing with Whitey. Everybody knew that. He was so shady.

"So you got my mans name on you?" smiled Arn with his southern accent. Arn wasn't from our hometown. He was from Rochester, New York.
"Yeah, yeah," I frowned.
"Why you gotta do all that?" asked Whitey.
"What?" I said.
"You act like you don't want my name on you or something," he smirked.
"It's not that Arn. I love Whitey. He can just be difficult at times. You know what I mean," I said.
"Yeah, I know," he agreed in a nice manner.
"Oh, go head wit' that bullshit," said Anirah to Whitey. She and Whitey had been close through the years because of Arn. She did her thing while he was in the penitentiary but she held shit down for Arn. She never let another nigga stop her from seeing him. She kept Arn with money on his books, she accepted all his collect calls, she took care of his kids and never complained. He had mad love and respect for her. Besides, he had many hoes while he was on the streets so he couldn't hate. "I love Arn but I would never get his name tattooed on me just to show him I love him. He knows that already without the bullshit. All the shit I been through wit' him."
"Whatever!" said Whitey. "My girl loves me. I wouldn't put up wit' your shit if you were my girl. That's why you have Arn and not me."
"You gotta good girl," smiled Arn. Whitey knew he was wrong about mistreating me. I was always in his corner. Living two lives was more than he could bear on top of all the other things surrounding him.

After Dave and Busters we toured the city until it got dark. Whitey was drunk and he wanted to do something daring. He put my loyalty to the test. He constantly compared Meena and me; some nights I fucked him better and other nights she did. He was getting all his royalties.

Whitey found a park of his choice and we got out. He wanted to do me in the park since that was one of the things I never did in my life. I was scared but Whitey put me out there and I wanted to prove my love to him so I pulled my linen skirt high and let him have his way.

Whitey's sperm met my egg that was laying in the cut ready to transform into a little human being. "It's time" thought the sperm hitting the egg. Little Whitey attached itself to my womb. I pulled my skirt down and Whitey zipped his jeans up then we ran to the car holding hands while people looked on and laughed too. We were crazy to them.

Candis calling the police on Whitey months ago, finally caught up to him, they stopped his car, searched him and locked him up, the next morning.

Whitey sat in a holding cell all night trippin'. Everything hit him instantly. He now needed me like never before. His mom was the one that would be there for him aside from his girl, but mom was expired.

The first chance Whitey got, he dialed me to get in touch with his lawyer and whoever else he needed. I got on my job right away. I couldn't let Whitey down. I had to move fast or he'd be disappointed.

With an old bench warrant hanging over Whitey's head, he couldn't be released right away. In fact, the judge wanted to make sure he'd be around to go to court. In knowing this, I waited for no one, not even the lawyer because he wasn't moving fast enough. Whitey had no patience. He couldn't stand jail.

Whitey put all faith in me. I moved out quickly making calls and visits. With Whitey never being convicted before, I arranged house arrest for him with the agreement of the court.

I lay in the bed tired and stressed from running around taking care of Whitey's business.

"I been awfully tired and extra hungry lately. Maybe it's from running and stressing, but this has been going on for about a week now. It can't be," I thought. Moments later my eyes closed gently. I had no problem falling asleep. The phone rang early waking me from my dream.

"Hello."

"It's a collect call," said the operator. I pressed the button before she could finish.

"Did you take care of what I asked you to do?" Whitey asked.

"Yes. You should be home in a day or two. They already came out and approved everything," I said.

"Good. What's up?" he asked.

"I just had a dream and I think it may be accurate," I said.

"What?" he asked.

"I had a dream that you were cheating and it was a baby in the dream. I don't know if it was my baby or the girl's baby, but I think I'm pregnant," I said.

"Are you serious?" he said, raising his voice now.

"Yeah. Do you have someone else?" I asked him.

"I don't need that right now," he said, cutting me short.

"Well, what about the pregnancy?" I asked.

"You aren't sure yet," he said.

"It is more than likely I am. My dreams are usually accurate and I know when I'm pregnant. I've been eating and sleeping a lot for the past week. Every time I eat something I get hungry again right away. I thought I was tired from running, but I'm tired all the time," I said.

"We'll deal with that when I get home," he said.

"Alright," I said as I rubbed my stomach gently.

"Ring, ring, ring," sounded my cell phone, thirty minutes later.

"Hello."

"What's up nigga?" said Tank.

"Nothing," I answered.

"What's new?"

"Nothing much."

"How's your situation goin'?" he wanted to know.

"Not too good. Whitey is locked up and I think I might be pregnant," I announced.

"Get the fuck outta here! So what are you gonna do?"

"I don't know yet. He's gonna be on house arrest here when he gets out," I let him know.

"I really don't think that's a good idea."

"Why?" I asked.

"Because it's not. That means y'all are gonna be around each other too much. Imagine being locked in the house with someone all day. I really don't think it's gonna work. He came in the relationship with drama. I told you before. Now you have to do something different. You can't have no baby by that cat. Imagine raising another child without a father. You can't do it. Look at his situation. Nothing good is gonna come out of it," he seriously said.

Tank sounds right, but who wants to accept the truth. "Let me call you from now on. I don't want him to trip," I told Tank.

"What! You mean to tell me you are cutting me off," he said loudly.

"No. I'm not saying that," I said softly.

"What are you saying then? You are telling me in a nice way. See that's what I'm talking about. You can't even keep it real being around that nigga. You have to cut yourself off from society and that's not cool. And I don't think it will be a good thing for my godson. You say you don't like the way he treats him when he's mad at you. How do you think he is gonna act being around y'all all the time? When he looks at Job, he sees you, he said.

I don't think you should do it. Let him get house arrest at his spot," Tank insisted.

"He wants to be here," I said and I wanted him here too.

"Whatever man! I'm gonna be here for you regardless, but don't say I didn't tell you," he said angrily.

"I love you, Tank."

"I love you, too. Keep in touch."

"Okay," I said as I looked at my phone.

Eleven days later I stared out the window crying. Tank was right. My kids and I were living in complete misery and I was pregnant with Whitey's baby. Whitey turned on everybody. He hated being confined. It was getting the best of him no matter what I did to make his bid comfortable. I labored over the stove making different dishes if he said he didn't like what I cooked. I fucked him when he wanted to be fucked and oral sex was horrible now. I hated to do it. I would gag and almost throw up sometimes because he went too far and his scent was unpleasant now. I began to hate this nigga I claimed I once loved. He turned me into a witch. I wanted so far away from him some nights. I was living in torture. His money simply wasn't good enough. Whenever he felt guilty, he tried to send me out shopping and while I was out, he'd talk to Meena on my phone. He promised her he'd be out of the halfway house and on house release soon so they would be able to see each other again. She couldn't wait. Whitey was her man. Cinnamon didn't exist in her world.

Whitey was out in the public finally and less tensed. He still had an attitude against the world like everybody put him where he was. He never looked at the real problem, him. He was so fast to blame everyone for what went on in his life, but he was happy to be moving around again. Handling his own business worked out better for him because niggas always had a story to tell. Nobody handled business like Whitey. He was the brain of everybody around him.

Whitey got up extra early on Monday. He put on his basketball Jersey, a cap to match, a pair of Guess jean shorts and a pair of red and white Jordans. He kissed Danielle and me good-bye, then he left out to hit the highway to see Meena. He knew he had enough time to get there, kick it with her for a few hours and get back before nine.

Whitey opened the door at nine o'clock sharp.

"I tried to call you all day because your house arrest lady was looking for you," I explained.

"For what?" he asked.

"She said she needed the address to the job again."

"Did you give it to her?" He asked nastily.

"Yes. You normally answer your phone. What happened?"

303

"I was at The Rucker playground with my cousin," he smirked like he didn't want to be bothered.

"The Rucker," I said.

"Yeah. You know. The Polo Grounds. You wanna ask him," he said, now more irritated, for me even questioning him.

"No," I said, now smirking back at him.

"Go 'head if you think I'm lyin'," he said out of guilt. He knew the main event didn't start until 8:00 so why didn't he answer his phone all day.

"I don't need to ask him."

"Is my food ready?"

"It been ready," I responded with my lips twisted hard now. I was sick of his lying ass. I knew what time it really was. Whitey wasn't shit.

"Alright. Well, I'm ready to eat," he said rudely like I was his personal chief, maid, whatever the hell he wanted me to be.

"Okay."

I walked into the bathroom only to realize I was spotting. My heart raced. I walked back into the room to tell Whitey. He called Ms. Gray to see if he could go with me to the hospital and she said no so I went alone.

I prayed for my baby while I lay on the hospital bed. I wanted a part of Whitey so badly even though he was treating me messed up. If we had a girl, I was to name her after his mother.

After all my testing was complete, the doctor sent me home on bed rest if I wanted to keep my baby.

Whitey sat on the bed in the middle of the night discussing his concerns about my pregnancy, a week later. What he once thought he wanted. He wanted no more. He was confused. He feared not being there for the baby so he gave me an ultimatum. I couldn't believe the man that said he wouldn't mind marrying or having a child with me. He actually changed up on me. I couldn't understand Whitey to save my life.

He used his mother not being there as an excuse, then his own life. Then he said it was too soon because Danielle was still a baby. Then he confused me by saying he didn't want his twins but they were here so I had to do what I thought was right and I actually got attached to my baby. Then he said it was the baby or he and I said, *fuck* him period. Whatever I did, I wanted to do alone because he wasn't any support to me.

Who's to Blame?
What are you asking me to do?
How can I terminate a special part of you?
I understand how you must feel, but respect what is real.
You don't know what it feels like, to bond inside,
I feel this life, and now you wanna suggest how we should ride.
No disrespect to you,
If I wasn't in love, it would be no problem to get rid of you
and all the above.
I knew from day one how deep I could fall,
And you entering my circle of love, is stronger than all.
I wish this was easy for both of us now,
But things seem a little difficult and someone is gonna wear a frown.
Whether it is you or me, I pray that the other can see,
That it's all good and simply what it has to be.
If it was up to me,
I would have thee,
Seeing your big, pretty eyes through another life,
would be more than special to me.
But unfortunately, I have to do what I have to,
And I don't know if I'll ever look at you the same,
without forever, placing the blame.

    In the morning I got up and drove to mom's. I had so much to think about and Tank thought it was best for me to get an abortion too. Whitey just wasn't worthy of me. He wasn't ready to be my *black King*.
    As I turned my ignition off Saleem pulled up to my window and said, "Can I speak to you for a moment?"
This pussy! "What about?" I said.
"Look, I just came home and while I was away, I felt so bad about all the things you were going through and what I did to hurt you. You didn't deserve those things and I wasn't a man. I wanted you so bad and I went about it the wrong way," he said.
"Well, it's the past and I'm not trying to relive it," I said. I deeply prayed to forgive him because I knew I couldn't get into the heavenly gates with anger, hatred, bitterness and other sins in my heart but seeing him made me realize I still wanted revenge.
"I'm on my hustle. I still have my properties that I had before I went away, so I just wanna make things right," he said.
"Really," I smirked. How could he make what he did right?
"Yeah. I wanna give you some money," he said.
"For what?"
"I just do," he said. "Here. Take my number and call me."

305

I took his number and he pulled off.

Inside mom's she gave me a number to call. I knew the first three digits were the same as my hospital but I wasn't sure who it could be so I called. The same doctor that waited on me the day I went into the emergency room for my bleeding let me know I had a STD and I had it for a while and whoever gave it to me, I needed to leave his trifling ass alone because if he jeopardized my health once, he'd do it twice. Besides, I didn't need a man that ran around fucking without protecting himself. *Some men thought with their pockets and dick.*

The doctor called in prescriptions for Whitey and me. I picked the medication up from the pharmacy and drove home in tears. In all my years, I never had a man give me a STD, no disease for that matter. Whitey was causing me more grief than any man I'd ever known. He was my worst nightmare. One I wished away badly.

"I haven't been fuckin' nobody," Whitey said as he sat on our plush suede, dining room chairs. *Men always flip the script when things come to the forefront and they look at us like we're villains most of the time when they bring out the beast in us and cause us to go astray.*

"Well, I know I haven't Whitey. Do you remember I used to bleed sometimes while having intercourse with you?" I said.

"Yeah. I remember a little," he answered.

"Well, you must have had it for a while now," I said, giving him the benefit of the doubt.

"Yeah, Candis must of gave me that shit."

"Whatever the case is, here are some pills for you and me," I said, giving him the pills with a glass of water.

"Can I drink while on this medicine?" he asked because he knew Meena was coming down and he had to fuck her or she'd think he was cheating and he couldn't lose her, not his future wife. He had no plans on marrying me anymore that's why he didn't want me to have his baby because he knew he didn't want me like that. Meena was his future. I was his past.

"Yeah, but you can't have sex," I told him. Whitey and I took the pills together.

"What about the abortion?" he said. I looked at him with disgust.

"What about it?" I asked him.

"When are you getting it?"

"Soon. Why do you care anyway?" I went to the room and shut the door behind me.

After days of mental abuse, I had to do what was best for me. Whitey really wasn't shit. He claimed he messed up the medication by drinking with his boys but I knew better, he fucked Meena then he had the nerve to flip out and say I gave him a STD and he distrusted me.

306

I got on the phone and made an appointment to terminate my pregnancy even though I had plans for another girl. After overhearing my conversation with the receptionist, Whitey asked to join me for the procedure and I told him I wanted no parts of him after all he put me through. I gave him my all and he took me for granted. Now I had to put me first.

After Whitey slammed the door behind him, I called Saleem to see what he had for me. I wanted all that was due to me since I didn't get his old ass locked up and put away. The system would've loved keeping him behind bars for good.

"Can you meet me at the hotel?" he said.

"Which one?" I asked.

"The Marriot," he said. I knew which Marriot from being around Saleem back then. I got dressed and he headed right over there.

Inside the room Saleem gave me a measly three thousand dollars for the heartache and pain he caused me back then.

"What the fuck can I do with this?" I said nastily.

"I'm gonna give you more as soon as I get back. That's just a little something to start off," he said. I snatched the stacks wrapped in rubber bands and placed them in my purse.

"Okay. You know I deserve something nice after what you took me through," I said.

"I got you. Trust me. I got you," he said. I walked toward the door and Saleem said, "can you just jerk me off for another thousand dollars?"

"What the fuck do you think I am?" I asked him. "I'm not pressed motherfucka."

"I know. I know. I know you got the bull Whitey. I heard about y'all while I was in jail. You know that niggas a snitch," he said.

"What?"

"Yeah. He told on the boy Gee that killed Bizzy. Gee is getting out soon and he's gonna kill Whitey. And I heard his man Todd had your car set on fire," he said.

"Oh yeah. I didn't know that and he talks all that shit about snitches and he's a fuckin' rat himself. Todd didn't do that to my car," I said.

"You loved that nigga that much that you don't believe that," he said. "I know fo sure. My mans wouldn't lie," he said.

"Well, if you know so much about all these niggas, tell me who killed Job. I know you know that much."

"I heard the bull Josh had something to do with it," he said.

"Well, he got killed in a car accident so he paid his dues. That sneaky motherfucka. I had a feeling he had something to do with that. It was something about his words I didn't trust," I said, thinking back to the day I went to his baby's mamas. "Who else besides brother Mike, I know he was the one who put it together but who were the other guys?"

307

"The dude Shariff is locked up for life with a hole in his face. They say your baby father shot him while they were kidnaping him. He was a good dude. I heard Black Mike robbed y'all too but niggas is on his head so he moved back to Baltimore with his peoples. You had good baby fathers'. I heard your daugther's father was thorough too. My young boy Ja used to fuck with him on the business tip," he said. I got so irked. This was too much in one day. Saleem was trying to gain points with me but I wanted revenge on everybody. I said fuck morals because the game wasn't right. Some men looked at us as PP anyway.

"I'll give you more than a hand job. I'll give you one of my old fashion massages but it's gonna cost you more than a thousand dollars. You have to triple that price," I said. Saleem went in his pocket and pulled out three more stacks.

"So you had more money and all I'm worth is three thousand for what you caused me," I spat in his face.

"I got you shorty," he smiled. "Believe me. I got you."

I pulled Vaseline from my Gucci drawstring bag and put it on his little pencil dick. I hated this motherfucka but I would be leaving the room with six thousand dollars and more later. I was about to take him for a ride. Whitey was going to pay too. I was tired of everybody. Me just jerking Saleem was cheating on Whitey in my mind. I was getting him back for cheating on me. It wasn't right but oh, well.

I gave Saleem the best massage he ever had. The oriental chick he went to in town couldn't fuck with me. I made Saleem crawl all over the hotel room. I had him climbing the curtains begging me for more. He got so turned out that he offered me another two thousand just to lick my pussy and another seven if I just sat on his dick. I did both. I left the hotel with fifteen thousand in my pocket book. Whitey made a good girl, go bad. I was tired of being trampled on. I made the calls now.

At home I put the fifteen thousand dollars with the fifty thousand I had stashed of Whitey's that he gave me for emergencies and my schooling so he wouldn't have to keep giving me from his pockets or when he wasn't at my reach.

At midnight Whitey walked in the house with an attitude like usual but I didn't care. I got him back in my mind and I was getting rid of the problem in a couple days. As bad as I wanted my child, I knew he would be so relieved and less stressed once I did what he asked me to do. I shut Whitey out and went to sleep.

I woke up in the hotel's king size bed, the day of my appointment with a queasy stomach and aching heart. I didn't want to spend my last night pregnant with Whitey. I wanted no parts of him.

I put on my stretch Betsy Johnson Capri's, a tee shirt and a pair of comfortable mules', then I left the hotel to go home.

I pulled up the block only to see an empty parking spot where Whitey's truck normally sat. *He's gone.* I jumped out the car and ran in the house hoping Whitey got the letter I left on the dresser the night before. I knew what I wrote and what we agreed upon, but I hoped he changed his mind about our baby.

A stack of bills lay next to the letter. I read the letter over. I put the money in my Gucci bag, then I left out the door lonely and sad, knowing what I had to take care of.

I talked to my baby girl the entire ride over Jersey to the abortion clinic. I asked her for forgiveness. I cried and I prayed. I wanted so badly to keep my baby then again I wanted nothing to do with the man I was pregnant for. I hated the thought of him.

I drove back to the city feeling miserable and sick. I wanted nothing to do with Whitey after my abortion. He didn't make me do it, but he gave me a choice and although I was confused, I should've followed my heart. But God forgave all and my baby girl rested in His presence.

At home there was no discussion about the pregnancy. I lay in bed crying all night to myself. I woke up crying. Whitey didn't understand my pain. Whitey only cared about Whitey. He didn't have to live with the guilt that I had to live with. He was used to paying for abortions. He didn't care about anything. It was all fun and play with him. He stuck and moved. He caught feelings for certain women, but he lived for himself. Whoever fulfilled his needs at the given moment, was who he clung to. He had to have someone around him at all times. He couldn't stand being alone. Even as a grown man, he hated the dark.

For the next two days I withdrew. I blamed myself and the hate grew deeper. School wasn't an issue for me and Whitey drilled me about getting the abortion during the week of school. Although he was jealous of what I was doing, he knew how much school meant to me.

Whitey gave me money for Danielle's party and left out early the next morning. He planned to return for the Rugrats crew but he had to check in with Meena to make sure she was straight at the Condo. The selfish nigga was crossin' all the lines.

While Whitey enjoyed anal sex with Meena, my niece Nancy and her brother Nick raided our room looking for Whitey's stash. They didn't respect him anymore because of his attitude, how he mistreated their aunt and simply because that was their twist now.

Once I heard footsteps over my head, I ran upstairs to find my door cracked. For the life of me I couldn't understand my own. Did they even think twice about jeopardizing me and mine? Whitey would kill somebody about his dough.

I didn't mention anything to my family because some would think I was tripping but I knew what was going on and I wasn't down with the bullshit.

In the morning I jumped out of bed once Whitey pulled off to attend Easie's funeral. Easie and Whitey grew up together but they fell out about the chick Fall. Now Whitey had to sit with Easie's mother because she asked him to and in the same room with the girl that they both loved.

Inside the bathroom I pulled Whitey's striped boxers from the hamper searching for evidence. If Whitey was fucking the night before, I would find a sign telling me so. I knew Whitey all too well. If he was rushing to get home, he fucked with his boxers on.

I examined Whitey's boxers carefully to find a few pee drips and a stain that looked like cum. My heart dropped lower once I smelled the same scent on his boxers that I smelled on him in our bed hours before. I could go to Easie's funeral and bust his ass but it wouldn't stop him from cheating on me. I threw his funky ass drawers back in the hamper and buried them for later evidence in case I needed it.

It was truly on now. I called Saleem's old ass to give him another dick massage for three thousand dollars. I wasn't about to sit on his pencil dick for extras. It was a massage only. I had to stack my dough.

While I drove home, Whitey slid his number into Fall's purse and asked her to call him sometimes. Although she was grieving over Easie, Whitey's come back was right on time because she needed his dough now. Easie left his baby mama with everything he owned and Fall was hurt because she was used to high quality living.

Chapter 9
The End
"The Final Product"

Whitey became an aggressive beast who wanted ruler over my entire universe. My family and I were to remain captive in his jungle being mistreated, shamed and tormented. What I thought love stood for didn't. I was to breathe him and only I could set my family free from bondage. I had to let Whitey go whether it would hurt or not. He wasn't healthy for our unit. He wasn't a positive force in our lives anymore. All that faded away. I now had to choose between him and my children or somebody was gonna lose their sense of worth or respect. Better yet, somebody was gonna get seriously hurt.

Whitey grabbed his Louis Vuitton suitcase out the hallway closet containing more than a million dollars. He took his jewelry from our jewelry box. He snatched my keys and pass to his condo from my night stand. He unplugged his box the way Ms. Gray instructed him to then him and his brother left without saying a word. He was upset with me, just as much as I was upset with him. No woman ever put him out before. I was the first and we were definitely enemies now.

Whitey left his clothes, some sneaks, the stash that he gave me months before, hoping things would someday get better. He really didn't want to part on bad terms because after all, we went through hell together and he'd never forget the shit I put up with for him.

Seven days later I opened the door of my spot only to have tears drop constantly. I began to wonder if I made a mistake. The house was silent. There was no sudden burst of laughter coming from the master bedroom. There were no new Vibe magazines laying on the glass coffee table. There were no Corona bottles on the counter and there definitely wasn't any food on the stove simmering for Whitey. Whitey was gone and the adjustment period had not yet taken its course. It was no doubt Whitey wasn't good for me because God had a better man in the plan for me but it was the getting used to being alone that was hard. I'd become so lax with Whitey around. It was the convenience of having him near that was important.

I fell into Whitey's trap again and we started seeing each other but things definitely weren't the same. I couldn't have his house number. I could only use the key when he told me to and I didn't stay at the Condo on the weekends so I did what I had to do and investigated the situation for myself. I didn't care if it was going to hurt me again because this time, I was out for good.

Around ten in the morning I called the house number that was left on Whitey's refrigerator from the Chinese store receipt and a woman with a soft voice answered so I hung up. I was hoping I was wrong about the number.

I called Whitey's cell phone to get no answer so I beeped him a few times, 911 then I sat on the bed and waited for him to call.

Twenty minutes and no call back. I got up and threw on a pair of Sergio's, a black tee and black Prada walking shoes. I unwrapped my hair and left out the door prepared for whatever.

Outside the misty morning air smacked me directly in the face. I jumped in my ride and hit the expressway. I pondered the entire ride up to Whitey's spot. I could only think the worst. My gut made me nervous. I really couldn't prepare myself for what I didn't know.

Minutes later I rolled up to the side of the complex and parked for a moment to get my thoughts together for the last time. I grabbed my cell phone from between my legs and called the number I remembered again. "Hello," said the same innocent, soft voice. I hung up quickly. It had to be the right number. It was no way I was mistaking. I wasn't that stupid.

I called my cousin, my hair dresser Carol. We confided in each other about our men all the time.

"Hello," she said hyped up and perky on her black leather stool, finishing up her first client for the early Saturday morning rush.

"Girl, you will never believe what I am doing," I said as I looked around me.

"What?" she laughed.

"I am on the side of Whitey's complex."

"For what?" she asked.

I told her everything in detail.

"Well, if someone is there, you need to let her feel what you are feeling. If she doesn't know about you, let her find out now. You been with him too long and you have taken too much off him. Not the way you been by his side and every and anything he wants, you do for him. You go to the moon and back for his arrogant ass. Go up in there. That is your man. Don't let no other woman come between you and him. Uh, un. You hear me! And she had the nerve to answer the phone. He let her answer his phone! See. I'm gonna hurt him for you this time. I'm tired of him taking you through all these different changes. Niggas don't get enough. Do whatcha' gotta. I'm tellin' you. Do you want me to meet you?" she asked. She wasn't playing with his narrow behind. She was sick and tired of how he was treating me.

"Okay. I'll go. I'll call you back to let you know what happened," I said. She really got to me and I was ready to face whatever.

"Oh, yeah Cinnamon," she paused.

"Yes," I said.

"That nigga Saleem just got locked up again girl. And you know he's a three-time felon so he'll never see the streets again," she said. She was the only one that knew about my secret. I never told anyone what Saleem had did to me and I didn't tell anyone I was tricking him either. I was so relieved that I didn't have to bump into him on the streets anymore. I didn't care

312

about his dough. I didn't want his filthy money no longer. I knew what mom instilled in me. I was trippin' anyway.

"I know that's right. I'll call you back," I said.

While I called the number one more time to make sure it was his spot before trippin' out, Whitey called my house to see why I called him *911*. He knew he wasn't right so he needed to talk to me badly. After Luke told him I left, he panicked. He knew the shit was about to hit the fan but he wasn't coming to his Condo to get it hands on.

The same young lady answered the phone again so I kindly asked for Mr. Shaw like I was Ms. Gray and the woman fell for it so it was time to go up in the joint. Whitey was busted. It was time for me to let go.

I rang Whitey's door bell and stood back. Once the woman asked my name and I said I was Whitey's girlfriend, she opened the door in shock. How could I be his girlfriend and she was? I felt like such an idiot on the outside of Whitey's door. It was apparent that Whitey and this woman Meena had more than him and I had together but I had to keep in mind that things were shaky between us.

Once Meena told me her and Whitey had been seeing each other since Cancun, I was devastated and so was she. This grimy nigga was playing house with both of us. He had her and her children there while he had my children and me at my house and he had the nerve to have all her belongings there and hid them when I came. He was good but that's why he stayed stressed because he had too much going on. His game was up.

I cried once I found out everything in detail. Meena and I actually had a lot in common. She was just as sympathetic toward me as I was toward her but I obviously had more to lose than she did. I spent years with Whitey building and losing and she spent months of gaining. I definitely got cheated.

Meena and I had similar taste too. Whitey got us the same anklet we found out. It was amazing how much Meena and I looked and acted alike but Whitey treated Meena with more respect and once she called him and told him I was there, he fronted on me so I went home and packed his things. It was no way I was putting up with his shit any longer. The only thing was, he wasn't getting his money because I deserved that after all the abuse he took me through. Money could be replaced but me, I was a priceless stone that he could never afford and some of his money would help cover my tattoos and some of his debts. It was no way he was walking away from his responsibilities. He had to pay his share of everything because I damn sure couldn't.

I stood in my mirror a week later talking to myself while putting on clothes that Whitey purchased for me to go out in. Yeah, I fell back into his trap again. Meena broke off their engagement so he wanted me back. The phone rang interrupting the mood.

"Hello."

"Are you ready?" asked Whitey.

"Not quite," I said as I turned and looked at the back of me.

"Are you still going?" he said.

"Yes."

"Well, me and my boys are going down. They are impatient. I'll meet you there," he said.

"Cool."

"How does the outfit fit?" I asked him.

"I love it and I look good in it," he smiled. He loved anything I picked out for him.

"That's good. I'm glad you like it," I laughed.

I finished dressing, then I called Tara to see if she was ready.

"Where are we going again?" Tara asked.

"To First Friday's."

"I know, but where is it this time?"

"It's in town."

"Okay, come get me."

I picked Tara up and hit the expressway. I parked in the crowded lot full of cars from all over.

"This is my first time at one of their events," I said as I fixed my hair in the mirror.

"Mine, too, but I heard they be nice. It's workin' class people. Not too many hustlers," said Tara.

We walked up to a long line all the way around the corner.

"Come on. Let's go up front so I can see if I know anybody. I'm not waiting in this long line," I said as I looked around.

"Okay," said Tara, following right behind me.

We walked up to the door.

"Hey, Cinnamon," said my friend Tony from 125th Street. It was good to see old friends at times like these. After graduation, he moved to NY.

"What's up, baby?" I said, throwing my arms around his neck.

"How've you been?" he asked.

"Fine," I smiled.

"You still lookin' good," he said, checking me from head to toe.

"Thank you. So are you," I said.

"Are y'all goin' in?"

"Yes, but I'm kinda waiting for my friend. Let me call him," I said as I reached in my purse for my cell phone. I called Whitey's cell phone.

"Where are you at?" I asked him.

"Where are you?" he asked me.

"I'm in front of the club."

314

"I'm across the street from the club waiting for Mack," he said as he stood by the curb. I glanced across the street only to see him standing tall and sexy in all black which complimented his skin tone.

"Oh, I see you right there. Well, we're at the door and my friend is gonna get us in. If y'all don't want to wait in the long line, come on."

"I can't leave my boy. We'll be all right. We'll get in," he said as he looked around to spot Mack.

"Are you sure?" I asked before going in.

"I'm positive."

Inside the club was packed with different types of people. You had the working class, high class and ghetto class. Tara claimed not too many hustlers came to their events but they were there checking for anything available.

As soon as Whitey and his boys came in, he stopped by the bar and ordered me an Alize and Belvi Vodka, on ice. He knew I wasn't a regular drinker but he loved me under the influence because it brought out the freak in me.

Before two o'clock arrived, I had another drink, then the lights flashed around the club to let everyone know it was time to get it moving. Guys searched through the crowd for a piece of pussy for the night and the chicks searched for anything available. I wanted no one. Nobody interested me. No one could do anything for me in the state of mind I remained in. I couldn't get over what happened to me the week before. Meena kept crossing my mind. I couldn't fault her for anything. She really didn't know. I could fault Whitey, but I was in the midst of his presence this night. I didn't know what to do. I thought forgiving him was only right because God forgave us all the time, but I also knew enough was enough and God didn't want me to play the fool. He knew my worth if no one else did.

Outside the club Whitey called my cell phone to see where I was. He told me to drop Tara off and meet him and his boys at the Hikaru Japanese restaurant. I did just that.

I walked into the restaurant at three a.m. feeling uneasy. In fact, I was a little angry and embarrassed. All Whitey's friends knew what happened. I didn't feel comfortable around them anymore after knowing they sat around Meena and me. They knew Whitey wasn't right, but he was their boy. They weren't gonna tell on him, although some tried to give me hints. They simply couldn't go up against the hand that fed them. They just couldn't.

After eating Whitey paid the tab then he grabbed me tight and we left out the door. I let him hold me, but I really didn't like it much because everything he did remained fresh in my memory.

"Do you have a dollar Miss?" said a man in dreads laying on a vent outside the restaurant.

"Fuck no!" said Whitey as he kicked the man.

"Stop Whitey. Don't be mean. You never know why he's out here. You don't know what drove him to this point," I said as I reached in my purse for five dollars. This man was stinkin', beat, and half dressed. I pulled the five dollars from my purse and passed it to the man.

"Cinnamon," he said. I looked closer to see this man's face.

"Is that you Cinnamon?" he said as he rose up. Nahum was smoked out and homeless. My heart sank into the concrete.

"What are you doing out here?" I asked him.

"I went crazy in jail after losing my boys. You know I lost one of my triplets too," he said.

"Come on wit' the bullshit," Whitey said, pulling me away.

"Wait a minute babe, hold up one second," I said.

"Who the fuck is this bum ass nigga you're talkin' to?" he said coldly.

"My nephew's father," I said.

"Well, hurry up. You can't help his bum ass," he said.

"I didn't know you lost another son. I'm sorry to hear that," I said. Even though Nahum took us through hell, I had a forgiving heart. God had his way of making people suffer for their wrongdoings. Nahum touched his anointed one and he had to answer for that. Mom was God chosen and Nahum did her wrong. And we suffered greatly because of him too and God never forgot that. Jail wasn't enough for him. He had to do what he needed to for him to cry out to God. God dealt with everybody differently. We all paid for our wrongdoings some sort of way.

"You know I shanked that nigga Bones for you while I was upstate," he said.

"What!"

"Yeah. I cut that nigga something nice. He was near death. Oh, that nigga has a death wish. He's out and I'm gonna kill him," he said. Although I wanted revenge some years ago, time healed all wounds and the devil was really winning in the end when our people killed one another. I really wanted peace in the world. I didn't want to keep seeing our people die at the foot of our enemy. I heard many stories of niggas going upside Bones's head about Luke. *You reap what you sow for sure.*

"Come the fuck on," Whitey said lastly.

"Nahum I gots to go. Take care and call on God. He can set you free from this bondage," I sincerely said.

"Thanks. Tell your mom and them I said hi and I'm sorry for all I put y'all through," he cried.

"I will," I said then Whitey and I jumped in the car and drove two blocks down to the center of attraction.

"Pull over and park," said Whitey.

"For what?" I asked.

"Are you questioning your man? Pull over," he said. I pulled the car over and parked.

"Get out!" he demanded.

"What are you doing?" I asked him.

"I wanna do something. Just be quiet," he said as he lowered his voice. He grabbed me, he pulled his dick out, he pulled my pants down to the middle of my thighs, then he threw me against the car and did it to me from the back in the middle of Broad and Cherry. He stuck every inch of him deeply inside me without my consent. He didn't care what I said. He wanted what he wanted, at any cost and I was so embarrassed.

"Where is he?" Agent Powell asked angrily. "I know you've been seeing him." I was victim No. 1, numero uno. It had been weeks that Whitey and I had been running from the FBI. He got caught up in an altercation with an old associate about an old debt and instead of putting the pressure on Fall. Her sister December put it on me. She knew Whitey was playing both of us but she wasn't about to rat on her own. She kept sending the Feds my way. And Agent Powell thought I would break once he mentioned Fall being tight with Whitey but I was breaking for no one, not even him. They could run up in my spot fifteen times, I wasn't folding regardless of the risk I was taking for his no-good ass.

"So you're not going to talk?" He asked angrily, hitting my counter top. I stared him in the eyes. "We'll be back ten times if need be. Here's my number. Call me when you see him," he said as he turned away to call his men off after ransacking my crib. He was pissed with me for still being loyal to the men I loved. He knew my devotion. He especially remembered my loyalty to Snoop. He indicted their entire clique although Butch was his nephew.

Whitey spent more time in Jersey City because he was too hot in Philly. Some of his so-called friends began to despise him because of his funky attitude. He thought he was the invincible man.

When Whitey did come through his gold mine, he realized he was being got. His right-hand man was stealing from him. Fall was dipping in his stash. And his family, they didn't care either. Everybody was fed up with Whitey, even me. I got pregnant by Whitey again and aborted it. What I once strongly disagreed with, became too familiar. I had to put an end to the misery.

Distance came between Whitey and me while Fall and Whitey got tighter. He thought he was using her for information and she thought she was draining his stash. They both had a motive and I had one too, and that was to put my kids and me first again. My mind was made up. Whitey would fall behind me just like the clouds hid the sun. He would be my past and no longer my present or future.

Two months later, spring of 2000. The plan to leave Whitey behind was a slow progress. Instead of pulling away completely like I said, I lingered on. I didn't know how to tell Whitey I didn't care about him anymore nor did

I not want to be bothered with him at all. He called like usual to ask me to meet him and I did. I met him at the Embassy Suites on a beautiful May morning.

Inside the suite Whitey did something he didn't do in a while. In fact, he stepped his game up a notch. Fall showed him some new tricks and he made me feel some type of way about the moment, but I couldn't think with my pussy. I had to think with my heart and mind. I was there to get my shit off and nothing else. I couldn't get caught up in the moment because our relationship to me, turned out to be a fuck, instead of a loving and caring one. I actually hated the man, I thought I once loved. I deeply regretted him.

The next day Whitey called and told me to fly out of town to be with him. I made reservations. I got a baby sitter for the kids, then I boarded US AIR at five p.m. sharp.

My flight landed in Boston before I could open my eyes. An older man sitting beside me tapped me on the arm.
"Honey," he whispered.
I opened my eyes gently.
"We're here," he smiled while reaching for his briefcase.
"Thank you," I said. I exited off the plane last. I walked down the escalator, then I called Whitey from my cell phone to let him know I was there. Why was I there, I didn't know? I didn't know if I was there because I wanted a change for the weekend or if I was there hoping things would be different for us out of town because of all the tension surrounding us back home. Anyway, I waited patiently for Whitey to pull up.

Ten minutes later Whitey, Mack and his friend Tyrese that played basketball overseas pulled up in a brand new shiny, black Hummer pumping Jigga's cd. Whitey swung the back door open. I stepped off the curb and jumped in the back of the truck with Whitey. Tyrese drove back to the hotel to pick up his female friend and Mack's female friend to go to Sullivan's Steakhouse for dinner.

At dinner everything was quiet between Whitey and me. I wasn't allowed to discuss our issues in front of people so I fed Whitey his steak while his friends fed themselves. They couldn't believe I was still obedient to Whitey and he was nothing but a dawg but they weren't any better. Tyrese had a wife back home and Mack had a fiancee so none of them was shit.

Back at the hotel Whitey and I did our thing, but his mind was on Fall. He was in Boston because of the basketball summer camp and his boy, but he wanted Fall to be with him instead of me and she chose to be in The Big Apple with her girlfriends spending his money. She gave Whitey a run for his dollars. She did to him, what he did to me.

In the morning Whitey and I hit the mall. Whitey got a few things. He purchased a few items for me, too, nothing expensive, just some cargos and tees to chill in from the Gap then we went to the food court to kick it. Things he lied to me about in the past, he confessed to. He told me things he never wanted me to know and I respected him for finally letting it all out. This made me look at him differently.

At two o'clock we walked into the gym. I spotted a man that looked just like Maurice Cheeks sitting in the front watching the game closely.

I walked up the bleachers and sat close to Whitey. A couple of familiar ball players walked in, moments later then a ball player that I'd never saw before walked in and sat down beside me, looking good as ever. While he looked me up and down on the sly, I did the same. *Hey. Damn! Whitey just doesn't know.*

"What the fuck are you doin'?" asked Whitey. "You being sneaky again."

"What! What are you talkin' about?" I asked, knowing what I was feeling. I liked this dude and Whitey really did nothing for me anymore.

"Move closer to me," he demanded. I slid closer to him while the sexy, caramel complexion athlete looked at me once again with a grin. I watched his tight, sexy calves from the corner of my eyes while Whitey talked trash about the game. He dawged his man for not being on his job while I wanted to *meow* at this fine motherfucka sitting next to me. Damn he looked good as pie and sweet enough to eat.

Moments later the athlete that caught my attention got up with his gym bag to change in the locker room for the next game. His platinum and ice glimmered with the lights above as he walked across the shiny, gym floor.

I could only imagine what it could've been if Whitey wasn't around. The thought of fucking someone new did something to me although I knew it wasn't right. It wasn't about the status or anything material. I was just tired of Whitey's dick. Like I said, it was just a fuck. There were no feelings involved anymore. I could care less about the relationship. It was just something to pass time. I outgrew his tired ass.

After the game everybody went out to eat, drink and be merry. And when the night ended, Whitey managed to get mad at me for something. The real problem was with Fall, but he took it out on me because I was close to him. I changed my flight ticket to an earlier flight, then Whitey drove me to the airport with a nasty attitude.

In front of the airport I leaned in the window and begged Whitey not to let me board the plane with him being mad at me, but his stubbornness wouldn't allow him to bend a little. He let me know he would be okay and to call him when I reached home, but that was it.

I felt like a nut during the entire flight. He cracked me once again. This instance made me realize his feelings still mattered to me to some degree. I had even gotten another tattoo with his name because he cried when I covered the other ones but I planned to do the same once again. I wanted a husband and having his name all over me, wasn't acceptable.

As soon as I reached home, I called Whitey to let him know I made it. The attitude still remained so I thought, "forget him" and went to sleep.

I ducked Whitey's calls for weeks. I told him if I ever found out about Fall, he was cut. My girl Ebony's man Cee spilled the beans about Whitey and Fall. Now was the time to concentrate on my family and me.

I sat at the computer with my long time family friend Welsh reading the final draft of, *3 Men I Chose to Love*. Welsh encouraged me through the years to finish my story after Daniel's death but I held it up because of Whitey. Now was the time to put closure on my life and print my book.

The reality is, all that I went through with men, it's only three I really loved; Luke, Job and Daniel will always pump through my vessels while everyone else will fall off and fade. Love is more than physical. It's the mental bond that stuck with me through my travels. When my heart pumps with joy and pain, I think of them, when I look at my children, I see them through their eyes. When I breathe in, I remember the sweet presence of love that they shared with me. When my nostrils flare wide, I capture their scent and smile gracefully. I even hear their voices in my mind and know that we'll meet again someday where nothing can stand between the love God has bestowed on our beings.

Before Welsh left out the door, he passed me, *A Divine Revelation of Hell*, that my mother asked him to give me. I heard so many positive reviews about the book. I knew it could only be a blessing to my children and me although the devil was going to try to torment our souls for reading it. But I wanted my children to get a feel of hell so they could keep their eyes on God and not fall into the trap of the enemy.

My cell phone rang out of control once I let Welsh out. I looked at the restricted number on my caller ID. It was Whitey. I let my voice mail pick up and he called again so I answered it. He begged me to meet him.

I sat in the parking lot of the hotel waiting for Whitey to pull up. Ten minutes later he did in his work van. I looked around to make sure I saw no unfamiliar cars, then I jumped out and stood by the curb and waited for Whitey to step out the van. He stepped out with a two piece, navy blue Dickies set on and a pair of tan Timberlands.

"Damn. I missed you," he smiled. "Did you miss me?"

"What's wrong?" I asked with a smirk. I wanted to know why he wanted to see me so badly. I didn't feel like the, *I missed you, shit.*

"I just needed to see you. I was thinking about you so much. I know you are a good girl. If I thought any differently, I wouldn't care whether I saw you or not. I know you have been in my corner. I know this. How's my baby girl?" he asked.

"She's fine," I mumbled.

"Can you go in and pay for a room so we can chill?" he asked.

I looked at him like, "I don't believe this motherfucka."

320

"Is something wrong?" he asked.

"No. I just can't stay long," I said.

"What time do you have to pick up the kids?" he asked, now irking me.

"Around two."

"Okay. We'll be out before then."

Inside the room Whitey and I talked for hours, then we laid in the bed together. Whitey assured me he didn't want to do it to me, he just wanted to soak in my presence. He realized what he had been missing. Whitey and Fall were tight, but she wasn't me. We were different. What I did she didn't do and what she did I didn't do. We served different purposes for sure. Whitey knew with age brought wisdom. With age brought listening and understanding. With age brought spending wisely. With age brought respect and loyalty. I was like, *"fine wine."* I would only get better with time. He knew I wanted my own and I didn't have to take when told *no* and if I asked, it was needed. I would never go in his pockets without permission. He knew I didn't need him because I could make shit happen too. I just graduated and received my degree in Psychology. I didn't become the doctor I wanted to be but I did something positive with my life.

Whitey took the soul food meal I made him home because he knew Fall wouldn't have anything cooked waiting for him. He promised me he'd be back. Whitey never showed because Fall was on to him. He left me in the hotel bed alone finishing up, *For the Love of Money* by Omar Tyree.

The next night I had a trick for Whitey, I put the code 69 in his two-way pager hoping whoever the girl he was messing with would call me back. And surely she did. Fall begged Whitey to tell me he didn't want me but he wouldn't do it so I did it for them. I hung up with intentions on never turning back. I now knew my true value. The answer was, *self.* I found Cinnamon.

I sat at the computer writing speeches on a Friday. Before I could finish, my cell phone rang. It was Whitey trying to make peace with me but Fall caught him and I laid them both out nicely. I turned Case & Joe's, *Faded Pictures* up then I wrote this in reference to Whitey.

Lovin' You Boy

Boy if you only knew what you did to me,
you would turn back the hands of time to set me free.
I was your friend, your lover to the end,
but you took advantage of my tender heart,
and I knew you didn't deserve it from the very start.
Now all I have are regrets, anger and pain,
wishing I never, ever have to hear your name.
You turned my love into hate,
being so sneaky and deceitful,
lacking trust, always wanting to fuss,

being so controlling over what I do,
making me so unhappy, knowing it wasn't me, it was you.
Always pointing the finger, straight at me,
afraid of looking in the mirror because of what you might see.
But it's all over now, and yes I was blind and now I am free.
You are the one that always told me to keep it real,
so I poured my love all over you, then I watched how it made you feel.
You were there for the moment,
then you turned and walked away.
You simply couldn't deal boy,
it was too much for you to stay.
My realness, my love was something you just couldn't understand.
So the next time you ask,
make sure you're not a little boy and be ready to be a real man.

I stood proudly on the stage of my High School speaking to the young girls and boys. I had to come back to my community first to shed a little knowledge about my experiences. Then I went back to the group home for girls where I did community service at. I had a special bond with the girls over there, especially Christina.

I had to save somebody else's daughter from going through what I went through or somebody else's son, if my story could help them become a better man and not die at the hands of the enemy for some worthless cause. I had to do what was right. I had to be a living example. I had to walk it, not only talk it.

Sometimes we think we're not worthy of the best but that's not so. We're all worthy of happiness, peace and joy. We sometimes look to the left or right to find security and it's in our innermost beings. We're not all blessed to have a secure foundation coming up but that doesn't mean we have to settle for anything. We hold the key to our own destiny. Yes, we may do foolish things but that doesn't mean we have to stay bound by our past or present situations. Life is what we make it for sure so don't fall for anything because what will we stand for in the end. Love yourself. Whoever said, "love don't love nobody." I can't agree with that. Love does love somebody. If we love ourselves, we can love others. Love self and others will do the same with all respect.

THE END, *class adjourned*

In life we make choices and I made mine. I chose to love the game more than myself and it caused me, **A Lifetime of Pain** *until I woke up and realized what I was here for. God chose me to do His work, not the work of the enemy so with that, I am whole and ten steps ahead of the game. I no longer have to look for love in all the wrong places because it'll only cause me so much pain and that I don't need anymore. God said He'd never leave me nor forsake me and He never lied. Hallelujah! All praises to the mighty ONE! I'm blessed, delivered and free. My soul soars high. I love you all!*

Epilogue

Life, Death, Choices . . . One Month Later

Job's uncle Brent felt bad about everything concerning his brother's only child. He finally broke me off eighty thousand dollars, forty to help with Job's college expenses and forty for the here and now. Two days later he died in a plane crash. Now tell me that isn't crazy. Lil Job needed a man in his life and as soon as his uncle reached out to him, God took him away too. Nobody could have told me nine years ago that Lil Job's father, his grandfather and his fathers only brother would die leaving him to carry their family name, not even God. That's why He couldn't reveal it to me but I know He makes no mistakes. Everything happens for a reason.

The invincible man Whitey, is behind bars for the rest of his natural life. His girl Fall surely did come up this time around. She has everything Whitey owned.

Candis said her farewells. Her kids will be grown when she hits the streets of Philadelphia again.

Kalif didn't receive the death penalty for killing Daniel because of his age but he received a life sentence. His old head Ty remains a mystery man. Nobody on the streets knows who he is.

And me, I vow to keep the *3 Men I Chose to Love* legacies alive. I travel around the country to different colleges, halfway houses, prisons, shelters and churches, giving speeches about my life, sharing the gospel of the Holy Ghost and cheerfully giving out copies of my book, *3 Men I Chose to Love* that I was able to print from the money I had while doing my do in the streets and I opened up a shelter for women and young girls that are battered, runaways, molested, raped, or sold themselves for money, or sold the product at some point or that is on, the product itself. God said, "the wealth of the wicked is laid up for the righteous" so I took all that filthy money and invested it into something worthy. I feed, cloth and counsel these girls and women. If I can help somebody else's child. I am so grateful. My heart is overwhelmed with joy and at peace. *Amen!*

Excerpt of *"A Lifetime of Pain"*

Chapter Ten
Back at the Ranch

Summer of 1997, four years later. Teala pulled her brand-new black on black 850Ci BMW up to her five bedrooms, two and a half bathroom single brick house in Bear, Delaware with a deck, pool and basketball court in the back. She let Tim talk her into selling Taylor's house and his vehicles to use the money for their new house. And the extra money left over they used toward new vehicles and Tim's hustle.

The music industry wasn't feeling Tim anymore and he wasn't willing to work legally so hustling became his number one priority. Teala hated what she stood for. She couldn't believe herself and didn't want a hustler for a man either. She knew what that life would bring her but Tim didn't care though. He wanted to be on top one way or another. He wasn't new to the game, he just didn't have to work for the notorious Kiss anymore like he did back in the day. He was doing his own thing.

Teala walked around to the back of the house where Tim sat chilling by the pool with a cold Heineken in one hand and a blunt in the other. Nothing changed through the years. He was stuck on stupid without a clue. All he thought about were new cars and gadgets and Teala didn't know why she was still putting up with his shit.

Teala spoke to Tim quickly and proceeded through the sliding glass doors where the cd player blasted hardcore rap music. Tim was so immature. Teala didn't find anything wrong with rap music, but Tim just didn't know when to wind down. He played it day and night and the neighbors already wondered what they did for a living. Nobody was really in a position to point fingers but people were always ready to judge a book by its cover. Tim and Teala were young, African American, stylish, they had a 850 BMW, a Mercedes S600 and 4.6 Range, little Bryanna had a Suzuki Quad Runner, go cart and game room in the basement. All the kids in their development envied her. She was following her father's footstep too. This was her second year playing for different basketball leagues and she was good. Her game was tight.

Teala popped in her Toni Braxton's Secrets cd then she ran to the exercise room to get on the treadmill. Since she wasn't working anywhere she had a lot of free time on her hands and spent most of her time at the house writing, cooking and eating so she had to exercise to keep her body tight or else it would be hard to catch anymore. The young girls had it sowed up and at twenty-eight, Teala was tight but she was getting old and the older, the harder it would be to keep the fat off so she had to keep it right like good money.

Tim couldn't wait until he finished his blunt so he could go in and fuck with Teala. His day wouldn't be right if he didn't find something to pick a fight about. He loved her for certain but didn't feel the same from her. Teala hardly made love to him anymore and when they did do it, Teala's mind was elsewhere and Tim couldn't stand rejection. He wanted a baby more than anything now and Teala couldn't see it. He had his chance years before and Teala simply couldn't let that one rest. She held that over Tim's head, repeatedly telling him she didn't want to have a baby with him. She didn't want Tim to father her children and didn't understand why she was allowing him to raise Bryanna either.

Although Bryan got Bryanna a lot, she spent most of her days with Tim; they shopped the malls together, they played basketball together, he took her to Gymnastics and basketball practice when Teala couldn't, their relationship came a long way and Teala didn't know how she let it get like that. She knew she wasn't feeling Tim and was unhappy. She would never take a ring from him. Wouldn't marry him to save her life. She simply wanted out and was living a lie for his sake, not hers.

Teala felt sorry for Tim and as much as she tried to pull away, he lingered on and was persistent. The relationship should've ended years before but because of his determined ways, Teala did something that would destroy her internally. Tim made her not want to do anything. She put all her projects off because of him. She turned down many jobs because of his insecurities. She sat home listening to Tim tell her to let him take care of her instead of working when she loved working. She couldn't stand to be sheltered by someone that she didn't want. She became as cold as he was because that's all she knew. She began to take on his attitude. She became a real bitch. Tim created a monster and she turned on him.

"What did you turn my cd off for?" Tim asked Teala as he stood next to the treadmill.

"Excuse me," she turned and said to him.

"You heard me! Why do you always have to come in fuckin' up the mood?" he said, waggling a crusty weed finger. Teala looked at Tim. She looked at the door. She just knew he wasn't talking to her. Tim had no kids in 25 For Sure Lane.

"Oh, you don't hear me now?" Tim got louder as he got closer. If he got any closer, he'd be running on the treadmill too.

"Pardon me," Teala smirked, trying not to inhale his now irritating scent.

"I hate when you play stupid. Didn't you hear me? Why the fuck did you turn my cd off and put on that bullshit? I don't wanna hear no fuckin' Toni Braxton. Ain't no love makin' goin' on in this joint," he said, breathing down her neck.

"Come on now. Why do you always have to find something to argue about? I'm sorry," Teala said then she jumped off the treadmill and walked away.

"Don't walk away when I'm talking to you," Tim said, grabbing Teala's wife beater. "I wasn't finished. I wanna fuck." Teala looked at Tim and rolled her eyes. If eyes could kill, he'd be dead.

"I don't feel like it," she said.

"You never feel like it. You used to love for me to put it in you. You used to love to hear me make love to you. Now you wanna act like you don't like it," Tim said then he gripped Teala up and kissed her in the mouth.

"Come on now," she said, pushing Tim. "Let me go." Tim kissed and kissed until Teala gave in and why did Tim do that. She didn't move, wiggle or pump a bit. She stayed still until he came then she got up and ran to the bathroom to wash.

Inside the bathroom Teala cried like a baby that needed to be fed and changed. She was really tired and would do anything to go back to living by herself. She hated Tim's controlling ways. She couldn't stand waking up to him. She didn't want to wash his clothes or cook for him anymore. It wasn't a pleasure now, it was a task and she wanted out. He wasn't her breath of fresh air like the good old days. He was polluting her temple and she had to find herself again.

After washing Teala called Mrs. Teena to talk. She just needed an ear to hear because Tim was draining her and wouldn't listen when Teala said she needed space.

"Hello," Mrs. Teena said pleasantly as she watered her flowers in the garden.

"Hey mom," Teala sadly said.

"What's wrong baby?" asked her mother. She knew her daughter all too well.

"Mom," she hesitated. "I...I need to come stay with you for a while."

"What's wrong? What did Tim do?" she asked.

"I just need some space," Teala said.

"Okay. You know the door is open," smiled Mrs. Teena. She liked Tim as a person, but she knew he wasn't the one for her baby. Parents always seemed to know who's for their babies and Teala just wasn't quite happy with Tim, especially since they moved together.

Teala packed clothes for Bryanna and herself then she skidded out the driveway in the Mercedes. Once Tim woke up and noticed Teala gone, he flipped. He couldn't believe she left without consulting him. She never even asked if he was using the Benz or not and normally she would. What did Teala care about what car she was to take now. Two of them had her name on them so that was enough. It was like picking candy; you take what you have a taste for and she felt like driving the Mercedes.

Teala pulled the Benz up to Mrs. Teena's house and parked. It was late and she knew Bryanna was asleep so she planned on creeping in and going straight to her old room.

Teala reached in the back to grab her Moschino bag. She felt someone watching her. Tim mentioned her getting a licensed gun but she was lunching and hadn't done so yet.

Teala slid her hand inside her bag as if she had a gun while looking out the corner of her eye. The tinted window of the Navigator slowly went down. Kiss smiled at her while singing Rick James, *Cold Blooded.* Teala cut her eyes and continued to grab her things from the back seat.

"You need some help," asked Kiss. Teala ignored him.

"I'm sorry if I scared you," Kiss said after picking up on the vibe. "I was riding and I seen you."

Teala looked to her left and said, "Excuse me."

"I was riding by and I saw you sitting. I wanted to make sure you was cool. It's not good for a beautiful lady to be out here late like this," he said.

"Yeah. I know," Teala said short and sweet. She just wanted him to leave so she could jump out and run in the house but she knew she had to unlock the door and take the alarm off.

"Why are you so cold beautiful? You are too pretty to be so moody. Can I take you out sometimes?" he smiled. Although it was dark, Teala noticed his eyes. They were catchy. He was handsome too. From what she could see, he had sandy brown, soft curly hair that complimented his caramel skin tone.

"No," she blatantly said.

"Why not? I'll show you a good time," he assured her. Teala thought about the way her and Tim's relationship was going. It wouldn't hurt to have a friend on the side.

"Look, it's late and I need to get to my daughter."

"Can you just take my number again?" he asked. Teala hesitated then she said, "yes."

Kiss wrote his number down neatly and passed it to Teala. She didn't even look at the paper, she threw it in her bag and jumped out the car.

Kiss shook his head as he watched Teala. She was getting better with time. Through the years she maintained and wasn't going backwards. Her booty was a little fuller from working out. Her hips were maybe a quarter of an inch wider from aging. Her stomach was as flat as a washboard and you know her hair was tight. Jae'Von was still doing his thing with his gayness. He added a touch of blonde to Teala's hair and it complimented her skin tone and eyes.

Kiss skidded off happy. He knew he was getting closer and closer to Teala. He felt it in his cold blood and really wanted to rock Tim now. Tim was hustling and wasn't getting his product from him. Tim had the girl he wanted too. Tim really didn't have a place in Kiss's eyes. If he was out of the picture, he could have Teala.

Inside Teala's room she felt at peace for a change. She didn't have to hear any bullshit. She could kick up her feet and relax without a worry.

Teala slept until the afternoon while Bryanna and Mrs. Teena went to the market for dinner.

Inside the market Mrs. Teena bumped into Solomon.

"Hey, how've you been?" Solomon smiled. Bryanna looked him up and down. "And you got so big."

"I'm fine. Thank you," Mrs. Teena said. "It's been a long time."

"Yeah, yeah. Everything is great. I just came from Chicago. I have a production company and I own my own record label," he smiled.

"Good for you, I'm glad to hear that," said Mrs. Teena.

"So what's Teala doing now? I haven't heard from her in a while," he said.

"Nothing much," said Mrs. Teena. She wasn't disappointed with her daughter's choices, she just wanted her to follow through with her dreams instead of letting them go to waste.

"I have to go. It was good seeing you. Give Teala my card please," he said, passing her his business card. "And take care beautiful."

"Bye," Bryanna smiled.

"Okay. Take care," said Mrs. Teena as she began to push the cart forward. Solomon brought back good old memories.

When Mrs. Teena and Bryanna got back to the house, Teala was sitting in living room flipping through old pictures.

"Mommy," Bryanna smiled, reaching for Teala.

"Hey, baby. Where are you coming from?" Teala asked her.

"I went to the market with mom-mom."

"Okay. What did you get?"

"We got a lot of things. I'm helping mom-mom make dinner tonight," she smiled then she walked to the kitchen with her bag.

"You would never believe who was at the market," Mrs. Teena smiled, passing Teala Solomon's card. Teala looked at the card.

"No, you didn't. I haven't talked to him in so long," Teala smiled. She kinda missed Solomon's presence. He could be a little moody too when he didn't get his way but he was a well-rounded dude for the most part, a good provider, a go-getter and knew how to treat his lady. Teala was so happy for him. While she sat home doing nothing with her work, he stepped his game up six notches.

"He looked great too, clean cut, smelling good. I'm proud to see young black men rising to the top," Mrs. Teena said as she walked away. She could only think of where her boy would've been if he was living. He was a go-getter too. He just wasn't as lucky. Some turned their dirty money into honest money and made it, some didn't.

"I know. Isn't it beautiful?" smiled Teala. Sure she had luxuries but her man wasn't living right. She wanted all the fine things that came with honest living. She didn't like feeling uncomfortable with what she had. She wanted to enjoy life without looking over her shoulder. She didn't want to be nervous every time the phone rang. A message saying Tim went to jail or died on the streets. Either Tim had to give the game up, or she was out. She didn't want that life anymore, especially after knowing what Solomon accomplished. He was no different from Tim. He hustled before he got into the music industry. He did jail time for shooting others. He was even shot and robbed before too but he made a choice. He knew jail or an early death wasn't for him. He was talented and his brain could make him big, legal money. He wasn't going to take no for an answer but Tim used the bullshit lines as cop outs. He didn't have to stop with the music. He could've done anything else but hustle and he chose hustling because he thought it was fast, easy money and he could master it without going to jail or dying behind it.

Teala went to her room and called Solomon. She wasn't going to play the waiting game; I won't call him right away. I'll wait for a couple days, bullshit. She wanted to know everything. She wanted to hear what he was doing.

"Hey," Teala said as soon as she heard Solomon's voice over the loud music.

"Who's this?" Solomon asked.

"It's Teala," she smiled, looking in the mirror.

"Hey baby. How's it going?" he laughed. "I missed you."

"I missed you too. I see you are doing your thing," she said.

"Yeah. I got a little something going on," he said.

"A little something, you got a lot going on there baby. I'm so happy for you," she said.

"So tell me something first. Are you still with that nigga?" he smirked.

"Not really."

"Come on now. You can keep it gansta' wit' me. Do you still fuck wit' the bull or what?" he wanted to seriously know because if she wasn't with Tim, he had a proposal for her.

"Well, I just came to my mother's for a few days. I'm tired of the bull," she said.

"What do you mean? Is he fuckin' up or are you giving him a hard way to go? I remember the last time we talked. Your spirit just wasn't right. He had you fucked up. I know when you're with him and when you're not. You are so much happier when you're not with him. Why did you keep taking him back? And you refused to give a good nigga like me a chance. What was wrong with me?" he said.

"You know what it was. First of all, you were married," she said.

"You know I would've never needed anybody else if I had you. I would've never cheated. I would've just loved you girl and I still love you, nothings changed. Through all the years, I never forgot about you. I dreamed about you. I smelled you in my mind. I don't know what it was about you but you did something to me. You had me fucked up and you know it. You know what you did. You are something special," he said, reminiscing.

"So are you with your wife now?" Teala asked him. Even though she had the marriage rule, she was thinking about what it would be like to have Solomon as her man. She knew he loved her and would treat her like a Nubian Queen. Maybe this time around she would at least give him a chance.

"Yes. We're a family now. We have three girls," he said, proudly. Teala's heart sank into the carpet. She was happy and disappointed at the same time, happy that he had his family but disappointed because she was seriously thinking about bending the rules for this man and he told her that he would never have his ex back and he ate those very words. Some women were so lucky. They could betray their men and they would take them back. Teala was a good girl and couldn't seem to find that. What was wrong with her?

"I'm glad you have your family. That's a beautiful thing," she said.

"Yeah, it is. I'm so grateful. God has been good to me. I'm so blessed," he said but he knew in the back of his mind that Teala would've been the perfect one for him. He would've made her his wife but he had to settle for what he already had and if he could, he'd have both of them because he loved his wife for bearing his seed but he loved Teala too. She was everything he dreamed of. She would've built with him. She was the perfect wife and she loved the wrong men.

"Yes, God is always good," Teala said. Although she wasn't happy like Solomon, she had to be grateful that she had her life. She was still living so she had a chance at happiness. Someday she would be happily married too.

"Can I take you out later?" Solomon asked her. He wanted Teala as a close friend because they were hard to come by but his wife couldn't know about him and Teala because when they got back together they told each other all of the things they did while they were separated and Teala was the one and only woman that Solomon would've made love to so his wife wasn't about to accept their friendship. It had to be a secret.

Teala thought about Solomon's proposal, then she said, "yes. You can take me out. Where are we going so I can know what to put on?"

"One of my artists is opening up a new club up New York. It's invitation only so I need to know if you're serious," he said.

"Yes. I'm going," Teala said. She knew it had been years since she went out to a set of that kind so she was a little nervous but it was time to do some networking. She knew it would be a lot of important people there and maybe she could tell somebody about her book that she had been sitting on for so long.

"Okay, call me around four so we can do dinner first and bring your clothes with you and we'll get dressed at the hotel," Solomon said.

"Sounds good to me," Teala smiled with joy.

Teala ran to the kitchen and told her mother what her moves were. She kissed Bryanna and out the door she went.

Teala arrived to Nieman Marcus. The attendant happily took her car and parked it. Teala felt great walking up in the store. She knew her night with Solomon would be everything she imagined.

Teala stopped by the Chanel section first to see what pocketbooks and glasses they had then she took the escalator to the first floor.

In the shoe department she purchased a pair of Gucci and Chanel evening shoes. She didn't know what she was wearing yet but it didn't make a difference either. The shoes would only add to the collection if she didn't need them for the night.

Teala walked out of Nieman's and over to the Versace store. And who did she see as soon as she walked in? An old classmate. He stood mesmerized. He thought Teala was the shit in Cherry Hill High but she looked even better as she got older.

"Damn," he said, looking her up and down. He had a girl but he would've loved to have one night with Teala, maybe every night if she had let him. He didn't want anyone in the store but him to help her. He showed her everything new that came in.

At the counter Ronaldo asked about Taylor. Teala paused for a moment then she told him Taylor was killed years ago. Ronaldo was shocked by Teala's words. He thought she would've said Taylor was living in another State or something but not dead. Ronaldo gave Teala a big hug, his card then she left out the store. He made a nice commission off Teala's twenty-five hundred dollars. She really didn't have it like that anymore because of all the money she had been spending through the years. Tim wasn't that generous with his drug money. He paid some of the bills but he didn't give Teala money to blow. Anything extra she wanted, she had to go into her account and buy and spending foolishly with no income coming in wasn't wise. Teala's account was getting smaller and smaller.

Outside Teala gave the parking attendant her stamped parking ticket and while he ran to get her car, she dialed Jae'Von's number to let him know she was on her way.

As Teala pushed the end button the parking attendant pulled up to her and opened the door for her to get in. She threw her bags in the back seat, she gave him a five-dollar bill then she sped off.

Inside the salon it was thick on a Wednesday afternoon. Everybody had to have a function to go to or something because it was never that crowded on a Wednesday that's why Teala chose Wednesday's to get her hair done.

Teala and Jae'Von did their favorite greeting, she spoke to everybody else then she sat at the shampoo bowl.

Jae'Von was just finishing up Teala's hair when Kiss walked in. Through all the years at the salon, Teala never, ever heard about Kiss coming to the shop. Was he a stalker or just an old clown? Teala wondered.

"Jae who is he here for?" Teala asked.

"Oh, his cousin gets her hair done here," he said. "Girl, ain't he fine."

"Who's his cousin?" Teala wanted to know.

"Trina Price," he said. Teala's heart hit the brown marble floors. Not only did Trina sleep with her ex, she was the cousin to Kiss and she never knew it. How did that slip by her and they went to college together? Teala was sure to make Trina upset now. Teala was going to take Kiss up on his offer and screw him over. This would be the perfect get back. She could finally hit Trina where it would hurt. Although Kiss was Trina's cousin, Trina would be upset at the fact that Kiss was doing Teala period.

"Oh, really. You know she did it to Bryan right," Teala said.

"Oh, yeah. Umm, I didn't know that shit," Jae'Von said, smacking his lips hard. "No, that bitch didn't. I don't like the stink ho anyway. She comes up in here like she is the fuckin' President or something. She messes with that tennis playa' from up north. Her peoples has something to do with him or something."

"Good for her. I hope I don't run into her in here. As a matter of fact, hurry up so I can get outta here," Teala smirked.

Kiss looked at Teala with a silly grin. She spoke to him and Jae'Von turned the chair the other way.

"Fuck him and his cousin," Jae'Von said. "Where are you going tonight girl?"

"I'm going to New York with a friend," she smiled.

"What's up NY?"

"A friend of mine artist is opening up a club up there," she said.

"Oh, the guy from Altoru Records," Jae'Von said.

"I'm not sure," said Teala.

"If so, that's going to be nice. I might see you there. I was invited too," he said.

"Please come. I'll feel so much better with you there," she smiled.

"Will do. I'll see you there," he said, taking the cape from around Teala's neck.

Although it was 85 degrees outside, a little breeze was sweeping through. Kiss stood by the curb admiring Teala's hair blowing with the wind.

"What's up for the night?" he asked Teala as she put her right leg in the car.

"Nothing," she said.

"Where's the party?"

"What party?" she asked him.

"Oh, I just thought you were going to a party or something."

"No, I'm not."

"Can I take you to Atlantic City to dinner or maybe down Baltimore? I know I'm asking you late but we can catch a late dinner if you have something to do right now," he smiled.

"Maybe some other time, I have somewhere to go right now," she said.

"Okay. I'll wait on you," he said, walking away. Teala shut her door then she called Solomon to let him know she was ready.

"Meet me at the Holiday Inn by the airport and we'll get in my mans car," he said.

"Oh, your man is going too," she said.

"We're riding with him and his girl okay. It's cool," he assured her.

"Okay."

Teala jumped on the highway, straight to the Holiday Inn and parked. Ten minutes later Solomon and his man pulled up in a white 4.6 Range Rover with black seats trimmed in white leather.

Solomon took Teala bags and put them in the back for her, then he shut the door like a real gentleman.

"This is my man Earl Wonder and his girl Kiera," Solomon said to Teala. "Earl and Kiera, this is Teala."

"Please to meet you," Earl and Kiera smiled then he pulled off.

Teala sat back and read the June Issue of Essence while Solomon and his man kicked it about business. They had been friends for years and shared some of the same interest. They both hustled in the early eighties, invested their illegal money into legal businesses. They came a long way but some dudes' they hustled with back in the day didn't like what they'd become. While they moved up, they stayed in the hood hugging corners, smoking weed, watching the sun come up. Now they were jealous and wanted their heads because they were successful. They didn't just talk it. They did it. *Respect comes from doing, not saying*, Teala remembered Taylor preaching constantly. That's why he executed his dream early on instead of waiting until he was thirty like most unwise men do. *Who's gonna respect a man coming into the game late? You grow old in the game, not come in old.*

You know the ride to New York was mad crazy. It was seven o'clock once they got there. That meant no dinner because that would take too much time and Solomon wanted to get to the club by 8:30.

Earl pulled his truck into the Marriott hotel. The attendant gave him a ticket while the bellboy loaded their things on the cart.

Solomon and Teala stopped by the front desk to get the keys to the room then they caught the elevator up to the 49th floor while Earl and his girl stopped at the bar to get a few drinks before getting dressed. He had to go up in the club with two up in him to get it started.

Teala showered up while Solomon checked his messages. He didn't feel like taking any calls because people would be begging for a favor. He couldn't get everybody in the club for free. And people didn't know how to take no for an answer so he had to lie to them or ignore them and he chose to ignore them. They were going to feel how they wanted to anyway. They had a guess list and if you weren't on it, then you had to deal with that on your own time.

Solomon knocked on the door once to see if Teala would open it. He had to try at least. She heard his knock but ignored him and kept drying off. She knew he would be waiting for her once she opened the door. She hated to get dressed in front of him but it could be no other way.

Teala opened the door with the towel tightly wrapped around her.
"It's cool. I'm not paying you no mind," Solomon smiled. "It's late and I showered before I picked you up so all I have to do is get dressed."
"Okay." Teala sat on the bed to lotion up. She didn't want to stand because Solomon would be all over her naked frame. Her phone rang. She looked at the number to see who it was. Tim would call while she was in the room naked with another man. There was no way she could answer the phone so she let the voice mail do the talking, and besides, she wasn't talking to him anyway.

Once Teala got dressed, Solomon's breath was taken away. She was more beautiful than ever. She had a slit from her cleavage all the way down to her navel. The chiffon fabric revealed Teala's pussy print but she didn't look like a slut. She looked sexy, and of course, enticing.
"Damn, girl. You look beautiful. See that's what I'm talkin' 'bout. I can see us getting a grammy together, you on my arms, damn! That nigga don't know what he got," Solomon said, shaking his shiny, round head.
"Stop it," Teala smiled. She was feeling good but Solomon made her feel wonderful. He felt like her man this night.

Teala and Solomon stopped by Earl's room to see if he and his girl were ready. Of course, they weren't. After drinking they had to get a quickie in so Teala and Solomon went to the bar to get spring water while they waited for them.

Thirty minutes later Earl and his girl walked to the bar smiling. They were ready to party. The four of them jumped in the cab instead of taking the truck. It was better that way. They made it just in time. Had they been a minute later, they wouldn't have gotten in.

All the cameras and videos were rolling. Teala didn't want to walk on the red carpet while the video was taping because Tim would see her on tv later and she didn't want to fight with him. He would never believe she and Solomon were just friends. It's no way she could explain the relationship. He would believe they were sexing and she knew she hadn't slept with Solomon.

Teala managed to duck the camera while Solomon got caught and boy was she glad. Solomon grabbed Teala's hand before she walked into the club. He knew he couldn't have her but he didn't want anyone else to have her either. He knew he was unfair and she deserved to be happy but he couldn't see her with anyone else, especially not anyone he was all right with.

Teala looked around at all the different colored bright lights and people socializing. It was definitely an upscale set, packed with entertainers, designers and athletes. Everybody that was somebody was there. The atmosphere was pleasant, the food, exquisite. The lounge chairs were different colored leather and suede, mint green, yellow, mauve, powdered blue, fuchsia with monitors everywhere. Three bars. Two kitchens. Private rooms, the place was extravagant. *This is what I'm talking about. I likes this*, Teala smiled, moving through closely with Solomon gripping her hand tight.

Solomon was stopped every ten feet. He practically knew everybody in the club. They respected him and he definitely respected them. Teala felt wonderful.

Solomon escorted Teala upstairs where it was less crowded and a few seats available. He knew she wasn't used to the set so he wanted her to feel comfortable.

"I'll be right back. Do you want anything to eat?" he asked her over the loud music.

"No, I'm fine," she said. As soon as Solomon walked away, a tall fine brown skinned brother came over to Teala.

"Are you here with your man?" he politely asked her.

"No," she smiled, looking him up and down.

"Do you have a man?" he asked.

She thought about Tim then she said, "yes."

"Well, he's very lucky to have a lady like you. You look very nice," he said and why did Teala say she had a man. This man looked good, smelled good, and from the look of things, he was legally stable. Different women and men kept approaching him so she knew he was somebody important. Probably a football or basketball player but she didn't recognize him from basketball.

"Thank you," she smiled.

"Are you a model?"

"No."

"What do you do?"

"I'm a writer," she answered quickly.

"That's very interesting. Maybe we can do something together," he said.

"I'm a young Entrepreneur and I may be able to show you some things."

"Oh, really. I'm impressed," she smiled harder now.

"Here, take my card and give me a call sometime. My name is Clyde," he said as Solomon approached.

"What's up brotha?" he said to Solomon.

"Hey. What's going on? It's good to see you," Solomon said.

"Yeah, good seeing you too, y'all have a good night," he said, walking away.

"I see you met Clyde, huh?"

"Yeah, he's pretty nice," Teala smiled.

"Yeah, he's a good dude. He's a multimillionaire now. That brother came a long way," Solomon said, reflecting back to when he first met Clyde at one of his sessions.

At the end of the night Teala had twenty business cards in her bag and she left the club with a five thousand-dollar bracelet in a gift bag that Altoru Records were giving out as gifts.

At least she got a buzz out about her book. People could be looking for, *A Lifetime of Pain* in stores soon. She wasn't about to wait any longer, forget a publisher, forget all the promises that people were making her. She would self publish until something bigger happened for her. She had little time to waste. If she was going to keep blowing money, she could print up her own material and hustle it herself. Maybe even get a movie deal. She was simply tired of looking in places that had no way out.

End of Sneak Preview

A Lifetime of Pain

A Novel by Cinnamon/Author Alyce C. Thompson

Coming to you soon

***Watching Over Us* /The sequel to 3 Men
Through Eyes of A Black Man
All My Honeys'
&**

THE GIFT

3
Men

Alyce C. Thompson

ORDER FORM

Alyce C. Thompson Books
P.O. BOX 28827
Philadelphia, PA 19151-0827

Purchaser Information

NAME:

If incarcerated, please provide #

Address:

City&State:

Zip Code:

Number of Copies: ___($16.00 plus $2.00 for shipping & handling of *3 Men I Chose to Love.*)

Please make checks or money orders payable to: *Alyce C. Thompson*